Deep

Heavy Hearts Book Two

Sarah Jane Duncan

SJ Duncan

ISBN-13: 978-0-9945177-3-9

PA: Obsidian Author Services (Bibiane Lybaek)
Cover by Simply Defined Art

Many thanks to my Beta Readers: Alana, Anoesjka, Belinda, Jocelyn, Melinda & Melissa.
Many thanks to my proof reader: Jennifer

DEEP

I am Lexi West, and this is my torment!

Content Warning & Playlist

This book contains adult themes and scenes which may cause trigger reactions for some readers, which include, but aren't limited to:
abusive and sexually abusive situations, non-consensual acts, demeaning acts, emotional and physical blackmail, drug and alcohol use, and foul language.

For my mum
A woman who fought her demons daily,
bet the odds so many times I lost count,
and endured unimaginable pain that
couldn't always be seen.
She was a woman who knew strength
and never gave up fighting.
Here's to you mum!

"Damned if you do, and damned if you don't."

Christine Filmer

1947-2008

One

Peering through the sheer curtain, my eyes lock onto the car parked in the shadows outside my house. It's been there for a few minutes, and no one has climbed out. Whoever parked the car there is still inside.

"Can you see it?"

Valarie's voice reminds me I still have her on speakerphone.

"Yep Val, I can see it. It's different from the one last night, though." I've deliberately left my bedroom light off to make it harder for whoever is out there to see me as I spy.

"It's different, but I'm pretty sure I've seen that car before, Lexi." Valarie huffs into the phone. I can just imagine her stretching up on her toes, trying to get a better view of the car from her vantage point in her bedroom next door.

Straining my eyes in the darkness, I try to get a better look. The car does look familiar.

"I think it's the one I saw drive off early on Sunday morning, but now that I think of it, that's not the only time I've seen this car." Valarie's small twelve-year-old voice raises in pitch.

"Are you sure, Val? I need to be sure before I go out there."

"What?" Valarie shrieks through the phone. "You can't go out there, Lexi. There have been different cars each night. We don't know who it is. For all we know, it could be Mike or his creepy friends."

My twelve-year-old neighbour is both a pain in my arse and the closest thing to a loyal friend I have right now. She was the one who filmed the abuse that my half brother, Mike, dished out on me a couple of weeks ago and alerted the police. I won't lie. I'm still pissed about that because I didn't want the world to know. In saying that, I don't hate her for it. She technically did the right thing, which is more than I can say for most of the people in my life.

When I dragged my sorry self back home on Saturday after leaving Ayden's dad's apartment in the city, Valarie was the first person to see me approach my house. Of course she was. That kid is the street sticky nose!

I'd been standing on the path, staring at my beige rendered two-story house, trying to figure out if it was safe to go inside, when my nosey little neighbour dragged her mum out to see me. It's then that I found out that Valarie's mum, Shen, had the locks changed on the house, and had also cleaned up inside. Shen even filled my freezer with frozen meals so that I'd have food for when I came home. If I hadn't been so consumed with anger from everything that had happened, I most likely would have cried.

Apparently, after seeing a car drive off early Sunday morning, Valarie stayed up late on Sunday night to investigate. It had confused her when she discovered a car parked out the front again that night because it was different from the car she saw that morning, but the problem was still the same. Someone had parked their car outside my house and stayed in it all night, only to drive off as the sun rose over Fox Pines the next morning. Valarie alerted me to the situation once she realised it was actually a situation.

It's now been five days since I've been back home, and each night this week a different car has parked outside my house. Whoever is in the car doesn't get out. They stay inside until sunrise the next morning when they drive off.

It's creeping me the fuck out!

Tonight, however, just as Valarie said, the car does seem familiar.

"Val, if it's the same car that I think it is, then it's not Mike or his friends. Tell me where you think you've seen it before?"

"I feel like it's the same car that drove past the night that Mike attacked you. I noticed it because it was going really slow as it drove past. Then it went around the corner, and a minute later, two boys came sneaking up to your house and snuck in the front door," Valarie explains.

"That's what I thought."

"Lexi, who..." I cut Valarie off by hanging up, and my phone immediately starts buzzing with another incoming call from Val. I ignore it because I know all she's going to do is try to talk me into staying inside my house.

Letting the curtain fall back in place, I push down my nerves and walk silently down the stairs to the front door. I'm nervous, but not because I'm about to leave the safety of my house to approach a suspicious car in the dark. My heart is racing for another reason. It aches just thinking about Ayden and the possibility that he might be sitting outside my house right now. I haven't spoken to him since he told me to leave him alone.

"You asked me to tell you if I ever needed space, so listen carefully because I'm not going to repeat myself. I fucking want space, Lexi! Get the fuck out!"

Those words have replayed over and over in my head for days now. So too has the text message he sent me on Sunday night.

Ayden Mitchell
I'm so fucking sorry!

I wanted to tell him it was okay, but I didn't. It would have been a lie. It's not okay that he promised he would protect me from anyone hurting me, only to be the one to hurt me the most. I get it. He was pretty fucked in the head at the time, and I really had no right to go into his parents' room to see him after I was told not to, but it doesn't make it hurt any less.

Even though it's only been five days since I've seen or spoken to him, it feels like a lifetime. As much as my heart aches for Ayden, I'm not all that keen to lay eyes on him yet, especially if he's parked outside my house like a creepy fucking stalker. This shit has to stop. Now!

Turning on my phone torch, I pick up the baseball bat propped next to the front door and quietly step out into the chilly night. My eyes shift to Valarie's bedroom window, and I see the silhouette of my nosey twelve-year-old neighbour as she follows my movements. With her bedroom located at the front corner of her second-story box-like house, she has the prime location to see my house and the rest of the street.

Taking a deep breath, I push forward with determination and approach the car. Darkness casts a shadow inside, but I can still make out the masculine figure of a male sitting behind the steering wheel. It's clear whoever is in there notices my approach because they start shifting around in the seat.

Rounding the back of the car, I come to stand by the driver's door and tap on the window not so gently with the bat before shining my torchlight in through the glass.

Marcus Grady. Marcus fucking Grady sits in the car looking up at me like a deer in headlights.

"What the fuck!" I tap the window again, and Marcus opens the door, looking up at me.

"Ah, hey Lex." His dark hair looks longer than usual, like he's skipped his regular haircut. It's also a little messier, but that's probably from sleeping in a car like a stalker.

"What are you doing?"

"Um… I was just coming to see how you are." Marcus glances at the bat in my hand, worry contorting his face. Good, he should be fucking worried. I shove the bat in his face just to make a point.

"Don't fucking lie to me, Marcus!"

"Jesus, Lexi," he puts his hands up to fend off my threatening assault before hitting the bat away, frowning. "You planning on hitting me with that?"

"If you keep lying to me, then you can bet your balls I'm going to hit you with it!"

Marcus sighs and runs his hands through his hair in frustration, messing it up more.

"I'm just here to keep an eye on things, Lexi. I just want to make sure you're not alone if your brother comes back."

Well shit. I hadn't even considered that would be his reason. I don't know why. It makes perfect sense. He is my friend, after all. I guess I'm just so paranoid right now that I'm expecting everyone to turn into a monster.

"It's been you out here every night?" My voice is soft and portrays my weak emotions. Emotions I've done a damn good job at shoving down from the moment I stepped on the train to come back to Fox Pines.

Marcus shakes his head, "No, not just me. The guys have been taking turns each night as well."

"The guys?"

"Simon, Gaz, Shaun and Jar." Marcus looks up at me from his seat in the car, and I see the honesty in his brown eyes.

The boys from our circle of friends have been the ones sitting outside my house each night? I'm not sure what to make of that, but it does weird things to my insides, and I suddenly miss each one of them. A tear slips from my eye before I can stop it.

For fuck's sake, I'd been doing so well for days until Marcus turns up and shows me the slightest bit of compassion, transforming me into a stupid prissy girl again. Ugh!

Marcus swings his legs out of the car, and I step back so he can stand, towering over me like most people do. He doesn't say anything but reaches out and gently pulls me to his chest. I don't refuse the comfort he is offering and silently let a few more tears fall before fighting them back. I'm sick of crying. I don't want to shed any more tears over this fucked up situation.

I'm not used to being on the receiving end of Marcus' cuddles. He smells nice, like spicy cinnamon, but it's not the same as Ayden, and his chest doesn't seem as firm as Ayden's does either. I know I shouldn't be thinking of Ayden right now. The main reason being that it rips my heart open each time I do, but the other is because Ayden isn't the one here, checking on me and wanting to make sure I'm safe.

Pulling back, I look up at Ayden's cousin and take in the concern etched across his face.

"Were you planning on staying out here all night?" I ask.

"Yeah." Marcus doesn't elaborate.

I sigh. "Come inside. If you're staying all night, you may as well stay in the house where it's warm."

Marcus shifts nervously, looking over the top of the car at my house. "Ah... no, that's okay. I can just stay out here."

"Jesus Marcus, I don't bite. Come on." I don't wait for him to reply and start walking briskly back towards my house. Apparently, wearing my PJ shorts and Metallica t-shirt outside is a bad idea on a chilly August winter night.

The squeak of a car door slamming shut is followed by heavy footsteps behind me as Marcus gives in to come inside. As I walk up the path to my house, I glance up to Valarie's window and give her a quick wave, hoping she will understand and know that I'm okay. A moment later the dark silhouette waves back, and I turn my head quickly to hide my grin. I love that kid!

Once inside, I lead Marcus to the kitchen and turn on the kettle.

"You want a hot drink? Coffee? Tea? Hot Chocolate?" Just saying the words hot chocolate sends a pang to my heart. Ayden and I drank hot chocolate in the rooftop garden of his dad's apartment building right before I gave him my virginity.

"Hot chocolate would be great, thanks." Taking a seat at the kitchen bench, Marcus looks around the room as I make the hot drinks. Now that I can see him better under the warm lighting, I notice his normally tanned skin looks a little pale. I can't really talk, though. My skin is more pallid than it's ever been.

It's a little weird to have Marcus here again. He stopped coming over a few years ago, which is apparently when he started crushing on me. That's what Ayden told me, anyway. Marcus has never said anything to me about it, and if I'm being honest, I'd be happy for him to keep that secret to himself. I love him in a friendly way, nothing more.

Handing Marcus his drink, I lean against the opposite bench to take a sip of the hot sweet goodness and watch as Marcus does the same, looking everywhere but at me.

"How did you know I was back?"

Marcus startles at my question. I guess he was hoping to avoid my interrogation. Ha! As if I am going to be that easy on him!

Marcus keeps his eyes locked on mine for a few moments while the wheels noticeably turn in his head.

"The truth is always a good place to start, Marcus." I verbally nudge, raising a blonde brow at him.

"I should have known you wouldn't make this easy for me." He shakes his head and grins, looking down at his hot drink, his cheeks turning a light shade of pink.

"Exactly. Now spill."

"Fine." Marcus huffs, "Ayden called me on Saturday night freaking out because you had gone. He told me what happened with that Muz guy and the drugs, or at least what he could remember about it. He said he lost his shit at you when he was coming down from his high. Crashing, I believe was the word he used. He said you probably wouldn't have anywhere to go because Abbey's parents seem to have an issue with you. He was worried. I called Abbey, and she said she hadn't heard from you, so I got my sister to do a drive-by that night, and the lights were on." He shrugs, "I figured it was you here."

It hurts to hear him speak about Ayden. Why hadn't Ayden just called me himself? I guess he was happy that I'd left, but the caring side of him just wanted to make sure I had somewhere safe to go. Why hadn't Abbey called me either? I know her parents are blocking me from calling her, but she could have called me. I've tried reaching her by phone daily and sent her numerous SnapChats that have remained unanswered. I can see she has read them, yet she's made no attempt to respond since we last spoke on Saturday.

Fucking Saturday. Everything went to hell that day!

"I'm sorry, Lexi. As if you didn't already have enough to deal with before, then Ayden's past caught up with the both of you."

The consuming rage I've felt since leaving Melbourne bubbles near the surface, fighting to break free. My hand twitches with the need to grab the baseball bat and start swinging it at the walls and furniture. I've been tempted daily to take my anger out on this house but have managed to hold back... just.

"You're not eighteen, Marcus. How did you drive here?" I deflect from talking about Ayden, "Or the others for that fact. How did they drive here? You are all seventeen."

Marcus shrugs, "We've been waiting until it's safe enough to take the cars without getting caught. Just after dark or after the olds go to bed seems to be the best time. The streets are quiet, and no cops are patrolling at that time of night."

"Are you shitting me? You stole your parents' cars and drove them here without a licence?"

"Well, the car I drove is my sister's shit box she leaves at home while she's in the city. I'm sure if I told her what's going on, she would let me take it."

"Marcus, that's not the point!"

He laughs, "I guess not."

"And the others all did the same?" My voice is pitched high in disbelief.

"Yep." Marcus nods.

"You guys are a pack of idiots!" I put my mug down on the counter, no longer interested in finishing it. Food hasn't been a high priority lately, anyway.

"Probably, but we mean well, Lex." He shrugs.

"I guess. Did Ayden ask you to do this? To watch me?" Saying his name crushes my chest. The pain is unlike anything I've felt before. It's consuming and never-ending.

Marcus shifts nervously on the chair and puts his drink aside too. "Not exactly. He just wanted to know you were somewhere safe. I didn't tell him you were back at home by yourself. He kinda needs to sort his own shit out, and if he knew you were alone, he would flip."

"So, what did you tell him?"

"Not much, actually. I just sent him a text saying that you were safe, and told him to do what he needs to, so he can get better."

"Whose idea was it to sit outside my house?" I ask, shooting Marcus a brief glare.

"Mine, I guess." He shrugs again as if it's no big deal.

"So, you thought it would be better to sit out on the street, like a stalker, instead of knocking on the door?"

He looks away, his face red. "I never claimed to be smart."

I laugh this time, and he joins in, looking a little more at ease than he was when he walked in earlier. When our laughter dies down, I tip my drink down the sink and start washing the mug.

"If I ask you to leave, will you?"

When I look up, Marcus is staring at me, his expression serious.

"If you don't want me in your house, Lexi, that's fine, but I'm not leaving. I'll stay out in my car."

I shake my head, "How long is this going to go on for Marcus? Until my mum comes home? She won't be back for a while."

"For as long as it takes for the cops to find your fucking brother and lock him up." The angry admission from Marcus shocks me. I've never really heard him sound so serious and demanding. He reminds me of Ayden when he's like that.

"So even if my mum comes home, you're still going to be here babysitting me?"

"It's not babysitting. And yes. She can't protect you. If she could, then this would never have happened." His lip curls when he speaks of my mum. Wow! I haven't seen this side of Marcus before.

But he has a point.

"You can't give up your life to watch over me, Marcus." My hands land on my hips before I can stop the movement, and I see Marcus try to hide his smirk. Smart arse.

"Well, that's why it's not just me. It's the other guys too, and we aren't giving up anything. Your safety is more important than anything else."

"I can look after myself."

"Maybe, but we're going to be here anyway," Marcus declares.

I can see that I won't win this argument tonight, and if I'm being honest with myself, having him here does make me feel safer and less lonely. My mind wanders to Ayden again. The stupid thing is controlled by my broken heart. All I can think about is Ayden and what I've lost.

"He's okay, you know," Marcus says softly, gaining my attention again. "He checked himself into rehab on Monday, so he's doing the right thing and getting the help he needs."

"But... He didn't relapse. He was forced." Muz had threatened to shoot him and then have his way with me before shooting me if Ayden didn't inhale whatever the white powdered lines were. If I ever see Muz again, I'm going to take that gun and ram it up his arse and smile while I pull the trigger!

"Even so, the addiction is strong, and now he needs to get his head right so he can get back on track. The place he's at has great counsellors to help with that. It's a voluntary clinic. He can leave whenever he wants."

I turn away from Marcus as my eyes glass over, my anger waning briefly as I consider what Ayden must be going through. I didn't know my heart could break anymore, but in this moment, it does.

Two

A warm body shifting behind me pulls me from sleep the next morning. My mind instantly thinks of Ayden, and it takes a moment for my brain to remember that Ayden isn't here. I stiffen as the scent of Marcus reaches me, and my eyes shoot open.

"You don't have to look so terrified to be waking up next to me." Marcus nudges my shoulder, and I glance over it to see a foot. My confusion must show on my face, which is obviously why Marcus starts pissing himself laughing.

Sitting up, I push my messy blonde waves off my face to take in the situation. We are on the couch in the front living room. Marcus is up one end of the couch, and I'm up the other, and we share the same blanket. Did I sleep next to his big smelly feet all night?

"What happened?" My voice is hoarse, not ready to be used yet. I don't miss the way Marcus' eyes darken and lock onto my lips. Shit! Ayden really wasn't kidding about Marcus having a crush on me. I need to make sure he doesn't get the wrong idea about what's going on here.

"You fell asleep ten minutes into the movie. I wasn't sure if I should wake you and tell you to go to bed." Marcus pulls himself up to sit, dragging his hand through his dark hair to try and tame it. It's no use, though. He's going to need a shit ton of water to get rid of that bed hair.

My memory slowly clears as I watch Marcus. Last night we decided to watch a movie after I revealed I'd been having trouble sleeping. Knowing me better than I thought, Marcus put on Guardians of the Galaxy, one of my favourite movies. That's all I remember.

"So why didn't you wake me?" Keeping my eyes trained on his, I search for the truth in his response.

He shrugs. "You said you hadn't been sleeping lately. If I had woken you, then maybe you wouldn't have gone back to sleep. Turns out you slept all night, so not waking you was the right decision." Marcus grins smugly.

It's true. I slept all night. The last time that happened was when I was in Ayden's bed, wrapped in his arms. Memories of my time with

Ayden fight to devour me, but I push them away, not ready to feel the slicing pain in my heart.

Looking across my living room to the other couch lining the wall, my brows shoot up before returning my glare to Marcus.

"You could have slept on that couch." I point to the very empty, unused couch.

"Nah, you were kind of hugging my feet, so I couldn't move without waking you. I paused the movie and went to sleep too." Marcus smirks, "Well first, I watched you drool for about ten minutes, and then I went to sleep."

I instinctively grab the cushion I'd used as a pillow to sleep on, and chuck it at Marcus, hitting him in the head.

"The fact that you watched me sleep is creepy as fuck Marcus!" I leap up from the couch, righting my Metallica t-shirt that twisted in sleep, and ignore the deep laughter filling the room.

Storming out, I head to the kitchen to boil the kettle. Over the last week, I have discovered coffee, and now I crave it. Who needs food when you have coffee in your life?

Marcus lets out a long, drawn-out yawn and follows me, going to the fridge. His black sweatpants and grey hoodie are a little creased, but with his bird's nest hair, it all ties together.

"How is the fridge full? Did you go to the shops when you got back?"

"Supermarket delivery. I didn't even have to set foot outside my house." I hold a mug up to Marcus, "Coffee?"

"Yes, please," he nods, "You want me to cook some eggs?"

"You cook?"

Marcus straightens from the fridge, grinning, "I'm not just a pretty face. I can do shit."

Jesus, he's like his cousin. Well, kind of. They look different, but you can tell they are related. They are apparently the same smug arseholes, though. How did I not pick up on that when I was getting to know Ayden? What am I thinking? I hardly know Ayden. I was in his life for not even two weeks before he kicked me out of it.

"Sure, knock yourself out. But you clean what you dirty. I hate doing dishes." I turn away from him and fix his coffee.

"Yes, ma'am."

While Marcus cooks, I sit at the kitchen bench and watch. I've missed having him around over the last few years. I mean, he's still been around, but not in the same way. It's never just the two of us shooting the shit anymore.

"Are you going to school today?" I ask. It's only 7:30, so he has plenty of time to get there for the last day of school for the week.

"Yep. I have a Maths assessment today, so I can't ditch." He looks up from the pan where he's scrambling eggs on the stove. "When are you coming back to school?"

School. Not a place I want to be, but I know I have to return. I reluctantly called them on Monday, thinking I would have to speak to that useless piece of shit Principal Ryland, but he wasn't there. Instead, my call was put through to the new Acting Principal Rogan.

Cynthia Rogan definitely took me by surprise. She doesn't sound like the typical Catholic principal. This lady openly swore down the line and confessed that the old principal was the scum of the earth who needs to be locked up with paedophiles and murderers.

I loved this woman instantly!

She knew who I was and what had happened to me when she got placed in the role after Miss Dice put in a formal complaint to the board of education and the police. The office ladies had told Miss Dice that Principal Ryland turned a blind eye and allowed my dad to drug me and basically kidnap me. I guess there are some decent people out there after all. At least Fox Pines Catholic College has a decent principal now.

"Ah, yeah, I'll be back next week, I guess. Just waiting for this bruising to go away."

Marcus turns the stove off and moves to stand in front of me on the other side of the bench.

"It's still pretty bad. What if it's not gone by next week?"

I shrug, "Then I go with a bruised face."

Marcus is quiet for a moment, his eyes roaming my face, and something like guilt twists his expression. "I'm sorry I didn't notice sooner, Lex."

I don't like seeing the pain in his eyes as he stares at me. I also don't like or want pity.

"I made sure no one noticed Marcus. Even Abbey didn't notice."

"Ayden did."

I cringe, hearing his cousin's name.

"New rule!" I slide down off the stool and rummage through the cupboards to get plates for our food. "No saying his name."

"What? You don't want me to say A-,"

"Ahhh!" I yell, causing Marcus to stop what he was about to say.

He frowns, "I can't say my cousin's name?"

"Correct." I place two plates on the bench trying to avoid Marcus' eyes.

"Why?" He dishes up the eggs while I start on the toast.

"It doesn't matter why. I just don't need to hear his name right now."

Marcus pauses briefly, watching me, probably trying to gauge if I'm being serious. He must get the hint because he keeps his mouth shut as we continue moving about the kitchen to finish making breakfast.

We eat silently. It's not a comfortable silence like it was with Andrea, Ayden's mum, when I was with her in Melbourne. I guess Marcus and I really do have some mending to do in our friendship. When he looks at me, he sees a girl with boobs. But when I look at him, all I see is the friend I grew up with.

After breakfast, I reluctantly go up to my room while Marcus does the dishes. Yes, I was serious about that. I hate doing dishes.

Since I don't have anywhere to be today, I slip on my jeans and throw on my SlipKnot hoodie over my Metallica t-shirt that I slept in. I don't care if I smell or look like shit; that's the least of my problems. My hair gets thrown up in a careless, messy bun, and I slide my feet into my black Ugg boots. I don't have anyone to impress.

I hate my room now. It's a real struggle just to step inside it. The door is still missing, and everything in it reminds me of the night that Mike assaulted me. I've been sleeping, or at least trying to sleep, on the couch every night, and I use my mum's bathroom downstairs. There's no way I'll be stepping foot inside the upstairs bathroom anytime soon, not after what happened with Mike. Most of my clothes are still in my bedroom, though. Maybe I should move them down to my mum's room. At least until she gets home from the hospital. Whenever that will be.

At first, I didn't know why I came back to the house that holds all of my nightmares. I knew I had to come back to Fox Pines because that's where my life is. I had intended to stay in the town's only motel, The Foxy Pine. I was wrong. Once my feet left the train, they led me back here. This house may hold memories I'd like to forget, but it used to feel like home, and it's the only home I have. Mike's attempt to break me failed. This is my house, and that fucker better not think he can come back here ever again.

"Lex?"

Marcus startles me out of my thoughts, making me jump. I hadn't realised that I was staring at myself in my dresser mirror, and I don't know how long I've been like that, or how long Marcus has been witnessing it. I do that sometimes now. Lose time. I think I just fall so deeply into my thoughts that I don't pay attention to what I'm doing. Who knows? My head is screwed up worse than it's ever been.

I turn to Marcus, trying to appear normal, so he doesn't see how embarrassed I am.

"The doors." Marcus looks over his shoulder towards the bathroom. Not only haven't I been back in there, but I avoid looking through the open doorway because the shower is the first thing I see. I also avoid looking at the brownish-red bloodstains on the carpet in the hall, which Valarie's mum obviously couldn't successfully scrub out.

Marcus turns back to me, looking uncomfortable, raking his hand through his thick brown hair. "I'll fix them this weekend. Or maybe tonight. Do you know where the doors are?"

"In the back shed." My voice sounds dead, and my heart feels cold.

Marcus frowns at me, worry etched across his face, "You okay?"

I give my head a single shake before moving past him out of my room.

"You can shower in my mum's ensuite if you need to before you leave." I keep walking, descending the stairs, and Marcus calls out.

"That's okay. I'll sneak back home and shower there before school."

Going upstairs always succeeds to push my rage to the surface. It's all-consuming, and I make no attempt to push it down. It's as if I need to feel the anger. I can't say that I like it, but I just know that I need it right now.

Marcus leaves for school after following me upstairs and trying to make conversation with me. It's no good, though. I'm in a dark place again, and he can't reach me.

I spend the day the same way I have every other day since getting back. I go for a run on my mum's treadmill that she used twice before using it to hang washing on. I pound the shit out of Mike's boxing bag in the garage and use his weights to push the limits of my weak girly muscles until the burning gets too much. I troll the internet while eating lunch to see if there's any news on my dad or Mike. So far there's nothing. Both of those fuckers are still out there, just waiting for the right moment to pounce. I can feel it in my bones. I haven't heard from either of them, but I know it's only a matter of time before I do.

As with every other day, I call the hospital where my mum is staying, only to be told that she's still not accepting calls. I try to reach out to Abbey again via email since that's what worked the other time. Still nothing from her either.

Just when the loneliness and isolation start to overwhelm me, I get a message from Marcus in our group chat that includes Simon, Garrett, Jared and Shaun.

Marcus-Grady
Heads up, Lexi. We'll be over around 5 pm.

Lexi-West
Who's we?

I know he means the guys in the group message, but what can I say? I'm lonely and want a conversation, even if it's brief.

Simon-Hastings
All you need to know is that I'll be there.
No one else matters.

Shaun-Bossier
Dude. She won't care about you once
I walk through the door.

Garrett-Cole

Marcus man, maybe you should have sent Lexi a PM. Having these idiots in the chat isn't a good idea!

Marcus-Grady

I'm beginning to see that!
Shut up, dickheads!

Jared-Crowley

Don't worry, Lex. Stick with me.
I'll protect you from these idiots.

Simon-Hastings

Who are you calling an idiot? Idiot!

Garrett-Cole

That's it, boys, keep showing Lexi how smart you are!
#digyourowngrave

Simon-Hastings

Did you just use a hashtag on me, Cole?

Marcus-Grady

I'm pretty sure Gaz used a hashtag on all of you.

Jared-Crowley
How are you anyway, Lex?
Ready for a night of gaming? If I recall correctly, you owe me a rematch of Fortnite.

Wow, he has a good memory. We spent an entire weekend playing it at Simon's months ago.

Lexi-West
Firstly, you're all idiots!
Secondly, Jar, isn't Fortnite like, so last year?

Simon-Hastings
Ha! Burn!

Jared-Crowley
Shut up, Hastings!
Lexi, Lexi, Lexi. Fortnite will never die!

Shaun-Bossier
Fortnite is totally dead!

Jared-Crowley
Says the tosser who still pulls himself over Mario Kart and his ancient Nintendo console!

Lexi-West
All right, guys. Piss off and do your schoolwork.
Stop interrupting me.

Garrett-Cole
What are you up to anyway, Lex?

Lexi-West
Homework.

It's a total lie. While I have been keeping up with the work my teachers have emailed me, it's not what I'm doing now. I'm not about to admit to them that the rage consuming me is sending me down a dark and lonely path, and today I'm plotting my revenge against Mike in my head.

Simon-Hastings
Of course, you are Lex. You're always the A-grader.

Not for a while now, but he doesn't need to know that.

Garrett-Cole
That's great, Lex!
Simon's sour because you haven't
been around for him to copy work off.

Simon-Hastings
Shut up, idiot!
I don't need to copy anyone. I'm a genius.

Marcus-Grady
If you're a genius, then I'm a fucking supermodel.

Shaun-Bossier
A genius at being an idiot!

Simon-Hastings
Shut up Bossi, at least I'm not too chickenshit
to slip my hand down a chick's pants!

Lexi-West
Ah, guys? Maybe you can take this
conversation somewhere else?
To a different chat, perhaps?
I don't want to hear about where
your hands have been.

Simon-Hastings
In Bossi's case, it's where his hands haven't been.

Shaun-Bossier
Shut up, idiot!

Lexi-West
Bye!!!!!!

I'm laughing as I put my phone down. I hate to admit it, but I miss those guys. I've always gravitated to boys, and no, I'm not talking about being attracted to them. I mean that I feel more myself around males. Well, those ones anyway.

With girls things always feel like a competition, or like anything I say will be used against me later in a bitch fight. Take Tasha, for example; whenever I've shown an interest in a new guy, it's like she or Allison suddenly have an interest in the same guy. Last year I even pretended to have a crush on Travis. I succeeded in my little experiment to see that both girls went after him once I'd declared I thought he was cute and wanted to kiss him. If those girls knew me at all, they would know Travis is not my type. *Eww!* I was also with Nathan at the time, so why they thought I would stray is beyond me because I never have and never will be that type of girl.

Just thinking about Tasha and Allison irks me. I don't know why I put up with them. It was Abbey that became friends with them and wanted to bring them into our circle. At the time, it was just me, Abbey and the boys. Things were so much simpler back then.

Anger still bubbles near the surface and thinking about Tasha and Allison isn't helping. I need to get it under control before the guys get here. I consider another run or boxing bag session, but when my eyes land on the baseball bat by the front door, I stop thinking and just act.

With the bat firmly in my grip, I climb the stairs two at a time and storm to Mike's bedroom. Lifting the bat, I start swinging at his door, the only door that still remains secured on its hinges upstairs. It's not locked. I could have just opened it, but that would be too easy, and this fucker doesn't deserve to have a door since he revelled in mine being taken away.

I slam all of my anger into each swing, growling screams bellowing from deep within me. My vision turns red as I splinter the door apart until most of it is gone, laying in jagged pieces on the carpet below. I don't stop there, stepping into Mike's room, I swing the bat at every piece of furniture or belonging he left behind.

When I'd first returned from Melbourne, I'd crept into this room looking for my laptop and phone but only found my laptop. It was then that I discovered he took his drug stash with him when he fled, which disappointed me because I would have loved to watch it flush down the toilet.

I'm so angry. Straight up, motherfucking angry. There's really no other way to describe it. After leaving Ayden's dad's apartment, I walked around the city for about an hour crying, feeling sad and sorry for myself, all while fearing that my dad or brother would jump out from every corner I approached. Just when I thought I couldn't take anymore, the tears dried up and what was left was anger.

I'm angry at my mum for never loving me enough to put me first and for looking the other way when I know she must have known Mike was harassing me. I'm also angry at her for being too weak to see what her husband, my dad, was doing to her.

Speaking of, I'm angry at that arsehole of a so-called dad for leaving me to live another life in the city and for getting mad at me for calling him out on it when I interrupted him and his mistress. I'm angry at him for laying his hand on me with so much force that he left bruises. And I'm fucking furious that he so easily told my principal lies and then drugged me to remove me from school so I couldn't fight for myself and make a scene. Let's not forget how he knew exactly what he was doing when he left me in the hands of his sick, twisted son and knowingly walked away without an ounce of regret.

That moment when he left me with Mike, that's something I'll never be able to forget for as long as I live. Motherfucking Mike! My dad's love child. He's always been odd and strange, and my dad left him in charge to teach me a lesson. The word angry doesn't even begin to cut it when I think of the crude, vulgar things my half brother did to me. Murderous is a good fucking word for it!

Nope, not even that feels right!

This anger, this rage that bubbles in my heart like molten lava, even extends to Abbey's parents and their fucked up religious beliefs. The fact that even though the police had announced to the world that they are looking for my dad, her parents still believed the crap he told them about me being mentally ill. I need Abbey, damn it! What the actual fuck is wrong with them?

Ahhhhhhh!

Principal Ryland doesn't escape my anger either! That chickenshit arsehole is just as guilty by letting my dad carry me out without even questioning things. If he had been doing his job, then I would have never been put in the situation that led to

Ayden having to rescue me and whisk me away to Melbourne to hide at his dad's place.

Ayden... I try not to think about him, but I can't help it. Out of all the fucked up shit that has happened to me, the fact that I put him in a situation which he'd been working so hard to free himself from, rips my heart in two. Our beautiful happy love bubble burst the moment that thug, Muz, forced us into his car, which led to Ayden snorting drugs and a gun being pointed at my head. That has to take the motherfucking cake!

That gun! I want that gun so I can shove it in Muz's open mouth and pull the trigger for no other reason than the fact that he hurt my Ayden.

Wait! No!

Not my Ayden. He made that clear when he kicked me out.

Like I said, I am angry as fuck, and I can't seem to simmer down my rage.

When my arms become heavy from lashing out my fury on anything and everything in my path, I let the pain in my heart take over and crumble to the floor, crying. What I really want to do is set this house on fire and watch it burn to the ground, ideally with Mike still inside. I think of his death daily now, of ways I can inflict pain on him. A quick death won't be satisfying enough. I think I need to torture him first. Strip away his pride and humiliate him until he's begging me to stop. Then, maybe I could happily finish the job and rid him from this earth.

Images flash through my head. Some are of Mike's face and the way he looked almost euphoric as he laid his disgusting, hateful hands on me. Some are images of my hand reaching up and slicing his throat open with a blade. Yes, I like those images. They are my favourite.

"Lexi?"

I jump up instinctively at the sound of my name, the bat in my hand, ready to swing. The room has darkened considerably, and I can only see a man's silhouette standing in the doorway. The only sound I can hear is the rushing of my blood and the pounding of my heart, my body ready for a fight.

Light suddenly fills the room, and I notice more than one body is standing before me. Instinctively, I take a step back, bat still in the air at the ready.

"Stay back!"

"Lexi. It's just us."

"Stay back!" I scream, wishing my eyes would function properly so I can see who's in front of me.

"Guys, back out of the room. Give her some space."

I know that voice. I know I know it, so why can't I make the connection?

The bodies slowly step backwards out of the room, all except one.

"Lexi," the voice is low and cautious, "it's okay. It's just us idiots. You remember us, right? You remember me? We have a Fortnite battle to play."

My eyes glass over with hot angry tears, while my chest heaves, attempting to gain control of my breathing. I swipe at my eyes with one hand, briefly letting go of my death grip on the bat.

"Lex, it's Jar. You know me."

I blink my eyes, and the red rage fuelled by my anger starts to fade, and in its place is Jared, the boy I grew up with.

My bottom lip quivers, and the fight leaves my body.

"Jared?" A shaky whisper leaves my lips.

"Yeah, Lex, it's me." Jared's face clears in my vision, and I can see his familiar kind blue eyes.

I let the bat fall from my hand and go to step towards my old friend.

"Wait!" Jared holds his hand up. "Don't move, Lex. I'll come to you."

Confused, I follow his eyes to the floor at my feet and the shards of glass and splinters of wood covering every inch of carpet. My bare feet are bleeding, and scratches cover my legs and arms, some freshly bleeding while others are crusted over.

What the fuck have I done?

The crunching of broken glass under foot gains my attention, and I watch Jared take the few steps across the room to where I stand.

"Lex, I'm gonna pick you up and carry you out of here, okay?"

I look up to Jared's towering height. He's the tallest of the boys, and just as manly as Ayden, even though there's a year between them in age. Jared gets a lot of attention from the girls at school, and if he weren't my close friend, I would probably deem him boyfriend material.

I nod up at him, letting more tears fall from my eyes. I'm so confused. I feel like a fucking freak! I don't know how I let myself get so out of control. Jesus, how long was I like that? I must have been in Mike's room for hours since the boys are here now, yet it feels like it was only minutes.

Perhaps I belong in the same hospital as my mum.

Jared wipes the tears from my wet cheeks and then reaches down to lift me in his arms. I curl into him as I'm cradled to his chest, and then he carries me out, stepping over the debris that used to make up Mike's bedroom.

Three

Gentle hands make quick work of cleaning up my scrapes, Jared's face deep in concentration as he glides a warm washcloth over my skin. He is kneeled before me on the beige tiles of my mum's bathroom floor. I barely notice the chill of the bench-top that Jared placed me on after carrying me downstairs from the destruction I inflicted on Mike's room because my mind is too consumed with shame.

"That should do it." Jared declares before tossing the washer in the sink, his blue eyes filled with concern.

"Thanks," I whisper, feeling embarrassed at being caught in the rage that saw me trash Mike's bedroom.

With sympathy etched across his face, Jared gives me a small smile, "It's okay, Six. Don't worry about what happened."

Six is my secret code name from when we were kids. We had turned our names backwards and used the first three letters, thinking we were so cool back then. Alexis turned into Six, Abbey turned into Yeb, Jared turned into Der, and Marcus turned into Suc. We used to love teasing Marcus about his secret code name. Mine is still the best. Well, I think so, anyway.

"I don't know what happened," I whisper, feeling self-disgust darken my mood.

Jared sighs. "You've been through a lot, Lex. Best not to overthink it. Besides," reaching out, Jared takes my hand, "That motherfucker has it coming to him. Trashing his room is the least of his problems."

I grin at the ferocity of Jared's voice. He's always been protective of me, even when we were kids.

"Lex," he hesitates before sighing again, "why didn't you tell me? Or Abbey? We could have done something. Helped in some way."

My cheeks heat in humiliation, and I drop my eyes from his intense gaze.

"I don't really know how to answer that." I shrug. "I guess I felt so ashamed. I couldn't comprehend saying the words out loud. I didn't know how to."

I don't feel like my words make any sense, but Jared nods anyway and stands from the floor to tower over me. Like the other guys, Jared isn't wearing his school uniform, so they must have gone home to get changed before they came over.

"We can't change the past, Lexi. But we can sure as shit make sure you're looked after from now on."

"I don't need looking after, Jar." I force strength into my voice this time. I'm not weak, and I need him to know that.

"Maybe. But it doesn't mean we don't want to look after you."

He has me there.

Reaching up, Jared runs the backs of his fingers over my bruised face. It feels intimate. Too intimate. Without even thinking, I jerk back, ultimately showing Jared that I'm not comfortable with him touching me like that. His gentle touch reminds me of Ayden, but he's not Ayden. He's my childhood friend. I struggle to hold back my tears but somehow manage and silently high five myself for winning that internal battle.

Jared probably thinks I'm upset about what Mike did to me, and while that is part of it, a hell of a lot of my emotional turmoil is all for the blue eyed, dark haired, dimple cheeked guy I left behind in Melbourne. The guy who took a chunk of my heart.

Not acting offended by my reaction, Jared offers me a lopsided grin which reminds me very much of the blonde haired, blue eyed, bratty boy I grew up with.

"Come on. The boys have pizza. We better get out there before they eat it all without us."

Tugging on my hand, Jared eases me down from the bench and leads the way out of my mum's room. It's easy to tell where the boys are as we head towards the front living room, where they argue loudly over something to do with football.

"If Bombers win, you have to strip off and run to the corner of the street and back."

A small grin tugs at my mouth as we enter the living room. I love the stupid banter between these guys. Simon is a diehard Bombers fan and is adamant that they will beat Sydney in tonight's game airing live on TV. He would never make such a bet if he didn't believe his team would win.

"You sick bastard, you just want to get a look at my mammoth cock! We all know Bombers are gonna win tonight." Shaun, or as the girls refer to him, Spanish Casanova, grabs his crotch, giving it a shake as he answers Simon.

"Fuck off man. I don't want to see your crooked sausage."

Everyone laughs at Simon's response before they notice my presence.

"Here, Lexi. We saved you some pizza." Garrett offers, jumping up from the couch to hand me a small pizza box. His eyes are just as intense as Jared's as he passes me the box, so I break the eye contact, quickly muttering "thanks" before taking a seat on the other couch along the back wall.

I ignore their silent stares and nibble at the pizza before Marcus re-directs their attention to their footy debate. *Thank you, Marcus!*

I take my sweet time nibbling on the same slice of pizza until I'm sure they won't notice that I've hardly eaten any of it and then slip it back into the box. My appetite is still lacking, and eating right now just isn't something I can fathom.

I'm quiet. Too quiet. The boys notice but say nothing and instead keep the conversation light. I feel embarrassed that they witnessed me losing my shit. I loathe myself for it. I'm drowning in a deep cold abyss that chills my heart, and it's almost impossible to hide the effects now.

I feel myself spiralling from my own thoughts, but this time a strange numbness takes over me, and I no longer hear the conversations around me. Dark thoughts consume my mind, and even though I can still see the guys talking and throwing the occasional arm *corkie,* I can't hear much else but white noise. I see the moment when Marcus and Jared notice. They share a look before Jared moves across my living room and sits next to me on the couch, wrapping his arm around my shoulders and pulling me into his side. I don't protest because honestly, the contact is comforting. My heart wishes it was Ayden, but my brain knows that isn't going to happen. Ayden made it clear that he was done with me.

At some point, I fall asleep. It isn't a heavy sleep because I swear, I can hear the boys bicker right through the evening, but I rest just below the surface of knowing what they are saying. It's oddly comforting to be surrounded by the noise after being alone in this quiet house for most of the week.

Sometime later, I'm pulled awake to the sounds of... well, sex. Moaning and panting shocks me into staying silent, and I pop one eye open to peek at whatever the hell is going on. I'm no longer in Jared's arms but laying on the couch I'd been sitting on earlier. I dart my open eye quickly around the room to take stock of what's happening. Then, I have to fight to hold back my laugh.

While I've been curled up on the couch at the back of the room, the five boys have been huddled on the floor in front of my wide-screen TV. Watching porn!

I sit up slowly, but they are so engrossed in what they are watching that they don't hear me. A lady, as naked as the day she was born, is gyrating against a man's hand while another chick takes him deep into her mouth. Fucking hell. If this isn't awkward, then I don't know what is. Watching porn with a group of guys is definitely not on my list of things I ever wanted to do.

"See Bossi, that's what you have to do when you put your hand down a girl's pants." Simon chuckles, always the clown of the group stirring up shit.

Shaun turns and punches Simon in the arm. "Shut the fuck up idiot, I've been down a girl's pants plenty of times. I just have no interest in going down Tasha's filthy pants."

My ears prick up at hearing Tasha's name.

"Yeah, wise choice man. She's one piece of pussy that you want to stay away from." Marcus states, keeping his eyes glued to the TV screen.

I don't flinch at their choice of words or the way they speak. Growing up surrounded by guys means you have no choice but to get used to how they act.

"You say that after you've already gone for a test drive." Garrett chuckles, and Marcus shrugs.

"It was a moment of weakness. I couldn't have the one I wanted, so I just imagined it was her and used Tasha for it."

Jesus! I didn't know Marcus could be so cold towards a girl. Or that he hooked up with Tasha. When the hell did that happen?

The boys go quiet and nod in understanding at Marcus before each one slowly turns to look back at me.

The deer in headlights look they all sport would be funny if it weren't for the fact that they just made something deadly obvious. Marcus had been wishing it was me when he was with Tasha.

Jesus! Fuck!

One thing I'm extremely good at is deflection, so I put that baby in motion.

"You arseholes better not be sporting wood while you watch that filth in my house."

One by one, grins take over their faces, and Simon leaps up, giving his ash-blonde hair his signature Bieber flick.

"There she is, our sassy little Lexi throwing her weight around." Simon stalks towards me, and my eyes widen at what I see before I squeal.

"Eww! Stop!" I leap up on the couch cushions, trying to keep Simon from reaching me, and put my hands out to stop him.

"What?" Simon looks confused and turns back to his mates in question.

They all see what freaked me out and roar in laughter. Simon turns his hazel eyes back to me, confused.

"You need to fix that." I point my eyes in the direction of his crotch, and he looks down to see what we are all aware of. He laughs and tries to push his erection down or something. I don't really know, but the damn thing bounces back up in the loose grey trackies he is wearing. OMG, is he even wearing jocks underneath?

"There's only one thing that's going to fix this, Lexi," Simon says with a devilish look on his face.

"Hastings, man! Not fucking cool!" Garrett snaps, leaping up from the floor, his face reddening in anger, but I don't flinch at Simon's provocative suggestion.

"Oh, yeah?" I smile seductively at Simon and step down off the couch. "Shall we?" I put my hand out and watch the internal battle twist his baby face.

The boys stare wide-eyed at us, and I hear Marcus curse under his breath when Simon puts his hand in mine. As I lead Simon out of the room, I give the boys a wink which Simon doesn't see, and I guide him to the front door ignoring the confused looks I receive from them all.

"Let's go out here where we can have some privacy."

Simon just nods eagerly at me as I open the door and drop his hand, gesturing for him to go out first. Because he is thinking with his dick and not his head, he doesn't even question why I'm leading him out the front door. *Idiot!*

"You can come back in when your wood has gone."

Simon turns to look at me in confusion before I slam the door in his face and lock it.

Laughter roars from the boys in the living room, but I ignore it, as well as Simon's persistent banging on the door, while I walk away to use my mum's bathroom.

My trip to use the bathroom alerts me to the fact that my dreaded monthly has reared its ugly crimson head. The thing is, for once, I'm damn happy to see the red monster, and I slump with a sigh of relief.

It was over a week ago that I gave Ayden my virginity. A night I will never forget, and even though things didn't end so well between us, I will always cherish it. I may not have known Ayden that well, or for very long, but for the briefest time, we shared a bond, a connection that I'm quite certain I will never find again.

We were careful and used protection, but the bitch devil in the back of my mind has been reminding me that condoms aren't 100% foolproof, and I've been fearing that with my luck, I may have fallen pregnant. The whole having to flee to Melbourne thing left me without my birth control pills, so yes, seeing the blood is a huge relief. It also may explain why I've been finding it harder to control my emotions today.

I take a moment to splash water on my face in the hopes it will make me feel better. It doesn't. Sunken dull blue eyes look back at me in the mirror. I hardly recognise them or the face they live on. There is no more swelling on the left side of my face, but the bruising is still there, more green than purple now, which must mean it's getting better. Under each eye sits dark shadows, which looks worse because of the sickly paleness of my skin. My cheeks hold no colour, and my lips are the lightest shade of pink I've ever seen them. Even the waves in my blonde hair look like they can't be bothered, and fall limp.

I should probably care a little more about my appearance. Maybe brush on some mascara or dust on a little blush, but it all seems too much, too hard. The outside of me looks just as lifeless as the inside of me feels.

When I force myself to leave my mum's room a few minutes later, the sound of porn has been replaced by gunfire on the PlayStation, and Simon no longer pounds on the door. My phone vibrates in my pocket with a message, and I smile, already knowing it's from Simon.

Simon Hastings

I'm sorry. It's gone. Promise.

I don't respond, but instead, walk back past the living area to the front door and open it. Simon has his arms wrapped around his shoulders, trying to stay warm.

"Sorry, Lex." Simon's usual clown grin has vanished, replaced with worry and shame.

Shit! Guilt hits me like a Mack Truck. He probably didn't deserve how I treated him.

"I'm sorry for being a bitch, Simon. Word of warning. It's hard for me not to be one right now."

Simon steps inside and closes the door behind him. "You have every reason to be a bitch. I mean... not that you are a bitch. I'm not saying you're one. I mean..."

I laugh at Simon's fumbled words. "It's okay, Simon. I am a bitch. I'm not in denial about that." I shift nervously and grin, "What exactly would you have done if I had gone out there with you?"

A blush creeps over Simon's face, and his dimpled chin sinks in further. I chew the inside of my cheek to hide my grin, but I can tell his bright hazel eyes pick up on it.

"Fucked if I know. I was hoping you would take the lead." I laugh at his honesty, and he joins in.

"Come on, Woodie," I turn and go back into the living room with Simon on my tail.

"Hey! No way! That's not going to be my new nickname." Simon protests, gaining everyone's attention.

"What's that, Woodie? You say something?" Garrett teases, sending everyone into fits of laughter.

"Serves you right for watching porn on my TV while I was in the same room!" I snap, trying to sound angry. I fail. They can see my grin.

"Bossi just needed a few tips to brush up on his lack of game." Simon steers the conversation away from him again. Smart boy.

"Fuck off, Hastings! I get more pussy than anyone in this room!" Spanish Casanova, AKA Shaun gloats.

And this argument goes on and on.

Considering how the boys found me when they came over earlier, I'm in a better mood with every passing hour. Their presence makes me feel lighter, and I eventually join in and play Fortnite with Jared before we all call it a night.

I thought they would go home, but I was wrong. Confused, I watch the boys disappear into my house, and I shoot Jared a questioning glare, but he shrugs and gives me a knowing smirk. Marcus and Garrett stroll back into the living room a moment later, their arms clutching piles of pillows and blankets.

"Ah... what's going on?" I squeak.

Marcus drops the blankets to the floor as Shaun and Simon enter the room with their arms packed with blankets too.

"Slumber party!" Jared announces.

Marcus hands me the blanket we'd used the night before and leans in to whisper. "You want to cuddle my feet again?"

Raising my brow, I snatch the blanket off him. "You can sleep on the floor or on the other couch, just like you should have last night!"

Marcus chuckles and moves to the other couch without argument. I don't miss the questioning looks Marcus gets from the guys, but thankfully, no one asks us to elaborate.

"Hey, guys?" I ask, gaining five sets of eyes. "Where do your parents think you are?"

"Their parents think they are at my house." Simon declares, puffing his chest out like he's proud.

"Where do your parents think you are then, Simon?" I ask, eyeing where he has just dumped his armful of blankets on the floor.

"They think I'm at home. You know what they're like, Lex, too busy attending snobby parties in the city to pay much attention to what I'm doing."

Pity sits heavy in my chest at the reminder of what Simon's parents are like. They are lovely people, always nice and welcoming, but they often go on trips away, leaving Simon to his own devices. The wink, which is more like a blink that Simon gives me, is his way of saying don't think too much about it because he doesn't.

Simon, Garrett and Shaun make their beds for the night side by side where they had been sitting earlier to watch porn, while Jared makes his bed at the foot of the couch I am occupying. Marcus shakes his head from the other couch, grinning before laying down and scrolling on his phone.

"Ah- Jared." I whisper, not wanting to get everyone's attention, "If I need to pee in the middle of the night, I might step on you."

Looking up in amusement, Jared simply shrugs, "I'll take that chance."

"Der, there's plenty of space in this room. You don't have to sleep under my feet."

Jared grins at my use of his childhood code name and sits down on his makeshift bed, shuffling his legs under the blanket.

"Well Six, there may be plenty of space, but I figure if I sleep here, then no one can get to you without getting past me first."

My brows shoot up, nearly reaching my hairline, and I frown, looking from Jared to the other guys in the room. What's Jared talking about? These boys won't hurt me.

"Not them," Jared interjects, "If your fuckhead brother or dad comes here, then they'll have to kill me before they can get anywhere near you."

I don't know what to say to that. I don't want Jared to get hurt. I don't want any of them to get hurt, but I am also scared. I'll never admit how scared I am out loud. I'm too stubborn for that.

"We're here for you, Lex. Each one of us. We will never let anyone hurt you again." The certainty in Jared's voice is convincing, yet I worry that his statement has more than one meaning. He knows, hell, they all know that I'm hurting from the way things ended with Ayden. The guys can't protect my heart from that sort of pain, although right now, I kinda wish they could.

I give Jared a small smile before laying down on my side to get comfy on the couch, and he follows suit on the floor below me. With the faint glow of the TV filling the room, I look down over my friends as they shuffle around, trying to get comfy on the floor. I feel bad. There's no way it's comfortable for them down there, but I desperately don't want them to leave, so I stay quiet.

They each have their phones in their hands, either silently playing a game or checking their SnapChats. I join them and take my phone out to recheck my emails—still nothing from Abbey. I don't understand why I haven't heard from her. Maybe her parents have taken all of her devices off her. But that can't be right. Marcus said he contacted her last weekend. It's now Friday, so anything could have happened in that time, I guess. Ugh, it's eating me up not knowing what's going on with Abbey. Maybe I will take a walk to her house on the weekend. Surely her parents won't be rude enough to my face and turn me away.

As if my heart isn't quite aching enough already, I decide to torture myself again and look back over Ayden's messages. I go back to our first messages when we were two strangers. Looking at them again shows me how fast we connected. It was instant, really. Sure, I pushed him away at first, but he never gave up. I scroll past the video he sent of his version of a lap dance from a magazine cut out, and then past the video I sent him in return of my crack house. I know now that it was my way of trying to tell him I was in trouble without admitting it. Most of our messages make me smile, but not the last one he sent.

I'm so fucking sorry!

I have to fight every instinct in me not to reply to him. I can't let my selfish needs get in the way of what's best for him, though, and what's best for him isn't me. A single silent tear rolls from my eye without warning, and I brush it away quickly, hoping no one witnessed my moment of weakness.

Shaun is the first to put his phone down and close his eyes. Marcus and Simon are next, giving in to the need to sleep. Garrett stays awake longer. I can see that he's reading something on his phone. Maybe a kindle book? It's a long while before he turns his phone off and rolls on his side to fall asleep, so I'm surprised when Jared's hand reaches up to grip mine from where he is laying on the floor in front of the couch.

I let him pull it down to rest on his chest and peer over the edge of the couch to see his sleepy eyes looking up at me.

"Try to sleep, Six."

I shouldn't keep holding his hand, but I do, and that's how I fall asleep.

Four

I might just be feeling paranoid, but I'm fairly certain everyone is looking at me. I didn't want to come to the boys' footy, but they weren't taking no for an answer. Staying at home hidden away suited me much better than coming out into the world where my bruises are visible to everyone.

I'd overheard Marcus and Jared talking in the kitchen this morning when I was in my mum's room getting dressed after my shower. They were worried about leaving me on my own and not just because my brother could show up at any time. I'm pretty sure they think I'm a nutcase.

They wouldn't be wrong. I'm all kinds of fucked in the head right now, but I'm not a danger to myself... At least, I don't think I am. My eyes move to my hands, where small scratches remind me of my meltdown in Mike's room yesterday afternoon. I wonder how long I would have stayed in that crazed state if the boys hadn't come over. Shit, maybe they're right to be concerned.

"You cold Lex?" An arm wraps around me, and I welcome its warmth. Spring is due to start tomorrow, but you wouldn't know it from the arctic blast hitting us today. I glance up to meet Garrett's warm smile and push out a fake one in return. Garrett doesn't smile often, so when he gifts me one, I always return it.

"It's bloody freezing today." I tug on my black beanie, making sure my ears are covered.

"You want my coat?" Garrett asks, and I immediately shake my head. He looks warm in the puffy coat he wears.

"So, what did you do to your finger, anyway?" I shift the attention to Garrett's finger, which is taped up and secured to a metal rod to keep it straight. I hadn't wanted to pry yesterday when I saw it, but I have no problem prying today. Like I've said before, I'm good at deflecting.

Garrett's blue-grey eyes dart to his bandaged hand before he shakes his head. "Let's just say the other guy's face is worse than my finger."

My brows shoot up. "Now I really want to know what happened. Who'd you hit?"

Garrett shifts uncomfortably but doesn't remove his arm from me. "Tony Anders." He doesn't elaborate.

"And what did Tony Anders do to piss you off?"

"Let's just watch the game." He keeps his eyes trained on the oval where Fox Pines is playing Woodall Ridge. All the guys are in the side today, apart from Garrett. His injured finger means he has to sit on the sidelines and support his teammates.

Unlike Marcus and Jared, Garrett didn't grow up with us. He moved to Fox Pines a few years ago from Redfield and fell into the boys' group through footy. He's always been kind to me, even though I know he has a temper. I'm not sure if his temper is just a trait he's always had or if something happened to make him feel anger so consuming that he has to release it. I totally understand that sort of anger now.

Unfortunately for Garrett, if he doesn't already know that I'm not going to give up so easily, then he's about to learn. Not because I'm nosey, but because I have a feeling that it has something to do with me.

"We can watch the game while you tell me about your run-in with Tony." I insist, working to keep a straight face.

Garrett chuckles, looking down at me, a strand of his wavy brown hair falling over his right eye. He's about the same height as Ayden. His eyes are blue like Jared's and Ayden's, but Garrett's has light flecks through his, making them appear more grey. Neither Garrett's nor Jared's eyes seize my heart the way Ayden's do, though.

"What are the chances that you're going to let this drop?"

"Zero chances, buddy. Spill." I give him a toothy grin, and he chuckles before clearing his throat.

"Tony is currently receiving dental treatment from my fist because the fucker stood by and watched your dad carry you unconscious out of the school. He saw you go into the office. He even overheard the office ladies speaking about how it's wrong that your dad is trying to force you to leave with him, and then he watched your dad carry you out. The little prick is fucking lucky dental work is all he needs."

Holy shit! I'm actually lost for words. Not because Tony Anders is a dipshit that didn't man up, but because Garrett stood up for me, and even now as he speaks, sounds so fiercely protective. My stupid eyes fill with hot tears, so I quickly turn my head and blink them away, but Garrett notices and tugs me closer to his side.

"Thank you," I whisper.

"I'd do it again in a heartbeat, Lex."

These guys. I don't know what I've done to be lucky enough to deserve their loyalty. I knew we were all friends, but I never knew until this week how much our friendship means. Hell, it feels like more than friendship. These guys feel like my family.

It's hard to concentrate on the football game playing before me. My mind is a mess flitting between memories, both good and bad, and the new things I've learnt since coming back home. Glancing around the oval boundary, I search to see if Abbey or any of the girls from school are here, but I don't spot any of them. Abbey's boyfriend, Daniel, doesn't play football, so I assume she is with him somewhere, and since it's cold as fuck outside today, I'd say the weather probably kept the other girls away.

Thankful the footy finally finishes, I'm surprised when the boys announce that we're going to Simon's for the night while his parents are away. I think about arguing my case to go back home for a night of silence, but it's for that reason that I don't. I don't want to be alone.

It's not uncommon for the guys to have people over for a night of celebrating after a footy win or even a loss. The difference with tonight is that they don't invite anyone else. It's just us in Simon's big house, and every time they get a message or call from one of the girls from school, they ignore them or shut them down, refusing to let anyone else join us. I'm sure they are doing it for my benefit, and I love them for it.

For the second night in a row, we have pizza for dinner. I have a single slice, and the boys try to force more into me, but they lose that battle. Stubborn should be my middle name! After eating, Simon brings out a box filled with bottles of alcohol, and the boys start drinking. Even though my mood is flat, I join them to have a few drinks hoping it will numb my pain. When the relaxing buzz kicks in, it has the desired effect and calms my anger giving me a sense of peace as I sit lazily in a beanbag, happily watching the boys hang shit on each other and talk footy while trying to play pool in Simon's rumpus room.

"Jesus, now Abbey wants to come over," Simon complains, tossing his phone on the bar counter.

"Abbey?" I shoot upright in the beanbag. "Chuck me your phone, Simon."

"Ah, that might not be a good idea, Lex." Marcus tries to intervene, but Simon has already launched his phone in the air towards me.

I catch it easily and tap Abbey's number. It starts to ring.

"Hey, Simon. So, can me and the girls come over? Tasha really wants to see Marcus." Hearing Abbey's voice is a relief until I take in what she just said. She doesn't sound like a girl who is missing or concerned for her best friend.

"Abbey?"

I'm met with silence. It's so quiet down the line that I pull the phone back to check if we are still connected. We are, so I try again.

"Abbey, it's Lex."

I hear Abbey curse right before the line goes dead.

"What the fuck?" I look up at the boys.

Simon's hazel eyes are round and playful like he is in some faraway land, rather than here with us. Garrett's grey eyes are shooting daggers into the side of Simon's head. Jared's eyes are wide, staring at me with god damn pity. Shaun's slick dark brown hair falls out of its well-styled place as he darts his head around the room, looking anywhere but at me, and Marcus is fascinated with his own feet.

What the actual fuck?

"What's going on?" No one answers me.

Standing quickly from the beanbag, I sway a little as the alcohol pulsing through my veins messes with my balance. Jared reaches for me, but I right myself and shoot him a dagger.

"Someone better start talking right the fuck now!"

No one does.

"Right, so I'll call Abbey back then." I lift the phone to press call again, and the five boys yell *"NO"* simultaneously.

Their response causes me to stumble back a little. Something is going on that they clearly know about, yet are keeping me in the dark. I thought I could trust them. I thought they were my friends. Apparently, I thought fucking wrong!

I drop Simon's phone to the floor, not caring if I damage it, and storm out of the room. Cursing and whispering quickly fades behind me as I put distance between us, heading for the front of Simon's big house. Just as I reach the foyer—*yes, he has a fucking foyer, this house is so big*—five sets of heavy feet rush towards me, and I abruptly skid to stop when Marcus and Jared block my path to leave the house.

"Move!" My yell echoes off the walls, and the guys flinch back a little.

"No, Lex. Don't leave." Jared is the one that dares to speak.

Tears threaten, and I fight them back by letting my anger come to the surface.

"Why the fuck would I stay here with a bunch of arseholes who are lying to me? Who are keeping fucking secrets from me? Fuck that! MOVE!" My scream, although louder this time, doesn't have the same effect, and instead, Jared steps forward.

"We aren't trying to lie. Just trying to save your feelings, Lexi."

The sincerity on Jared's face stuns me, and I turn in a circle to take in the same sincerity on all of their faces.

"Tell me why my best friend just hung up on me." My voice is soft, and my bottom lip wobbles as I speak.

"We aren't exactly sure what's happened, Lex, but Tasha has some sort of vendetta against you, and the girls have jumped on board... even Abbey." Jared offers, reluctance evident in his tone.

"Abbey?" I barely whisper it, but the boys nod, so they must have heard me.

"W-what did I do?" The fact that Tasha is running the show isn't surprising. Having me out of the way is something I think she's always wanted. She has some sort of Queen Bee mentality going on, and it looks like she's just amped it up. But why would Abbey side with her?

Jared steps forward and takes my hand in his, "You haven't done anything, Lex. You know what Tasha's like; she finds people's weaknesses and uses it against them to make herself feel better."

"B-but Abbey?" The tears fall. I hate them as much as I hate my dad and Mike.

"We don't know why Abbey is going along with it." Marcus takes my other hand, and I now have two very caring friends standing before me, showing me how sorry they are. "We have asked her, but she won't tell us anything. We've stopped hanging around them at school and noticeably shut them out. We hoped that would be enough to get Abbey to see sense, but it hasn't. I'm sorry."

Their closeness makes me uncomfortable, so I step back, pulling my hands from their grip and turn to Simon.

"That's why you wouldn't answer their calls? Because of what they are doing?"

"Yep," he nods, "We only accepted those bitches into our circle because of you. They fuck with you, then they fuck with us, Lex. They are out!"

Well, damn, who needs those bitches when I have these guys? Right?

"I'm going to need more alcohol."

The boys chuckle, although it's strained, and we make our way back to the rumpus room. They think I'm joking, but I'm deadly serious. I need a good stiff drink. I don't care anymore. I'm sick of trying to do the right thing all the time, only to be shit on.

Simon pours me a vodka and lemonade, but I grab the bottle and take a swig, trying not to gag on the burn as it goes down. I pass the bottle to Jared, who takes a couple of gulps and then hands it to Garrett. We share it around, and it vanishes quickly. It's not long before I'm stupidly drunk, and with that stupidity is the thought that drinking even more Vodka is a good idea.

There's a lot of yahooing and handstand comps, and after they act out some sort of dance battle, they eventually stop jumping around with me and fall back onto the couches framing the rumpus room. I don't stop dancing, though. I close my eyes and let myself feel the music and sway my hips, allowing myself to enjoy the lightness that I haven't felt in so long.

Any time thoughts of Abbey creep their way in, I visualise a stop sign and slam her out of my thoughts. I can't stop the thoughts about Ayden, though. His intense blue eyes, his smile, those soft lips, and let's not forget those adorable dimples. Any time I close my eyes, it's like he's here with me. I wish he was here.

"You wish who was here?" Simon asks, and my eyes snap open.

Did I say that out loud?

I look over at the three couches that seat my friends and regret it instantly. They are all watching me. Their gazes are different from usual, but I recognise the look. It's the same heated look that Ayden used to give me during our brief time together.

"Who do you reckon?" The distaste in Marcus' tone gains my attention.

"Oh," Simon sits up, leaning forward, a few strands of his ash blonde hair falling over his hazel eyes, "You wish Ayden was here?"

Hearing his name cracks my heart open, and I spin away from my friends, hoping they didn't see the pain on my face.

"Shut up, dickhead. No saying his name, remember!" Shaun interjects, and Simon curses under his breath.

I compose myself and decide to pretend that little slip up didn't happen on my behalf or Simon's.

"I'm tired. Where can I sleep?"

The room is quiet, and all five boys regard me before Jared pipes up.

"I'm beat too. Are we all sleeping in here, Hastings?"

"I mean, there are a thousand bedrooms in this house. If you want your own beds, then have at it, but if you're happy to sleep in here, then we can." Simon offers, glancing at me as he speaks.

"Where do you want to sleep, Lex?" Marcus asks, standing from the couch, stumbling a little. Good, he's drunk too. I'm not the only one.

The guys look at me expectantly, and I hate how vulnerable I feel right now. Maybe drinking wasn't such a good idea.

"If I sleep in here, will someone stay in here with me?" I shift nervously under their gazes.

"Of course Lex, we will all stay in here," Jared answers for the group, and the others agree with nods.

I nod back, and they all start to move when Simon tells them where there are extra mattresses and blankets. While they are all busy, I sneak off to the powder room, which is just off the rumpus room, and as soon as I've locked the door, I start to cry.

It's stupid, pathetic drunk crying. I have never been a drunk crier, but apparently, I am now. With the need to rid my body of this emotion-weakening alcohol, I pull the hair tie from around my wrist and tie my hair in some sort of mess on top of my head before moving to the toilet, hovering over the bowl. I stick my fingers down my throat, but it takes a few tries before my body responds, and I heave the burning contents of my stomach into the toilet.

Sweat beads over my forehead when I'm done, and I flush the evidence away before sticking my head in the sink to drink the cold water falling from the faucet. The cool fluid eases my burning throat, and I guzzle it down until I feel full and bloated.

Not ready to face the boys yet, I sink to the floor and sit in a defeated heap leaning against the vanity. I know it's only been a week since I left Ayden behind, but the pain in my heart feels like it's been a lifetime. I can hardly handle the constant ache, and I don't know how to make it go away.

Voices whispering on the other side of the door drag me out of my head, and I realise my face is wet with tears. Again.

"She needs help, man. More than we can give her." Marcus' deep voice is recognisable.

"It's because of your fucking cousin. He's broken her heart. I'm gonna kick his arse when he comes back," Jared bites back.

"He's been through a lot too, Jar. He didn't mean what he said to her."

"And what did he say? You haven't exactly been forthcoming about what went down between them." Jared sounds pissed.

"It's not my story to tell, and you know it," Marcus hisses.

"This is fucked. Yesterday when we found her trashing Mike's room, it was all about that sick motherfucker. Last night when she cried herself to sleep, and tonight... well, those things are all about her broken heart, man. That's your cousin's doing!"

"Shit! I know. What are we meant to do? It's killing me seeing her so broken." Marcus sounds genuinely upset.

I can't take hearing the pity. I feel pathetic enough as it is. Reaching up, I unlock the door, swinging it open from where I sit on the floor.

"Would you two shut up already?" My tone is flat, hardly matching the words I speak.

Their eyes widen, looking down at me. I must look a sight, but I just don't care anymore. Jared holds out a bottle of water, and I take it eagerly, making quick work of the lid and drinking the cool liquid down.

"Sorry, Lex. I didn't realise you were so drunk that you felt sick." Marcus squats in front of me and pushes my hair back off my forehead. Sometime throughout the night, I must have taken my beanie off. My hair probably resembles a bird's nest.

"I didn't feel sick. I just want the alcohol out of my body. It's making me a weak, whiny girl."

Both boys chuckle and Jared moves into the small space to sit on the floor next to me.

"I don't know if you missed the memo, Lex, but you are a girl."

"Yeah well, I'll take angry me over sad me any day," I utter before taking another swig of water.

Marcus joins us on the floor, sitting in front of me in the doorway.

"Angry you scares me." He admits, and Jared chuckles and nods in agreement.

"Sorry," I whisper, and Jared nudges my shoulder with his.

"Don't be sorry, Lex. You do what you need to. We are here for you no matter if you are angry, sad, or happy."

I sigh and drop my head against Jared's arm. Marcus keeps his pitying eyes on mine, and I break, letting the tears fall silently.

"My heart hurts." It's barely a whisper, but both Marcus and Jared hear me. Jared lifts his arm around my shoulders and pulls me into his side, where I cry silently, while Marcus holds my hand, stroking his thumb over the back of it just like Ayden used to. That makes me cry even more.

We sit like that for a long time, on the floor of the little bathroom. The other boys don't interrupt us, which I'm grateful for. I decide to let my stupid weakness out, for now, determined that tomorrow when I wake, I will keep it locked away forever and never let it free again.

Five

Have you ever had that feeling when you wake up from having a night on the booze that you think you did something you shouldn't have, but you just can't remember? It takes me a few minutes to try to sort through the bits and pieces floating through my head before I recall what I did. Honestly, last night was a clusterfuck of regrets.

Firstly, I regret grabbing Simon's phone and calling Abbey. I think I would have rather not know just a little longer. I can handle Tasha and Allison and whoever else is going against me. But Abbey? No. It's something I don't know how to deal with, and I'm not sure what to do about it. Abbey not responding to my texts, emails, and calls obviously has nothing to do with her parents like I initially thought and everything to do with Tasha's vendetta against me. The only problem is, it's so out of character for Abbey.

Secondly, I regret drinking so much alcohol. Yes, I had a fun night which I really needed, but the fun had to end, and it was my pathetic alcohol weakened emotions that ended it. Getting drunk broke down my walls, and I let the guys see my broken heart. I wish I hadn't. My broken heart is for me and me alone to bear. Now, these amazing five guys know I let myself fall for Ayden and let myself get hurt.

Thirdly, and at this point, this is the biggest regret that I'm sure a lot of people have to deal with after a night on the drink... The drunk text!

Fuck me. I sent a drunk text!

Trying to be quiet so I don't wake any of the boys, I sit up on the couch I claimed as my bed and pull out my phone from my hoodie pocket. Taking a deep breath, I hesitate to open it. I almost don't want to confirm my worst fear. Of course, I give in because curiosity has the better of me. When I unlock my phone, it's still open in the messages.

Oh, my god! I sent a drunk text to Ayden!

Lexi West

Firstly, your cousin is a good guy.
I wish you hadn't told me about his crush on me,
because now I can tell!!!!!!!!
He doesn't know, I know, though.
So there's no awkwardness... Well kind of.
But still, it would have been better not knowing.
Like, did you know he fucked Tasha, and while he was boning her, he was thinking of me?
That's fucked up!! EXTRA!!!
B) My friends are weirdos, but I love them for it.
Yes, they all have penises, but I've learnt that penises are better than vaginas.
Vaginas are bitches that are going to get what's coming to them!
One vagina in particular. Tasha!
I don't know what I've done to piss her off,
but the cow has it out for me, apparently.
Did you know she has turned Abbey against me?
That's another vagina that isn't worth my time!
3. Alcohol is a trick to make people weak,
and I will not fall for its trickery again!
C. I'm sorry too.

Oh. My. Fucking. God!

I am a loser! A pathetic, worthless loser! No wonder Ayden hasn't replied to my message.

He's probably thanking his lucky stars that things ended with us when they did.

I need the earth to open up and let me fall into its deep dark depths now.

Jesus Lexi!

Hating myself, I creep off the couch and carefully climb over Garrett's sleeping form on the floor of the rumpus room. He slept at the foot of the couch I was on, effectively protecting me the same way that Jared had the night before. Garrett's chiselled face is usually twisted in brooding anger, with his big smile only reserved for those closest to him. Now, however, his handsome features are soft, not angry, not happy, just relaxed. He almost looks innocent. I like seeing him free of his internal torment for once. I know he struggles. I also know he tries to hide it from everyone. Perhaps we are more alike than I thought.

I tiptoe out of the large rumpus room, leaving behind the faint snores of my friends in search of a shower. I desperately need to wash away last night and pull myself together and get my shit sorted. It takes me a few minutes to navigate the mansion Simon lives in. I have no idea what his parents do for a living, but whatever it is, I wish they'd share their secret to success. It must be nice to live in such luxury.

Finally, finding two bathrooms on the second floor, I choose the one that looks more like a guest bathroom. The other looks like it's Simon's bathroom, and it just feels too weird to use it. Of all the stupid things I did last night, I remember thinking that I would allow myself the night to be emotional, and then push it down and never let it out again as of today. So, that's what I do. I push thoughts of Ayden to the back of my mind, even further back than Mike and my dad, because I need the anger they bring to keep me strong, to keep me focused.

Stripping down quickly, I try to ignore the nerves that poke at me each time I use a shower. I had little trouble showering when I stayed with Ayd... that guy and his parents in Melbourne. Since coming back home, though, it's been a daily struggle.

Glancing back at the bathroom door, I double-check that it's closed. There's no lock on the door, but the guys will hear the shower running and know not to come in, so I turn and step under the warm water closing myself in. Trying my best to ignore my stomach-churning anxiety, I make quick work of the shampoo and conditioner I pinch from the shower ledge and wash away the drunken night.

I'm about to turn off the water and get out of the shower when I hear the door click open. Frozen in place, standing under the hot stream of water, I wait for whoever it is to hear the shower running and retreat.

They don't.

Through the steamed-up shower screen, I see the figure of a man enter. Blinking rapidly to clear the steam, I'm about to tell whoever it is to get out, but then I see Mike's face.

I scream, throwing myself back until I hit the cold tiled wall of the shower. Mike moves towards me, and I continue screaming in the hopes one of the boys will hear and come to help me. Thrusting my hands out in front, I ready myself to try and hold him off. I won't let him hurt me again. I won't let him succeed in what he failed at last time.

Deep voices are somewhere nearby. Someone is yelling. Mike stops, turning back to the door that is still open before turning back to look at me.

"No! Stay away from me!" I roar. My voice unrecognisable.

Mike retreats then, stumbling from the room before Marcus and Jared rush in.

I'm still screaming, terrified; my body tries to retreat, only it has nowhere else to go. Losing my balance, I slip to the floor of the shower as the screen door flies open and the water shuts off. A white towel is thrown over me, but I thrash my arms out, my fists connecting with someone.

"Lexi stop!" Jared's voice finally registers, and I freeze, sobs shaking my body.

"J-j-jar?"

Jared's face comes into view, and I can see the red mark just under his eye. Did I do that?

"It's okay Lex. You're safe. No one here will hurt you." I can see the sincerity in his eyes like I always do, and I force myself to relax a little knowing that I'm safe.

"M-mike was h-here."

Jared turns to look over his shoulder at Marcus.

"Mike's not here, Lex." Marcus steps forward.

Confusion creases my brow as I take in their faces.

"W-what?"

"Mike isn't here. It's just us. You're safe." Jared confirms what Marcus said.

"B-but he w-walked i-in." I'm shaking now as I look between the two of them. Am I shaking because I'm cold or because I'm scared?

Jared reaches out and wipes the drops of water running down my forehead from my wet hair.

"Lex, that was Garrett. He accidentally walked in, not realising you were in here. He had his earphones in, so he didn't hear the shower running."

I look down at my feet, peeking out from the white towel that covers the front of my naked body, "But I saw Mike's face." I whisper.

"Lex, I promise you that Mike isn't here. I think maybe you have PTSD or something. Maybe you should see a doctor." I take in Jared's concerned face. He knows all about PTSD after being in the same car crash that killed his older brother when he was twelve. I remember going to his house every day after the funeral. He would try to get me and Marcus to leave because he didn't want to come out and play. But we never left him. We stayed and just sat with him until eventually, he started smiling again. I know he had nightmares and was seeing a psychologist. No one should have to go through what he went through, especially not a twelve-year-old.

"Do you still see a doctor?" Jared's brows shoot up in surprise at my question.

"Sometimes." He shrugs, "It's gotten easier to deal with over the years."

I nod, hoping it's true. I need this to get easier sooner rather than later because if it doesn't, I'm pretty sure I'm destined to be locked away in a psych ward.

"It was really just Garrett?" I ask, needing to hear them confirm it one more time.

They both nod, "Yes, Lex. Just Garrett, who's gonna get my fist in his face for scaring you like that." Jared's words are honest, but I don't want that to happen.

"No Jar. It's not Garrett's fault. I bet he feels bad enough." I watch as Jared and Marcus both nod, still squatting down in front of me in the shower door. God, I'm a fuckup. "I'll uh, be out soon."

Taking my hint, Jared and Marcus give me a sympathetic smile before leaving me in the bathroom.

I'm mortified. I don't care that they saw me naked, but I do care that they saw me freak out like that. I've probably just sealed my fate with them. They will join Tasha and her minions soon enough. I need to get control of my freak-outs, but I just don't know how. Maybe Jared is right. Maybe I do need to see a doctor.

Perhaps I should offer the boys the same courtesy I'm offering Ayden? I should stay out of their lives so I don't drag them down with me. They don't need someone like me cramping their style. They are only seventeen. They should be partying and hooking up with girls and running wild instead of babysitting a lost cause like me.

My heart pounds with anxiety as I take my time drying myself and getting dressed in the same clothes I had on yesterday. My hands shake through the whole process, and I can't seem to get them to stop. One glance in the mirror shows me that the bruising is still visible on my face, although a little lighter than yesterday. Each day it gets lighter, and each day I wish it would just fuck off already. Every time I see it in the mirror, I think of Mike.

When I'm finally done, I wander through the mansion and eventually find the boys in the kitchen eating pancakes. I don't know who cooked, but I love them for it, realising that for the first time in days I'm eager to eat something. When the guys notice me standing in the doorway, their chatter dies down, and the room goes quiet. I hate it. I don't want the uncomfortable silence to be a part of our group. Maybe they are already done with me, ready to cut ties and have fun with the likes of Tasha and her minions.

In an effort to change the feel of the room, I decide to use humour to disguise my discomfort.

"So how many of you got a look at my rack?"

All the boys chuckle. Well, all except for Garrett.

"You got a nice rack, Lex." Simon offers his opinion, and I smile.

"Thanks. I hope you got a good look because that's the first and last time you will see it, Simon." I move to the kitchen bench and snatch up a pancake, smearing Nutella on it and roll it up.

"Oh, don't worry. I got those babies saved into the spank bank." Simon taps the side of his head; his smug look gets rewarded with a punch in the arm from Jared. "Ouch."

The boys laugh again, and we all relax. I'm about to bite into my Nutella pancake when I notice Garrett sitting at the end of the bench, staring at his uneaten plate of pancakes. He won't look at me or anyone else for that matter.

Putting my pancake down on Shaun's plate, he glances at me and shoots me a wink, and I respond with a small grin as I pass by to where Garrett is sitting on the barstool. I can tell he's freaking out still, but I need him to look at me because I really want things to be okay between us. I stand in his peripheral, but he doesn't look at me, so I nudge his shoulder, trying to get his attention. He still doesn't look at me, but I hear his quiet words.

"I'm sorry, Lexi."

Needing him to know that I'm okay, I spin his barstool to face me and watch the surprise on his chiselled face as I step between his legs. His blue-grey eyes are drowning in pain as they roam my face. Moving slowly, because I feel like he's a caged animal that will startle at any moment, I wrap my arms around his neck and pull him in for a hug. Instantly, as if relief suddenly washes over him, Garrett's arms wrap around my waist, tugging me closer into his chest as he buries his head into the crook of my neck.

I didn't intend on my emotions showing too much, but when I feel Garrett's slight shudders, I can tell he's crying. That undoes me, and we both cry silently in each other's arms. We pull each other tight, and Garrett's firm athletic body moulds to mine, his woody scent wrapping around me like a blanket. It's nice, not Ayden nice, but nice all the same.

Someone's hand pushes between us at some point, leaving a handful of tissues behind. Still wrapped in each other's arms, we pull back enough to use the tissues, and it's like we are in our own little cocoon, not letting everyone else see our faces as we keep our heads low, tucked into each other's chests. It feels intimate in a way. Not sexually so, but intimate, nevertheless.

"I'm sorry I freaked out, Garrett. It's not your fault. My head is all fucked up." I whisper, needing him to understand. I'm so worried that I have scared him and the other boys from wanting to stay involved with me. I know they are better off without me, but I don't want to let them go.

"I'm going to kill anyone who has ever hurt you." Garrett breathes, the warmth of it fluttering over my cheek. The fierceness in his tone is so sure that I believe every word he said. If there's one thing I know about Garrett, it's that he wears his heart on his sleeve, and combined with his struggles to keep his anger in check, killing someone could certainly be on his cards. That thought should scare me, but it doesn't. I know he would never hurt me.

"You know, I'm getting kind of jealous watching you hug Cole like that." Using Garrett's surname, Simon's playful voice breaks our bubble.

Reluctantly, I step back from Garrett. I can tell he doesn't want to let me go, but he does. Wiping my face again, I make sure all the tears are gone before moving back to Shaun so I can grab my pancake from his plate. He gives me a classic cheeky Shaun grin that would make most girls melt, and another wink as I take a bite of my Nutella pancake. I can't hold back the moan that escapes me as the sweet goodness hits my tongue, and it's almost as if I'm possessed, not able to control myself.

"Jesus, Lex. You'll make a man hard, moaning like that." Shaun's dark gaze is on my mouth, and I roll my eyes while the other guys chuckle. Turning away from them, I shove the pancake in my mouth in a very unladylike manner, and once I've devoured it, I turn back to see five sets of eyes still looking at me. It reminds me of a fuzzy moment from last night when they looked at me the same way. An uncomfortable weight sits in my chest as I take in my friends. I'm not trying to toot my own horn here, but I'm fairly sure that if I was interested, I could kiss any of these guys, and they would happily comply. As nice as it is to feel wanted like that, I don't want that from any of them. I need their friendship, their loyalty. I need their support.

"We need to talk." My voice echoes in the silent room as their eyes remain on me.

"You guys are my friends, right?" They all nod at my question. "Like just friends. Nothing more?" They slowly nod. "Because if you guys can't do the friend only thing with me, then I need to know now."

"What makes you think we can't?" Marcus asks, his dark brows furrowing.

I step up to the kitchen table and lean against it, putting a little more distance between me and the guys.

"Look, I don't have a problem with sexual innuendos or a bit of harmless flirting, but I'm getting some..." Jesus, how do I say this? "Vibes, I guess. If I have overstepped by doing something misleading, I need you to tell me because I don't want to give any of you the wrong impression."

The boys are quiet for a few moments, and I'm sure I've fucked up. I've either hurt their feelings or made a fool of myself.

Jared breaks the silence. "I'm not gonna lie, Lex. If you came to any of us and asked us to be your guy, then we would without hesitation, but we know the deal here. We are here for you, with you, as friends, as family. We are also guys who think with our dicks way too much, and it's hard to deny our attraction to you. So yeah, we flirt like the dicks we are. If you ask us to stop, we will. It will be a challenge, but we would do anything for you." They all nod in agreement at Jared's words, and I feel like crying again. I don't though.

"We also know your heart belongs to someone else, Lex," Marcus speaks this time, and I'm glad he added that bit in because it's true. Ayden may not want me, understandably so, but my heart belongs to him, and until it doesn't, then anyone taking his place is out of the question.

I nod, "Okay. Good." And then I shake my head, "Sorry."

"Don't be sorry. You can talk to us about anything." Shaun, the playboy of the group, looks genuine and serious for a change.

"Anything?" I ask, shooting Shaun a cheeky grin.

"Yes, anything." He smiles back.

"Oh good, because I've got mad cramps and need to go get some tampons."

A round of curses spill from the boys, and Shaun sticks his fingers in his ears, cringing. And just like that, all is right in the world... for now.

Six

I spend my Sunday afternoon at home alone. Marcus had to go home earlier since he hadn't been there in three nights and the other boys followed not long after to make appearances with their parents too. Jared drew the short straw for babysitting duty tonight, even though I tried to tell the boys that they don't have to keep doing this. They ignored me like my opinion is irrelevant. I hate putting people out, but I'm quietly thankful that they insist.

I do my usual run on the treadmill and kick the shit out of the boxing bag before Jared arrives back just before 6 pm. He comes bearing steaming hot fries and fresh bread, so we have hot chip sandwiches for dinner and then do some homework at my kitchen table before retreating to the living room to watch TV.

"You remember those forts we used to build over near the hockey fields?" Jared asks, sitting next to me on the couch eating Salt n' Vinegar chips from a bowl.

"Yep. We thought they were so sick." I laugh, "They were so bad."

Jared laughs too, "They never held when the wind picked up. Remember when it fell in on Marcus."

"Oh my god, that was hilarious. He hated us for ages after that. Said we bullied him." My tummy hurts from laughing, but it's the good type of pain.

"He's always been a wuss." Jared chuckles and offers me the chips, but I shake my head, "Remember when we were in the fort, and my brother turned up with his girlfriend, and he didn't know we were inside?"

"Oh yeah. That's when we got our first closeup of teenage love." I remember wishing I was the girl Jared's brother, Tim, was kissing. I'll keep that little memory to myself, though.

"I wouldn't call it love. Lust definitely. I remember getting the biggest woodie watching them kiss."

"Ew, Jared!" I whack him with a cushion, "TMI! I didn't need to know that!"

He throws his head back in hysterics causing the bowl of chips to slip off his lap, but I leap over to save it just in time.

"It wasn't just me, you know?" Jared continues through chuckles, "Marcus did too. Told me he nearly blew his load in his pants when my brother touched the girl's boob."

"Eww! Stop Jared! I don't want to hear this!" I stick my fingers in my ears and aggressively shake my head, effectively giving myself a mouthful of my wayward hair.

Moving to his knees before me, Jared grabs my wrists and pulls them away from my ears so I can't block him out. "He also told me that day that when your boobs grow, he wanted to touch them."

Lifting my knees to my chest, I push my legs back out and kick Jared off the couch. He falls to the floor, laughing and clutching his tummy as if the act causes him pain. I take the cushion and start beating him with it, making him squeal like a girl, or a pig, it's hard to decide which one it sounds the closest to, and eventually, I fall in a heap beside him on the floor in my own fit of laughter. It feels good. Really good.

"I'll kick you in the nuts if you ever repeat that story again." I manage to say when I gain my control.

Jared chuckles, laying back on the floor, looking up at the ceiling before a sombre look washes over his face.

"My brother died a week later. Poor guy didn't even get the chance to lose his virginity."

I lay down next to Jared taking his hand in mine like I used to when we were kids. "He'd be proud of you, Jar. You're a decent guy, and he'd be proud to call you his brother."

Jared turns his head to look at me, and I don't miss how his blue gaze quickly flicks to my lips before meeting my eyes.

"Thanks for saying that, Lex. Sometimes I wonder if I'm a fuckup."

"Why would you think that?" My frown is so deep that I can feel the tension in my temples.

Jared shrugs, "I guess my opinion of myself isn't that great."

"You still think it should have been you who died in the car accident, don't you?" I remember Jared telling me that about a year after his brother died. It was just him and me at the park near my house. Marcus had been sick and couldn't come out, and Abbey was at some weird bible camp, so Jared and I spent the entire day together. I didn't want him to be alone.

Jared nods at my question, his ashen hair a tousled mess, bobbing as his head moves. I desperately want to lighten the mood, so I decide to admit something to him.

"I wanted to kiss you the day you told me that."

"What?" Jared sits up quickly, looking down at me with his intense blue eyes. Looking up at him like this, I can see the boy I grew up with hidden underneath the manly features overtaking his body. His eyes are the same shade of blue they've always been, but his eye shape isn't as round as it used to be. Maybe it's because he frowns more these days. His bone structure is sharper now; a chiselled chin sits more prominent than his boyish one did. He also has the faintest blonde stubble framing his jawline. He's buff. Jesus, when did he get so buff? How did I miss that?

"Uh-yeah, I had a crush on you. This probably makes me a bad person, but I was secretly glad that Marcus was sick that day because I got you to myself." I feel my cheeks heat at the admission and hate that my blush has made an appearance for someone other than Ayden.

"Jesus! Fuck! Motherfucking prick!"

"Uh... say what?" I'm confused at Jared's outburst.

He rakes a hand through his hair, and I sit up too. "Fuck, Lexi! I should have made a move that day because I wanted to kiss you too, but I knew how Marcus felt about you, so I didn't."

I laugh, and he shakes his head in frustration.

"I lost my chance, I guess." He looks hopeful at me like he wants me to tell him he hasn't lost his chance. I hate that I have to let him down.

"Yep, you sure did." I slap him on the shoulder and get up from the floor, trying to pretend like this conversation hasn't affected me.

"I call fucking dibs when you're ready to move on from Ay..."

"Don't say his name!" I lean down and slap my hand over his mouth.

Jared grins behind my hand and then darts his tongue out, licking my palm. I squeal in disgust, ripping my hand away to wipe it on his shoulder, causing him to laugh again.

The rest of the night is a mixture of reminiscing and laughter, and it feels so good. We sleep in the living room again with the glow of the TV lighting the room, just the way I've become accustomed to. This time we both sleep on the floor next to each other, under our own blankets.

I wake early on Monday morning with anxiety pulling me from sleep. Today is the day I return to school. It's the date I agreed I would return when I spoke with the new acting principal. The other condition of my return is that I visit with the school counsellor every week. I tried to get out of that one, but Principal Rogan was very insistent and wouldn't budge on the idea, so I reluctantly agreed.

I know today is going to be a shit show. Not only am I facing everyone after my secret and shame aired on the news, but Tasha is out for my blood, and my best friend has joined her ranks. I have no idea what's going on with Abbey, but I no longer feel sad about her betrayal. I feel pissed.

Last night, Jared told me he and Garrett bailed Abbey's boyfriend, Daniel, up at school last week wanting answers because Abbey has refused to tell them anything. Daniel was tight-lipped and said it wasn't any of his business or theirs, and then Jared had to hold Garrett back from punching Daniel. I kind of wish he had let him now. Something is going on, and being left in the dark about it contributes to my anxiety.

I quietly get ready for school while Jared sleeps, slipping into my uptight, formal uniform and pulling my hair back into a not so polished ponytail. Using concealer and a little foundation, I attempt to cover the bruising hoping to appear *not* like the walking dead with the dark shadows under my eyes. I use a little mascara to wake my eyes and a dusting of bronzer on my cheeks to add some colour. The end result is a natural look, and knowing there's not much else I can do to fix my appearance, I head to the kitchen for my morning coffee, which is where Jared finds me once he wakes.

"Nervous?" He asks, finding himself a mug to make his own coffee. I just nod.

"We got you. You know that, right?" I nod at his question again.

"Can I have a blow job?"

I turn and glare at him, and he shrugs.

"Well, you were nodding at everything I said. It was worth a try." He grins, and I'm helpless not to smile back.

"Go get ready, loser." I roll my eyes at him, and he smiles again, giving my cheek a peck before taking his coffee into my mum's room to get ready.

While I wait, I check my emails to see if there's anything from Abbey. Still nothing. I need to accept that she isn't going to reply to me. I need to remember that she hung up on me on Saturday night when she realised it was me calling, not Simon.

As if I haven't tortured myself enough, I scroll through my messages from Ayden for the next ten minutes. He hasn't responded to my drunk text. I'm partially happy about that because WTF was I thinking? I'm also somewhat annoyed because if he hasn't messaged me, it obviously means he isn't thinking about me.

As if I have the power to summon him, little bubbles pop up in our message chat to indicate that he is typing a reply. My heart stops. My lungs cease working, and my head spins. Holy shit! Is Ayden replying to me? I shouldn't want him to as much as I do, but fuck, I really, really do. The bubbles keep scrolling over and over before they stop and disappear, and I wait a moment for a message to come through, but it never comes.

My eyes burn, and my heart kicks in at a rapid pace while air seeps into my lungs. If Ayden had written a reply, then he must have deleted it and moved on. *Shit!* That knowledge sends sharp pain to the centre of my chest, and I have to fight to remain quiet and not scream.

I'm thankful when Jared is ready because I need his distraction. Digging deep, I muster up the mask I used to wear to fool everyone into thinking that I had a good life. I don't want Jared or anyone else to see how upset I am over Ayden.

We head to school and stop at the mouth of Marcus' street to pick him up. I'm quiet as the boys talk about footy and some new PlayStation game that's coming out this week as we walk. They must sense that I'm not in a chatty mood, so they don't force the issue, but I can see them glancing at me frequently from the corner of my eye. As we get closer to school, clusters of students enter the grounds together, and my anxiety soars. I desperately want to turn around and go back home.

Deep breaths, Lexi.

For once, I listen to myself and take steady deep breaths, trying to slow my racing heart. My eyes focus on the ground in front of me as we walk, and I repeat over and over in my head, *keep going Lexi, you can do this!* It helps me push forward, and I hope like hell that my fear doesn't show on my face.

Simon, Shaun and Garrett are lingering just outside the gates when we arrive. Garrett doesn't wait for us to reach them. Instead, he approaches me, swinging his arm around my shoulders and grins down, giving me a wink. Christ, did they all learn that wink from Ayden?

"We got you, Lex," Garrett repeats the words Jared said earlier this morning, reminding me I'm not alone. They are right here by my side.

Hushed whispers float through the air as we make our way into the schoolyard. It's tough, but I hold my head high despite how visible my fading bruises still are, and I ignore the stares from basically everyone we walk past.

The moment I lay eyes on Tasha, Allison, Amanda, Sophie and Abbey, I start to struggle, and the need to flee or go ape shit on their arses begins to consume me.

"Looks like the trash has arrived." Tasha's whiney voice holds no fear. "You should let go of her, Garrett. You might catch something."

On instinct, I start towards her, but Garrett bunches his muscled arm and holds me firmly to his side.

"Hey look, Marcus," Garrett's raised voice commands everyone's attention, "Isn't she that Tasha bitch who gave you crabs?"

I nearly choke, shocked. I've never heard Garrett speak to or about a girl like that.

The boys stop walking, and Marcus glares over at Tasha, looking at her from head to toe, curling his lip in disgust.

"Yep, that's her. She also has the smelliest cunt I've ever come across." Marcus gags, and the rest of the boys screw their faces up before they walk again.

Holy shit! Did that really happen? I hate the word Marcus used, and I'm shocked that he spoke like that too, but I don't feel sorry for Tasha. Not one bit.

Laughter carries across the crowd of onlookers, and they join in throwing taunts at Tasha. I can't help but feel happy about it. If that makes me a bad person, then so be it. I've been through too much shit to care about Tasha's feelings right now.

I don't miss the way my former friends glare at me as we walk past, scrunching their noses up at me like I'm a foul smell. Not Abbey, though. She doesn't have the balls to look at me. She keeps her brown eyes cast down at her feet. Coward!

My school day starts at the principal's office. She requested to meet with me in person before I go to class, and I have to dig really fucking deep to walk through the door that last time held my dad behind it, right before he drugged me.

"Miss West. It's lovely to finally meet you in person." Principal Rogan is dressed in a navy pin skirt and suit jacket that matches the school uniform. Her chocolate brown hair is long and straight, and her dark brown eyes are kind.

I offer her a small but fake smile and sit in the seat she gestures to. Instead of sitting behind her desk like the previous principal always did, she takes the seat next to mine, turning it on an angle to face me.

"So, how are you feeling about today?" I regard Mrs Rogan for a moment before responding, needing the time to clear the panic rising in my chest.

"The old me would say that I'm feeling eager to get stuck back into my work." I relax back in the chair, trying to appear unbothered, my usual prim and proper mask long gone.

"And what would the *you* that is sitting here now say?" She asks, her eyes never leaving mine.

"Honestly?" I ask, and she nods. "That I couldn't care less about my school work right now, but I know I can't afford to fall behind."

She nods, "Well, that's good enough for me, Miss West." Reaching out to the desk, she picks up a piece of paper. "Here is your new schedule. Unfortunately, a few changes had to be made at the request of some parents."

I accept the paper and glance over the schedule, seeing clearly which classes I am no longer a part of.

"You mean Abbey Delany's parents?" Most of the classes that I had with Abbey have now changed on my schedule.

"It's complicated." Mrs Rogan states without elaborating.

"In other words, yes!" I hiss, "Let me get this straight. Because the old arsehole principal allowed my dad to come into this very office and drug me, knocking me unconscious, which inevitably led to my assault, the school has agreed with Mr and Mrs Delany's request to move me out of classes with their daughter?"

Mrs Rogan sighs, "I'm sorry, Lexi. This decision was approved before I took over. I have tried to advocate for you, but there are a few things I haven't been successful with. This is one."

"This is bullshit!"

"Yes, it is bullshit! And I will keep fighting for you. But for now, we have to follow the rules." Principal Rogan sounds stern, but not in a scary way. She's kind of intimidating, like one of those successful businesswomen who have had to wade through all the bullshit to rise through the ranks and prove that she is just as good, if not better, than her male colleagues. I bet she's had to sacrifice a lot over the years. Maybe she's one of those forty-something career women who chose not to have kids. She doesn't look like a school principal, that's for sure. Cynthia Rogan looks like the rich and powerful CEO of a multi-million dollar company.

"The rules suck dog's balls." I don't care how immature I sound right now. It's not fair that I have to suffer because other people are uncomfortable with what happened to me. Fuck them! I didn't ask for any of this to happen to me!

"That they do." Mrs Rogan laughs before turning serious again. "You will also see your counsellor appointments on your schedule. If you miss one, then we have to review your enrollment here. This is also a stipulation that is out of my hands."

"So, someone is waiting for me to fuck up, basically? Not go to an appointment and then boot me out?" My blood is boiling. I'm getting more and more pissed off by the second, and Mrs Rogan can tell.

"You can't be booted out for that, but it will keep you unnecessarily busy attending red tape meetings with the school counsellor and Child Services. Let's try our best to avoid that, hey?" Principal Rogan gives me a sympathetic smile, so I nod.

"Can I go?"

"Yes." I stand when Mrs Rogan confirms I can leave but stop as she speaks again, "Oh, and Lexi. Given what you've been through, I don't mind that you swear and release some of that pent up anger while you're in this office with me. And it's okay to do the same when you're with the counsellor," She points to her door, "but out there in the rest of the school, you need to reel it in. Talk to the counsellor if you are struggling to do that."

I should probably tell her now that I am already struggling and will likely fail at keeping it reeled in as she asked. I don't, though, and nod before leaving the office, wanting nothing more than to burn the entire school to the ground.

I don't bother with my locker and go straight to Maths with Miss Dice. I'm lucky to have her for a couple of classes. Not only is she a good teacher, but she is also a good person. She welcomes me back when I walk into her class, and I sit at the empty table at the back of the room. It's the same table Ayden and I sat at a couple of weeks ago when he shared his music with me. The ache in my heart feels like it's slicing me open from the inside as I recall the memory. I don't even care when I notice Allison glaring at me from across the room throughout the lesson. I don't do any work. I can't concentrate. All I can think about is Ayden.

I remember how I had tried to ignore him, but he was having none of that, making sure I would talk to him even though I treated him like crap at first. His smile captivated me. The way it turned up and sunk in his dimples that were partially hidden by the light dusting of dark hair over his jawline. I also remember how it felt when I realised that he listens to the same music as me. It was nice knowing we had that in common.

I miss you, Ayden.

Tears threaten, so I fight them back through most of the class, and when the bell rings, I practically bolt from my seat to escape. I don't get far. Allison steps in front of me wearing a bitchy smug look, so I raise my brow, waiting for her to say something. She doesn't.

"What's your problem, Allison?" Distaste drips from my tone. I'm done hiding the truth.

"My problem is you." Crossing her arms over her chest, she continues to block my path. The first time I met Allison, I thought she was cute because she was so short. At just over five foot, with chocolate skin and dark wavy hair, her small frame carried a big personality. Now that I'm on the receiving end of her wrath, I am reminded how alone I am in the world. I never imagined losing my friends.

My brows lift again. I'm unsure of what she is trying to prove right now.

"You say that as if I care. Move the fuck out of my way before I make you."

Allison's smile drops, and she almost looks as if she's going to cave, but the stupid girl doesn't.

Luckily for her, Miss Dice approaches right before I get the chance to make her move.

"Off to your next class, Allison."

Allison shoots me a brown-eyed dagger before she throws on a fake smile and turns to Miss Dice, passing by her.

Miss Dice frowns before looking at me.

I shake my head. "Don't ask."

Shooting me a sympathetic smile as I pass by my favourite teacher, I make my way to PE class. As I walk, I try my best to ignore the whispers and stares. When people stare too long, I shoot them a glare that makes them turn away, and when I see Sophie and Abbey, I look each of them in the eye as I pass. Abbey looks away immediately, but Sophie mutters, "Skank." I just shoot her a toothy grin trying to show her she doesn't affect me, even though she does.

Marcus and Shaun catch up with me on the way to PE and flank me, giving me a little more confidence as we walk. Abbey is meant to be in this PE class, but she isn't anymore. Her parents must have moved her out, which is fine by me. All my boys are in this PE class, and for once, I actually enjoy playing today's activity of basketball.

Unfortunately, there's a little problem. These boys, my boys, are being a little too overprotective. Dylan Brent, a guy I have always been friends with, gets totally blocked from talking to me on the court. When he approaches me, Marcus steps in front of him while Garrett leads me away. At first, I thought I imagined it, but I know for sure that these guys are up to something after the third time it happens. It does nothing but piss me off. By the end of class, I'm so angry that I storm off the court and into the girls' change room before the boys can catch up with me, and I'm thankful for the breather from their intense hovering.

After I change back into the uptight FP Catholic formal uniform, I shoot the group chat a message to say that I'll catch up with them, and I wait patiently in a toilet cubicle for everyone to clear out so I can sneak off to the library to hide out during recess. When the coast is clear, I go straight to my usual spot in the back corner and force myself not to think about my time there with Ayden when he sat with me while I slept and hid from going to class. It's hard not to think of him while I'm here, though. I swear I can almost smell his spicy scent lingering in the air.

It doesn't take long for my phone to blow up with messages from the boys. They're worried, and it makes me feel like shit for ditching them.

Not enough to go to them, but enough to send them a message to let them know I'm okay and I'll see them later.

After recess, instead of double Art, I have my first counsellor's appointment, so I reluctantly drag my feet to the administration building to get it over and done with.

The door to the counsellor's office is open when I approach, so I tap on it popping my head in. A tall man with a shaven head, dark facial hair, and ear-piercing stretchers sits behind a desk in the far corner.

"Ah, you must be Lexi. Come on in." He has a deep friendly voice and blue eyes that are nearly as blue as Ayden's.

Damn it! Why do I compare everything to Ayden?

Walking in, I close the door behind me, taking a seat in the one he gestures to as he comes to join me in the seat opposite.

"I'm Mr Matthews, but in this room, you are welcome to call me Stephen." In his hands, he holds a red clipboard that has a file attached. Great. He's going to be taking notes. This whole situation makes me uncomfortable, so I keep my mouth shut and cross my arms over my chest.

Mr Matthews chuckles quietly. "I get it. Seeing the school counsellor isn't your sort of thing, but we have to meet for at least thirty minutes every week, so let's talk about something."

"Like what?" I ask, unimpressed.

"Well, anything. You can talk to me about how you are feeling today, or about what happened a couple of weeks ago at home, or even what boys you are crushing on." Mr Matthews seems like an okay guy, but that doesn't mean I'm going to divulge all of my secrets to him.

"What if I'm crushing on girls?" I smirk, and he smiles back.

"It's fine if you are. Is there a girl you're interested in?"

"Nope. That's gross."

Mr Matthews laughs. "You're not going to make this easy for me, are you?"

"Nope." I shake my head again.

"You don't trust me?" He asks, and I shake my head. "Do you trust anyone?"

I shrug.

"I'm guessing you have more people in your life that you don't trust, than you do. Is that right?"

I shrug again, looking away because he's hit a nerve, and I don't want him to see. When I look back, he's writing something in the file.

"What does my file say?" He looks up, surprised at my question.

"I'm sorry, that's confidential."

"But it's my file. Shouldn't I be privy to what it says? How am I meant to trust you when you're keeping things from me?"

Mr Matthews regards me for a moment and then nods his head. "Okay, Lexi, I'll read you what is in the file if you tell me how you are feeling today. Deal?"

He's good at what he does. For all I know, this is how he gets all the kids to talk. I nod because I really want to know what the hell is in the file.

"Okay. The file says your name, Alexis, in brackets Lexi, Amity West. Born on the 13th of May 2002. Parents are Ruth and Maxwell West. Sibling is Mike West. You live at-."

"Stop. I know all that shit. Read what it says about my personal situation." I'm struggling to keep my anger in check. I'm getting sick of people tiptoeing around the issues.

"Okay, then. Claudia from Child Services has reported that Miss Alexis West was in a dangerous situation on Thursday the 15th of August 2019, which involved her father, Mr Maxwell West, and her brother, Mr Mike West. The situation is of a sensitive nature that has resulted in an ongoing investigation with an alleged physical assault, crude acts and possible molestation."

"Okay, stop!" I hold my hand up, sucking in air as nausea hits, "I don't want to hear any more."

Mr Matthews looks up from my file with soft eyes. "I'm sorry, Lexi, I should have warned you before I read that."

I take a few moments to breathe away the tears that burn the back of my eyes and shake my head.

"I asked, and you answered. It's fine." My voice is raspy as I try to swallow down the lump in my throat.

Placing the file down on the little table next to his chair, Mr Matthews leans forward, resting his arms on his knees. "I didn't want you to know what it said, but I want you to trust me, Lexi. I want to help you. What happened to you will affect you for a long time. I know you know that. What you tell me is just between us. I do have to give a report to Child Services, but it's only a summary report. Nothing of detail will be included. I don't expect you to talk about what happened with your father and brother, not today, but I hope you will tell me something that I can try to help you with."

"I'm angry." I can't even hold the words in. They come out on their own as if someone else spoke them.

Mr Matthews nods, "Anger is expected."

"I'm really fucking angry," I admit, letting the strange voice inside me speak again.

He nods again. "Do you feel violent?"

I shrug. I don't want to tell him the truth and say yes, but I can't say no, either.

"Do you want to talk about the violent thoughts you have? Who are they directed at?"

"Who do you think?" I glare at him feeling too pissed off to be nice.

"Well, if I had to guess, I would say your brother and your father."

"Bingo," I say, sarcasm lacing my tone.

"Have you heard from either of them?"

I frown at Mr Matthews, "No! And I better not either!"

He nods, "My records show you are in the care of a family friend. Do you feel safe with them?"

I nod, blatantly lying to him, and when he looks relieved, I feel the same way. I'd thought Andrea, Ayden's mum, would have contacted Claudia at Child Services to let her know I left their care. But obviously, that hasn't happened, which must be why I haven't had Child Services on my doorstep.

"Our time is nearly up, Lexi, but I want you to know that you can come and talk to me anytime. No need to wait for your next appointment if you need to see me before then. In the meantime, I think it would be a good idea for you to write in a journal every day. It may help to get your anger out of your head and onto paper."

Mr Matthews' suggestion is disappointing. Of course, he would suggest journal writing, just like every other typical school counsellor. The only thing is, there is no way in hell I am writing down my dark thoughts. Writing that I want to slice Mike's throat open with a blade is as good as a confession.

Seven

I'm too pissed off to go to Art, so I hide away in the library again, which is where I stay right through lunch. I should really just go home. It's pointless for me to be here. I can't concentrate in class. My ex-friends are out to crush me, and the boys are suffocating me. I don't go home, though. Home is lonely. Home doesn't feel like home because my heart still thinks my home is Ayden.

It's not even halfway through lunch when my phone blows up with messages again from the boys. The messages start out as simple questions asking where I am and if I need one of the boys to come to me. By the end of lunch, Marcus declares that he's coming to check the library, so I flee like a bat out of hell to the girls' toilets. I'm a coward, I know. I should just face the boys and ask them to take it easy with their possessive behaviour, but I also don't want to push them away because they really are all I have. I just need some space right now.

As if my day hasn't already been a shit show of cluster fucks, the moment I fly through the door of the girls' bathroom, I come face to face with Tasha and her gang of merry bitches. *Fucking perfect!*

"Well, well. If it isn't the fallen queen." Tasha slides a cruel smirk on her average-looking face and crosses her arms across her chest. I know that move. She's been doing it ever since we grew boobs, and hers didn't compare. She uses her arms to push what little cleavage she has together, trying and failing to look like she is more endowed. When is she ever going to realise that no one cares about her ugly tits?

I don't know why she is referring to me as the fallen queen. I was never the queen, nor do I ever want to be. While there are cliques and social groups within our school, we've never had a hierarchy amongst the students at Fox Pines Catholic College. Tasha may think she is living in a Hollywood high school movie, but she's going to feel the sting of disappointment really soon.

"What's wrong, Lexi? Got nothing to say now that you have been dethroned?" Yep. Tasha is delusional.

I don't miss how Abbey takes a step back as Tasha addresses me. She keeps her brown eyes on me, though, which is a change from earlier when she couldn't bring herself to look at me. As usual, her white-blonde hair is in a perfect braid, a style she has worn since we were in primary school.

Sophie, Allison and Amanda puff out their chests and mimic Tasha's stance. It's a struggle, but I manage not to laugh at the sight.

"What's your problem?" I turn my eyes back to Tasha. For some reason, she is under the impression that I'm scared of her, but my tone causes the briefest shift in her confidence. Did she think I would just take her bullshit?

"You and your filth is my problem! I can't believe they actually allowed you to come back to school here after the depravity you've done." Tasha's pale face turns red as she speaks, which is a telltale sign that she's struggling with her emotions. She's not the only one. Her words are meant to cut deep, and they succeed.

My eyes shoot to Abbey in question, and she looks away, staring at the back of Tasha's dull brown frizzy-haired head. She looks guilty, and she knows I can tell. What has she been telling Tasha? Surely she didn't tell these girls all the details of what happened to me. She knew that information was private. Shit, I even sent her pictures of what Mike did to me, of my battered body. Would she really break my trust like that? Betray our friendship? As much as I don't want to believe it, I know it's true. I can see the guilt in her eyes.

A knot forms in my throat, and I lose my ability to speak as I try to fight back my weak emotions. I don't want Tasha or any of them to see how they are affecting me. It's nearly impossible to hide my anguish. Biting the inside of my cheek, I push the sadness, the hurt, and the tears down and let the anger take over.

Red rims my vision. Rage boils inside me, and I know if I let it take over completely, then I'll have no control over what I do. I'm yet to decide if that would be a bad thing or not.

"You must be confused, Tasha. I have done nothing wrong." I am strangely calm as I direct my question to Tasha but look at Abbey when I speak. A small frown draws her blonde brows together before worry settles over her face.

Tasha scoffs, "You filthy whore! You allowed your brother..." Her words are cut off when my hand wraps around her throat and squeezes.

"Let's get one thing straight, you fucking bitch! I did not allow my brother to do anything to me!" My face is so close to Tasha's that I can feel her warm gasps of breath on my lips. It happens so quickly that I don't even remember moving.

Rough hands grab at my arms and, much to my disappointment, pull me off Tasha. Twisting forcefully, I struggle free to see it was Allison and Sophie that came to their friend's aid. I shove at the bitches needing to get distance from them before I move towards the sink at the far end of the bathroom so I can splash cold water on my face. I don't make it that far.

A heavy weight shoves me to the ground before a fist slams into the back of my head. The impact makes my head swim for a moment, but the blow doesn't hold the strength to do any real damage. Not like it did when Mike was behind the punch.

Trying to move my arms up to shield my head or potentially throw my own punches back, the weight on my back abruptly disappears, and Tasha screeches.

"Playing fair, as usual, I see Trashy Tashy. We all know if Lexi had the chance to fight you face to face, she would kick your arse."

I jump up quickly from the grimy bathroom floor and turn to the new voice. It takes me a moment to focus my eyes. I guess the hit to my head rattled me more than I thought.

Tasha sneers from her position on the floor, where she landed on her arse after Rhys George pulled her off me. I bite back a laugh knowing how pissed Tasha must be right now, especially after the tripping incident a couple of weeks ago when Rhys, not so accidentally, tripped Tasha in front of a group of guys. I saw the video that went viral around the school, but man, I wish I had been there to see it in person.

Rhys George is as individual as they come in a Catholic school. With hair as dark as night and lips to match, she is every Catholic teacher's nightmare. I have always admired her from a distance, wishing I could be as bold as her and show the world who I really am. Her hair is in two side buns which seems to be her signature style, and her eyes are painted with thick dark liner on the top and bottom with perfectly defined winged tips. To top off her look, and as much against the school dress code as the rest of her look, she has a septum piercing in her nose that I haven't seen before. It must be new.

"This is none of your business Goth Girl." Tasha hisses, shooting daggers that are more laughable than scary as she stands up off the floor. I notice her bitch brigade didn't step in to help her this time.

"Oh, don't mind me Trash, I was just making sure the playing field was even. Please continue." Rhys gestures between us, and when she looks at me, she smirks.

"Fuck off then." Allison finally speaks up for Tasha. It took her long enough.

Rhys laughs, "As if I'm going to miss Lexi messing up Trashy Tashy's ugly face. Who knows, she may be able to rearrange it so Trashy actually looks pretty."

I think I love this girl!

"Stop calling me that!" Tasha hisses, turning her focus on Rhys.

"I'd like to know something." I interrupt, gaining everyone's attention.

"What?" Tasha practically spits, throwing her hands on her hips to look at me again. Her usually well put together façade is a mess. Her navy uniform is twisted a little, and I'm sure mine is the same.

"What makes you think I care about whatever your problem is with me? What are you trying to achieve?" I look at each of my ex-friends as I speak, wanting them to know that I'm talking to each of them.

"I just think people should know about your depravity. They should know how sick you are. That you like it rough, and with your brother nevertheless." My nostrils flare at Tasha's words. "Tell me, Lexi, how long have you been getting off on fucking your brother?"

Her words are harsh, but because they are so wrong, it just confuses me, and I automatically look at Abbey. Like a coward, she looks away again.

"Don't look at Abbey. She was traumatised after you told her what happened. After you sent her those pictures of the bruises you so sickly boasted about to her. What was she meant to do? Just sit back and accept that her best friend has lied to her about being in an incestuous relationship?"

I almost laugh at the lies she is spewing, but my eyes are drawn to Abbey because part of what Tasha just said is true.

"You showed them the pictures?" I ask Abbey, but she won't look at me. "Abbey!"

At my roar, Abbey looks up to meet my eyes. She doesn't need to speak; her eyes tell me the truth. Why would she do that to me? A pesky tear slips free, revealing my weakness, and I hate myself for it.

Something cold and wet slaps hard against my face right before Tasha lunges for me. I quickly reach up and grab the wet wad of toilet paper off my cheek before I throw myself towards Tasha meeting her face with my fist as her own fist meets the side of my head. With the wet toilet paper still in my hand, I shove it into her open screaming mouth and stuff the wad down her throat. Leaping back from me, Tasha grabs her own throat before she sticks her fingers in her mouth, trying to dislodge the paper. She starts gagging and Allison and Sophie rush to her aid, moving her into a stall right before she starts to vomit.

Amanda wraps her arm around Abbey, comforting her as if she hasn't done a thing wrong. I feel the overwhelming need to cry clawing at me, so I do everything I can to push it down and replace it with anger.

"That was brilliant! Best fucking movie I've ever seen." Rhys gains my attention, and I see that she is holding her phone up. Did she record that?

Fuck my life! I need to get out of here, now!

As I storm toward the door, I stop abruptly, causing Amanda and Abbey to jump before I get all up in Abbey's face.

"I don't know what's going on, Abbey, but what you have done is irreversible. There's nothing you can ever do to make this right. I hope it's worth it. I really do." I step back, laughing in disbelief and shaking my head. "I've had some pretty vile things done to me, Abbey, but this by far is the worst. You make me sick."

I let Abbey see all of my anger and all of my pain before I hold my head up high and walk out of the girls' bathrooms. While I look calm and unfazed on the outside, I am anything but. On the inside, I'm screaming, crying, and dying slowly.

"This is the best day I've had at school ever." Rhys' voice gets louder as she catches up with me, still holding her phone up recording.

"Stop fucking recording me, or you'll join that bitch in the toilets."

Rhys laughs, throwing her head back before putting her phone away. I don't know why she's still walking with me.

"Girl, you are the best. I always knew there was more to you than good grades and popularity."

I scoff, "My grades are shit, and I've never had an interest in popularity."

"Why be someone you're not then if not for a social status?" Rhys matches my strides. Doesn't she have somewhere to be?

I stop walking and turn to her, "Why do you think?"

She considers my questions and nods, "Okay, I get it. Secrets to hide and shit?"

"Exactly," I walk again, and so does she, "What are you doing?"

"Walking."

Smart arse!

"Shouldn't you be in class or something?"

"Shouldn't you?" Rhys is quick to come back. She kind of reminds me of Valarie, just not as innocent.

"Touché."

That makes her giggle.

"Look, I get that your life is on a fast train to fuck town right now, but if you need somewhere to hang out besides the girls' toilets, you're welcome to come chill with me and mine. You can find us behind the stadium hall at the back of the school."

"Ah, okay, thanks." I stop outside my English class and turn to Rhys, who looks over my shoulder at something.

"Your pack looks pissed."

Frowning, I turn to see what she is referring to. Through the window of the classroom door, Marcus and Jared are glaring at me from the back of the room. Rhys is right, they do look pissed. *Great!*

"My pack?" I ask, turning away from their glares and back to Rhys.

She waggles her eyebrows, "You know, your shadow pack. They walked into school with you and followed you around all morning."

"Right." I cringe.

"Good luck. Oh, and you might need to get someone to look at your head." Rhys walks away grinning, and I move my hand to my head. It's sore all over the back and the side where that bitch clocked me. A little blood comes away with my fingers, and I groan. How am I going to explain this?

I quickly pull my ponytail out and brush my fingers through my hair, hoping that Miss Dice isn't going to have a problem with my hair being down. Hopefully, I have earned the right to do a little rule-breaking.

When I walk into English, I throw an apology to Miss Dice, who has the rare ability to teach both Maths and English. She nods and smiles before turning her attention back to a student she is helping. Making my way to the only seat left, I ignore Marcus and Jared's glares as I sit between them and glance to the board at the front of the class. Shit. I didn't even bring my books or laptop. I left them in the library. Fuck, I'm totally losing it.

"Wanna explain where you've been?" Marcus demands under his breath, and I shake my head. "Let me rephrase that. Where have you been?"

My brows reach my hairline at his tone. He's speaking to me like I'm a fucking child!

"Wanna tell me why you think you have the right to speak to me like that?" I hiss under my breath, hoping Miss Dice doesn't hear.

"I've been worried, Lexi. For all I knew, Mike or your dad had taken you again." His words cause instant guilt at my stubbornness. Yeah, I probably should have messaged Marcus back instead of dodging him. Does it give him the right to speak to me like that, though? Hell no!

"As you can see, I'm fine. I needed some space, if you must know. Don't forget, I'm hormonal right now. I'm not opposed to eye-gouging you if you keep speaking to me like that!"

Jared chuckles, and Marcus sighs.

"Sorry, Lex. I was worried, that's all."

"Well, worry in a nicer tone!" I hiss, and Jared chuckles again, so I shoot him a warning glare.

Marcus just nods and turns to his work, giving me a brief reprieve.

Phones start chiming throughout the room, and when Bianca Tact pulls hers out, Miss Dice practically pounces on her snatching up her phone.

"If I see any of you take out your phones to see whatever it is you all just received, I will confiscate every phone in this room and have them held in the school safe for the rest of the week!"

Grumpy mumbles filter through the air, but no one moves to get their phone out.

"Shit Lex," Jared leans forward, brushing my hair back off the left side of my head, obviously eyeing the damage Tasha did. I flinch away from his touch. "What happened?" He whispers in my ear.

When I don't answer him, I feel his hand slide into mine under the table, and he gives it a gentle squeeze. "Lexi?" He pleads, and I can't help but turn to him. I want to tell him to bugger off and mind his own business, but the concern in his blue eyes breaks me, and I cave.

"Tasha happened," I whisper.

"Shit." Jared says too loud, and Marcus mouths a "What?" in question over the top of my head.

"What did she do Lex?" Jared asks in a whisper, and I just shrug, not wanting to talk about it, because holy shit. Did that really just happen? Did Tasha really just hit me?

"I'll tell you later," I whisper before snatching up his English novel and opening it to chapter nine. Jared takes the hint.

I can't believe what happened in the girls' toilets. I've never been in a fight with anyone before. Well, that is, anyone other than fighting to free myself from Mike or my dad. I can't believe that Tasha is behaving the way she is. More than anything, though, I can't believe the way Abbey is acting. What in the hell have I done to her to make her turn against me so brutally?

I completely zone out for most of the lesson until Mr Matthews, my new counsellor, comes into the classroom and asks me to go with him to the principal's office.

For fuck's sake! What now?

I continue to ignore Marcus and Jared as I stand and leave their sides. Miss Dice, my fierce protector, joins me just outside the classroom with Mr Matthews.

"Stephen, what's going on?" For a small petite lady, she sure as shit can be scary when she directs her wrath on you.

"Yeah, Stephen, what's going on? The last time I was asked to leave class and go to the principal's office was when my dad kidnapped me." It's a low blow to the school, but I can't seem to find it in me to care.

"That won't happen again, Lexi." Mr Matthews responds sternly and then directs his attention to Miss Dice, "It seems that Lexi has been in a bit of a scuffle with another student."

Miss Dice doesn't look surprised. She chews on her bottom lip, looking very much like she wants to say something in response, but instead, she turns to me.

"Would you like me to come with you, Lexi? Or perhaps one of your friends?"

I shake my head, "No need. It's all good." I lie.

"Principal Rogan just wants to have a discussion with Lexi. Nothing more." Mr Matthews sounds convincing.

Miss Dice looks between the both of us before choosing him to address this time, "Lexi is not to leave this campus with anyone but her current guardian. Not her mother, not her father, and absolutely not her brother!"

"Of course, Amy. That won't happen on my watch, nor Cynthia's," Mr Matthews declares, his blue eyes looking fiercely at Miss Dice, and then her face goes red.

Oh, what do we have here? Do I sense something more between Miss Dice and Mr

Matthews? When their eyes meet, I can tell they are very familiar with each other. I try to hide my smirk, which is in no way appropriate for the current conversation.

Miss Dice nods, her brown bob bouncing as she does so, apparently satisfied with his response, before giving me a small smile and returning to the classroom.

Mr Matthews and I start walking down the hall, and he grins, "I know what you're thinking, and you need to stop."

"What?" I ask innocently.

He shakes his head, chuckling under his breath but doesn't answer my question.

"Oh, come on. Is she your girlfriend? Are you two *lovers*?" I wag my eyebrows at him, and he just smirks and shakes his head.

"Lexi, you should stop being concerned about my life and start showing concern for your own. You haven't even been back a whole day, and you've already gotten into a fight."

"I plead the fifth."

"We live in Australia, not the US. The Amendments don't apply here." Mr Matthews offers, even while trying not to laugh at me.

When we reach Principal Rogan's office, I get the same nervous sick feeling like I had this morning, so I gesture for Mr Matthews to lead the way and let him walk in before I do, hoping this isn't another trap.

Sitting in one of the chairs is Tasha Pritchard.

Did that cow lag?

Principal Rogan approaches, looking down at me from her height, concern etched over her face.

"Lexi, do you give me permission to look at your head?"

Well, I guess I'm not hiding this from her. I shrug, and she gently lifts my blonde waves up off the side of my face. I hear the moment she sees the cut or whatever it is, by her sharp intake of air. She steps back, dropping my hair and gestures to a seat.

"Please sit."

I do as I'm told, and I don't at all feel unsafe like I did a couple of weeks ago when my dad was in this office with me.

The smell of vomit wafts over, and I turn in the direction it's coming from. Ha! Tasha, the bitch, vomited on herself. Serves her right. I wrinkle my nose at the stench and make sure she sees.

"I could ask you both what happened, but I'll save you the trouble of lying to me. We have a video of the incident in the toilets that occurred at the end of lunch today." Principal Rogan turns to me, "Lexi, I understand that you have been through an extremely traumatic ordeal of late, but we do not condone violence."

"But..." I try to defend myself.

"No," Principal Rogan holds her hand up, "We will have further discussions about that later. For now, you will attend after school detention for the rest of the week." She moves her attention to Tasha shaking her head, "I may be new to this school, Natasha, but make no mistake, I am not new to this sort of bullying behaviour. The words you spoke and the way you have treated Lexi and also contributed to the physical violence of the situation is absolutely disturbing." Principal Rogan takes a deep breath before speaking more calmly. "You too will attend after school detention for the rest of the week. I want you both to understand that this is not over. I will be making further consultations on this matter, and we will readdress the punishment."

"Just suspend us already. That's what usually happens." Tasha apparently has balls I didn't know about, and her comment gets a glare off Principal Rogan.

"I know that's what normally happens, but I'm in charge now, and I do things differently. So, for now, your punishment is in limbo."

I like this principal. I don't like the fact that I have to go to detention, but let's be honest, what the hell else do I have to do?

"Lexi, here is a pass to the school nurse," Principal Rogan hands me a slip of paper, "Please go and get your head cleaned up before you do anything else."

I accept the slip of paper with a nod and stand, turning my back on Tasha. As I leave the principal's office and the stench of Tasha behind, I get a message on my phone.

Marcus Grady
Lex! WTF is this about you getting in a fight with Tasha?

And then my inbox blows up with messages from the rest of the guys.

Eight

Detention is a bitch! Mainly because I'd rather be anywhere else than in a room with Tasha Pritchard. The good thing about it, though, is that Rhys is also in detention, and she entertains the shit out of me as she sits next to me, across the room from Tasha, taunting her by pulling faces and blowing her kisses. This chick is hilarious. I don't know why I haven't paid more attention to her before. Probably because it would have raised red flags on my prim and proper status. I can't believe how superficial I used to be!

It surprises me that they allow us to use our phones in detention, but I'm thankful to use it as a distraction from Tasha's daggers. I read over the messages from the boys, who aren't happy. Well, most of them anyway. Simon seems pretty pleased he got to watch my catfight on video.

"Wanna explain how the video of that cow and me fighting got out?" I whisper to Rhys.

"What video? I know nothing about a video." Rhys flutters her dark lashes innocently before poking out her tongue.

"Did you really need to send it out to everyone?" I complain, but Rhys just smirks.

"By everyone, do you really mean why did I send it to your pack of hot saucy guys?" She shoots me a cheeky grin and wags her dark brows, her voice too loud to be classified as a whisper.

I roll my eyes, "Sure. Whatever."

"You can thank me later." She winks, "The lighting in the toilets really brought out the blue in your eyes, don't you think?" She doesn't even try to be quiet as she speaks. I shake my head and try to hide my smirk.

"How did you edit it so quickly?" I ask, genuinely interested. Apparently, the video got sent out about fifteen minutes after Rhys and I parted ways outside my English class. It had been edited to cut out some of the words I had with Tasha and her bunch of bitches. Like when I asked Abbey if she'd shown Tasha the pictures I sent her. For some reason, Rhys had cut that out. She had cut out anything too personal to my situation, and for that, I am thankful.

"It's my jam. It's what I do. Easy peasy." Rhys skites, shrugging her shoulders, "I sent the full version to Cynthia, though."

I almost choke. "What!"

"Quiet please, Miss West." Mr Ellis, the sub teacher, glares at me from his desk.

Rhys giggles, "I know you got in trouble for fighting too, but that cow over there will be dealt a bigger punishment for it, and for that, it's well worth spending every day after school in detention with me. Don't you think?" She smiles wide, extremely proud of herself.

Shaking my head in disbelief, I stay quiet for a few minutes taking in everything that's happened today. I'm exhausted, and it isn't even 4pm yet. As if I've willed it, Mr Ellis announces that detention is over, and I watch as Tasha practically runs out of the room, nearly tripping over twice on her way out. Does she think I'm going to do something, like chase her and grab a fistful of her hair before slamming her head into a concrete pole?

Okay, so maybe I really do need professional help!

Strolling out of the room behind Rhys, my tummy drops, knowing that I have to go back to an empty house. What if it isn't empty? What if Mike is back? Maybe I can ask Rhys to come home with me?

"Oooh, look at your fellas all lined up in a row." Rhys smiles wide, and I glance up to see Marcus, Jared, Simon, Garrett and Shaun waiting for me, leaning against the walkway railing. Rhys walks up to each of the guys and checks them out from head to toe, raking her dark eyes over them like they are a smorgasbord. She doesn't even try to hide what she's doing, and they just watch her curiously.

Have they been waiting out here the whole time I was in detention?

"Tell me, Lexi, which one makes you scream the loudest?" Rhys asks, raising a black painted nail to her lips in thought.

I would have gasped in shock if it weren't for the looks on the boys' faces. Jared frowns and then directs his blue gaze down the line as if wondering which one of his mates is the one that makes me scream. Garrett's blue-grey eyes widen, and then I swear I see a pink blush heat his cheeks. Of course, Shaun looks like his usual smug Casanova self and nods his head like he's imagining making me scream. Poor Simon looks flustered, and Marcus eyes Rhys with heat in his dark gaze.

Well, well, well. I think Marcus likes what he sees.

"Rhys stop. They're only friends. Stop conjuring up bullshit that isn't real." I try to scold her, but in true Rhys style, it doesn't faze her one bit, and she shoots me another cheeky grin. Rhys George is a little troublemaker who likes to stir up shit. I think I like her even more.

"The guy who makes her scream isn't here."

I swing my attention to Marcus, not missing the bitterness in his deep voice.

"What the fuck, Marcus!" I yell, not able to hold back.

Rhys turns to me, blocking Marcus from my view, "Oh, do tell. Who is the guy that makes the one and only, Lexi West, scream?"

"You know what, I thought I liked you, but I was wrong," I say through gritted teeth to Rhys before storming off.

"Oh, you still like me, girl! I'll see you tomorrow." I ignore Rhys when she calls out as I head straight for the school exit.

The boys' voices and footsteps sound behind me, so I know they are following, but I continue to ignore them. My emotions are all over the place, and Rhys has successfully made me think about Ayden. Or maybe it was Marcus who did that since he referred to him. Either way, Ayden is on my mind, and as much as it hurts, I don't want the thoughts to go away. I want to drown deep in the memories I'll forever cherish.

Stuffing my earphones in my ears, I hit my Heavy playlist on my phone and let the music flow through my chaotic mind. I haven't listened to it for a while. Most of the time, when I'm alone now, I'm too scared to have too much sound going on around me in case I don't hear the moment that Mike or my dad try to pounce. I know the boys are behind me right now, so I allow myself this moment while we walk to listen to the music that speaks to my soul.

In my peripheral, I notice Jared step up beside me before he pulls me to his side while we walk. Although his scent isn't the same, I try to pretend that for a moment, it's Ayden who is walking with me. *I miss him so much.*

I kind of expect the boys to veer off to head to their own houses, but they don't. When I walk through the door of my house ten minutes later, so do the five of them. I don't tell them, but I'm so grateful they are here. I don't want to be alone, especially in this house.

Knowing that they'll be hungry, I go to the kitchen and start cooking up some meaty party pies and sausage rolls before heading up to my room to change. As I pass the living room, I continue ignoring them because I'm still pissed about their overkill smothering earlier. I'm also trying to avoid talking about my run-in with Tasha.

When I reach my bedroom, I hesitate outside the door like I always do since returning from Melbourne. My mind flashes with a memory of flying over my bed when Mike threw me across my room. As the images engulf my mind, I sway on my feet a little. Will I ever stop seeing the night Mike attacked me when I walk into this room? Probably not.

Taking a deep breath, I push forward and step over my threshold that remains door-less. Since I have no privacy with an open doorway, I hide in the corner of my room and change into my black leggings, a crop top and throw my black zip-up hoodie over the top. Since I have 20 minutes to kill while the food cooks, I slip on my sneakers and make my way back downstairs to the garage.

I ignore Marcus when he asks where I'm going because he's still on my shit list from his comment to Rhys earlier. Shutting myself in the garage, I slide the gloves on and start pounding away at the bag hanging from a ceiling beam. Every time I throw punches at it, I picture Mike's face, followed by my dad's, and then finish with the scary face of

Muz. I beat the crap out of them in my mind, giving in to the anger that has been trying to break free all day. It's only when my alarm goes off on my phone to alert me about the food cooking that I'm reminded I'm not alone in my house.

"If you ever want a sparring partner, let me know. I'd be happy to let you beat the shit out of me."

I turn to Garrett's voice and see him sitting on the floor just inside the access door that leads back into the house.

"You been here long?" I tug the gloves off and use a towel to wipe the sweat from the back of my neck.

"About fifteen minutes. I hope you don't mind?" Garrett's large hands are linked together, hanging lazily from his knees. It looks kind of funny with his hand bandaged up around a metal rod.

I shrug, not really caring, even though I probably should. Throwing the towel down by the treadmill, a strange noise floats through the walls, followed by arguing.

"What's going on in there?"

Garrett grins, "They're trying to put the doors back on upstairs. Marcus reckons he knows what he's doing. It turns out he doesn't."

We both laugh.

"I'm going to need a repairman to fix their mistakes, aren't I?"

"Probably." Garrett stands from the concrete floor. "For the record, I'm glad you were able to hold your own against Tasha."

I cringe, "I wouldn't say that I held my own at all."

"Oh, you did, trust me." I'm pretty sure he's just saying that to make me feel better, so I accept it with a smile.

Garrett follows me back into the house and heads upstairs to sort out the idiots who think they can hang a door while I go into the kitchen. Taking the food out of the oven, I let it cool on the bench and then grab six cans of soft drink out of the fridge. When I close the fridge, I notice that the pictures of me and mum that have lived on the fridge for like, years, are gone.

That's weird; I could have sworn they were there this morning. Maybe I just thought they were there because I'm so used to seeing them. Maybe mum took them off a couple of weeks ago, or perhaps they got damaged when Mike trashed the house. Valarie's mum might remember if she came across them when she was cleaning up.

"Oh honey, did you cook for us?"

I turn from the fridge, poking my tongue out at Shaun before piling the hot food on a plate.

"Tell your moron friends that their food is ready."

"Hey morons, come get some grub!" Shaun yells from the seat he claims at the table.

"I could have done *that,* Shaun!" Shaking my head and fighting back a grin, I place the plate on the table as well as the ketchup.

"Done what?" He asks innocently.

"Yelled at the top of my lungs." My hands are on my hips as I scold Shaun, and I've never felt more domesticated than in this moment. For fuck's sake, I feel like their damn mum or something!

Shaun chuckles right before the room fills with male laughter. One by one, they file in and grin at me, giving me a "Thanks" or a wink before sitting down to eat. I shake my head at them and turn to hide my grin. I really enjoy having them around, even if I do feel like their mum. No, mum isn't right. Maybe their wife, just without the sex.

"Here, Lex, I grabbed you some before these pigs ate it all."

Turning back at Marcus' voice, he stands awkwardly holding out a plate piled with party pies and sausage rolls. Stepping forward slowly, I take the plate with a small smile. There's too much on it for me to eat, but I don't want to be rude, so I keep that to myself.

"Sorry, Lex," Marcus whispers.

Looking up to his pained face, I realise that the plate of food is a peace offering. I sigh.

"I don't know what your problem is, Marcus, but you need to stop having digs at me about Ayden. I know I should never have let him get mixed up in my bullshit. I know he is suffering now because of me. But you have to know that I care about him, and for a moment there, I was selfish and gave into my emotions for him. For a moment, I thought I could have something more than what I deserve."

Marcus gapes at me, "Is that what you really think, Lex? That what he is going through now is because of you?"

"Well, isn't it? And isn't that why you keep having digs at me?" Part of me knows it's because he has a thing for me, but that can't be the whole reason.

"Jesus, no. What happened at that party in Melbourne has nothing to do with you, Lexi. If anything, it's fucked up that you were dragged into *his* bullshit." Marcus drags his hand through his thick hair, "I hate admitting this, and I know you know why, but you and Ayden are good for each other. Ignore my bullshit. I'll get over it."

Wow. He is basically admitting to liking me as more than a friend, without actually admitting it.

"I'm sorry," I whisper this time, shuffling my feet anxiously where I stand beside the kitchen bench.

"What for?" Marcus asks, confusion drawing in his dark brows.

I shrug. "I don't know. Maybe dragging all of you guys into my bullshit."

"If you remember correctly, we didn't give you much of a choice." Marcus reminds me before he steps towards me and then stops himself.

"True." I smile, and Marcus returns it with his own.

Ayden did the same thing, he didn't really give me a choice. He was adamant that we would be friends, or more than friends. He was right. It was right... until it wasn't.

I end up eating more than I thought I would. I know I've lost weight lately from my lack of appetite. It hasn't been intentional; my appetite just kind of disappeared. Now, it seems to be back, a little.

The boys manage to get the doors back on upstairs after a lot of arguing and noise. Of course, Mike's bedroom door is toast after I beat the shit out of it the other day, much like everything in his room. Maybe I should board it up, so I don't have to see that there is even a room there.

By sunset, some of the boys go home, leaving Garrett and Simon, who are on tonight's babysitting duty. I don't know why I get two babysitters tonight, but I'm not complaining. I welcome the company. Being alone in this house isn't good for me. When I'm alone here, my mind goes to dark places. Places so dark that it scares me.

Simon's parents are still away apparently, and Garrett told his mum that he's doing a joint assignment with Simon, so he was staying at his house to try and get it finished before school tomorrow. I feel bad that the boys are lying to their parents just to babysit me. I can't let this go on for much longer. They will eventually get caught, and I can't bear to be why they get grounded or something like that. Maybe I should talk to them about it tomorrow.

Coward Lexi!

The right thing to do is send them home tonight!

Shut up, inner evil voice!!!

Simon is like an Eveready battery. He just doesn't stop. He is full of energy and ideas of things to do. I could easily curl up on the couch and watch a movie with these two guys, but Simon isn't having any of that. He insists we play poker.

It's fun despite having to constantly remind Simon that we're playing regular poker, not strip poker. The idiot takes an item of clothing off each time he loses, and an hour into it, when he's about to pull his jocks down, I stand and walk away laughing. I don't want to see that! I leave Garrett to deal with Simon, exiting the room with tears, good tears this time, streaming down my face.

Leaving both of the boys to argue over things, I duck into my mum's room to shower and get changed for bed. I have on my usual PJ shorts, but I can't find my Metallica t-shirt, so I settle with my Three Days Grace t-shirt. Don't get me wrong, it's a good t-shirt, but my Metallica one is so worn that it's thin and soft and feels weightless to sleep in. I really love it, so yeah, I'm kinda bummed that I can't find it. I could have sworn I left it over the towel rack this morning.

"What's this?" I ask when I walk down to the front living room and see the set-up Simon has made on the floor.

"Your bed awaits my queen." Simon does some sort of bow or curtsy and gestures to the bed of blankets and pillows.

I raise a brow in question, and Garrett stands from the couch glaring at Simon.

"Told you she wouldn't want to sleep on the floor."

"Nah, Lexi doesn't care about sleeping on the floor, do ya, Lex?" Simon's hazel eyes lock onto mine for confirmation.

"Where are you sleeping?" I ask, confused. Looking at the pile of blankets and pillows. It appears very much like we are all sleeping on the floor. Together.

"Oh, come on. It'll be just like camping." Simon approaches me, grabbing my hand and leads me to the pile of blankets.

"You want us all to sleep on the floor? Together?" I frown, confused and let him drag me down to the floor, to sit on top of the cushioned blankets.

"Yes." Simon lays one of the blankets over my bare legs.

I'm a little stunned. I don't move as I watch Simon practically skip across the room to turn off the light, leaving only the glow of the TV to fill the space. With a grin tugging at his thin lips, Simon moves back to our bed on the floor, sitting down next to me.

"You want me to sleep here, Lex?" Garrett asks, sitting next to me on the opposite side Simon takes. "If you're uncomfortable with Simon's suggestion, I can move."

"Just to be clear, if either one of you touches me, I'll rip your fucking balls off."

Garrett chuckles and leans in to kiss my cheek, "Noted."

Simon flicks his ash-blonde hair off his brow and throws his hand against his chest in horror, "As if I would ever do such a thing."

"I'm serious, Simon," I growl.

He laughs, settling down under the blankets, "I know, Lex. Relax. We're just here to protect you and make you feel safe."

I look from one side to the other, at my two friends who have snuggled down under the blankets. I do trust these boys, so I slide down under the blanket and stare up at the roof. It should feel weird, right? Having a boy sleeping on each side of me? It doesn't, though. It feels safe. Not as safe as when I'm in Ayden's arms, but still safe. For once, it doesn't take me long to fall asleep.

Nine

I wake to the smell of bacon on Tuesday morning. My mouth waters and I can't hold in my moan. Simon can stay over every night if he cooks bacon for me each morning. It's definitely a weakness of mine. The smug smirk on his face tells me he knows damn well how much I like it, which is why he cooked it. He's trying to win brownie points, although I don't know why.

After Simon, Garrett and I go through our usual morning rituals, we walk to school, meeting up with Marcus on the way, followed by Shaun and Jared just outside the school grounds. My anxiety plagues me as we approach with all eyes on us, but unlike yesterday, today the onlookers smile in my direction, and a girl that I don't even know says, "it's about time that someone put Tasha back in her box."

Tasha isn't at school, which helps me breathe easier, but her bitch crew are, and they have no problem glaring daggers at me every chance they get. Abbey even dares to shoot me a bitch glare. *Ballsy!*

My first two classes are double Photography. It's a new class that the school has moved me into, so Abbey doesn't have to endure a class with me. Her parents are arseholes and are on my list of people who need to pay! I like the Photography class, though, so maybe they did me a favour.

Rhys, the smart bitch, bows down upon seeing me enter the Photography room like I'm royalty and then doesn't take no for an answer at partnering up with me. I don't complain. I'm already enjoying her company. She catches me up with the course work, and I feel oddly inspired about what theme I'm going to choose for my portfolio.

We part ways after class, and I find the boys hovering at my locker waiting for me.

"You look happy." Shaun nudges me with his shoulder as I squeeze past to get to my locker. I exaggerate my smile in response.

"She looks too happy." Marcus frowns, and I poke my tongue out at him.

"What gives?" Marcus asks.

I shrug. "I had a good class, I guess. I'm looking forward to doing the work."

"Shit, she really is a dork." Jared teases and winks at me.

I need to ask them to stop winking at me like that. It reminds me too much of Ayden, which makes my heart hurt. After my locker is full and my arms are empty, I start walking towards the canteen, and the boys flank me, drawing attention from the other students.

As we pass Dylan Brent and Hayden Saunders, they say hi to me, which is totally normal because they are my friends, but I don't miss the glare that Garrett and Jared shoot their way. When we're far enough away from Dylan and Hayden, I stop and turn on the boys, hands on my hips in a huff.

"What the hell is your problem with Dylan and Hayden?"

"What do you mean?" Jared asks innocently, but I can see the guilt on his face.

"Don't give me that. You know what I mean. Yesterday in PE, Marcus and Garrett kept blocking Dylan from talking to me, and just now you and Garrett shot daggers their way when they said hi to me."

"It isn't just them two. Marcus and Shaun were killing them with their eyes just now as well." Simon, always the helpful guy adds. The four other boys turn to him to shoot him with their murderous looks.

"Want to explain to me why?" I ask them, not willing to let this go.

"We're just trying to protect you, Lex." Marcus shrugs.

"It's overkill!" I snap, "The only person I need protection from is my brother. Back off everyone else!"

Five sets of puppy dog eyes look back at me. Ugh, this is hopeless. I turn, storming off in the other direction.

"Hey, where are you going?" Simon asks.

"The toilet. Meet you in the canteen." I lie, not looking back until I turn the corner at the end of the passage. Peeking back, I see the boys walking in the opposite direction from me, towards the canteen. Thank fuck they aren't trying to follow me.

I don't go to the toilets, though; I walk straight outside and along the side of the stadium building to the back of the school to find my new crazy friend.

When I round the corner, I'm met with the distinct smell of weed and the sound of music and laughter. As I get closer to the small crowd, I smile inwardly when I hear the music playing is Breaking Benjamin's Failure. It soothes my soul instantly.

"All hail Queen Lexi!" Rhys cheers, spotting me before anyone else, kneeling on the grass to bow as silence sweeps over the small group of students.

"Get up, you idiot," I say, feeling self-conscious all of a sudden.

"Oh now, don't be modest. You are our worthy queen, and we, your loyal servants." Rhys stays on the ground smiling up at me with a ridiculous toothy grin.

All eyes are on me, making me squirm. Maybe this wasn't such a good idea. I feel like I've just walked into a private party uninvited. But that's not true, is it? Rhys invited me.

"Is she always like this?" I direct my question to the group, hoping to break the ice.

An auburn-haired girl with a pixie cut, and a sandy blonde boy wearing pink lip gloss turn to each other and grin.

"Unfortunately, yes." Pixie girl steps around Rhys, who's still bowing to me on the ground. "I'm Tillie. Rhys said she made a new friend. A word of advice, turn around and run now because once she gets her claws in you, you'll never be able to escape." Tillie holds out her hand, and I take it in a very formal handshake that doesn't suit the current situation.

I laugh, "I'll take my chances, thanks."

"Oh, come on now. Lexi loves me, don't you, girl?" Standing, Rhys brushes some blades of grass off her knees and moves to my side, giving me a hip bump.

"Ah... Sure." I say, and the rest of the group laughs.

"So how did you manage to ditch your reverse harem?" Rhys asks, grinning widely.

"Reverse harem?" I'm confused. What is this girl on about?

"Yeah, you know, like a harem but filled with delicious guys instead of girls. A reverse harem. Where are they?" Rhys turns to look where I came from, disappointment flashing over her face when she realises that I'm alone. She pouts in my face.

"You have a reverse harem?" A girl that reminds me of Wednesday Addams approaches with an indifferent expression on her face.

"Um, no. The boys Rhys is referring to are just my friends." I shove my hands in my blazer pockets, feeling nervous under her glare.

"Oh, well, that's boring." The Wednesday Addams look-alike turns, retreating, quickly losing interest in me.

"Don't mind Bell; she has some questionable interests," Tillie explains, and Bell glances back at us with the same indifferent expression and shrugs.

"Come on now, Lexi, which one are you banging?" Rhys throws her arm over my shoulders and leads me to the emergency exit stairs that descend from the rear entrance of the stadium.

"I'm not banging anyone. My boyfriend... well, I mean the guy that was my boyfriend for like a second isn't here." I don't know why I revealed that, and I inwardly kick myself. By the looks of it, I need to be careful around Rhys. She seems to have a way of prying information out of me. Either that or my walls are slipping.

"Oh. My. God. You were seeing that hot new guy, weren't you?" Rhys' jaw drops open before morphing into a grin.

Damn it! How did she put that together?

"OMG, really? That tall, dark and fuckably handsome new guy?" Lip gloss boy speaks up for the first time. I've seen him before around school. His name is Dale Martin, I think. He's been openly gay since seventh grade and doesn't care what people think of him. It's admirable.

Eager eyes stay focused on me, obviously waiting for more information. Even Bell's eyes glint in interest. Leaning against a tree just off to the side is another guy that looks more like a dark-haired vampire with skin as pale as snow. He's been quiet, but even he's paying attention now.

"If you're talking about Ayden Mitchell, then yes. Ayden and I were... a thing. Briefly." I shrug and swallow down the lump that forms in my throat from speaking his name out loud.

"Oh, damn girl! You lucky little bitch. I was hoping he was gay. I'd totally let him top me." Lip gloss boy, Dale, declares.

"Jesus Dale, that's TMI, dude." Tillie cringes.

Rhys roars with laughter, and Bell steps close to me, invading my personal space. I try to move back, but there's nowhere to go, and Bell, who's a couple of inches taller than me, looks into my eyes like she can see inside my soul.

"You love him," Bell states, and I flinch.

"Ah, Bell, maybe Lexi doesn't want you all up in her business." Vampire boy speaks up, brushing hair as dark as coal off his face. He really is so pale. If I found him lying on the ground with his eyes closed, I'd be sure he was dead.

"You also have a broken heart. Did Ayden do that?" Bell tilts her head from side to side, studying me, so I close my eyes tight, needing to take a moment as pain, sorrow and anger bloom in my chest. When I open my eyes, Bell is still standing just as close, studying me.

"How about you take a few giant-sized steps back from me? I don't exactly have control over my temper lately, and I'd hate for you to get hurt." I hiss through gritted teeth, fisting my trembling hands in my blazer pockets, hoping no one notices.

No one speaks, and Bell continues to study me for a few more long moments before turning on her heel and moving away. "I like her. Can we keep her?" Her words sound oddly humoured, which is a stark contrast from the straight look on her face.

"Bell, if you keep showing Lexi your loopy side, then she's probably going to run very fast, very far away." Dale addresses Bell, and she simply shrugs, taking a seat on a log next to the tree where vampire guy is leaning. I still don't know his name.

Maybe coming here wasn't a good idea. Was ditching my boys really necessary? Just then, my phone starts to vibrate with incoming texts, and I pull it out of my pocket to read them.

Marcus-Grady
You're not in the toilets or the library.
Where are you hiding, Lexi?

Shaun-Bossier
Maybe she's behind the bike shed
kissing Dylan and Hayden!

Marcus-Grady
She better fucking not be!

Jared-Crowley
Not helping Bossi! But funny.

Simon-Hastings
We all know she's hiding from you
smothering arseholes.
Hey Lex, I won't smother you.
Where you at, girl?

Garrett-Cole
Your presence smothers everyone, Hastings!

Simon-Hastings
I'm standing right next to you. I'm not opposed
to punching that pretty face of yours, Cole!

Rhys nudges me with her hip, "Who's texting you? They seem keen. Or obsessive." She wags her dark brows and glances down at my phone.

Sighing, I move to sit on the step, and Rhys sits next to me, leaning in when I put my phone on my lap, so we are both able to read the bullshit from the guys.

Garrett-Cole
Try it, arsehole. I'll knock you out in one punch.

I glance at Rhys. "I need to do something. It's getting out of hand." She gives me a mischievous toothy grin, and I cave, joining in the boys' group chat.

Lexi-West
Garrett and Simon, keep your hands to yourselves!!!

Jared-Crowley
There's our girl!

"Ha! See! Our girl! You totally have a reverse harem." Rhys bounces around where she sits in excitement.

I roll my eyes.

Marcus-Grady
Where are you, Lex? We're worried.
The toilets were empty, and your not
so secret hideaway in the library was
taken by some year nine girls.

Lexi-West
How do you know the toilets are empty?

Shaun-Bossier
That was me!!
I'm a frequent visitor to the girls' toilets.

"It's true. I've walked in on Shaun getting blowjobs in there multiple times." Rhys fills me in, making me cringe. Does that boy have no shame?

Simon-Hastings
Yeah, because you have a pussy
where your dick should be.

Shaun-Bossier
Says the guy who checks me out when we
take a piss and even asked me how long
my giant cock gets when it's fully erect!

Rhys bursts out laughing, clutching her stomach right as the bell rings, indicating the end of recess.

Lexi-West
You lot are idiots!
FYI - I needed a breather. I'm okay.
I'll see you later.

Shaun-Bossier
Give Dylan and Hayden a parting kiss before you leave them, Lexi.

Marcus-Grady
Shut up, Bossi, she's not with them!

I know I'm about to throw fuel onto the fire, but Marcus deserves this! Where does he get off telling me who I can and can't fucking talk to?

Lexi-West
Oh, don't you worry, Shaun.
I gave them both more than a kiss xx

Marcus-Grady
What?

Jared-Crowley

Oh, shit!

"Girl, you're asking for trouble, and I love it!" Rhys rubs her hands together, and we stand to make our way to our lockers. "So, Ayden, hey?"

"I don't want to talk about it."

"Well, when you do, I'll give you my shoulder to cry on." Rhys stops walking and grabs my wrist pulling me to stop, and I witness her unusually serious expression.

"I may joke around and take the piss 90% of the time, but I know heartache, Lexi. I can stop being an immature fuck for the serious stuff. Just so you know." She shrugs, honesty shining in her dark eyes that are closer to black than brown.

I like that Rhys pretty much says what she thinks. It's refreshing. I wish more people were like that. I wish I could be like that.

"Thanks, Rhys." I smile, and she gives me another toothy grin showing off her straight white teeth.

Throwing her arm over my shoulder, we continue walking to our lockers, getting all sorts of looks from the other students. Once upon a time, I would have feared being seen with someone so different, someone from the school's out-cast misfits group. Now it feels like home.

Mr Matthews is waiting for me outside my Pastoral Care class when I get there and asks if I can come and chat with him. One look at Mrs Monaghan standing at the front of the Pastoral Care class sends chills down my spine. I was in her class when the secretary came to get me and lead me to my kidnapper a few weeks back. Naturally, I choose to go with Mr Matthews because not only is Pastoral Care a bullshit class, but I don't want to sit through it remembering that day.

"Let's talk about what happened in the girls' toilets yesterday." Mr Matthews starts after we take our designated seats in his office.

"You know, Stephen, it's kind of creepy that you want to know what happens in the girls' toilets."

He smirks, "Let me rephrase that, shall I? Let's talk about what happened between you and Natasha Pritchard in the girls' toilets yesterday."

I sigh dramatically, trying my best to annoy him. "I don't really want to. Let's talk about you and Miss Dice. That sounds like more fun."

"We aren't here to talk about Amy. We are here to talk about you." Mr Matthews grips the arm of his chair, trying to hide his frustration. He doesn't do it well.

"Amy, hey? First name basis. So how long have you two been dating?" I'm smug as fuck when I see pink flush his cheeks. I think it even travels up to his shiny bald scalp.

"Lexi, I'm here to help you." There goes his grip again. That poor chair! What did it ever do to him?

"And how are you helping me?" I sit forward, anger fuelling me. "Everything I say in this room will be recorded in that stupid file you have on your lap, and then the teachers can use it against me. Information is power, Mr Matthews."

"What you say to me is confidential, Lexi. It doesn't leave this room." He bites back.

"Yeah right, until Child Services wants to see it, or a court judge wants it for evidence when the cops finally catch up with my brother or my dad. Fuck, even the students could get a hold of it if they really wanted to."

"No students can get into the private files in here, Lexi."

Sitting back, I cross my arms over my chest. "Really? Wanna make a bet about that?"

He stands abruptly, anger etched across his face and walks over to his desk, turning back to look at me.

"Fine Lexi, you don't trust my ability to keep your records safe, then I'll destroy them. He leans down and flicks a switch, igniting a grinding sound. I watch, stunned, as Mr Matthews feeds my file into a shredder.

Shit! He's actually destroying the file. I didn't think he would do that.

When he's finished, he walks back to sit in his chair in front of me. I don't miss the poor chair getting assaulted by his grip again.

"What the hell, Mr M! You can't do that!" I protest, moving to the edge of the seat.

He shrugs, "Well, I just did it."

"That has to be illegal or something!" I'm completely shocked for a moment, but then wariness flutters through my head.

"Now anything you tell me will only be up here," he taps the side of his head, "and if it's ever disclosed, it will be hearsay."

He's totally bluffing. I mean, yeah, he shredded the files, but they are just pieces of paper. Everyone knows records are kept in the computer system.

"I'm not stupid; we live in the 21st century. You'll just update your files on your computer. How about you put that through the shredder as well, and then I'll talk?"

I expect him to get pissed off, but after a moment of his static stare, he erupts in a deep belly laugh. The rumbling sound goes on and on, and I fight against the urge to laugh too. He has one of those infectious laughs that affects everyone that hears it. Drawing in my top lip, I bite it hard to try and stop myself from reacting. When he calms, wiping at the tears in his eyes, he tries to compose himself.

"I say something funny?" I ask.

"Sorry, Lexi. I just never know what you're going to say. It's refreshing. You remind me of my sister. You both have the same quick wit and stubborn nature." He takes a deep breath and morphs back to his serious self again. "I am trying to help you. I'm concerned about your anger. You were very quick to lash out at Natasha when you first walked in the toilets yesterday."

"You'll have to excuse me for not knowing what you're talking about. The whole thing is a little fuzzy." I lie, and he knows it.

"I believe the words Tasha used to provoke you were *'you filthy whore, you allowed your brother'*." He doesn't miss the fury that engulfs my face at him repeating Tasha's words. "Then you reacted by trying to choke her."

I laugh, "Hardly. I didn't even squeeze tight enough to choke the bitch. I was going easy on her."

Mr Matthews studies me for a moment, obviously considering his words.

"I get that you're angry, Lexi. After what you've been subjected to, it's totally understandable, but you need to learn how to control your anger. Mrs Rogan and I want to support you. We want to show you that you can trust again—especially adults. The thing is, we also have a duty to keep everyone that walks onto our school grounds safe.

We aren't going to pursue further punishment for your part in what happened yesterday, but we can only do so much. If you show violence on the school grounds again, then we won't have any choice but to discipline you in the appropriate manner."

"Don't do me any favours. I didn't ask to be treated any differently." I snap, biting back tears.

"We know that, Lexi. We do, however, want you to feel safe. But we also have to make sure the other 987 students in this school feel safe too." Mr Matthews sounds genuine. If I wasn't being a stubborn bitch, I'd have to admit that I like the guy.

"Fine, I'll try to behave, but if anyone, male or female, student or teacher or even parent, tries to hurt me, then I will fight back in self-defence. I couldn't care less about the damn school rules."

"Agreed. Thank you." Mr Matthews relaxes.

We're both quiet for a few minutes. Mr Matthews is deep in thought, and I'm battling a war with my tear ducts. My emotions are shot lately. I'm totally blaming my monthly.

"Can we talk about something else?" I ask, needing to lighten the mood.

"Yes, of course, Lexi." He grins, pleased.

"Have you kissed Miss Dice yet?"

Ten

After I left Mr Matthews, I went straight to English and ignored Marcus and his sulking. Jared was okay, though, and I managed to concentrate and plan out my essay for the upcoming assessment. After that class, I didn't even go to my locker; I just bolted from the classroom to the back of the school and didn't look back.

I'm getting good at ditching my shadow pack, as Rhys likes to call them. I spend lunch with my new misfit friends and ignore the messages blowing up my phone from the boys. They are pissed at me, which just pisses me off more, tempting me to be more defiant. Who the hell do they think they are?

After lunch, Maths is a struggle because once again, I'm reminded of Ayden. When am I ever going to stop thinking about him? When will I ever stop longing to inhale his addictive scent or to feel his gentle touch? When will I ever stop replaying his kisses in my head or the way he lit my body on fire on that rooftop? It's safe to say that by the end of Maths, I'm a walking time bomb of mixed emotions, and even Rhys can't seem to reach me with her witty conversations during after school detention.

When I walk out of detention thirty minutes later, I'm surprised to see Garrett waiting for me. The boys have football training on Tuesdays and Thursdays after school, but I guess Garrett gets a pass with his injured hand.

"Oh, look, it's the dark, broody one," Rhys whispers too loudly in my ear as we approach Garrett. He smirks, and I roll my eyes.

"Hi dark and broody, I'm Lexi's bestie, Rhys." She offers her hand with dark cherry red painted nails, and Garrett hesitates a moment before taking it for a brief shake.

I'll admit, hearing Rhys use the term bestie to explain our very new friendship makes me smile inside but hurts a little at the same time. Abbey held the best friend title for like fifteen years. Now, she's my enemy.

"Hey, Rhys. I'm Garrett." He drops his hand back by his side and looks at me before looking back at Rhys. "You're her bestie, are you?"

"Sure am." She grins pleased and links her arm with mine.

"So, if you're her best friend, then I'm guessing you're the one she's been running off with at recess and lunch?"

"Of course. Lexi can't handle Dylan and Hayden behind the bike shed all on her own. Sharing is caring, after all."

I burst out laughing at Rhys' words, and Garrett's blue-grey eyes widen, looking completely stunned.

"Jesus Rhys, you're gonna give Gaz an aneurism. That's TMI. He doesn't need to know what we do with our spare time." It feels good to stir the pot. These boys deserve it, after all. I just wish they were all here to endure it.

"I really hope you're just trying to fuck with me, Lex." Turning his intense gaze on me, Garrett frowns.

"Why? What's it to you who I get down and dirty with?" I'm being a bitch, and Garrett's in the firing line, unfortunately for him.

His jaw ticks, "I'm just trying to look out for you."

"Why? You never looked out for me before when I was on and off with Nathan. You never looked out for me at Tasha's party a few weeks back when I was getting high and wandered off with Travis.

Why are you looking out for me now?" Why am I being such a bitch to him?

"You wandered off with Travis? Travis Watson? I wasn't even at that party. Otherwise, I totally would have stopped that shit from happening!" Garrett's anger shocks me. Shit, was he really not at that party? As if I would even know. I hardly remember anything.

"Lexi West has a dark past. I love it!" Rhys adds, clapping, but we both ignore her.

"Yes, Travis Watson, and before you ask, it's not like that. Nothing happened." Well, if you don't include breaking into and vandalising the very school we go to as nothing happening. Oh, and the kiss which I'm still in denial about since I can't remember it.

"Jesus, Lexi. You had me worried." If he only knew. What would he say if I told him what I did that night with Travis? Or the time I went to the party to give Travis the weed I stole from Mike in exchange for information. He'd finally see me for the trash that I am.

"Why are you looking out for me now?" My voice is low, just above a whisper. Shame twists like a knife in my heart. That night really was a turning point for me. The spiralling out of control started that night.

Garrett steps up to me and cups my face, his warm palm nearly breaking my walls down. I have to crane my head back to look up to his tall height, and I hear Rhys suck in a breath. She doesn't let go of my arm, and I can see her out of the corner of my eye, watching every moment that passes.

"We're looking out for you because we failed to do that before and look what happened. Me and the guys can't bear the thought of you getting hurt again, Lex." Still holding my head in his hand, Garrett's eyes bore deeply into mine, and I have the familiar urge to flee.

"I was right! You have a harem." Rhys' voice cuts through my emotions, and I push Garrett gently back from my personal space.

"I need to go." I pull away from Rhys, but she just chuckles, not taking it personally.

"See you tomorrow, bestie!" She calls.

I ignore her, knowing that my bitchy attitude could very well push her away and end our very brief friendship. I'm so over feeling so shit all the time. I feel like I'm on a rollercoaster getting whiplash every day.

Garrett doesn't let me get far and catches up with me taking my hand in his to stop me. I keep my eyes cast to the concrete path at our feet.

"Lex, come back to my house for a bit. Let's try to get you out of that head of yours."

Peering up at Garrett, his concerned eyes roam my face. He has his own demons to deal with, but here he is, trying to help me deal with mine. Sighing, I nod, letting him lead the way to his house, and we walk in comfortable silence. The walk isn't long, and less than fifteen minutes later, he leads me into a small generic red brick house in a part of town I've never been in.

I can tell he's a little uncomfortable with having me in his house. A look I've never seen him wear worries his face. I hope he doesn't think I'm so shallow to think less of him because he doesn't come from wealth. I certainly don't. My family is obviously better off financially than Garrett's. Marcus and Jared's families are much like mine, but Simon's parents are the richest of rich. I have no idea about Shaun's family, though. It changes nothing about the way I feel about any of these guys. My guys. Garrett included.

Garrett is totally right about getting me out of my own head. As soon as we walk through the door of his house, we are engulfed by his family. His younger sisters dote on me, and his mum is kind and eager to chat. I don't have a moment to think about my crappy life. I have no choice but to be in the here and now.

We help his sisters with their diorama project for school, and I find out that Garrett is actually quite creative. I even get roped into staying for dinner where Garrett insists I help him and his mum cook spaghetti bolognese. I consider telling him I don't like to cook, but I keep that to myself. He seems so happy and content in his small kitchen cooking with his mum and me, and in the end, I have to admit; I have fun.

It's after eight when Shaun drops by with his older brother to pick me up and take me home. Like Garrett, I've only known Shaun for a couple of years, and while I've been subject to his flirty ways many a time, I don't think I've ever been alone with him for long. Tonight, however, he's my babysitter, and it's just him and me alone in my house.

After Shaun's brother drops us off, I shower in my mum's bathroom while Shaun plays some online game on the PlayStation. Alone with my thoughts once again, Ayden comes to mind before Mike's attack rudely bursts in. I wonder if I'll ever be able to shower again without remembering his face or how he pleasured himself in front of me? I deliberately run the water scalding hot and let my skin turn pink under the burn while I cry silently, needing to take this moment alone to let it out.

Why haven't the police found him yet? Are they even looking? Knowing he's still out there somewhere is turning me into a crazed bitch. Surely he wouldn't be idiotic enough to stay in Fox Pines? He's on parole, for fuck's sake. He legally can't leave the state, although what he did to me wasn't legal either, so why would he care? With any luck, he will be caught soon, and then I will be free to try and live a normal life.

Getting out of the shower, I avoid looking at myself in the mirror and make no attempt to wipe away the fog. While going to Garrett's house was nice, I haven't had a chance to go for a run or punch out my frustrations on the boxing bag.

Glancing down, my eyes catch on the shaver resting on the sink. *Shit!* My heart races, and I brace my hands on the benchtop forcing my eyes away from it. There's a reason I started beating the shit out of the bag in the garage and running on the treadmill until the burning pain gets so intense that I can no longer feel anything. While it's helping me to feel stronger, the real reason I started doing it has everything to do with that razor.

My eyes flick to it again, and I feel like screaming. I don't understand why I feel like this, but I have an overwhelming need to remove the blade and slice it over my skin. It's completely fucked up and scares the shit out of me! I've never had such an impulse. Never considered physically harming myself until I arrived home from the city.

"You're so fucked in the head," I say out loud to myself, attempting to shake myself out of the funk I'm in right now. The few times I've had this feeling, I've managed to drag myself away before following through, and instead, burn off the emotions and impulses in the garage.

It's late now, though. I really need to be winding down for the day, and somehow try to turn off my overthinking brain, so I dig deep and turn away from the bench to snatch up my PJ shorts that are in a crumpled heap on the floor. Once they are on, I move to grab my Three Days Grace t-shirt that I hung over the towel rail this morning, only it isn't there.

"What the fuck!" I'm sure I put it there this morning. Just like I'm sure I put my Metallica t-shirt there the morning before.

Moving into my mum's room, I glance around searching for my missing clothes, but my t-shirt isn't here either. Shit, I have no top to put on.

Throwing on my crop top, I leave my mum's room and walk through the house, scanning every piece of furniture or bench-top for my t-shirt as I go. It's not in the kitchen, not in the laundry, or hanging out on the line under the patio either. Marching past the living room, and ignoring Shaun when he calls out to me, I go upstairs to my room.

The doors are back on now, thanks to the boys. I hesitate for a moment, anxiety racing my heart in fear of not knowing what's on the other side of the door. It's ridiculous. It makes no sense for me to be panicking about this, so I hold my breath and turn the knob, opening the door. My heartbeat pounds in my ears when I'm met with darkness. Snaking my quivering hand inside the door frame, I feel for the light switch and flick it on quickly.

"Wanna tell me why you're walking around half naked?" Shaun's voice causes me to jump, a scream ripping from my lips.

"What the fuck, Bossi!" I hiss, clutching my chest, turning to look at him standing behind me. "Did you have to sneak up on me?"

"Ah... I didn't sneak Lex. Those stairs are creaky as fuck. I couldn't sneak up them if I tried."

He has a point. They are creaky. I know exactly where to step to make little noise, but he doesn't.

"Sorry, Shaun." If I'm not careful, he's going to see right past my attempt at hiding how fucked up

I really am and do a runner, probably taking the other boys with him. Then I'll be all alone again.

"Ah, Lex? Why are you only wearing a bra and shorts?" Shaun's steel-grey gaze travels over my body.

"Did I say you could look at me like that?" I raise a brow at him and then return my sights to looking for my t-shirt.

"I'm a guy. Tits and arse turn my brain into mush. Besides, you've got it all going on, Lexi. It's hard to think straight around you when you're fully clothed. Don't expect much from me when you're wearing next to nothing."

I give up on looking for my t-shirt and grab my Slipknot one from my draw, quickly covering up.

"Better?" I ask Shaun, and he drags his eyes to my legs.

"I also like legs."

"Fucking hell Shaun." Shaking my head at him, I slip past and head to the upstairs bathroom. I put my hand on the doorknob to open it but freeze, unable to go through with it. Dropping my hand, I step back.

"Hey, what's wrong?" Shaun slips his hand in mine and wraps his other one over the top, drawing my attention from the bathroom door.

"I'm trying to find my t-shirt."

"You think it's in there?" He asks, looking at the closed door.

I shrug.

"You don't want to go in there?" His question is more like a statement. He's obviously putting two and two together. "How about I go in there and look for it?" He asks, and I nod gratefully.

"It's a black Three Days Grace t-shirt. While you're there, can you check if my Metallica one is in there too? It's also black."

"Sure, chickadee. Be right back." Shaun drops my hand, shooting me a wink, and opens the bathroom door slipping in. I turn my back to the door, not wanting to see anything inside that room. The thought alone is turning the pasta I had for dinner over in my stomach.

Shaun is back a minute later empty-handed. "There's nothing in there, Lex." He looks confused, his steel-grey eyes latching onto mine.

Looking away, I walk off towards Mike's room and look in through the splintered door frame. Nothing has changed from Friday when I trashed it, so I go to the last place left to look. The garage. It's a waste of time. My t-shirts aren't in there either, so I go back inside.

"I don't understand." I plonk down on the couch next to Shaun, taking in his Latino features. He's undoubtedly attractive, which helps his Casanova complex; with hair as rich as a black coffee, tanned skin, full lips and a sharp jawline, he is the boy all the girls dream of snagging. Well, all except me. My heart belongs to Ayden.

There goes my heart again.

Ayden, I miss you!

"When did you last see them?" Shaun asks, snapping me out of my Ayden daydream and reminding me that my t-shirts are missing.

"I'm certain that I hung my Three Days Grace t-shirt over the towel rail in my mum's bathroom this morning. And the same with my Metallica t-shirt the morning before. But they aren't there when I go to look for them each night. I don't know what the fuck is going on."

Shaun is quiet for a few minutes, his white teeth biting into his lip as he mulls over something, and then asks me to stay put while he does his own search. He doesn't do a man's look either. I hear him going through every room, every cupboard and drawer looking for my t-shirts. Fifteen minutes later, he is back with me on the couch, and I know without a doubt that I'm not imagining things. My stuff has gone missing.

"Has anything else gone missing?" Shaun asks, glancing around the living room.

I frown, "Ah, yeah—the pictures off the fridge. I noticed them gone a couple of days ago. They were of my mum and me."

Taking my jittery hands in one of his, Shaun looks concerned before releasing my hand again and pulling his phone out of his pocket.

"I'm just gonna pop into the garage and make a quick call. Will you be okay here?"

I frown but nod, unsure why he needs to go to the garage to make the call. A few minutes later, as he's walking back in, I get a private message on my phone from Marcus.

Marcus Grady

If you need me or any of us to come and stay with you and Shaun, we will be there in a heartbeat.

"Which one sent you a message?" Shaun asks, and I hold up my phone so he can see. Shaking his head, he sits back down with me on the couch, "I told them not to message you. He's fucking hopeless."

"Why? What's going on?"

"Nothing Lex. I just thought I'd check with them to see if any of the guys took your stuff as a joke."

"And?" I already know the answer.

"They didn't."

I must look worried because Shaun pulls me to his chest for a hug.

"It's okay Lex. We have your back. Everything is okay." I'm not sure if he's trying to convince me or himself.

"It's not really, but I appreciate you trying to make me feel better." My words make him smile.

"You know what you need?" Shaun looks devious. I should probably be scared.

"I'm almost afraid to ask."

He laughs, "Well honey, any time you want some of this," he gestures to himself, "Then just say the word, and I'll make you forget your own name. But for now, let's watch The Office."

So that's what we do. Huddling up in the blankets on the floor, we watch back-to-back episodes of The Office until I fall asleep next to him on the same makeshift bed Simon had made the night before.

Eleven

I don't sleep well. My mind goes to dark places in my sleep, and I end up in the garage by 4am beating the shit out of the bag. Shaun checks on me at one point but leaves me to my inner rage to get his own sleep.

By 6am, I send Valarie a message asking if her mum has been in my house to do any of my washing. By 7am, she replies with a "*no*" and wants to know if everything is okay. I don't want to worry her, so I tell her everything is fine and leave it at that.

I deliberately leave my Slipknot t-shirt over the end of my mum's bed when I dress for school, taking a picture of exactly where I leave it. I've got no idea what's going on, but I know I'm not going crazy. My t-shirts, and possibly the pictures off the fridge have gone missing. The only way that can happen is if someone has taken them. My boys haven't taken the items, in this, I am sure. But someone has.

Shaun's brother picks us up and drops us out the front of the school, where the other boys are waiting for us. When we approach, I get hugs from each of them, feeling a little overwhelmed at their unconditional support. It's nice to feel their arms around me. The only problem is the only person's arms I want to feel around me isn't here. He hasn't even responded to my drunk text, even though I know he's read it after seeing the response bubbles the other day. In all fairness, I don't blame him. It was a stupid text. But I said that I was sorry too, so surely that should mean something, right?

My exhaustion has me in a sour mood, and I don't talk much to the boys or anyone else for that matter. They respect my need to be quiet, but I can tell by the concern etched across their faces that something is going on. I suspect they're thinking the same thing as me but don't want to worry me, so they keep quiet. At this point, I'm sure that someone is coming into my house and stealing my things. The worrying part about it is that there's a high chance that it's Mike. It'd be just like him to try and screw with my head like this.

My first two classes are double Media, and for the first time, I notice that Tillie and Dale are in my class. I'm annoyed at myself for not noticing them before, the old me was too far up her own arse to see anyone but the bitch squad, apparently. Tillie and Dale sit with me, so I'm not alone. I'm thankful to have met them through Rhys. They are funny and manage to get me to smile a couple of times as we do our Media tasks. It probably helps that Tasha isn't in class today. I have no idea where she is, but her absence makes it easier for me to concentrate.

At the start of recess, I ditch my books in my locker, ready to dash away quickly to avoid the boys, when I come face to face with Tasha fucking Pritchard. Ugh, I had hoped since she wasn't in Media class that she was away again today.

"You think you're so good, don't you? Brainwashing the boys to follow you around like lost puppies. What did you do? Spread your legs for them like you did for your brother?"

I try. I really do try not to lose it, but the bitch knows how to push my buttons and her words are heard by swarms of students in the passageway. I have no control over my fist as it attempts to slam the bitch in her ugly beady-eyed face, but strong arms wrap around me and pull me back, my swing meeting thin air.

"No, Lex," Marcus growls in my ear as Rhys strolls in front of me, walking right up to Tasha, grabbing her face and planting a kiss on her lips.

"Eww! Get off me you freak!" Tasha screeches, shoving Rhys back into me, making her laugh.

"What's wrong, Tasha baby? Don't want people to know how you love to kiss my lips? Or should I say, both sets of my lips?" Rhys smiles like the smug bitch she is, and Tasha looks around at our audience, horrified before huffing and storming off.

Laughter fills the air from the bystanders, and Rhys turns to me.

"I guess she didn't want people to know how much she likes kissing me." She flutters her dark lashes at me, feigning innocence.

"Rhys, you are going to get yourself into trouble one day." I grin.

"I do hope so. Trouble is so much fun." The boys behind me chuckle, and I shove away from Marcus, who hasn't made an attempt to let go of me.

"Lexi?" Miss Dice steps into our circle, concerned brown eyes peering at me through her glasses. "I think maybe it would be a good idea for you to go and see Mr Matthews."

My shoulders drop, and I almost whine. "Why?"

"You know why, Lexi." Miss Dice glances around at my friends before returning her brown eyes to me. She seems unsure of how much she should say in front of them.

"You can speak in front of them. They're cool." I let her know, and Rhys hooks her arm in mine, dropping her head on my shoulder.

"Lexi," Miss Dice lowers her voice, "It's either to the counsellor or the principal."

"But why? I didn't do anything."

"Only because Marcus stopped you. If he hadn't, then we would have had a repeat of Monday. Please go and see Mr Matthews so we can avoid involving the principal."

I can see Miss Dice thinks she is helping. Mr Matthews had asked me to try to control my anger. I mean, I did try... Kind of.

"Can I go after recess?" I ask, wanting to avoid it altogether.

"No, now, please. I'll walk with you." Miss Dice isn't backing down, so I pry Rhys' hold off me and follow Miss Dice.

Glancing back, I see Rhys wiggle her fingers in a wave while Marcus and Jared stand arms crossed over their chests, frowns contorting their faces. It almost makes me want to run up and hug them and tell them everything will be alright. Rhys may be a new addition in my life, but she sure is a loyal addition, much like the boys. Or my pack, as Rhys calls them.

I sit and wait inside the counsellor's office as he and Miss Dice talk quietly outside the door before he shuts us in and joins me.

"Natasha Pritchard strikes again." Mr Matthews states, sitting down.

"Why isn't that bitch being hauled in here? Why is it always me?"

"Well, mainly because your first instinct is to use violence." Mr Matthews doesn't bother with a file or note pad. He knows how I feel about that.

"That's a crock of shit. She provoked me! Words can be just as harmful as physical violence, you know!" My face is burning with anger, and I feel like smashing things. I probably shouldn't admit that to my counsellor, though.

"Yes, I know, and we will follow up on her actions later, but right now, my concern is you."

"Why?" I grumble. I was looking forward to spending time with my new friends during recess, but instead, I'm spending it getting interrogated by the bald, yet kind of cool counsellor. He's lucky I like him!

"Because you're having trouble controlling your anger. Have you thought about doing some exercise to burn off the anger and clear your head?" Mr Matthews looks more relaxed in his chair today. Unlike me. I'm a ball of tension.

"I already do." I snap.

"Like what?"

"I run, most days, and I hit the bag at home."

"At home? Aren't you staying with a friend?"

Shit!

"Well yeah. I mean at their place. It's home for now."

Mr Matthews nods, happy with my answer; thank fuck.

"When was the last time you punched the bag?" He's studying me, and it's making me squirm.

"4am this morning."

His brows shoot up, "That's pretty early, or really late depending on the way you look at it. Shouldn't you have been asleep?"

"Sure, if sleep is easy to come by," I admit.

"You aren't sleeping?" He looks concerned, his bushy brows pulling together.

"It depends on the day." I'm being vague on purpose because I don't want to talk about it.

Next, he'll be asking about my nightmares and a whole heap of bullshit that is no one's business but mine.

"What happens on the days you can't sleep?" He asks, and I sigh.

"Can I go?"

"Not yet. Let's chat a little more." He's being sterner today, and I don't like it.

"I really don't want to. Haven't you figured that out by now?" I shoot him a glare, but he only grins.

"How about a change in conversation?" He suggests.

"Okay. How's Amy going? You two getting hot and heavy yet?" I cross my arms over my chest and grin.

"Deflecting won't help Lexi."

"Will walking out? Because I'm happy to do that." He's going to get sick of me and kick me out eventually, right?

"I hear you've made some new friends. That must be nice."

"Good deflection Stephen." My quick comeback makes him chuckle.

"Do you have a boyfriend?" He asks, and I frown.

"What business is that of yours?"

"It's none of my business, but I thought that might be a happy topic to talk about."

"You're shit out of luck there, Mr Matthews. That topic is nothing but heartbreak." I don't mean to reveal that. It just comes out on its own as if someone else is talking. I realise then that it's my heart talking and not my brain.

"So you have an ex-boyfriend?" He's tried to broach this subject with me before, but I pretended to be interested in girls. Why is this line of questioning even necessary? And why did he have to make me think about Ayden again?

"Yes. No. I don't know." I look at my hands fidgeting in my lap.

"What's his name?"

"You don't need to know his name." I snap, and he nods.

"Okay. How old is he?"

"He's eighteen."

"An older guy, hey? Does he go to this school?" The bell goes indicating the end of recess, and I'm about ready to flee.

"Maybe. Maybe not." That's the truth too. I have no idea if Ayden is coming back to Fox Pines.

"What did he do to break your heart, Lexi?"

I hesitate, feeling the burn of tears in the back of my eyes. I don't want to cry. I take a moment to fight them off, and when it lessens, I respond, "He didn't do anything. It was me that ruined his life.

Tainted it with the sick world I live in. He's better off without me."

Mr Matthews frowns, "Does he agree with that?"

A knock sounds at the door and Mr Matthews calls out, "Hold on a minute, please."

I stand ready to escape this man and his questions.

"Lexi, wait." He stands as well, looking serious. I raise a blonde brow waiting for him to continue.

"Next time you feel so angry that you need to explode, I want you to come straight to my office."

"If I do that, Mr Matthews, then I'll be in here all day." I ignore whatever he says after that and swing the door open to leave, but then I freeze.

My entire body heats, from my toes to the tip of my head, when I come face to face with eyes as blue as a summer sky. Ayden Mitchell, my Ayden Mitchell, is standing in front of me.

I want to speak, or yell, or cry, or do something, but I'm frozen on the spot drowning in those familiar eyes that draw me in and hypnotise me.

"Oh, hi, Ayden. Come on in."

Ayden's eyes flick over my shoulder to Mr Matthews and then back to mine. I wait for him to say something, but he doesn't.

"Ayden mate, you'll need to step aside so Lexi can leave." Mr Matthews says, unaware of what's going on before him.

The longer we stare at each other, the more his anger builds, turning those piercing blue eyes into a storm. That's okay though, I'm all about angry right now too. I step forward, not waiting for him to move, and I push past him, nudging my shoulder into his side on my way out of the room.

Part of me wants to go back and leap into his arms. Another part of me wants to scream in his face and let out all the hurt that surrounds my heart. The part that wins, though, is the part of me that feels the need to flee. I consider going home, but I'm too scared. What if Mike's there? Or whoever is stealing my stuff? I could go to the library, but the anger bubbling at the surface of my control is too intense, and I need to let it out.

Needing a distraction, I head to my double PE class. As I walk across the campus, my mind replays the expression on Ayden's face. What the fuck is his problem? Why the hell did he look so pissed? And why didn't anyone tell me he was coming back? Fuck him, and fuck everyone else.

PE has already started when I walk in, and I ignore Mr Foster and head to the girls' change rooms. I'm furious. I'm livid. I need to hurt someone, and I need to do it now. Once I'm changed, I go into the stadium and spot Allison. She wasn't here last time we had PE, and after today, she's going to wish she didn't show up.

Today's activity is soccer, and I can see that all my guys are on the same side, so I grab up a yellow bib to indicate that I'm on their team too, and run out into the game honing in on my target. What happens on the field stays on the field, right? Or I should say floor since we are playing indoors today.

I watch the ball in play and assess the situation quickly before running towards Allison. She sees me coming, her dark brown eyes widen, and I read her lips saying "Oh fuck" before she turns and runs in the other direction. She's not quick enough, and I leap on her back, tackling her to the ground.

I get a mouthful of her chocolate brown waves before the whistle sounds, and strong arms wrap around me just as I'm about to pound my fist into her. My legs flail, and I growl in frustration as I'm dragged in the other direction.

"Calm down, Lexi," Jared growls in my ear, so I relax a little, happy that for once, it isn't Marcus trying to control me. When we're far enough away, he puts me down and releases me.

"What was that, Miss West?" Mr Foster yells, his over sunned face reddening in anger.

"What? Aren't we playing football?" I ask innocently.

Snickers sound around me.

"Not Aussie rules football Lexi. This is soccer. No tackling!" Mr Foster shakes his head, walking off.

"Well, that's boring," I say before shooting Allison a glare.

The boys jog over to us, noticeably confused. Well, except for Simon, he seems happy.

"You okay, Lex?" Garrett asks, but I ignore him as I seek out Marcus. He's standing back, which is odd because he's always front and bloody centre in my face telling me what to do lately.

Stomping towards him, I let the anger show on my face and his eyes go wide just before I shove him in the chest.

"What the actual fuck Marcus!"

"What?" His brown eyes go round in innocence, and he takes a step back.

"Why the fuck didn't you tell me he was back?" My chest rises and falls with heavy breaths. I'm on the edge of a very steep cliff right now, and I'm not sure that I'm going to be able to step away from it.

"Who's back?" Simon asks from behind me.

I keep my focus on Marcus, and he opens and closes his mouth like a damn goldfish, obviously struggling with words.

"Who's back, Lex?" Jared asks, and I realise Marcus has kept this information from all of us.

The whistle blows, and Mr Foster calls for us to take positions again, but none of my boys move.

"You could have fucking warned me, Marcus." A tear slips free, and I turn from him, needing space between us. A lot of fucking space.

I push through the boys, but Jared grabs my hand halting me briefly.

"Six. Who's back?"

I look up into the eyes of one of my oldest friends and let him see the pain swimming in my own.

"Ayden," I whisper before pulling away and taking my spot for the game to resume.

I don't miss the round of curses falling from the boys' lips as I retreat or Garrett's voice as he tears strips off Marcus.

"What the fuck, man! That's information we should have all known about!"

I take my anger and focus it on the game, letting my competitive side come out in full force. While everyone else's aim is to kick the ball in the goal, mine is to hurt Allison. I am relentless in my endeavour to make her suffer. I stay near her for the whole game. Sticking my leg out to trip her or nudging her hard whenever Mr Foster isn't looking.

Even though I get concerned looks from the boys, they don't try to stop my attacks on Allison. It's like they know I need to get my aggression out, so they just watch on at the monster I unleash.

While my anger stems from my family and the way Tasha and her merry bitches have been treating me, I realise that I've been bottling up anger to do with Ayden as well. I've been telling myself that he is better off without me. That I tainted his world. But the selfish part of me is truly hurt by the cruel words he said with such distaste the day I walked away from him in Melbourne.

I know I should probably go to Mr Matthews instead of unleashing my wrath on Allison, but there's just one problem. I can't go to him because he is with Ayden right now. Ayden fucking Mitchell. The guy that took my virginity, took my heart, and then destroyed me.

That's not right, though, is it? I know I'm being irrational. If I were a better person, I'd admit that I was the one who happily gave him my virginity, who freely gave him my heart, and who tainted his life, leaving him no choice but to demand space.

Today, I'm not a better person. I am tired. Exhausted. Scared and confused. I am hurting so brutally on the inside that I almost wish I could come face to face with Mike and let him beat the shit out of me because it would be less painful than what my heart is suffering.

Ayden Mitchell pushed his way into my life and broke down my walls. He made me care about him. He made me think there could be a better life. He made me trust him. In this moment, I realise that what he did to my heart is the biggest betrayal I've endured.

Twelve

"Who pissed you off?" Bell stands before me with her midnight black hair in her Wednesday Addams braids, wearing her typical indifferent expression.

"You, if you don't get out of my face!" I snap, and holy shit, I get a fucking grin out of her.

"You're always pissed off. Today is different, though. Who do you want to kill?" Bell makes no attempt to move, so I step around her and sit on the steps at the back of the school stadium.

"Girl, are you on your period?" Dale sits next to me, screwing his nose up in a cringe while sweeping his hand through his mop of sandy curls.

"Maybe." I lie, not wanting to talk about the real reason I have 'fuck off' written across my forehead.

"Here, this might help." Dale offers me the joint he's smoking, and I don't even hesitate to take it.

Bringing it to my lips, I drag the smoke in, letting it seep into my lungs, and I close my eyes, savouring the feeling, eager for the effects to kick in.

"Queen Lexi is being naughty. Can I be naughty too?" I open my eyes to peer up at Rhys. She's grinning down at me, which makes me smile. "Sure, if you have your own joint."

"Girl, that's my joint you have." Dale quips, and I roll my eyes at him before taking another drag.

"You gave it to me because I'm on my period." I grin, blowing the smoke up into the sky as Dale makes a gagging noise.

"You little liar. You're not pissed because of your period. It's because of Ay-."

"Rhys, don't you dare say his fucking name!" I hiss.

"I like the angry version of you," Bell states matter-of-factly, and I roll my eyes.

"I do too. It's turning me on." Rhys smirks at me before snatching the joint and taking a drag.

I don't try to get it back. She probably just did me a favour. The last thing I need is to go to my next class baked out of my mind. I also don't want a repeat of losing my memory, or to become a drug fucked zombie like my mum and Mike.

Shit, why do I keep making bad choices?

“Everything turns you on, Rhys.” Tillie nudges Rhys with her shoulder before taking the joint from her and having her own fill.

“I’m a sexual being. What can I say?” Rhys seductively drags her hands over her breasts and cups them.

“You could keep it to yourself. I don’t want to hear that shit. Or see that. Stop groping your tits!” Dale hisses at Rhys, and she pokes her tongue out.

Dale and vampire boy, whose name I found out is Allister, starts talking about some game called D&D that they are going to play this weekend, and Rhys nudges Dale over with her foot so she can sit next to me.

“You okay?” She asks, taking my hand in hers. Her tone is serious, so I meet her gaze and shrug.

“I saw him just before lunch, coming out of the counsellor’s office. You didn’t know he was coming back?” Rhys’ voice is low, and I appreciate her not blabbing it to everyone. This shit is personal.

I shake my head and then rest it on her shoulder. Rhys lays her head on mine and takes the joint off Tillie to take another drag before holding it to my lips so I can have one last intake before it’s all gone.

"I can feel your phone vibrating in your pocket," Rhys giggles. "It'll be your reverse harem trying to find you again."

"Probably," I feel relaxed, but not as relaxed as I was on Saturday night when I got wasted at Simon's.

I purposely don't take my phone out of my pocket to check the messages. I can't deal with the guys right now. I just need a breather, so I selfishly enjoy the company of my new misfit friends for the rest of lunch.

When the bell goes for last period, I drag my feet to my new Psychology class. Another new class care of Abbey's stupid parents. I mean, why the hell would I be interested in psychology? This is just another class I'll probably fail because it has no relevance to my interests or my ability.

Miss Harding, my year eight science teacher, is standing at the whiteboard writing something that I don't understand when I walk in. A quick look around the room, and I'm ready to turn and walk the hell out.

Ayden is in this class. Seriously?

To make matters worse, the only empty seat is at the table next to his. Not happening.

I walk to the back of the room where Sally Davis is sitting and glare down at her.

"Move!"

"What?" She looks at me, confused.

"I want this seat, Sally. Move." I can feel eyes on me, but I ignore the onlookers and keep my focus on the red-headed girl cowering before me.

"But, there's a spare seat over there." She points and I smile. It's not a friendly smile.

"Yes, I know. That's your seat. Go fucking sit in it."

"Is there a problem, Lexi?" Ms Harding's voice travels from the front of the room, so I turn to her.

"Nope. Sally was just telling me she wants to sit closer to the front, so I'm being kind enough to swap with her."

Miss Harding smiles, "That's nice of you, Lexi. Thank you."

"Anytime," I smirk and turn back to Sally, who's bundling up her books to move.

When the desk is free, I sit and open my laptop. Unfortunately, even though I will myself not to, my eyes still seek Ayden out. I quickly regret that when I see the disappointment etched across his face. The frown he shoots me across the room almost breaks me, so I glance down at my laptop screen, fighting back tears and the need to scream.

Taking my phone out, needing to distract my thoughts, I go on the group chat and read through the usual messages that the boys send me when I do a runner from them. Then a notification lights up the screen with a message from Ayden.

I debate whether to open it. I've been waiting to hear from him since I sent the drunk text, and now that I have, I'm not sure I want to know what he has to say.

Of course, I'm lacking the ability to control my curiosity, so I open the message.

Ayden Mitchell
What was that?
Since when do you act like Tasha?"

Oh, he did not just compare me to Tasha fucking Pritchard.

Lexi West
*** middle finger emoji ***

Ayden Mitchell
We need to talk.

Lexi West
*** middle finger emoji ***

Ayden Mitchell
How old are you?

Lexi West
*** middle finger emoji ***

Ayden Mitchell
Lex, come on. We should talk.

Lexi West
To you, my name is Alexis!

I look up from my phone to watch Ayden as he reads my message, and he flinches before shooting me a glare. Oh man, even his glare is hot.

I stick my middle finger up at him and watch as his face turns from a glare to a grin.

Shit! I look away quickly, hoping he doesn't see how he affects me, knowing that a stupid blush is most likely on my face.

I decide to put my phone away and ignore him for the rest of the class, knowing that I need to learn whatever the hell one is meant to learn in a psychology class. I fail, though. By the time the bell goes, I realise I have no idea what Ms Harding was even speaking about.

I wait for Ayden to leave with the flow of students and then hurry out, eager to get detention over and done with so I can get out of this wretched school. Rhys is in detention once again. Apparently, detention is a daily ritual she performs due to ignoring the dress code rules to express her individuality. She hasn't *not* had a detention after school for a couple of years. I wonder what she'd do if she didn't get one?

Tasha is in detention as well, doing her time for her crimes. She does a good job of ignoring Rhys' attempts to stir her up. I, however, find the whole thing way too entertaining, and Rhys knows it. Just like with that boy I don't like to talk about, my friendship with Rhys has evolved quickly, and it makes me wonder why. Am I so needy that I latch onto someone so quickly? Or have I just had unheard-of luck in finding a friend I truly connect with? Whatever it is, it makes me both thankful and wary.

After detention Rhys and I walk out to find the boys waiting... and Ayden is with them. My heart somersaults in my chest at seeing him. Stupid heart! Looking over the boys' faces, I notice each one of them wears a look of unease or guilt. They know damn well that I wouldn't be happy that

Ayden is with them waiting for me, yet here he is, standing with them like he belongs there.

"Damn! Shit's about to get real, hey?" Rhys asks, not helping the situation since she says it so everyone can hear.

"Want to come over to my place?" I drag my eyes away from the boys and focus on Rhys.

She turns her head to the side to study me. I don't know what she sees, but she smiles and nods, linking her arm in mine. "Absolutely. Lead the way to your palace, my queen."

My hope that the boys will back off and let me have some time with Rhys quickly vanishes as they follow us out of school.

I spin to them, avoiding Ayden's eyes to address my friends.

"You guys can go home. Rhys will be with me."

"Nice try Lex." Jared chuckles, walking up to us, linking his arm with Rhys' and moving us forward again. Traitor.

The other boys chat away behind us as we walk, so I plead to Jared.

"Jar, please. I don't need you guys to come over tonight."

"You know we're not leaving you, Lexi. Save your breath." He doesn't even look at me when he speaks.

I huff, "You just come over then. There's no need for everyone to be there."

Rhys darts her head between Jared and me as we speak. I swear she's going to pull a neck muscle.

"Lex stop! You need to face him, eventually. May as well get it over with, hey?" Jared looks at me this time, his blue eyes firm and serious.

I want to cry.

"You smell really nice. How have I not met you before?" Rhys interrupts, and I'm grateful.

Jared smiles down at her, "I don't know. I'm Jared."

"Rhys," she introduces herself, "Lexi's new best friend."

"Pleased to meet you, Rhys. So where do you hang out at school?"

Rhys laughs, "Nice try, Jared. The only way I'm revealing that is while your head is between my legs, making me scream."

Laughter rips from Jared so forcefully that he nearly makes us stumble since he's still linked with Rhys, with me on her other side.

"Noted. I'll be sure to make that happen." Jared finally responds.

Rhys grins, "Are you jealous, Lexi? Because if you don't want one of your boys to make me come, you better say so now."

I laugh, "Have at it, Rhys."

Rhys grins at me while Jared frowns behind her before looking away. I want to ignore the look he gave me, but I know I won't be able to. I need to ask him about that later because I thought we had cleared up any confusion about our relationship. His look said otherwise.

When we reach my house, the boys flow in and make themselves at home like they usually do. The PlayStation gets turned on, music starts streaming from the stereo, and Marcus and Simon head to the kitchen to seek out food. I stand just inside the living room and watch Rhys as she demands control of the stereo over Shaun. Ayden comes to stand next to me, looking taken aback by the scene before him.

I try to assess what he's witnessing through his eyes. He's seeing how comfortable the boys are in my house, how we all seem to have a routine. He can also see the blankets on the living room floor. *Whoops.*

"Who slept there?" He asks, and I almost sigh at the sound of his voice. Or melt. Probably both.

"Last night, it was Shaun's turn to sleep there with Lexi. The night before, Gaz and I had the honours." Simon divulges, walking back in the room with a packet of potato chips.

My eyes widen in horror. He did not just say that. Did he?

Simon doesn't make it far into the room before Ayden reefs him back by his school blazer and throws him against the wall by the front window, potato chips flying through the air.

"You better be fucking kidding!" Ayden roars, and Marcus leaps into action to pull his cousin off Simon.

While I know I should be panicking, for some reason, I'm not. A strange calm comes over me, so I lean back against the door frame watching the scene before me like it's a good movie, while Marcus does damage control.

"Calm the fuck down, man!" Marcus gets up in Ayden's face forcing him to step back from Simon, who glares daggers at Ayden while he straightens his blazer.

"Why the fuck are you sleeping with her? That wasn't part of the fucking agreement!" Ayden glares at Simon, and then Garrett and Shaun. My ears perk up.

"What agreement?" Suddenly I don't feel so calm anymore.

"I thought you said this wasn't a reverse harem?" Rhys asks, coming to stand beside me.

"It's not!" I snap, not taking my eyes off a very guilty looking Marcus.

"If you're like, sleeping with all of them, then girl, you have yourself a harem."

"Jesus, Rhys," I turn to her, needing her to stop talking about this in front of Ayden, "I'm not fucking them. I'm not doing anything remotely sexual with them. There is no fucking harem!"

"What the fuck is she talking about?" Ayden asks, but I ignore him.

"What agreement, Marcus?" I ask Marcus because I don't want to speak to Ayden.

"Nothing," Marcus adds and turns his attention back to a still fuming Ayden. "I wouldn't have told you about Lexi's stuff going missing if I knew you would come back here and pick shit at everyone."

"You know what. Fuck you all! Get out of my house!" I yell, my patience snapping. No one is telling me the truth. I'm sick of being lied to. "Get the fuck out!"

No one makes a move to leave, so I turn to Rhys. "You should go."

"Um, no. I'm not leaving you here to deal with these douchecanoes on your own." Rhys frowns at me, looking more serious than I've ever seen her.

"Douchecan-what?" Shaun asks.

Rhys turns to him, "Douchecanoes. Google it."

"Rhys, seriously. It's okay. I'm used to these boys invading my space."

Rhys steps up to me, putting her hand on my shoulder. "I'm staying the night, Lexi. You can shut me out tomorrow, but I'm not leaving."

I can see her genuine concern, and my heart pangs a little. I nod, and she pecks me on the cheek before moving across the space to sit on the couch.

The room goes quiet, with a thousand unanswered questions still hanging over our heads.

"Ha! Douchecanoes. It's actually a word! An obnoxious or contemptible person, typically a man." Chuckles float around the room when Shaun reads out the meaning. "Hey, wait a minute. We're not douchecanoes."

"Aren't you?" I raise my brow in question, leaving Shaun with confusion twisting his handsome Latino face.

"Is anything missing today Lex?" Ayden asks, and I ignore him, not wanting to even look at his beautiful blue caring eyes.

"Come on, let's go have a look." Jared steps up to me, and I happily let him lead me out of the room by my wrist. I don't miss the glare Ayden throws him or the way Ayden hones in on where Jared is holding me.

We look in each room on both floors, but I don't notice anything out of place, so Jared relays that to the boys before making their plans for babysitting duty tonight. Marcus, of all people, gets the job, and I'm a little annoyed because he's the last person I want to be with since he's clearly been keeping secrets from me.

We have pizza once again, although I struggle to get through half a slice. There are attempts at doing homework, but it seems as though no one can concentrate. Just before the sun goes down, the boys say their goodbyes for the night and leave, but Ayden hovers and follows me out to the garage, invading my sacred space.

"Lex, can we talk?" His voice sends chills, of the good kind, all over my skin, and I fight hard not to let him see my body's reaction.

I not so subtly turn the volume up on the Bluetooth speaker and start pounding the shit out of the bag, letting myself fall into the zone where all that exists is my anger. I punch, kick, and throw my shoulders into the bag over and over, letting the sweat drench my body until I'm exhausted.

When I come up for air, I find myself alone in the garage. That's when I finally let myself go, collapsing to the cold concrete floor to cry.

Thirteen

Another sleepless night equals another grumpy Lexi. Part of me, and I must say, it's a very stupid part, wanted Ayden to still be in my house when I dragged myself in from the garage last night. Thankfully, Marcus didn't notice my disappointment, but Rhys did. Nothing seems to get past that girl.

Marcus and Rhys were doing homework together when I came in, which kind of blew my mind. I never imagined them getting along so well, but my judgement doesn't mean shit these days. By 10pm, Rhys insisted we watch Stranger Things on Netflix. I didn't think I would like it, but what can I say? Now I'm hooked.

By midnight I went to my mum's room to get changed for bed, still happy that I found my Slipknot t-shirt earlier where I left it on the bed that morning. I went through the motions of brushing my teeth and then went to take my birth control pill, however, when I went to get the packet out of my toilet bag I keep in my mum's bathroom now, it wasn't there.

That's why sleep evades me once again. Knowing my pill had been there the night before, and is now missing, turns me into an even bigger nutcase than I already was. I toss and turn on the couch for hours, waiting for sleep to come, but eventually give up, worried that I'll disturb Marcus and Rhys, who had taken the makeshift bed on the floor. I did point out to them that there was a second couch in the room for one of them, but they ignored me. It could be just me, but I think there's something brewing between them.

Creeping silently through my house in the dark, I peer out through the windows, looking for any signs that things aren't right. Even though everything appears as it should, nothing feels right. Something feels very wrong. When I found my pill was missing, I told Marcus, and he sent a message to someone. Probably Ayden.

It doesn't really matter that I didn't take my birth control pill since I'm pretty sure I won't be having sex for a while. My cycle is all up the shit anyway from my lack of taking it when I was in Melbourne. Marcus hadn't packed my pill the night they'd helped me escape, so I had to start again when I got back home, and now I'll have to get another script and start all over again.

Foul mood in full swing, I know I need to try and protect myself from the world. Or maybe I should be protecting the world from me and my bad mood. When I see Rhys and Marcus waking up for the day, I decide to block everything out with music using Ayden's blue earphones. Rhys doesn't seem fazed by my need to do this, but Marcus looks concerned, although he doesn't bother me. I'm fairly certain I have Rhys to thank for that.

Before we leave for school, I look around the house and try to memorise where everything is, so it's hopefully easier to spot if something is missing when I come home later. Part of me wants to stay home and catch whoever it is, but I'm also too scared, knowing deep down that the only person it could possibly be is Mike.

When we walk into school, boy pack in tow, Tasha sees me and steps towards me, ready to start shit. I dig deep for inner calm and simply shoulder her out of the way and glare at anyone who looks to challenge me.

We turn heads as we walk through the school, me up the front with Rhys and the boys following close behind. It must look ridiculous. I don't care, though, and I doubt the guys care either. I should turn around and tell them all to back off and give me some space, but I don't. If I'm honest with myself, I'd admit that I like their attention, but I'm in a foul mood and hating on everything today, so I ignore how much their need to protect me warms my heart and focus on how smothering it has been of late.

English is somewhat okay. I keep my headphones in, ignoring the world, and Miss Dice allows it as long as I do my work. Ayden doesn't try to sit with me, but I feel his eyes burning a hole into the side of my head throughout the whole class.

Art is a reprieve, and even Ms Holland doesn't ask me to remove my earphones. I throw myself into the grayscale canvas that I'm painting of a lake with reflections of the clouds in the water. It looks okay, I guess. I'm not going to be a famous artist anytime soon, but I might get a B for this piece.

I have no appetite once again, and at recess, I make my way straight to the back of the school to meet my new friends. When I reach my gang of misfits, instead of the normally happy welcome, I'm met with glares and daggers. Frowning, I tug my earphones out.

"What?" I ask, feeling the full force of their anger.

Rhys laughs standing from the steps, and points behind me, "Your wolf pack followed you."

My eyes widen, and I spin to see the smug as fuck faces of Marcus, Jared, Garrett, Simon, Shaun and Ayden.

"For fuck's sake! I'm fine here with these guys. You can go have a normal recess without babysitting me." I sweep my hand in a shooing motion.

Frowns tug at their faces, all except Ayden, who walks past me to the steps where my new friends sit, and then, he introduces himself to them.

What the actual fuck!

As if they are all possessed by the same idiocy, the other boys join Ayden and introduce themselves too. *No. Fucking. Way.*

I glare at them as they converse, making me feel overwhelmingly stupid for some reason. I never imagined my two groups of friends mingling and talking. It was enough for me to deal with Rhys hanging out with them last night. My new friends aren't the typical type of people the boys associate with. I'm anxious about this, but even as I look on, I see them chatting freely and even laughing. Probably at my expense.

Not wanting to join in on their invasion, I stuff the earphones back in my ears and ignore everyone as I take a seat on one of the logs on the grass and turn my back to them. It doesn't take long for Ayden to appear in my line of sight, and he leans down to offer me a choc chip muffin. Acting as stubborn as ever, I look away and ignore him as he stands before me, looking down with a frown. Dale's thin, lanky body comes into view, and he sits next to me on the log, offering me his joint. I mouth a 'thank you' to him and take it.

Ayden's frown deepens. I pretend I don't notice as I draw the smoke in and close my eyes, savouring the feeling. When I open my eyes, I can see confusion etched across his beautiful face. I get it. He's seeing the trashy version of me right now. He hasn't met her until now. I bet he's second-guessing ever taking me into his life.

With my eyes locked on his, I take another deep drag, silently challenging him to try and stop me. Apparently, I feel like playing with fire today!

Ayden takes his phone out and types something. A moment later, my phone vibrates with an incoming message. I roll my eyes at him, and his blue eyes practically glow as he glares at me in a silent challenge. I give in.

Taking my phone out, I read his message.

Ayden Mitchell
Talk to me, Lex.

Lexi West
*** middle finger emoji ***

This time Ayden rolls his eyes at me and starts to type out his response on his phone. I take another drag of the joint before handing it back to Dale, who gives me a wink before walking off, leaving me alone with Ayden.

Shit! I should call him back over.

My phone vibrates again, and I sigh before opening the message. It's a long one. Part of me doesn't want to read it because I'm a stubborn bitch, and I don't really know if I can handle knowing what he wants to say. The other part of me is practically frothing at the mouth to know, and that's the part of me that wins.

Ayden Mitchell
Since you won't talk to me, then I'll talk.
I need to tell you how sorry I am for so many things.
Mostly though, I need you to know how incredibly sorry I am for the way I treated you before you left.
I'm not trying to make excuses, but please believe me when I tell you, that person who was in that bedroom in Melbourne was not me!
He was a different version and someone I have worked so hard to be rid of.
I am not him, and yet I am.
That is the war I battle every day to beat the urges to turn to drugs and throw away my life again.
The me you spent time with before we ran into Muz, that's the real me.
Our time together was the most real thing I have ever experienced with another person Lexi.
It's you, Lexi. You make me real.
You make me want to be a better person.
Can you please find it in your heart to forgive me? I will spend every minute of every day, making it up to you. I swear!

Tears fall freely and blur my vision as I read his honest words. When he sees I'm done reading, he squats down in front of me, trying to catch my eyes. I slide my phone into my blazer pocket and wipe away my tears, keeping my eyes cast to the ground. Reaching out, Ayden places his hand on my knee, and I almost moan. It feels so good to have him touch me, and I just want to leap into his arms and fall into a world that is just him and me again.

But my world isn't just the two of us. My world is all kinds of fucked up, and he is too good of a person to be dragged into it.

"I'm sorry," I say before standing quickly and hightailing it away from every single one of my friends. I consider going to hide out in the girls' toilets, but instead, I find myself knocking on the school counsellor's door.

When Mr Matthews opens it, his brows shoot up, surprised to see me. When he holds the door open for me, I make my way in and sit on my usual chair. I tug out the earphones and wait while he sits. When he's settled, I can tell by his expression that he's concerned.

"Is everything okay, Lexi?"

And then I cry. It's all I can do. He tries to ask me questions and help me stop crying, but I can't. He's quiet for a few minutes before handing me the box of tissues, which I snatch up and make good use of.

"Lexi, are you here because you need to talk?"

I shake my head.

"Are you here because you need a safe place to take a few moments?"

I nod, and he nods back.

"Okay, that is totally okay. Do you want me to leave?" I consider his words for a moment before shaking my head. "Okay. Want to watch some funny cat videos?"

A snotty laugh rips from me, and Mr Matthews grins and sets up his laptop. I spend the rest of recess and all of period three in his office watching the most stupid, yet funny, cat videos. Mr Matthews is definitely one of the good ones. Although he continues to look concerned, he doesn't pressure me to talk. He just lets me be there in the moment, feeling safe.

I manage to pull myself together in time for Maths, and even though I know Ayden is in that class, I somehow will myself to walk in and ignore him through the whole lesson. I even finish two of my overdue Maths tasks and submit them, which makes me a little happy.

By the time lunch comes, I drag myself through the yard to the back of the school, going over my apology in my head to Rhys and the others for the intrusion at recess. I know it was hard enough for them to feel okay with me invading their sacred space, but to have six of the school's most popular guys invade it too, is going over the line.

They all watch me approach with neutral expressions, and I dig deep, summoning up the courage to speak. I hope they want me to continue being their friend.

Stopping in front of them, I pull out my earphones. Here goes nothing.

"Ah, sorry about earlier, guys. It won't happen again."

They all stare at me with straight faces for a beat before bursting out in fits of laughter. Frowning, I watch Rhys leap down from the steps and skip up to me.

"What's so fucking funny?"

"You are!" Rhys cackles, "Turn around." Grabbing my shoulders, she spins me, and I come face to face with my smirking pack.

"Seriously? Again?" I hiss at them, and I swear their grins grow wider. *Arseholes!*

"Your pack follows you everywhere, Lexi. Maybe instead of fighting it, you should embrace it!" Rhys whispers into my ear.

"Not likely," I growl, unable to contain my frustration and Rhys sighs.

"Here's the deal, dickheads. You can stay as long as you abide by some rules."

I snicker at Rhys' firm tone and climb the steps to take a seat next to Tillie. She gives my shoulder an 'I forgive you' nudge and we both smile, returning our attention back to the boys and Rhys.

"We don't follow rules; we make the rules," Simon grunts, puffing out his chest like a damn gorilla. I roll my eyes.

"Follow these rules or fuck off, Hastings." Rhys sneers, and I swear I see him flinch back.

I love this girl!

"We'll follow your rules, George." Marcus throws Rhys' surname back at her like she did with Simon's, but I don't miss the satisfied grin Rhys shares with him. Yep, something is definitely brewing there.

"What are the rules?" Ayden asks, sounding fed up. He looks over to me, and I notice for the first time that he has dark shadows under his eyes. Is he not sleeping?

"Firstly, you are here because we allow you to be here. This is our area, and if you don't like the rules, then you can fuck off." Rhys locks eyes with each one of the boys, getting a nod from each of them before continuing. "Do not, under any circumstances, bring anyone else here. If you have a clingy girlfriend, then I suggest you hang out with her friends instead because we don't want any of those self-entitled stuck-up bitches here. Got it?"

"You don't have to worry about that. We are all single and ready to mingle." Shaun wags his brows, and Rhys makes a gagging sound. Everyone laughs, except for me. I chew the inside of my cheek to stop myself.

"Dude, you sound like a creeper," Jared adds, making Shaun frown.

"Lastly, if we ask you to leave, you will, and without any bloody commotion," Rhys demands, her painted nails resting on her hips. Today's shade is a dark blue. I bet it's called midnight blue, or night sky, or something.

"Do we really look like we make commotion?" Simon asks.

"Hastings, your middle name is commotion." Rhys shoots another dig at Simon before addressing them all. "Do we have a deal?"

"Deal," Ayden speaks for all of them and strolls past Rhys to take a seat next to Dale on one of the logs under the trees.

The look Dale gives Ayden is priceless. It's obvious he didn't expect Ayden to sit next to him, but then his face melts into a satisfied smile, and they both start quietly chatting. Ayden is oblivious to the fact that Dale is totally checking him out.

"Should we warn him?" Rhys asks quietly, sitting down next to me.

"Hell no. This is too entertaining." Tillie quietly giggles, and I can't hide my smile this time.

"Till is right. This is way too entertaining. Let's watch Dale have his fun." I add.

"Girl, you're just as devious as me." Rhys throws her arm over my shoulder and plants a big kiss on my cheek.

Laughing, I push her away and notice Ayden watching. He looks so lost. I have to force myself to stay seated and not go over and climb onto his lap. The pull is ridiculous, but I have to keep fighting it. He deserves more than what I have to offer. He'll see that soon, and he'll be thankful I pushed him away.

"You okay, girl?" Rhys nudges my attention away from Ayden, and I look into her concerned gaze.

"I guess." I shrug.

"That's not very convincing. I know we haven't had any real deep and meaningfuls, but I'm here for you Lex, if you want to talk."

"Me too," Tillie adds, and I turn a small smile her way.

"I'm not very good at opening up." I look to my fidgeting hands in my lap and will them to stop.

"Maybe we should have a girls' night. Get drunk and spill all of our dark secrets to each other." Rhys rubs her hands together, excitement laced in her tone.

"That might not be such a good idea, Rhys. Remember what happened last time?" Tillie cringes, and Rhys laughs. I don't know what they are talking about, and they don't divulge the information.

"I think my secrets are too dark to share." It's only a whisper, but Tillie and Rhys stop laughing when they comprehend what I said.

Arms link with mine on both sides, and both of my new friends drop their heads to my shoulder.

"You'd be surprised, Lex. I've got some pretty fucking dark secrets as well," Rhys says in all seriousness.

"Same. Mine are as dark as a moonless night." Tillie says quietly.

A shiver travels up my spine as fear creeps its way into my heart at hearing both of their confessions. One thing I know for sure. My connection with these girls stems from lost souls finding each other through the darkness that roams this earth. They too, have come face to face with the blackened devil that has wrapped itself around my heart.

Fourteen

Tillie, Dale and I take our seats in Media class after lunch, minding our own business, eager to focus on the work we need to get done. That is until silence sweeps over the room, and I look up to see Tasha stroll in looking like a smug bitch. Then she opens her vile mouth.

"Look, it's the filthy whore who had her brother prepare her virgin body for all the boys to share. Did you beg your brother for more, Lexi?"

I see red!

My control is gone, and all I see is her face and how much I need to end its ugly existence. The table I'm at flips over as I leap from my chair across the room to reach Tasha before she even has time to turn and run. My fist meets her nose with a sickening crack, and blood sprays from it as she goes down. My fists keep flying as I follow her to the classroom floor, punching her face over and over.

I fucking hate her. She's just as bad as Mike, and she needs to be shown that she can't go around bullying people. As I land each punch, Tasha's face morphs into something else. Someone else. It's no longer Tasha I see. It's Mike.

He must die!

Strong arms come around my waist, reefing me away from my assault. I kick and scream in fury when I lose sight of my victim as I'm dragged out of the room. My screams don't stop, and neither do my fists as I punch at the strong male arms carrying me down the corridor towards the school hall. I try to kick my legs into the shins of whoever is carrying me, and I hear a deep grunt when one makes contact. Marcus runs past us and pushes open the stadium doors right before I'm dragged inside and carried deeper into the open space, my yells echoing through the empty building.

The arms holding me let go, and I tumble to the ground, still enraged from being manhandled. Leaping up, I spin to see Ayden looming over me, sucking in deep breaths and looking dishevelled.

My fists clench, and I scream, throwing a punch at him too. It meets his nose, which surprises me but also satisfies me, and I watch as he stumbles back a few steps with his own surprise evident on his face. Then, his eyes darken.

"Do it again." He growls. I don't know if it's meant as a command or warning not to do it again, but I do it anyway, this time making contact with his cheek.

Ayden steps forward, his chest rising and falling, "Again, Lexi!"

I do as he demands and hit him again. I hit him over and over on his chin, his shoulder, his chest, all while he stands before me just taking it until my arms weaken and a sob slips free. I try to swing again, but my punch is powerless, and I crumble to the floor in defeat. My girly emotions take over, and I clasp my hands into my hair and pull, letting out a scream much like I did the day I went to visit my mum in hospital.

Strong arms come around me, and for a few weak moments, I fall into them, needing the comfort they offer. Then, Ayden's scent engulfs me, and my senses kick in, making me stiffen.

"No!" I yell, pushing him off me and kicking myself back across the stadium floor to get distance between us.

"Lexi!" Mr Matthews booms across the hall, surprising me, "You need to come with me."

I hear Ayden curse, and Marcus comes into view, reaching his hand down to help me up. I don't move for a few moments, air struggles to get into my lungs, and I heave a few times before I get relief.

What have I done?

I'm a monster, just like my brother.

From my place on the floor, I look up to Marcus. The concern contorting his face matches Ayden's when I glance at him. They know now. They know who I am. What I am. They will choose now. Choose to walk away and rid themselves of me, of my darkness. They are better off without me. They know that now.

I wipe the tears from my eyes before taking Marcus' hand to help me stand up but drop my hold as soon as I've righted myself. I ignore the shame and embarrassment that heats my face. I deserve this. Tasha may be wrong about her insinuations, but she is right about one thing. Fox Pines Catholic College should have never let me come back.

More tears fall, so I give up trying to hide them, knowing that my whole Media class just witnessed me lose my shit, followed by taking it out on the guy that stole my heart. I am truly the scum of this earth. The school is probably about to kick me out, and rightly so. They don't need the likes of me here.

"Lex." Ayden reaches out for my hand as I go to move past him, and I let him take it, selfishly needing one last chance to feel his love before I'm kicked to the curb.

I look up to his deeply concerned gaze wishing for the thousandth time that I wasn't me, that I was someone else who is worthy of him.

"I'm so sorry," I whisper on a sob and release his hand, walking over to Mr Matthews, too ashamed to look up and see the disappointment in his eyes as well.

"Where are you going with Lexi?" Ayden asks, and I can feel both him and Marcus at my back.

"She's required at the principal's office." Mr Matthews gestures to move through the doors, and I step past him to make my final walk through my school.

"You'll understand if we need to come with you and stay with Lexi after what happened a few weeks back." Ayden's voice sounds stern and commanding, and not for the first time do I think of him more as an adult than a naïve teenager like the rest of us.

"You want to go with her after what she was just doing to you?" Mr Matthews asks, sounding surprised.

"She was doing what I asked her to do. Maybe the school should invest in some punching bags so students can take their anger out on those instead of other students." Ayden hisses.

"You have a good point. I'll bring it up at the next meeting." Mr Matthews sounds like he likes the idea. It's a good one. It's just a pity that I won't be around to see it happen.

We walk the rest of the way in silence, and as we pass my Media class, Tillie rushes out and hands me my books. She doesn't say anything but pulls me in for a hug before returning to class. I will miss seeing her when I'm gone.

We keep walking.

I imagine how terrifying it must be for a prisoner to walk on Death Row in America. I'm kind of terrified now, and all that's happening to me is getting kicked out of school. Hell, maybe the cops will be involved this time. If they are, I may as well confess I was with Travis during the school break-in and vandalism. It plagues me daily that he took the rap for it. I think now is the time for me to own up to my wrongdoings and stop having people suffer because of me.

Reaching the school office, Mr Matthews turns to the boys.

"If you two are insisting on staying, you need to keep quiet and not talk to Lexi. You are here only as support, so she knows she is safe and that no one will harm her."

Ayden and Marcus both mutter their agreement, and Mr Matthews points to seats in the small glass room off to the side, aptly called the vault. It's used to keep watch on students that are in trouble. A glass cell of sorts. Looks like my first visit will be my last visit.

The boys do as they're asked and don't speak to me. Their eyes dart to mine frequently, though, and I try to dodge them as much as possible. My shame, my discomfort, it has me prisoner. Nothing can help me now.

Raised voices and yelling spills out from the principal's office, drawing our attention. The door swings open with force, revealing a furious, very red-faced Mr and Mrs Pritchard. Tasha's parents.

Ayden and Marcus quickly stand and move in front of me. At first, I think they are trying to block my view so I can't see what's happening, but as the angry words from Tasha's hysterical mum greet my ears, I realise that Ayden and Marcus are trying to keep me hidden.

"If you don't do something about Alexis, then we will! I'm sure the news stations would love to hear how Fox Pines Catholic College did nothing to protect the rest of the students and let that little tramp walk the halls and bully everyone!"

I flinch back, guilt hitting me like a ton of bricks knowing that Tasha's mum's words speak true. I've come back to school, taking out my problems on everyone else. Sure, they may have played a part in harassing me, but doesn't it speak more to how I dealt with it. I am exactly what Mrs Pritchard says I am. I'm a bully.

The voices trail off and disappear down the hall, so Ayden and Marcus return to their seats in silence. I thought I felt shame before, but it is nothing compared to the shame I feel now. It's sickening, and I hate who I've become.

"Lexi, the principal will see you now." Mr Matthews appears in the door. Ayden and Marcus stand straight away. "No, guys. Lexi only."

"No way Mr Matthews. Lexi isn't going in there alone." Marcus beats Ayden at voicing his concern. He looks like he's ready to fight Mr Matthews on this one. I don't want him or Ayden to get into trouble because of me, though.

"It's okay, Marcus. If you and Ayden can just stay out here, I'll be okay."

Both the boys turn to face me, their eyes and grim expressions showing me how torn up they are by the idea of letting me go into the office alone. I love them. Both of them. They are my family—a family not by blood but by bond. I need to tell them they are my family, but it will have to wait. Right now, I have to face up to the things I have done, then later, if they'll listen, I'll tell them.

Ayden steps towards me and takes my hand. I shouldn't let him, but once again, I'm weak and need his touch as much as I need oxygen.

"If you need me, just call out. I'll break that fucking door down if I have to." He will too. I know it as much as I know the sun will rise tomorrow.

I give him a small nod, and he brushes his thumb over the back of my hand before dropping it so I can follow Mr Matthews. I feel their eyes on me as I walk, and it somehow helps me put one foot in front of the other, however, a sense of dread sweeps over me. I feel like I'm going to walk into this office and never walk out again. I know it's completely irrational. Of course, I will walk out again. Right?

Whatever happens, I need to make things right. Not just for me, but for my friends too.

I stop Mr Matthews outside the door before he opens it.

"Mr Matthews?" I ask, gaining his attention. "I'm sorry. I've let you down, I know that."

He sighs, raking a hand over his shiny shaven head, "Let's talk inside."

I nod, feeling so ashamed of letting him down and follow him inside to meet the eyes of a very unhappy Principal Rogan. Knowing the drill all too well, I take a seat and wait for Ms Rogan to speak. She doesn't, but Mr Matthews does.

"Lexi, please tell us, in your own words, what happened in the Media class this afternoon?"

For a few moments, I can't speak. Sadness, guilt, shame, and regret render me speechless. It takes everything I have to pull myself together enough to relay the comments that Tasha said and how it triggered something in me, and I lost control.

"I don't know any other way to explain it. It was like someone flicked a switch, and I started doing things. I couldn't seem to stop myself. I punched her. Several times, and eventually, I wasn't looking at Tasha's face anymore."

"Who were you looking at?" Mr Matthews asks.

"M-my brother. Mike." I can't stand to look at Mr Matthews or Mrs Rogan any longer and direct my focus to my shoes. They are old and dirty, and the stitching is coming apart on my right sole.

"A-Ayden came and pulled me off Tasha. I don't even know where he came from or why he was there because he isn't in my Media class. But he dragged me away and took me to the hall to-."

Mr Matthews finishes my sentence, "To cool off. Yeah, that's when I found you."

I look up at him, narrowing my eyes. Did he just cover up the fact that he saw me punching into Ayden?

Principal Rogan remains quiet, and it eventually makes me crack.

"I'm so sorry. I know I've let you both down, and I know that I have to pay for what I did. I understand that violence isn't tolerated, so do what you must do. I'm so bloody ashamed of myself. I hate that I'm the bully that Tasha's mum described me to be. I know I have to fix that somehow. I just don't know how. I don't even know who I am anymore." I cry for a moment looking at my hands as they lay defeated in my lap, "Maybe I'm just like him."

"Like who?" Principal Rogan asks, speaking for the first time.

"My brother," I whisper, feeling everything like the monster he is.

"I don't think you're like him, Lexi. I think you are struggling to deal with the horrible things that happened to you, and it's coming out in anger directed at anyone that gets in your way. You just need to accept the help people offer, so you can learn how to deal with what happened and manage your anger."

I nod, knowing she is right and wishing I wasn't about to get kicked out of school. I feel like I could learn a lot from her and Mr Matthews. Who will help me now?

"I'm sorry, Lexi, but I have to enforce the school's discipline for violence, especially given that the incident happened in a classroom in front of fifteen other students and Mr Bert." Mrs Rogan's words are laced with regret.

I nod, fighting back nausea, waiting for her to say the words that I'm no longer a student at Fox Pines Catholic College. The problem with this situation isn't just that I'm about to be kicked out of school; it's that the principal will have to call my guardian, which is Ayden's mum, who will then tell her I haven't been staying with them, and that will spark a call to Child Services, and I'll most likely be put in foster care. Of course, if for some reason I'm able to dodge that scenario, it means that I will be home alone every day in that house. The very house that is getting broken into each time I leave. If it is Mike, I'm likely to come face to face with him before too long.

Commotion draws our attention from outside the door, right before it flies open, and Andrea,

Ayden's mum, storms in. My breath hitches at seeing her again. It's almost as jarring as the first time I ran into Ayden when he arrived back. Andrea looks at the principal, then to Mr Matthews, before landing on me, and then her face softens. How did she know I was here? Did the school ring her already?

"Lexi." She says, stepping up to me with open arms, and I fall into them, bursting into more stupid tears. Andrea embraces me, hugging me close, rubbing her hand up and down my back while I seek her comfort.

Words are exchanged quietly as Mr Matthews fills Andrea in on today's events, thankfully leaving out the part where I took my anger out on her son.

"So what has to happen now?" Andrea asks, still holding me to her chest.

"Since there was very crude provocation on Tasha's behalf, something she has been doing since Lexi's return to school on Monday, we feel that expulsion is too harsh and are issuing a week's suspension. We expect Lexi to still attend her counselling sessions with Mr Matthews twice during the week and that she makes more of an effort to work with him so he can help her."

Lifting my head from Andrea's shoulder, I glance at the new principal, knowing deep down that I want to prove to her I'm a better person than I've been.

"I need to be frank, Mrs Mitchell." Principal Rogan addresses Andrea again.

"Of course," Andrea says, pulling back from me now that I'm no longer sobbing, and she hands me some tissues.

"I'm concerned that Lexi hasn't been getting the stability she needs right now."

Andrea nods, "Yes, I agree. Honestly, I have been giving Lexi space, so she doesn't feel so controlled given the situation she came from. However, now I see that perhaps it's been too much freedom." I stiffen a little as Andrea turns to address me. "Lexi, I know you like to be in control, but we need some rules. From now on, I would like you home at my dinner table by 6pm on school nights. We can negotiate weekends. You can still go home to your house to study after school if you like, but no more sleepovers with friends for a while. Let me and my family look after you the way you deserve to be."

I'm unsure if Andrea means what she is saying or if it's a ruse to get the principal off our backs. After all, when I fled her husband's apartment in the city, she didn't come after me or contact me. I hate rules, but I don't hate the idea of what she's insisting. I really want her words to be true. The only problem is Ayden.

"Can you agree to that, honey?" Andrea asks, looking sincere as she brushes back my wayward blonde hair.

I nod, "Yes."

I hear an audible sigh of relief come from both Principal Rogan and Mr Matthews, making Andrea smile.

"Okay, Lexi. I feel like we have a bit of a plan in place now, so that should start to help. Mr Matthews will email you your counselling times, and your teachers will email through your schoolwork for the next week. I'll expect you back in my office first thing next Friday morning for a briefing before you start back from your suspension."

With that, Principal Rogan hands Andrea some paperwork to sign, and we leave the office to find Ayden and Marcus waiting. They are quiet as they follow us out into the passage before Andrea swings around with a face full of fury. She looks from Marcus to Ayden, gritting her teeth.

"You two have a hell of a lot of explaining to do! No more god damn lies! This is what happens when people lie. Things escalate and get out of hand. We could have avoided this situation to an extent if you little shits had just been honest. Poor Lexi has suffered enough, and you two haven't helped. I'm fucking furious with the both of you. You can both bloody walk home." Andrea turns and grabs my hand, "Come on, honey. Lead the way to your locker so we can grab the rest of your books. You will need them all at home to stay up to date with your work."

I look over my shoulder at the two boys who just had strips torn off them by Andrea and kind of feel sorry for them. That's until Ayden gives me one of his signature winks, and I turn quickly to hide the telling blush, hoping like hell that he didn't see it.

Fifteen

Every picture frame in my house is empty. It doesn't matter if it's a frame hanging on the wall, or a frame sitting on a table. Every single one no longer has the pictures in them that were there this morning when I left for school.

"Seriously, can this day get any worse?" My whisper and shocked expression brings Andrea up short, and she looks around to see what I'm seeing.

"What's going on, Lexi?" She's confused, and rightfully so. I'm confused as hell too.

"Someone has taken all the pictures," I whisper, my eyes darting to each empty frame that I can see.

Andrea stands in front of me, a world of concern twisting her pretty face. "Lexi, I can see that. Where have the pictures gone? Who took them?"

I sigh. I don't want to tell her because then I'll have to admit that someone really is breaking into my house daily with the intent to freak me out. But since she is now dragged into this, I have to be honest.

"I'd say the pictures are with all the other things that have gone missing."

Andrea looks around again, and then as if a light bulb goes off, she grabs my arm and escorts me back outside to her car.

"Are you telling me that someone has been going into your house and taking things?" When I nod, Andrea continues, "How long has this been happening?"

I think back over the things that have gone missing. It all coincides with me leaving the house with the boys for the first time. I tell Andrea what she wants to know and sit in her car as she takes out her phone and relays the information to Officer Reynolds. Within ten minutes, Officers Reynolds and Zimora are at my house, checking through it to make sure no one is inside. Then they proceed to take photos and put some sort of dust stuff everywhere to pick up fingerprints.

Once they give the all-clear, I go inside to pack my bags. I hadn't been sure that Andrea was serious about what she agreed to in Principal

Rogan's office, but she absolutely was. As far as she is concerned, she is my temporary guardian and I'm moving into her place. Well, technically, it's Marcus' house, but it's where Andrea and Ayden are living, so I guess it's now where I'm going to be living.

The whole idea seems weird as fuck to me. Am I really meant to sleep in their house and eat their food? And rules? Am I meant to have rules? The thought both warms my heart and scares the crap out of me. So does the idea of living with Ayden. Jesus, how am I meant to keep my distance from him if we will be eating breakfast at the same table?

Knowing that I'm just working myself up, I try to force my overactive mind to calm down and focus on packing my things. I shoot Valarie a quick text to let her know that I'll be living somewhere else for a while and then lock up before meeting Andrea and the officers in the driveway.

"Lexi, I thought you should know that we have spoken to your father on the phone a couple of times, but so far, we haven't been able to convince him to hand himself in. We are still searching for his location." Officer Reynolds offers the information, and I just give him a nod. My dad will never hand himself in. It would hurt his pride too much.

"Do you have any more information about Lexi's dad's case?" Andrea asks.

"Yes actually. We are working with a team in the city who are building a very damning embezzling case against him." Officer Zimora offers, looking all sorts of yummy in his navy uniform with his gun sitting on his hip. Why is that so hot?

"Has he been in contact with his whore?" I ask in a flat, unimpressed tone.

"No, unfortunately, he hasn't made any further contact with Sally." Officer Zimora offers, and I just shrug like I don't care. I do care, though, a hell of a lot.

"Anything on Mike?" I ask, wishing like hell that they would just catch him already.

"No. He's a ghost." Officer Zimora says, "But there's a chance that these break-ins are him trying to torment you, and if so, it means we can concentrate our search locally. We will do drive-bys regularly to monitor the house. Please don't come back here alone, Lexi. Make sure you are with a couple of friends or an adult if you need to come back here for anything."

I nod, knowing I'll probably disobey his request. Why? Because it's my home, no matter how fucked up the situation is, and also, because I'm stubborn.

The officers talk with Andrea some more while I sit in her car waiting before she drives me away from my house. When we arrive at my new home, AKA Marcus' house, AKA Ayden's house, AKA my new place of torture, Andrea fusses over me and takes me upstairs to Rachel's old bedroom. It's strange being back in the house I used to play in for hours with Abbey, Marcus and Jared when we were little. I remember wanting to be like Rachel when I grew up. I was fascinated with her, but now as I stand in her bedroom, which hasn't been changed since she moved out, I wonder what the big deal was. After all, this room is all girly and frilly, and I am a no-frill, cover my walls with tattooed guys, type of girl. Rachel's room speaks Barbie, and I'm more Grand Theft Auto.

"Barb, my sister, said you can redecorate the room to suit your style. She asked Rachel if it was okay first, don't worry." Andrea carries one of my bags into the lilac bedroom, placing it on the pink floral bed. Jesus, this room gives me a headache.

"Lexi, I need to apologise to you." Andrea's pained voice draws my attention away from the bookshelf lined with creepy dolls. The first thing I need to do is remove those scary fucking things. "I should have chased after you that day when you left. I should never have accepted what Ayden said after he reached out to Marcus and told me you were staying with a friend. You were never staying with a friend, were you?"

I don't want to get Ayden and Marcus into trouble, but I also don't want to lie to Andrea. She is offering me a home, even if it is temporary. I owe her my honesty. I can only assume that Marcus and Ayden told her I was staying with a friend thinking they were helping me somehow.

"There was no friend. I went home."

"You mean you stayed in that house all alone for all that time?" Andrea's eyes turn glassy.

I shrug. "I wasn't alone the whole time. Marcus and the guys from school started staying with me last week. They've been looking out for me."

Tears fall from Andrea's eyes, and she pulls me in for a hug that I didn't realise how much I needed until this moment.

"I'm sorry, Lexi. I should have done more to help you."

I pull back and look at her. "You had already done so much for me, and I was just getting in the way. Ayden needed you more than I did. I was fine. I really was." I'm lying again. My honesty didn't even last a minute. I'm going to hell!

We both still when we hear voices downstairs, so I insist that I'm okay to unpack my things, and Andrea leaves me to it. When I hear raised voices, mainly Andrea's, I know the voices we heard must have been the boys, and now they are getting more strips torn off them. I feel bad. I don't want to cause anyone distress or get anyone into trouble. It's the last thing I want.

More voices come from downstairs, some I don't recognise, which just reminds me I'm an intruder in this house, so I focus on unpacking a few of my things into the empty dresser drawers.

"Can I come in?" Ayden's voice floats across the small bedroom, and I look up from the dresser to see his head peeking around the door. I give him a nod, and he steps in, closing the door behind him.

Nerves unsettle me now that we are closed in the small space together.

"Man, this room is hideous!" Ayden screws his face up, looking around, which makes me giggle.

"I can see why you were happy to take the loft above the garage when you moved here."

"Hell yeah. This is terrifying." Ayden leans down, examining the dolls on the bookshelf, making me laugh again.

Then awkward silence fills the space.

"Sorry about hitting you," Ayden looks away from the dolls to focus on me when I speak. "I hope I didn't hurt you?"

"I've got thick skin." He smiles, reminding me just how adorable his dimples are.

"Well, even so. I'm sorry. I guess I'm not coping the best. Maybe I should be locked up in a hospital like my mum instead of here with your family."

Two strides across the small space, and Ayden is before me, his gentle hands gripping my upper arms.

"Don't say that, Lex. You know that's not true. You belong here, and you should never have had to deal with the likes of Tasha."

I look down at our feet, too nervous to look him in the eye when we are standing so close. I can feel the warmth from his hands seeping past my shirt and heating my skin. I fight the urge to fall into him and take what I need. I won't though. I need to be strong. I need to give him the chance to move on and find his own happiness. It will be harder now that I'm here, but I have to make sure I stay strong, for him.

"Lex." He whispers when I don't respond to him. "I meant everything I said in that message this morning. I am sorry. So sorry. I can't even describe the pain I feel when I think of how I treated you. I know I don't deserve forgiveness, but fuck, I'm a selfish arsehole, and I want it because I want you."

A sob jumps up my throat, and I step back out of his hold, needing more space between us before I cave.

"Lex." Ayden's voice is pained, and it claws at my heart.

"I'm sorry, Ayden. I don't need to forgive you because you did nothing wrong. I don't hold any grudges against you."

"But you're so angry at me."

I look up to see the concern etched across his handsome face, and I swear my heart breaks all over again.

"Aren't you angry at me, Ayden? The way you looked at me at the counsellor's office yesterday... you looked like you hated me. Besides that," I suck in air because apparently, I've forgotten how to breathe, "I'm not angry at you. I thought I was, but really, I'm just angry at the world. At my life. I'm angry because I know that as much as I want you, I can't have you."

"What do you mean you can't have me? And if I looked angry yesterday, it wasn't directed at you. I was angry at myself. One look at you reminded me of how special you are and how much I fucked everything up. It also pissed me off that the bruising is still on your face." His dark brows furrow, and he takes a step towards me, but I take another step back, shaking my head.

"We both have demons we need to deal with, Ayden. Right now, we both need to focus on getting our own heads right before we even think about getting involved with each other."

He remains quiet for a few beats but doesn't once take his piercing blue eyes off mine. It's like he's trying to see into my soul, and it makes me squirm because I feel like he has the power to do just that. See deep into my soul.

Then he takes another step towards me, and I have nowhere to go, the dresser already pressing at the back of my legs. His gentle fingers lift to my face and stroke back some of my ever-present stray hairs. My heart stops or skips a beat. I can't really tell because I'm too busy trying to remember how to breathe again.

"So, I can't kiss you?" He whispers, his eyes flicking to my lips briefly. He is so close that the heat of his minty breath feathers over my face.

I've lost sight of his eyes because my gaze is locked onto his soft lips which are framed with the shadow of dark facial hair.

I slowly shake my head, working hard to keep my composure and not give in because damn, I want his lips on mine.

"We can be friends, though, right?" The smallest grin tugs at his lips when he says that. He knows damn well the effect he's having on me, but given the deep rise and fall of his chest, it looks like I'm having the same effect on him too. I draw my eyes away from those lips that call out to me like a siren and take in his caring blue eyes.

"I guess. I mean, I'll try my hardest not to kill you if that's what you mean?" I shrug, trying to come across like I don't care either way. *Lies! Lies! Lies!*

He laughs and considers my words. "I think we will be best friends." He gives me a full-blown grin then, dimples caving, white teeth making a brief appearance, his kissable lips turning up. Damn him! He's like my kryptonite! I'm powerless to stop my grin in return.

"Rhys is my best friend," I add, trying to throw him off.

"You can have more than one best friend." He smirks smugly.

I shrug again, folding my arms across my chest. He is so close that I can now feel the firm ridges of his abs under the touch of my arms.

"And when things settle down, and we sort our shit out, you'll let me kiss you again?" He sounds like a hopeful little boy asking to go to the fair.

"I really need to finish unpacking." I deflect and move past him to dig the rest of my clothes out of my bag.

"I'll take that as a yes." A huge grin spreads across his face before he turns to leave.

"I didn't say that, Ayden!"

"You didn't *not* say it either, Lexi." The smug prick walks out with a knowing smile leaving me flushed and frustrated.

This is going to be torture. I just know it.

I spot my reflection in the small dresser mirror and catch the ridiculous grin I'm wearing.

Get a grip, Lexi!

I turn my focus to unpacking, and when I'm done, the smell of something delicious wafts upstairs just before Andrea calls me down for dinner. I peek my head outside my new bedroom door and look down the narrow hall to the stairs where the sounds of family life flow up. Nerves make me uneasy, but I know I need to bite the bullet and go downstairs to face the family that has taken me in.

Reaching the bottom of the stairs, I catch sight of Marcus, and he gives me a grin waving me over to the dining table where he is laying out cutlery. He's still wearing his training gear from footy. I hadn't even realised he had gone to training.

I'm quickly reacquainted with Barbara and Tony Grady, Marcus' parents, as they carry plates of food over to the table. Barb frees up her hands and comes over to give me a hug, welcoming me to their family. Not to their house, but to their family. I offer a smile, unable to find words as the hustle of this family prepares the dinner table and sits down to eat.

"Sit here, Lex." Ayden pulls out a chair which I quietly take, looking at the plate of food before me. Bangers and mash with onion gravy. I swear I can hear the gargling drool of Homer Simpson in my head as the smell engulfs me, and when Ayden takes the seat to my left and Marcus takes the one to my right, I pick up my knife and fork at the same time they do, and dig in.

As I eat every crumb of food dished up to me, Marcus and his mum reminisce about the good old days when we were hyperactive kids causing havoc around the neighbourhood. I find out from their conversations that Ayden had been amongst some of our shenanigans, and we both hadn't realised that we shared those events. I'm disappointed that I don't remember. Sometimes we had a whole gang of kids from the area playing tag and water fights during our summers. I can't believe I didn't notice Ayden back then.

I'm quiet throughout dinner, happy to enjoy the discussions between everyone else. I feel out of place, even though I can tell Andrea is trying extra hard to make me feel welcome. I guess I'm just not used to so much happiness or normality going on around me.

I help wash up after dinner, working silently alongside Ayden and Marcus to get the job done, and when I'm about to escape up to my bedroom, I'm dragged into their living room to watch an Aussie Underworld Crime show. As much as I don't want to sit there and watch it, I do so quietly and watch like the outsider I am, as Marcus and Ayden's family gets drawn into the TV show.

My phone vibrates in my pocket, and at first, I don't want to be rude and take it out, but when I see Marcus and Ayden take theirs out, I do too. There are multiple messages from the boys' group chat, plus I have an unread message from Rhys. I open that first.

Rhys George

Girl, you are a fucking queen. Like seriously. Taking Tasha Pritchard down like that must have been so satisfying. I'll admit, I'm jealous as hell. But also proud. GO YOU!

Now I'm sorry that you got busted for it because that's legit sucky, but rumour has it you've moved in with Ayden.

You don't mess around, do you? I'm so proud!!!

Lexi West

I don't feel like a queen. I feel like a monster. Tasha deserved something, but not what I did to her.

I'll be lucky if her parents don't press charges!

I'm suspended for a week, so you'll have to endure detention without me.

I hope you'll survive.

Also, I have NOT moved in with Ayden!

His mum is my temporary guardian, so I have moved into her sister's house with her, which is Marcus' house.

Ayden sleeps in the loft garage out the back.

My bedroom here is creepy as fuck!

There are dolls, Rhys! Scary fucking dolls!

Rhys George

You are a queen, and I don't want to
hear another word about it!
Don't beat yourself up about what happened.
Tasha did deserve it!
I just wish it had been me doing it!
I'm sure I will survive without you,
but don't be a stranger.
You're my bestie now, remember.
You're stuck with me!!!
So, how easy is it to sneak out of the
house and into Ayden's loft?
Ooooh, and how far away from your
creepy bedroom is Marcus' room?
Send me a pic of the dolls!!!

Lexi West

You are so weird! But I love you for it!
I am NOT going to sneak into Ayden's loft.
We are not together.
And why do you want to know
where Marcus' bedroom is?

Rhys George

I mean, I'm Rhys George, I'm hard not to love!!
You're only human, Lexi!
$50 says you do end up sneaking
into Ayden's loft.
You know I'm right. Stop trying to deny it.
I want to know where Marcus' room is so that
when I come for a sleepover
(because that's what best friends do),
I can sneak out of your room and
into his, so I can ride him.

Lexi West

O... K... Thanks for sharing that with me.
Going now.

Rhys George

Going to sneak into Ayden's loft?

Lexi West

Good night, Rhys.

Rhys George

*** kissing emoji ***

I look up from my phone to see the boys still on their own phones. Marcus' dad is asleep in the armchair, and Andrea and Barb are still focused on the TV, so I open the boys' chat.

Simon-Hastings
I heard your mum handed you your arse Aydo.

Shaun-Bossier
She handed Marcus his arse too. She's a MILF!

Marcus-Grady
Dude. That's my aunt. Gross!

Ayden-Mitchell
Keep speaking about my mum like that, Bossi, and you'll really find out what getting your arse handed to you feels like.

Simon-Hastings
Yeah, Bossi. That's going too far, man!
So Aydo. You got an older sister?

Ayden-Mitchell
Fuck off, Hastings!

Jared-Crowley
You there, Lexi? Are you okay?

Ayden-Mitchell
She's fine!

Jared-Crowley
I wasn't asking you!

Garrett-Cole
I'd like to hear Lexi say she's okay.

Marcus-Grady
She's busy!

Jared-Crowley
Doing what?

Ayden-Mitchell
I'll tell you what she's not doing! You!

Jared-Crowley
Fuck you, arsehole!
Come and say that to my face!

Marcus-Grady
He can't, Jar. He's busy with Lexi.

Seriously. WTF!

Lexi-West
Hey dickheads! Calm down!
I am NOT busy with Ayden.
Thank you very much, Marcus!
How about you tell them the truth that we are sitting in your living room watching some TV show with Andrea and Barbara while your dad snores on the couch!

Simon-Hastings
Hahahaha, suck shit, arseholes!
Hi Lexi. How's our girl?

Ayden-Mitchell
She's not your girl! She's not anyone's girl!

Jared-Crowley
Including yours, bro!

Ayden mutters something and draws Andrea's attention. "You okay, buddy?"

Ayden looks up to his mum in confusion before realising that he's not doing a good job at hiding his emotions. I try to hide my smirk, but Marcus catches it.

"Ah, yeah. All good." Ayden responds to Andrea, who looks at Marcus and me before returning her focus to the TV.

Lexi-West
If you losers are going to keep starting shit with each other, then I am removing myself from this group chat!
I don't need this shit!
I have enough to deal with!

Jared-Crowley
You're right, Six. Sorry.

When Ayden doesn't respond in the group, I look up to him, and he mouths, "I'm sorry."

Jared-Crowley
You really not going to apologise, Ayden?

Ayden-Mitchell
I did. You just didn't see it because you're not in the same room as us.

Fuck me! What the hell is wrong with these guys?

Simon-Hastings
LOL burned Crowley!

Jared-Crowley
I'm going to bed. But first, Lexi.
Please tell us if you're okay?

No one jumps in this time with crude comments or any banter to stir the pot, so I respond.

Lexi-West
I need to apologise to you all.
I've not been myself.
I've turned into an angry bitch, and I've been acting like a psychopath. I'm sorry that you have had to witness it, and I'm sorry that I dragged you all into my mess.
In time, I'll get my head right.
One thing I know is that I'm so lucky to have each one of you in my life.
Good night. I'm going to bed too.

I switch off my screen and slip my phone into my pocket before standing from the couch.

"I'm going to head to bed." I turn to Andrea. "Good night... and thank you."

Andrea smiles up at me, "Good night, Lexi. I hope you're able to have a good sleep tonight knowing you are safe here with us."

I nod and smile before looking at Marcus and Ayden. Marcus smiles, and Ayden mouths "Goodnight", offering a soft smile.

I trudge up the stairs, and a moment later, hear the backdoor close. Ayden must be heading to bed too. It seems weird to me that he's out there alone while the rest of the family is in the main house. I know he likes it that way, though. I'm pretty sure I would, too, since right now I'm feeling a little claustrophobic in this strange house.

Sixteen

The buzz of a message on my phone catches my attention as I settle under the bed covers after changing into my PJs. Ayden's name lights up my screen, and I debate putting my phone down and trying to go to sleep.

Temptation is a bitch!

Ayden Mitchell
Are you okay?

Lexi West
Sure.

Ayden Mitchell
Cryptic!!

Lexi West
Not really.

Ayden Mitchell
What are you wearing?

Lexi West
Ayden!!!

Ayden Mitchell
What?

Lexi West
You know what!

Ayden Mitchell
I'm a guy. I don't know shit!

Lexi West
Playing dumb isn't your style.

Ayden Mitchell
How do you know?

He has a point. I don't know. Not really. We may have come together feeling like we're old friends, but what do I really know about the guy I gave my virginity to?

Lexi West
This conversation is irritating!

Ayden Mitchell
Yet you can't stop.

Lexi West
Cocky much?

Ayden Mitchell
Shit, I guess you do know me.

A giggle slips free, and I clamp my hand over my mouth, hoping that Marcus or his parents didn't hear me.

Ayden Mitchell
You haven't answered my question yet.
What are you wearing?

Lexi West
What I always wear.

Ayden Mitchell
A t-shirt or hoodie that's long enough to cover that perfect little arse of yours?

I can't help it. I blush like a fucking firecracker! Thank fuck he's not here to witness this.

Lexi West
Oh, no. That's only what I wear when you're around. When I'm alone, I wear little clothing.

Shit! How do I un-send that???

Ayden Mitchell
Now you've gone and done it!

Lexi West
Done what?

Ayden Mitchell
You don't want to know.

Lexi West
Actually, I do!!

Wait! Do I?

Ayden Mitchell
Let's just say I need a cold shower and leave it at that. I am a gentleman, after all. I have a rep to keep!

I snort, and the sound practically echoes in the quiet room. *Whoops!*

Lexi West
You need a cold shower like the one you needed that morning at your dad's?

Ayden Mitchell
Exactly like that!

Lexi West
Sorry.

Ayden Mitchell
No, you're not.

Lexi West
Okay, maybe I'm not.

Ayden Mitchell
Lexi?

Lexi West
Yeah?

Ayden Mitchell
Can I call you?

Lexi West
Now?

Ayden Mitchell
Yeah.

I don't know if saying yes is a good idea, but man, I want to hear his voice. I need to stay strong, though.

Lexi West
It's probably not a good idea.

Ayden Mitchell
What are you talking about?
It's a brilliant idea!!!
Please?

Fuck me, I can just imagine his face right now. All puppy dog eyes and sex wrapped into one. I should say no.

Lexi West
Okay.

I've barely pressed send on my reply when my phone starts buzzing with an incoming call from Ayden. My heart rate picks up, anticipation pumping through my veins.

"Hey." My voice is raspy when I answer the call.

"Hey," Ayden responds, his voice soft. "Thanks for letting me call. And for picking up."

"Ah... yeah. No problem." I'm awkward as hell. This guy does weird things to my insides.

"I wish I could be over there with you instead of stuck in this loft."

I wish I could be over in that loft with him instead of stuck in this creepy lilac bedroom... but I keep that to myself.

"I think that would overstep the whole friends thing. Besides, do you really want to be in this room with those creepy dolls?"

Ayden's deep chuckle comes through the phone and instantly warms my chest, relaxing me.

"Probably not." Ayden pauses, and I can hear the rustling of blankets through the line, "Tell me something honest, Lex. I know you have a thousand and one things on your mind right now but tell me one thing that is eating at you."

"Why?" I ask. I'm unsure if I should be opening up to him. He has enough to deal with as it is.

"Because I know from experience that talking about things helps," he says honestly.

Why does he have to be such a good guy? It would make it so much easier to stay away if he'd just be an arsehole.

"I'll make you a deal. I'll tell you about one thing that is bothering me if you let me ask you a question."

"Hmmm... I don't know if I like the sound of that." The wariness in Ayden's voice is a reminder that he is definitely still battling his own demons. I wish I could be the one to slay his dragons for him.

"It seems like a fair trade to me," I coax, and he chuckles.

"Fuck it. Let's do it. You first. Tell me something that's on your mind."

I giggle at how easily he caved, and then take a moment to think over all the shit that bothers me, but it doesn't take me long to decide. I haven't spoken about this much, but it has me fucked up pretty bad.

"Abbey." It's all I can say without the waterworks starting up. It's all I have to say for Ayden to understand as well.

"Yeah, Abbey. Something more is going on there. There's no way after the lifelong friendship you two have had, that she would turn her back on you like this without a reason. Not that any reason is good enough for her to do that."

"I think something more is going on too. At first, I thought it might be because of her parents. They obviously have a problem with me, but the Abbey I know would never do what she has done. She would find a way to stay in contact with me. She would fight for me. Instead, she has stood by and watched Tasha try to bring me down. I have no idea why Tasha is doing that either. It's just another one of the many mysteries fucking up my life right now."

"We'll get to the bottom of it. I know the guys noticed something going on before you even went back to school. So maybe they have more information. We should have a chat with them tomorrow or something."

I shrug, even though I know Ayden can't see.

"Ayden?"

"Yeah?"

"What was it like when you went to the rehab clinic after the party with Muz?" I ask, unsure if I am overstepping. Ayden tends to be tight-lipped about his past, about his drug use. The moment Muz inserted himself into our life, Ayden's past caught up with him, and now I've seen a glimpse at the person he's been trying to run from.

"Actually. It was good. I never thought I'd say that. Isolating from my parents and you guys was a hard decision to make, but I knew I needed to go through some of the steps, even though I didn't have to worry about a full-on withdrawal process this time. I needed to get my head right."

"Did it work? Is your head right?" My voice quivers as I ask that because I'm pretty sure I know the answer.

"It kinda worked. The party brought up a lot of old memories and feelings. Cravings. My biggest problem is anger, Lex. That potent shit I snorted turns me into a monster."

I hate the devastation in his voice. It cracks my heart wide open.

"You're not a monster," I whisper loud enough for him to hear.

Ayden is silent for a beat. These conversations really are too heavy. Too deep to have before going to sleep.

"Ayden?" I whisper.

"Yeah?" He whispers back.

"I'm wearing a white Crossfade t-shirt and navy bootie shorts."

The low rumble of his chuckle tops my heart up with a sprinkling of happiness.

"Thanks, Lex. I should let you get some sleep."

"Okay," sleep is hard to come by for me, but I agree anyway. "Goodnight, Ayden."

"Goodnight, Lex."

When the line goes dead, I lay back in the darkness and look up at the shadows that dance across the ceiling. My heart seems both happy and sad right now. Happy because I really needed to have a conversation with Ayden that wasn't me trying to fight him off, and sad because he hung up the phone, and now, I can't hear his voice.

Today has been a massive day from hell. This morning feels like it happened two days ago, and as I toss and turn in the floral bed in the lilac bedroom, I strangely wish that I was back in my house so I could go out to my garage and punch the crap out of the bag.

I try to force myself to go to sleep, but as soon as I start to drift off, the silhouette of a man standing in the doorway intrudes my sleepy haze. I almost scream, only to realise that there is no one there. It had been a dream, but after the fourth time it happens, I throw the blankets back and tiptoe around the bed to crack open the door, peering into the dark silent hallway.

Marcus' room is right across the narrow hall, so I close the door to the horrid lilac room and sneak through the one Marcus is behind.

"Marcus, are you awake?" I whisper-yell into the darkened room, unable to make out anything in the shadows. The sound of rustling sheets comes right before the bedside lamp clicks on, and I see Marcus sitting up in his bed, shirtless and his hair a tousled mess.

"You okay, Lex?" He asks, and I nod, but then shrug, and he chuckles.

"Can't sleep?" He asks, and I shake my head at him. He nods and kicks his blankets back to stand out of his bed.

"Nightmares again?"

"Kind of." I don't want to elaborate, but he knows how things have been for me.

Walking over to his wardrobe, he grabs out some blankets and a pillow and puts them on the floor on the other side of his bed.

"I'll take the floor." He says, laying out a makeshift bed.

"No, don't be silly. I'll take the floor, Marcus."

He scoffs. "Lexi, I'm taking the floor. Don't even try to disagree. It's what's happening, so suck it up."

I can see he's not going to budge on the idea, so I walk across the room to climb into his bed.

"Jesus Christ, Marcus, when did you get so grumpy?"

"Shut up." He chuckles, turning off the light and laying on the floor.

We are quiet for a few minutes as both of us try to get comfy.

"Marcus," I whisper in the dark, "when did you notice Abbey acting weird?" After speaking with Ayden about Abbey, I can't get her off my mind.

"On the Monday after you got back. Tasha was telling anyone that would listen that the news report was a lie and that your brother didn't assault you. She..." Marcus hesitates.

"She what?" I demand, my blood turning to ice in my veins.

"She was telling everyone that you've been trying to seduce your brother ever since he moved back in and that you got him drunk and made him fuck you. She said you cried rape after your parents sprung you, and you're trying to put the blame on your brother."

Tears stream down the side of my face at hearing what Tasha has been saying. The light flicks back on, and the bed dips before Marcus pulls me to his chest in a hug.

"Why would she say those things?" I whisper past my tears.

"I don't know, Lex. We've been trying to find out. Jared and I tried to speak with Abbey a few times, but she pretended to ignore us or would walk off and hide. Then Daniel grew some balls and started acting like her fucking bodyguard or something. We haven't been able to get close to her since. If it's not Daniel blocking us, it's Tasha."

Sitting up, effectively breaking Marcus' hug, I swipe away my tears and push my blonde waves back off my face.

"I don't understand what I did to Abbey to make her turn against me. It just doesn't make sense."

Marcus offers me a sympathetic smile. "We'll get to the bottom of it, Lex. The most important thing right now is keeping you safe."

I return the smile, "Thanks, Marcus."

Marcus stands from the bed, and I sink back down as he switches off the lamp again and resettles on the floor.

"Lex." He whispers. "Give me your hand."

I roll over onto my side, knowing what Marcus means, and I dangle my arm over the edge of his bed, my hand finding his in the dark.

"Marcus?" I whisper.

"Yeah?" I can just make out his shadowed form.

"Thank you."

Seventeen

"What the fuck!"

A familiar deep voice drags me out of sleep, and I crack my eyes open looking around, only no one is there. Did I dream that? Confused, I take in Marcus' bedroom, from the crumpled blankets on the floor where he had slept last night, to his open bedroom door.

I should sneak back to my room before Andrea or Barb find me in here. It probably won't go down too well if they find me in Marcus' bed, so I move to slip out of his bed but freeze when I hear a door bang down the hall, followed by shouting.

What the hell?

The next thing I know, I'm having a deer in headlights moment when Ayden drags a still dripping wet, barely covered by a towel Marcus into the bedroom.

"Wanna explain this to me?" Ayden hisses, his face turning red in fury as he points to me.

Well, fuck me. A fury faced Ayden is even hotter!

"Stop being a dick man! What the fuck is your problem?" Marcus hisses, clutching the towel to keep his junk covered.

Ayden growls, slamming Marcus up against his door, their faces mere centimetres apart.

"What the fuck do you think dickhead? Why is my girl in your fucking bed?"

Oh, Jesus. I know I shouldn't be getting all swoony about him calling me *his girl* since I'm the one pushing this whole friends only thing, but I'd be lying if I didn't admit that it makes my tummy do a stupid little flip.

Marcus shoves Ayden back off him, barely catching his towel in time when it slips down his hips.

"Look on the floor on the other side of the bed, cockhead!"

Ayden rips his glare away from Marcus to me before he takes the few steps past the end of the bed to see the pile of blankets on the floor.

"What in the hell is going on?" Great! Barb is here to join the party!

"Ayden, what is all the yelling about?" And… there's Andrea.

Kill. Me. Now!

"Why don't you ask this tool? He's the one carrying on like a dickhead." Marcus sneers, causing his mum to glare at him.

"Stop swearing, Marcus." She scolds with her hands firmly on her giraffe flannelette covered hips.

"Ayden?" Andrea snaps, glancing at me warily before turning her attention to her son.

Ayden's eyes are still locked on the floor where the blankets are, and then his face twists in torment. I hate seeing it. I really just want to climb across this bed and wrap my arms around him. But I won't, because he deserves more.

"Lexi slept in Marcus' bed," Ayden says quietly before looking at me in confusion.

"I can see that." Barb's curt tone draws my attention, and I silently wish I could shrink back into the shadows and disappear.

"Mum quit it, would you? Lexi gets nightmares, and if she's alone, she can't sleep. I offered her my bed because you bloody raised me to be a gentleman. I slept on the floor." Marcus pushes past his mum to grab some clothes out of his drawers, his pale arse exposed to everyone in the room. Meanwhile, I'm still huddled in his bed with Ayden, Andrea and Barb all staring at me.

My face heats, and I feel a whole new level of humiliation. Not only am I the girl that got assaulted by her brother, manhandled by her dad, forgotten by her mum, and pushed to breaking point by Tasha, but I'm also the girl that needs to co-sleep with someone just to get some fucking shut-eye.

I throw the blankets off me, sliding out of the bed on the opposite side where Ayden stands, and turn my glare on him.

"You know, instead of going all caveman Ayden, you could have just asked me what was going on."

Beyond embarrassed with four sets of eyes on me, I run out of Marcus' room and back into the one that is meant to be mine, locking the door behind me. I hide under the horrid floral blankets and ignore Ayden and Marcus each time they come to the door, asking if they can come in. I stay that way until the house goes silent, and I know that the boys have left for school, and the adults have left for work.

Deciding it's safe to come out now that the house is empty, I shower quickly, keeping my eye on the door the whole time, even though it's locked. After I'm clean, I stew over what to wear today since I don't know what to do with myself for my first day of suspension. Deciding to go with comfort, I slip into my red trackies and my black Billie Eilish tee, tucking it up under my bra at the back.

I've never been suspended before. It seems weird to me that the school thinks it's a punishment. Kids don't even want to be at school. This is totally not a punishment to me. I guess if I had to stay alone in my house, it might be a different story.

After readying myself for the day, I make my way downstairs, only to find Andrea in the kitchen doing dishes. I thought she had left earlier when the others did, but I guess I was wrong.

"Take a seat, honey. I'll cook you some toast." Andrea smiles warmly, and I give her a small smile trying hard to hide my embarrassment from earlier.

Sitting at the kitchen bar, I watch her cook the toast and pour me some juice before I give my thanks and nibble on the crust, not really feeling all that hungry.

"Was that true, what Marcus said this morning? Are you struggling with nightmares and sleep?"

I nod, not wanting to talk about it. Keeping my eyes cast down at my plate, I'm hoping to avoid the pity I know will be in Andrea's eyes. I hear her sigh, and she turns back to finish washing the dishes.

"I have the morning free. How about we go and buy some new bedsheets and things to make that bedroom less creepy?"

I can't help it. I laugh and nearly spit out the piece of vegemite toast that was in my mouth.

"That would be good, thank you. I have my card, so I'll pay for it."

"Lexi, you should keep your money. I can buy them for you." Andrea comes to stand in front of me on the other side of the counter, but I shake my head.

"Thank you, but I'd rather buy my own things if it's okay with you?"

Andrea studies me for a moment and then nods. "That's totally fine, honey."

So that's how I spend my Friday morning, my first day of suspension, with Andrea buying new things to help me turn Rachel's old room into my new temporary room. Even though it's not necessary, I appreciate Andrea trying to make me feel more welcome. Of course, it doesn't have her desired effect, but I'm not going to burst her bubble and tell her that I feel like an intruder.

While we're out, I get a new set of earphones and fill my pill script so I can try to get that back on track. We talk while we shop, and the whole experience makes me feel sad. Is this what it would be like if my mum were normal? Would we go on shopping trips together? It's not something I can ever picture my mum doing, but there's still a part of me that hopes we could have a better relationship.

Andrea uses our time together to ask about the things Tasha did to me at school, and I admit to her that I have been struggling to control my anger and that it feels like it's consuming me. She tries to make me feel better by reminding me it's probably normal to be feeling anger after what I've been through, and then she grins and lightens the mood telling me she couldn't stop laughing when she asked Ayden what happened to his nose yesterday and he told her I had clocked him.

"I know some of your anger is coming from what happened in Melbourne." In typical Andrea style, she says exactly what she's thinking. I can't even escape the conversation because we're in her car driving back home. "That's understandable too. We were meant to keep you safe when you were with us in Melbourne, Lexi, and we failed."

"No, that's not true." I insist, even though I do feel bitter about it. It shouldn't have surprised me, though. All the other adults in my life had let me down, so what was a couple more?

"It is true, Lexi. I also need you to know that Ayden isn't normally like how he was after the party with Muz. He's only ever like that when he's coming down off his high. That's what those drugs do to him. They change who he is."

"He should have let me take some of them too, so it didn't affect him so bad." Guilt squeezes my heart, remembering that night all too vividly. He had me kicked out of the room so I couldn't snort the white powder when Muz forced his hand.

"He thought he was doing the right thing, honey. He told me he was scared that you would like the drugs, and then he'd lose you like..." Andrea trails off, obviously unsure how much I know about Ayden's past.

"Like Dani?"

Her brows shoot up in surprise, and she nods, trying to keep her eyes on the road. "He told you about Dani?"

"Yeah, he did."

"Well, you get it then. He could never live with himself if something happened to you, Lexi."

I don't say anything to that, and she frowns, "I'm surprised he hasn't told you how sorry he is about everything that happened."

"He has, kind of. I haven't really given him much of a chance."

Andrea smiles, "Well, you have been through a lot. You take all the time you need. He can sweat it out a bit."

I smile back, grateful to have her in my life. I know I need to learn how to move past this bitterness that's weighing me down. It's fuel to my anger. Anger which scares me, to be honest. I don't want to lose control ever again like I did with Tasha yesterday. I don't want to become a monster like my brother.

When we get back to the house, Andrea helps me transform the creepy lilac bedroom into a contemporary lilac room with a hint of Lexi here and there. No more creepy dolls, no more floral, just white and grey tones that create a calmer space. I appreciate the time she has taken out of her day to spend with me, and it even surprises me when she makes me a sandwich before she leaves for her shift at the hospital. I never knew mums were like this.

Now alone in the house, I throw myself on my newly decorated bed and pull out my phone, noticing a voicemail, some messages from Rhys and Ayden, plus a heap of messages in the boys' group chat, which has been renamed to *Lexi's pack of hot beefcakes*. That has to be Simon's doing.

I open the group messages first.

Jared-Crowley
What does one do when they don't have to go to school, Lexi?

Simon-Hastings
We miss you! Do you miss us?

Shaun-Bossier
Of course, she misses us. We are HOT!

Marcus-Grady
You're an idiot, Bossi!

Simon-Hastings
We heard Marcus has snagged you, so you don't need us as bed buddies anymore.

Shaun-Bossier
That totally sucks, Lexi!
I'm gonna miss our cuddle times!

Ayden-Mitchell
Marcus has NOT snagged her!

Simon-Hastings
Bit touchy, are we Aydo?

Shaun-Bossier
Who's going to watch The Office with me now?

Marcus-Grady
She's going to be too busy watching
Stranger Things with me.

Ayden-Mitchell
Since when do you watch that shit, Marcus?
And if she's watching it with you,
then she's watching it with me too!

Marcus-Grady
Rhys got Lexi and me into it the other night.
Good show.
Don't dis' it until you've watched it!

Simon-Hastings
Lexi, when you get sick of these amateurs, you can always join Gaz and me for strip poker again.

Ayden-Mitchell
WTF! You better be fucking joking, Hastings!

Simon-Hastings

No joke, dude! The girl can play a mean hand of cards! She had me down to my jocks.
Little minx was checking me out too.
Weren't you Lexi?
That was right before we called it a night, and we slept on the floor.
Together.
Lexi was in the middle.

Ayden-Mitchell

Fuck off, prick! You better watch your back!

Garrett-Cole

Stop goading him, Hastings!

Simon-Hastings

What? Ain't you gonna tell him how you watched her take a shower, Gaz?

Ayden-Mitchell

Motherfucker!

Garrett-Cole

Well, no man! I'm pretty sure Lexi doesn't want that info public knowledge.

Ayden-Mitchell
Gaz man, you better be joking!!!!!!

Garrett-Cole
It's not what you think, so calm the fuck down!

Simon-Hastings
Well, I mean, Gaz watched, but Marcus and Jared got in the shower with her.

Shaun-Bossier
Simon man, cut the shit! Ayden has just walked out of class to hunt you fuckers down!!

Marcus-Grady
Ayden, they are just fucking with you. It didn't go down like that.

Simon-Hastings
That's a matter of opinion.

Marcus-Grady
Ayden?

Simon-Hastings
Are you serious, Shauno? Is he on his way here?

Shaun-Bossier
He's fucking gone man!

Holy shit! There are no more messages. I need to stop Ayden.

Lexi-West
Ayden, STAND DOWN, PLEASE!!
While some of that stuff is true, the dickheads
are twisting the truth to piss you off,
and you've just walked right into their trap!
Ayden?

Shaun-Bossier
Too late, Lexi.
They are all up at the principal's office.

Lexi-West
What? Who?

Shaun-Bossier
Ayden, Simon, Gaz and Jared.

Lexi-West
Fuck!

Marcus-Grady

Don't worry, Lex. I'll sort these dickheads out.

Lexi-West

I'm not speaking to any of you arseholes until you make this right!

Shaun-Bossier

Hey! I've been well behaved!!

Lexi-West

Fine! I'm only talking to you.

Shaun-Bossier

:)

I can't believe those arseholes stirred Ayden up like that! Wait. I take that back! I can totally believe it. Shitheads!

Shaking my head, I open Ayden's private message that he must have sent right after he left for school.

Ayden Mitchell
Sorry about this morning.
I guess I'm still pretty fucked up.
I really hope you are okay, and my mum isn't hovering too much.
She felt terrible about what happened at my dad's. She was so upset with herself when she noticed you had left.
Anyway, I know you aren't interested in talking to me right now because I was a total judgmental douche this morning, but I needed to reach out to apologise.
P.S. Knowing you are safe at my place is a load off my mind. X

I want to respond to Ayden's message, but I can't bring myself to do it. I'm scared. I'm not sure of what exactly, but I feel like I need to muster up some more courage before I have another heart to heart with him.

I decide to leave Ayden's message for a bit, and I open the one from Rhys.

Rhys George

Girl, you are a badass, you know that?
Someone from your media class caught the
best footage of you pummelling Tasha yesterday.
I swear it's the best moment of my life.
I thought the incident in the toilets was,
but I was wrong.
This definitely tops it!!!!
You are officially my best friend!!!
I know I've said that before,
but I mean it way more this time.
No other bitch will cut it like you do!
Oh, and don't forget about the party
tomorrow night. Wear something slutty.
I'll be in contact with times later.
Maybe we can have another sleepover?

I'd forgotten about the party. Rhys had told me about it a couple of days ago and said she wanted to take me. She tried to sell the idea by saying it would be way sicker than the type of parties I usually attend. I'm not sure how she knows what the parties are like that I normally go to, but I never asked her to explain.

Lexi West
I think psycho is a better word to describe me than badass! There's legit something wrong with me. I hardly even remember what I did. Can you send me the video?
I'll have to double-check with Andrea if it's okay for me to go to a party tomorrow night. It's weird as fuck having to ask someone for permission. I'll try to be convincing.

After I hit send, it occurs to me that Andrea could very well say no. If she is my acting guardian, then I have to follow her rules. Jesus, that sounds suffocating. I'm not used to anyone caring where I am unless it benefits them.

Shaking those thoughts off, I hit the voicemail button and wait to listen to the message.

"Alexis, it's Maxwell… ah, your dad. You need to ring me back. Your little victim charade has gone on for long enough. If you don't want to suffer the consequences of your actions, then you should probably think about behaving first. Call me. There are some things I need you to do for me."

What the actual fuck!

Eighteen

What a dick! My dad actually thinks I will call him back and do "things" for him! Hell fucking no! Who does he think he is? Calling me and leaving a message basically saying that I'm making shit up and then telling me, not asking, but telling me to do stuff for him.

I hate him.

"Hey, here's our girl." Simon's voice rips me from the toxic thoughts swirling in my head.

I've been sitting in the kitchen impatiently waiting for someone to get home. Being alone with my thoughts isn't good right now. It's re-sparked my anger, and I'm in a foul mood.

Following Simon through the back door, my pack, as Rhys likes to refer to them, quickly fills the small kitchen area in Marcus' house.

I roll my eyes, "I'm not your girl, Simon."

He gives me a hazel-eyed wink and leans down, pecking my cheek before dropping his school bag by the wall and going to the fridge. I'm about to tell him off for dumping his bag when Jared, Garrett and Shaun follow Simon's lead and slap kisses on my cheek as they make their way past into the kitchen.

Marcus and Ayden are left standing by the door looking at me with expressions I can't read, and I frown at Marcus, hoping to warn him off from doing what the other boys did.

I fail.

He gives Ayden a sideways smirk before stepping up and whacking his own kiss on my cheek.

"What the hell!" I hiss, shocked by the big hairy balls all the boys have grown overnight.

They all snicker to themselves from the kitchen while feeding their faces with fruit and potato chips.

"My turn," Ayden whispers in my ear, jolting me in surprise. I hadn't seen him approach.

Before I can push him away, warm lips press softly to my cheek. Well, not even really my cheek. More like his kiss lands on my lower cheek right next to my lips and then lingers a little too long. If I were to turn my head slightly, our lips would connect. I don't though. Ten points to me for showing restraint!

I stand as Ayden walks by, joining the boys in the kitchen that now looks even smaller, filled with all six of them. Maybe boys is the wrong word to describe them. They are definitely closer to men now!

That's when I notice Ayden's bandaged hand. I look from it to the others and notice that Jared and Simon have faint bruising on their left eyes. Garrett, however, seems to be unscathed.

"Really? You actually punched them?" I glare at Ayden, and he just shrugs, biting into an apple, his blue eyes sparkling with mischief. My temper rises, something that happens too easily these days. Why does he have to be so infuriating?

"My face hurts, Lexi. You should look after me." Simon pouts, and I notice the smallest tick in Ayden's jaw when my eyes flick back to him. He really doesn't like the way my pack flirts with me.

"Actually, Simon, I think you deserve what you got." Folding my arms across my chest, I shoot him a glare.

"What? Why?" Simon cries, slapping his hand over his heart as if what I said is the most preposterous thing ever. He looks a little more unkempt than usual. His longish ash-blonde hair is messy and falls over his eyes, and his uniform is creased and twisted.

"You poked the bear." Is all I say, and I don't miss the smirk Ayden tries to hide.

"Maybe he shouldn't be so easy to poke." Garrett sneers, shooting blue-grey daggers at Ayden, but Ayden doesn't bat an eyelid. He just continues to take bites out of his apple before clearing his throat.

"I need some answers." Ayden draws my attention as he looks from the guys to me, "Can someone please fill me in on the real details?"

"You don't need me for this." I turn to leave the room, not wanting to relive everything that's happened over the last couple of weeks, but Ayden moves quickly, darting out of the cramped kitchen to block my exit.

"Lex, please. Those pricks won't tell me the truth. Stay and talk to me." His ocean eyes draw me in like they have done so many times before, and I find myself nodding before I realise I'm doing it.

"Let's take this to the living room," Marcus announces, and the guys grab their food and file out behind him.

I follow reluctantly. It's not too late to do a runner, is it?

Jared and Garrett take a seat on the couch, while Marcus and Shaun take the armchairs, and Simon takes the floor. Even though I know it will annoy Ayden, I pop my arse in between Jared and Garrett on the couch, trying to avoid his glare.

"He's a touchy motherfucker, isn't he?" Garrett whispers in my ear, and I giggle.

If looks could kill, then Ayden would have just killed Garrett.

"Hurry up, bro. What do you want to know?" Shaun urges Ayden, only annoying him more.

"What's the shower incident?" Oh, he just had to go straight to the most humiliating thing first, didn't he?

No one speaks, all eyes falling on me. Okay, I'm ready for the earth to open up and swallow me now! Waiting... Waiting... Waiting... *Crap!*

Lifting my feet up onto the couch, I wrap my arms around my knees, resting my head on them.

"I don't want to talk about it." It's all I can manage, and Ayden comes to sit in front of me on the coffee table, concern etched over his beautiful face.

"Lex." He pleads, and Marcus sighs.

"I'll tell him, Lex. It will at least shut him up."

"Fuck you, Marcus!" Ayden hisses, shooting his cousin a death glare before dragging his eyes back to me. I duck my head and hide like the coward I am, staring into my lap.

"We were at Simon's for the night," Marcus speaks up, saving me. "The next morning, Lexi was taking a shower, and this dickhead was walking around with his earphones blaring in his ears, not paying attention."

"Fuck you, Grady!" Garrett hisses at Marcus.

I reach out and grab Garrett's hand, holding it in mine to try and calm him. I know how bad he feels about that whole incident. I don't blame him for it at all.

"Then he walked in the bathroom where Lexi was showering, not fucking cluing in that the bathroom was occupied until he heard her screaming over his music."

Garrett surges to his feet and goes to storm out, but I leap up and latch onto his arm, turning my glare to Marcus. "What the fuck, Marcus! What is your problem?"

"Hey, don't shoot the messenger. If you want to blame anyone for bringing this shit up, blame your boyfriend!" Marcus scoffs, holding his hands up in surrender.

"He's not my boyfriend. Why are you being such a prick?"

Ayden stands from the coffee table, ignoring my squabble with his cousin, and moves to Garrett's side, looking him dead in the eyes. I'm not sure what he's doing, but he stares hard and long at Garrett before a softness overtakes his features, and he looks to me in question.

"I'm still screwed in the head, Ayden. I didn't see Garrett walk into the bathroom. I saw Mike."

Realisation dawns on Ayden's face, and he shifts his eyes back to Garrett, offering him his hand. Garrett takes it, and they do some sort of bro hug. Then, saying nothing, Ayden takes my hand and leads me back to the couch.

Ugh. Guys are so weird!

Moving back to the coffee table, Ayden keeps his eyes on me, "You had another panic attack?"

Nodding, I feel the shame crawl up my spine like a hairy spider.

"Marcus and I helped Lexi. We made sure she was covered up and took care of her. No one mistreated her." Jared offers the information, which comes across a lot fucking kinder than how Marcus was re-telling it.

Ayden gives a nod before shooting his glare to Simon, "Strip poker?"

"Okay, okay, look." Simon puts up his hands in surrender, "I was the only one that stripped, and not just because Lexi was kicking my arse at the game, but because I was trying to be a funny bastard. She needed laughter in her life, and I delivered. There's no way I would have taken my jocks off, though. I'll only do that if she asks. Besides, if I had, there's no way she would have wanted you back."

In a blur of movement, Ayden is off the coffee table with Simon's feet barely touching the ground as he lifts him by the scruff of his school shirt. Curses fly, Garrett and Shaun leaping up to talk Ayden down while all I seem to be able to do is watch.

I don't remember Ayden being this aggressive or angry. Well, unless you count the day after the incident with Muz and the drugs. There was definitely aggression then.

Marcus, the arsehole, is still lounging back in the armchair, looking like a smug prick. What the fuck is his problem? What is going on?

Needing to get the situation under control, I speak up over their voices.

"I've got better things to do than watch you measure your dicks." I know they are my friends, but they are acting like jealous lovers, and I've had enough. In all fairness, Ayden should be the only one acting that way.

My outburst gets their attention, and Ayden, still with his eyes trained on Simon, drops his hold on him, letting him fall back to the floor.

"What else do you want to know, Ayden?" I ask, and everyone seems to calm down and return to their seats. Ayden turns to face me before stomping back to sit on the coffee table.

"Sleeping arrangements? There seems to be a lot of guys wanting to cosy up to you." He throws a glare at Marcus, and he bites.

"Fuck you, Ayden! You know why she was sleeping in my bed last night!" For a moment, it looks like Marcus is going to leap out of his seat, but he stays put, balancing on the edge.

"You slept with Lexi last night? I thought Simon was joking around about that earlier." Garrett adds, and I have to fight the urge to dick punch him.

"I slept beside her. On. The. Floor! There's a fucking difference!" Marcus hisses at Garrett.

"She looked pretty fucking cosy in your bed!" Ayden snaps.

"You know I slept on the floor, Ayden! You don't fucking own her. What gives you the right to swing your dick around?"

I stand, "Right well, I'm leaving since you are all swinging your dicks around."

"Wait, Lex." Ayden grabs my wrist as I try to move past him, and I hear the others mutter apologies.

"Sorry, Lex. I just need to know the details. Once I have them, I'll back off, I swear."

Simon scoffs, but Ayden ignores him.

"Please, Lex, fill in the blanks for me. Tell me what these pricks are leaving out."

Glancing around the small living room, I take in these boys, my so-called pack. They all mean well. They've been looking after me, and even though they have been borderline possessive, I can't hate them for it. I get that Ayden has walked into a strange situation, but I need him to understand because I really do need all of them in my life. Even if I don't deserve them.

"Fine," I sigh, snatching my wrist out of Ayden's grip and moving across the room. I don't want to sit down anymore. I'm feeling cagey, so I stand by the entrance, knowing I can make a quick escape if needed.

"You know about the shower incident already, and Garrett and I would rather never speak of it again, please."

Ayden nods, keeping his eyes on me from where he's still perched on the coffee table.

"I did kick Simon and Garrett's arse at poker. I remained fully clothed, not just because I was winning but because Simon was the only one playing strip poker. I don't take my clothes off for just anyone." I shoot Ayden a pointed glare and ignore the fact that the others notice it too. "The guys slept near me depending on the situation of each night, and yes, Ayden, it's because I've turned into a pathetic, needy wimp, but don't worry, I'll make sure not to sleep next to anyone again just to make you fucking happy!"

"You're angry?" Ayden asks softly.

"You think?" I snap.

"Good. You should be angry. That anger is what's going to help you get through this."

"This anger is what is destroying me!" I scream, not able to control the pained words ripping from my mouth. Silence fills the room as stupid hot tears burst free.

"That's why we're here, Lex." Jared speaks up, "We want to help. We want to protect you and make sure you come out the other end of this in one piece."

More tears come then, and Jared moves from the couch to wrap me in his arms. I relax into his hold, trying to fight the tears off because I'm so sick of crying. The room is still quiet around me while I stand in Jared's arms, trying to compose myself.

When I pull back, I can tell Ayden isn't happy. It's clear that he's struggling to see me receive comfort from Jared, but he doesn't share his annoyance with anyone this time. Smart man!

I look around the room at the guys, my family, knowing that Jared's words spoke the truth. They do want to help me. They do want to protect me. I don't deserve them.

"Since this seems to be a Q & A session, I have a question I'd like to ask you all, and I want the truth." Although my words are demanding, my tone isn't. I feel flat and sad again, and I'm just so sick of being kept in the dark.

"Absolutely. Anything." Ayden answers for all of them, watching me as I take a couple of steps away from Jared.

"What is the agreement Marcus was talking about yesterday?"

I'm met with silence, and I glance at each of the boys as they look anywhere, but at me, so I focus my glare on Marcus and Ayden.

"It's not fair to keep me in the dark, you know?" I add, hoping they will cave.

Ayden does.

"I asked Marcus to look out for you when I realised you had left my dad's apartment. The prick lied to me and told me you were okay, though. Then on Monday, I received a video of you and Tasha fighting in the girls' bathroom at school. I wasn't meant to be looking at my phone while staying at the clinic, but I couldn't help but keep reading over the message you sent on Saturday night whenever I got a free moment. That's how I came across the video."

"What message did you get?" Marcus asks, confused, his dark brows furrowing.

Ayden chuckles when I feel my cheeks heat before he looks at Marcus. "Nothing you need to worry about, man."

Marcus frowns, but Ayden ignores it and continues. "When I saw that fucking video, I called Marcus and made him tell me the truth this time. So, that's when I asked him to stick to you like glue and make sure no one else messed with you. I didn't ask these other fuckers to join in, and I sure as shit didn't ask anyone to fucking sleep with you!"

"Dude, we were already sticking to Lexi like glue before you even asked." Shaun's grey eyes are fierce as he glares at Ayden.

"You didn't do a good fucking job at sticking then, did you? She managed to ditch you fuckers at school more than once." Ayden retorts, but Shaun just rolls his eyes.

I guess that explains the whole agreement thing. At the end of the day, they all meant well. They just forgot that we live in the 21st century and that girls don't need guys to do everything for them.

"Ayden?" My voice is soft, and he looks at me with hopeful eyes, "Did you really have to punch them?"

Ayden grins, "Yep."

The boys snicker.

"Man, Ayden, your face looked crazy as fuck when you stormed into Mr Hall's class. You're lucky he didn't see you swing that punch, or you would be stuck at home sharing a suspension with Lexi." Simon laughs, and the boys join him. Ayden tries to hide his grin by turning away, but I see it.

"I bet that's exactly what he was trying to do." Marcus teases, triggering more laughter. Ayden doesn't deny it.

Males are weird. How can they be punching on one minute and then joking around the next? It's a pity girls can't be more like that.

Marcus turns on the TV, and before I know it, Simon and Shaun are setting up some car racing game on the PlayStation. That's my cue to leave. I'm sure they've been eager for some boy time without having to worry about me, and now that

I'm here under Andrea's care, they can have their lives back.

"Come talk with me for a bit?" Ayden's voice is close, and I jump a little, surprised to see him at my side. I give him a nod and follow him back out to the kitchen, joining him at the kitchen counter on one of the bar stools. He seems nervous, which is unusual for Ayden, but I wait. He doesn't say anything.

"So, you gonna talk?" I push, biting the inside of my cheek to fight off a smirk.

"Well, now that I have you alone, I don't really know what to say." His blue eyes look up at me through dark lashes.

I move to stand, "I can do us both a favour and leave." I'm in a bitch of a mood right now. Ayden is better off not having to endure it.

I don't even make it off my seat before Ayden has me caged in, trapped on the barstool.

"Don't do that, Lex. Don't act like you hate me."

"Maybe I do." I lean back on the stool, crossing my arms over my chest, trying to get a little space.

"No, you don't." Ayden gives me a dimply grin.

"How do you know Ayden? We hardly know each other."

"You know that's not true. You didn't sound like you hated me last night on the phone. I may not know all of your history Lex, but I know you. I know your heart. I know you think I betrayed you in Melbourne…" Ayden sucks in a breath looking down for a moment before returning his blue eyes to mine. "I was just trying to stop you from being dragged into that world. I know you said I did nothing wrong, but I disagree. I should have fought harder to keep you from getting in the car with Muz."

"I'm pretty sure he would have shot us if we tried to fight," I whisper, my mind instantly going back to the moment when Muz grabbed me and ran his filthy hands over my body.

Ayden goes quiet, too, probably reliving the same scene.

"You want to know what I'm mad about?" I ask, and Ayden nods. "You took away my right to choose. You got me thrown out of that room, Ayden. I get why you did it, but it wasn't your decision to make." Having me thrown out also meant I didn't know what was going on inside the room, and I was so scared that I'd find him dead.

"I disagree," Ayden says with confidence causing my brows to shoot up. "I won't apologise for that part, Lexi. I'd make the same decision again and again if it meant that you were safe."

"You're infuriating." I can feel my blood boiling thick in my veins, ready to explode.

"Ditto!" Ayden hisses, pushing me over the edge.

"I'm not a weak damsel Ayden!" I hiss through clenched teeth.

"Fuck no. I know you're not! You are fierce, Lexi. I know you will obliterate anything that stands in your way, but I can't help needing to protect you."

I get what he's saying, but it doesn't make me feel better.

"I'm just so angry, Ayden. At everything, especially myself."

"Why at yourself?" His brow creases in the centre, making him look all kinds of adorable.

"For letting you in. You made me weak." I admit in a soft whisper.

Ayden flinches at my words; a look of hurt contorts his face before it's replaced by resolve.

"For the record. You have never been weak, and I don't think letting me in has done anything but make you stronger. But I get it. Things are fucked up right now, so I'll stand back and give you space like you've asked. Hopefully, it will give you the control you think you have lost by being with me. I can see you need to feel in control. I'll do whatever you want me to Lexi, I just ask that you please don't push me away."

I don't want to push him away, but I don't know how to have him in my life without it being more. He's also different since coming back from Melbourne, and now I understand that I don't really know him, even though my body seems to think it does.

"You've been a dick to the guys. They have been there for me when you weren't Ayden."

"I know. I will make it up to them, I promise." Ayden finally lets go of the arm of my chair and drags his hands through his dark hair. "I just have trouble thinking straight when it comes to you."

I know how he feels. I feel the same way around him.

"You don't need that in your life Ayden, not right now. You have your own problems to work through, and you need time to heal on your own. Being with me won't help you move on from your past."

Ayden is quiet for a moment, and my heart sinks. Stupid heart. It wants him even though it knows I'm not good enough for him.

"Please don't use that as an excuse Lex." His whispered plea almost breaks me. I remind myself once again how much better off he will be when he moves on from me. He has the chance to find someone that isn't damaged, isn't broken.

"I can't do anything more than this right now," I admit.

"I know," he sighs, "but I can't *not* see you, *not* talk to you, *not* be involved in your life."

"Didn't we agree to be friends last night?" I ask, and he goes quiet again, casting his eyes to his hands in his lap.

"We did." He nods before raising those blue eyes again, "But that's just for now. When the time is right, I'm totally stepping back over the line and kissing the fuck out of you."

Red. Hot. Blush.

There's no way I can hide it, and his knowing smirk only makes it worse.

"Fuck, it's going to be a long hard road if you keep blushing like that."

"Stop," I slap his arm, "That's not helping!"

Ayden raises his hands in surrender, "Okay, backing off. Friendzone. Got it." He crosses his heart.

As sincere as his voice sounds, his eyes are anything but.

He isn't going to make this easy for me at all.

Nineteen

I need my punching bag! Sleep is evading me, and of course, it's because I'm so pathetic that I need someone to sleep next to me to keep the fucking dreams at bay. Too scared to start more drama and possibly get myself thrown out of Andrea's sister's house, I don't go to Marcus or even Ayden to help me sleep. Instead, I stay confined in the lilac bedroom, going out of my mind with the overwhelming need to vent my pent-up anger.

My mind wanders to Ayden so many times that I'm beginning to think I'm becoming obsessive. His promise to kiss me again one day has me all hot and bothered, which only adds to my festering frustration.

At my wit's end, I try to read, hoping it will put me to sleep or pass the time until morning. The only book that Rachel left behind in her room is boring and confusing, and it's not long before I give up trying to comprehend it. Trolling the internet for something to read, I come across Amazon, and before I know it, I've created an account and downloaded my first kindle book. At first, the amount of book options nearly sends me packing, but I persevere and start searching for Reverse Harem books. Rhys is so obsessed with that topic. She keeps saying that the guys are my reverse harem which is ridiculous. While I adore them, my heart belongs to only one, even if I won't admit that to his face. My first kindle book is Uppercut Princess by E.M. Moore, and I'm blown away and instantly hooked. As I read, a part of me wishes I could be more like Kyla. She is a true heroine, strong and determined on her quest for vengeance. Uppercut Princess definitely gets me through the remaining hours of the night. I can't put it down.

By 6am, I drag myself out of bed, my arms and legs feeling heavy. I take a long hot shower, once again watching the door the whole time with my heart racing, and by 7am, I'm sitting at the kitchen table taking small bites from the pancake stack that Barbara whipped up. Ayden comes in from the loft not long after that, and he and Marcus join me at the table. It's a struggle to look up from my plate of food as I pretend to eat. Making eye contact with the guys and Barbara is uncomfortable because I feel like an intruder. I really just want to go home, which makes no sense since that house holds nothing but nightmares for me.

I'm utterly exhausted by the time breaky is done. Sleep tugs at me, filling my lethargic brain with dark, swirling clouds. All I want to do is go to sleep, yet if I give in to the need, I risk falling into the nightmares.

Unfortunately, the boys have other ideas about how I'm going to spend my Saturday and drag me to the footy again. The sun is out today, and the air doesn't have as much chill in it. It's already a week into spring, and finally, the weather is acting like it. Spring is my favourite season. With the days becoming warmer and the sun staying in the sky longer, it brings me a sense of hope.

"You're pretty tired today," Garrett observes from next to me, his blue-grey eyes seeing what I was hoping to hide. We are sitting on the same bench seat we sat on last weekend at the footy; the only difference is that today, Ayden is sitting on my other side.

"Yeah, I didn't get much sleep." Well, I didn't get any sleep, but Garrett doesn't need to know that.

"Maybe you should have stayed in bed, Lex." The concern in Garrett's voice is evident, which sparks Ayden's interest.

Ayden's head suddenly blocks my view of the footy oval as ocean eyes study my face. His dark brows pull together when he sees what I've been trying to hide from him all morning. I close my lids blocking out his intense gaze and take a deep breath. I prepare for criticism, but it never comes.

"I can take you back home, Lex," Ayden's soft tone oozes into my pores and wraps itself around my heart.

I shake my head, digging deep to open my eyes again. I'm here; I may as well watch the game.

Ayden's mouth thins, but he turns back to the game. A moment later, I feel him slide closer to me on the bench seat.

"You can rest your head on me if you need to." He doesn't look at me when he speaks, but I glance up at him.

His face is a mix of emotions. I can see he's struggling to figure out if his comment oversteps the friendzone line I've drawn. His worry makes me grin. Why does he have to be so adorable?

"Maybe just for a few minutes," I say, and his head whips in my direction, his brows reaching his hairline. I've surprised him. I'd laugh if I weren't so tired.

I offer him a small smile before a yawn engulfs me. He grins then, reaching across my back to pull me into his side, where I melt right into his heat.

I swear I only intend to shut my eyes for a power nap, ten minutes tops. My body has other ideas, though, and it's the third quarter siren that rips me from sleep again. I can't believe I slept through the first three-quarters of the game. Not to mention sleeping while sitting up drooling on Ayden's hoodie.

Feeling more alert, I move casually away from Ayden's side. Garrett's blue-grey eyes catch mine when he turns to me and welcomes me back to the land of the living. When I give him a small smile, he shoots me a wink before continuing his conversation with Ayden about how the umpires are one-sided today. I have no idea what that even means.

After footy, we congregate at Simon's for lunch and gaming, which is when I notice a new voicemail, as well as a text from Rhys on my phone. Sneaking off to the toilet, I listen to the voicemail. Part of me hopes that it's from Rhys, but part of me already knows it's another one from my dad.

"Alexis, I had to go to great lengths to find out your new number. The least you can do is call me back. I have a few errands I need you to run for me. Call me back today!"

My dad's voice does nothing but make me cringe. Why the fuck does he think I'll do anything for him? And how did he find my number? It hadn't even occurred to me yesterday when I received his first message. I should probably contact the police and tell them he's been calling. Not that it will do any good. Unless he comes out of hiding, then they can't get to him.

Not wanting to think about that arsehole any longer, I move on to the text from Rhys.

Rhys George

Bitch, you ready to party with me tonight?

I spoke with Andrea about going to the party with Rhys last night. She was reluctant to let me go, but she caved and told me to be home by midnight. Of course, then she said that if I change my mind and stay with Marcus and Ayden instead of going to the party, I could do whatever I wanted.

She really should have chosen her words better because it leaves my possibilities wide open.

It's foreign to me this whole having rules thing. My mum has been so away with the fairies over the last couple of years that she forgot a teenager needs them. I've always been pretty well behaved except as of late. Now the idea of rules just feels like more people trying to control me.

Lexi West
Of course. What are the plans?

Rhys George
Can you meet me at your place?
There's no olds there, right?
It will make pre-party drinking easier, although if you're not comfortable going back there, we can totally find a park to hang out in for a bit. Sometimes that's more fun. You know, taking the risk that we might get caught by the cops.

I know I shouldn't go back there without one of the guys, but I really need this with Rhys tonight, and I'd rather not risk getting busted by the cops. I need a night to have fun and forget about the bullshit that my life has become, so if Rhys is with me, I should be fine.

Lexi West

Yeah, sure, we can go to my place.
Definitely no olds there. What time?

Rhys George

I can be there around 6.
We can get ready together and have some shots before we head to the party.
I can stay the night at your place, right?
I can't go home if I've been drinking, you'll understand why later. But if I can't stay, Lexi, my dear queen, don't worry your pretty little head about it. I'll have one drink and be your designated wing woman for the night, anyway. After all, Rhys George knows how to party no matter the situation!!!

Shit. I hadn't thought of Rhys staying. Maybe I can convince her to come back to my new place. Either that or I somehow have to convince Andrea to let me stay out all night. I'll think of something, I guess. I'd really like to spend the night with my new friend and get to know her better.

Lexi West

Sure, you can stay the night.

Rhys George

Fuck yeah! We are gonna have the best time tonight! Make sure you ditch your wolf pack. No jocks allowed!!!
Tonight, I am your knight in shining armour!
I will protect your life with my own, my fair queen!

Lexi West

You're an idiot! But it sounds perfect. :)

Leaving my hiding place, the toilet, I now have to figure out how to ditch the guys, grab my things from Marcus', and get to my house before 6 pm.

"Where have you been hiding?" Shaun alerts everyone to my presence when I walk back into the rumpus room. I shoot him an annoyed glare, but he just gives me one of his cheesy, white-toothed grins.

"Women's business." I snap, pretending I'm moody, even though I'm not.

"Say no more. I get it." Shaun raises his hands like he's trying to tame a wild animal, making the boys chuckle. Even Ayden.

"Well, I'll see you guys later." I move toward the back door, and they all go quiet.

"Where are you going, Lex?" Jared asks the question.

"Just going home. I'm tired. Didn't get much sleep last night." I slide the door open and get one foot out the door before Ayden's voice makes me hesitate.

"I'll walk you back." His voice comes from behind me, and I have to take a deep breath to calm my racing heart before looking over my shoulder at him.

Part of me wants to stand firm and determined like Kyla does from the book I'm reading, but who am I kidding. I'm not Kyla, I'm Alexis Amity West, and I'm yet to find the strength Kyla wields.

"Uh-okay. Thanks."

Ayden's eyes soften around the edges at my response. I guess he'd been waiting for me to refuse.

Stepping outside, Ayden follows behind, calling out to the others that he will be back soon, and we walk side by side towards Marcus' house.

"You've been quiet today." Breaking the silence, Ayden's deep tone instantly calms me while giving me stupid butterflies at the same time.

"I'm tired." It's a typical response, isn't it? I'm tired. When really, we mean emotionally exhausted. Would it be so bad to be honest when someone asks this question?

"I know you're tired, Lex. But something else is wrong; I can see the worry in your eyes. Has something happened?"

My shoulders drop, and I sigh. I don't know why I thought I could keep anything from this guy. After all, he's the only one that saw past the façade I was trying to trick everyone with when he first came to Fox Pines.

"My dad called."

"What!" Ayden hisses, stopping me with his hand on my arm. "When? What did he say? Why didn't you tell me?"

I take a step back from him and the anger flashing across his face, and my hackles instantly go up.

"I am telling you, so stop freaking out! I *was* going to keep it to myself, Ayden, for the simple reason that I don't want anyone freaking out any more than I am. It's just a call... well, two calls, actually. I haven't spoken to him. He left messages."

Ayden regards me for a moment while he chews the corner of his mouth. I wish he wouldn't do that. It draws my attention to those kissable lips that I work so hard to avoid.

"Did you save the messages?" His tone is calmer this time, so I nod and pull my phone out of my pocket.

Going into my message bank, I pass my phone to Ayden and watch his expression as he listens to my dad's voice, each second, his face becoming redder and redder. His nostrils flare, and his breathing quickens, and the hand holding my phone is squeezing it so tight that I think he's going to crush it.

When he's done, he slowly hands me back my phone while taking a couple of deep breaths. I can see what he's doing. He's angry but is trying to calm himself, so it doesn't upset me. The thing is, seeing him so affected by it upsets me enough. This is why I keep things to myself. I hate dragging other people into my bullshit.

"What do you think he wants you to do?" Ayden asks, calmer than I expected.

I shrug, "No idea. He's shit out of luck, though. I'm not calling him back."

Ayden smiles, pleased with my response before it slowly falls from his face.

"You know, friends talk to each other, Lex. This is the sort of thing you should be telling me or one of the others."

My brows shoot up, "You wouldn't care if I told one of them and not you?"

"Of course, I'd care. I'd be pissed. But this isn't about me. This is about you and your safety."

Shit. I was totally going to try to pull the wool over his eyes about my plans for tonight. There are two problems with that. The first, which is obvious. It's too dangerous for me to be running around the street without letting someone know my plans. The other is, I don't want to lie to Ayden.

Ayden starts walking again, so I fall in beside him, trying to figure out how to tell him about my night with Rhys without him hijacking my plans.

His deep chuckle draws my attention, and I find him looking down at me as he walks.

"What else is going through that mind of yours?"

"Nothing," I say way too quickly, making him chuckle again.

"Lexi, Lexi, Lexi. Don't you know that the pretty pink blush you get whenever I get too close, also pops out when you lie?"

Without thinking, my hands fly to my cheeks, finding them warm and confirming what Ayden just said. Shit. I had no idea that happens. Ayden tosses his head back in a belly laugh at the look on my face.

"Give it up Lex. Tell me what's eating you."

I wish you were eating me!

Whoa! Down girl!

My face heats at the thought, and his dark brows reach his hairline.

"Fuck, Lexi. You have no idea how expressive you are, do you?"

"W-what?" Why am I stuttering?

Ayden stops walking again and leans in close enough that I feel his warm breath on my cheek and his addictive scent wraps around me. "Tell me what you were just thinking about."

O. K. Time for deflection!

"If you must know, I wasn't going to tell you the real reason that I wanted to go back to your place, but since you are so nosey, and because you have a point about the danger I'm in..." I hesitate when I see the surprise flit across his face.

"You have to tell me now." His tone is playful, but I can see the concern in his blue eyes. I'm not the only one that is expressive. He is too!

"I'm going to a party with Rhys tonight. It's not in Fox Pines, but it's not far. I'm going back to grab my things and meet Rhys at my house to get ready together before we leave."

"Like hell!" He hisses, his beautiful face contorting in anger.

"Excuse me?" I hiss back, my ever-present anger instantly eager to unleash.

"You're not going to a party with that girl."

"You mean Rhys? Why not?" I demand, shoving my hands on my hips.

"You hardly know her, Lexi. She can't protect you."

"Ayden, the whole thing with tonight is to get to know her better, plus my other friends will be there too. We will stay together. It will be fine."

"It's a bad idea, Lexi."

"I need some *me*-time Ayden," I look up into his eyes, my hands falling from my hips. I need him to understand. "I need to feel normal," I whisper.

Intense blue eyes analyse my face, worry making them appear lighter. With frustration, he drags his hand through his dark hair and turns away from me, obviously needing a moment.

When he turns back, he's frowning. I hate seeing the disappointment on his face. I wasn't lying when I said I needed some *me*-time. I really do. I need some space from all the testosterone and the magnetic pull he has on my heart.

"Fine, but I'm walking you to your house, and I'm having a long fucking conversation with Rhys before I even agree to leave you alone with her."

Tears burn my eyes, and I turn away in frustration this time. He doesn't get it. He doesn't see what his demands do to me. They make me want to run.

"Hey." His warm hand slowly turns me by my arm to face him again, but I keep my eyes cast low. "Look at me, Lex."

He flinches when I look up at him. He obviously wasn't expecting to see the anger.

"I get that you want to protect me, Ayden, but let's make one thing really fucking clear. No one, including you, has the right to demand what I should do or with whom I should do it with. I need to take control of my own life."

He steps towards me, moving to reach out to my face, but then stops himself dropping his hand back by his side.

"I'm sorry. I'm not trying to control you. I'm just worried. I want to protect you." The sincerity in Ayden's tone is unmistakable.

"I know." I nod, "I get that. And I know I probably sound like an ungrateful bitch, but he..." I look away, trying to bite back my tears. When I feel like I have them and my voice under control, I look back to his ocean eyes. "Mike may not have succeeded in what he set out to do, but he took something from me that day. Probably before that day. I need to get it back. I don't know any other way to explain it. I don't need you to be a dad to me Ayden, I need you to be a friend."

Dark brows pull together as Ayden takes in my words, and then he steps forward, pulling me to his chest. I have no control over my reaction. My arms wrap around his waist, and I hold him just as tight, not wanting to let go.

"I just need to know you are safe." His deep voice rumbles through his chest to meet my ear.

"How bout I check in with you through the night? And if I want to leave, I'll call you."

Ayden sighs, "I guess that will have to do, but I'm still having a chat with Rhys. I worry she doesn't understand the seriousness of the situation."

"She's seen the news, Ayden."

"The news didn't even cover half of the danger you're in."

"Fine." I concede. It's as good as I'm going to get with him, and honestly, I'm okay with that.

When we arrive back at Ayden's, I pack a small bag while Ayden waits downstairs, and then he escorts me to my house. He goes inside first to do a sweep of the house while I wait just outside the front door, listening for any noise that isn't meant to be there.

"Lexi!" Valarie's voice is a loud shout, and I turn and watch as the scrawny little twelve-year-old runs up the front path to greet me.

"Hey, Val."

"It's so good to see you." She flings herself at me, wrapping her arms around my waist in a tight hug. I laugh into her jet-black hair, hugging her back.

"It's good to see you too, kid." I ruffle her hair, and she steps back, grinning up at me.

"So, you have a new family now?" She asks excitedly.

"Ah, not really. It's a friend's mum who's taken me in until my mum gets better, I guess."

"That must be fun. Do you have to share a bedroom?" Val is almost frothing at the mouth with excitement.

If only it were that exciting. Really, it's kind of awkward and uncomfortable. As much as I'm grateful, I just really want my own space back. I feel like I don't belong there. I feel like I don't belong anywhere.

"No, I don't have to share a bedroom." I look up at my house to my bedroom window. It looks the same as it always does. It doesn't look like anything sinister ever goes on behind the window. "Have you noticed any weird activity at my place since I've been gone?"

Valarie shakes her head, "Nope. It's been quiet. What are you doing here, anyway?"

That's Valarie for you, always the snoop.

"I'm meeting a friend here. We're getting ready to go to a party later."

"Oh, cool. Will you be drinking alcohol?" Val asks, looking up at me with eager brown eyes.

"No. I'm not old enough."

She rolls her eyes. "Like that's stopped you before."

I laugh, "nothing gets past you, does it?"

"Nope." Val's grin is wide and proud. "I'd better go back inside. Mum doesn't know I snuck out to see you."

"You should definitely go back in then." I smile, and she smiles back. "See ya Val."

She giggles, waving as she runs off, leaving me to wait anxiously for Ayden.

I listen hard again, not hearing any noise coming from inside my house. Is Ayden okay?

"Are you going to go in?"

I scream and spin at hearing the voice behind me, my fists raised, ready to fight.

Rhys' dark eyes widen before she smirks.

"Damn, girl. I don't want to fight you, but I will if I have to."

"Fuck me, Rhys! Why the hell did you sneak up on me?" I drop my hands to my sides, waiting for my heart to slow its pace.

"I didn't sneak. I called out to you like three times after that little Asian girl ran off. You're stuck in your head again, aren't you?" Rhys pops her hand on her hip, showing me her sass. "You really need to get drunk."

"Shit!" Running my hand down my face, I try to calm my racing heart. If it keeps racing like this so frequently, will I give myself a heart attack?

"You need to get drunk and get laid, girl," Rhys adds.

She's not totally wrong. I do need to get drunk!

"She doesn't need to get either!" Ayden's voice booms from behind me.

Whoops. Busted!

Twenty

“I’m starting to second guess bringing you with me.” Rhys pouts, her black lips matching her nails tonight. She told me the shade is called *Haunt Me* and the polish and lipstick came as a set. I don’t know where this girl shops. There are no retail outlets in Fox Pines that would sell something so mint!

“Why is that?” Eyes are on me. I can feel them coming from every direction. This party is nothing like the usual parties I get dragged to. Normally the music resembles viral TikToks or whatever is playing on Australia’s top 40, but not this party. My heart instantly feels at home, hearing the soothing voice of Aaron Lewis from Staind. *Fuck yes!* This is my sort of party!

“Well, besides the fact that you look so fuckable that I’m fighting to restrain myself,” Rhys turns in a circle gesturing to everyone else around us, her short black skirt twirling out a little as she turns. "They all want to fuck you too."

I laugh, "Stop being dramatic."

Her head snaps in my direction, her dark eyes annoyed at my comment. But then she cringes, "Shit, head spin."

I laugh again.

"Ignore her, Lexi. Rhys is just used to getting all the attention and having her pick from the crowd. She's just going to have to learn how to share tonight." Tillie gives me a wink that sparkles with the movement from her glittery lids and proceeds to scull down her beer. She looks cuter than ever, wearing a peach-coloured top under her shredded denim jacket which brings out the peach glitter colour on her cheeks. This girl is all about the glitter. She even has some in her cute pixie hair.

"Fine, I'll share, but only because I love you, Lexi." Rhys flashes her teeth at me, throwing her arms around my neck in a hug. I stumble a little, the three vodkas and two fireball shots already oozing through my veins.

"How much have you bitches had to drink?" Dale asks, pulling out a joint and offering it to me. I shake my head, refusing.

"We've had enough to drink for now." Rhys grabs the joint out of Dale's hand and pops it between her lips, leaning into Allister when he offers her a light.

"Oh, joy. Rhys is going to be drunk and stoned. What a lovely combination." Bell complains, looking basically the same as she does at school, just without the ugly navy uniform. In its place is nothing but black. Her lips are as dark as Rhys' tonight, and her eyes are smoky with shadow. She looks hot. Shit, they all do. Even Allister, who usually looks like death, has colour in his cheeks tonight. I wonder why. Maybe he's taken something. Or perhaps he's just had a tumble with Dale in the bushes. I know they're both gay, but I don't think they are into each other. I could be wrong.

Courtesy Call by Thousand Foot Krutch blasts through the speakers, and we can't help but start dancing right there in the backyard of the party. Most of the people here are older, maybe Uni students, since we are at Redfield, a town that basically butts up against Fox Pines in Timberland Valley. Very few people here look like they are our age. I don't care, though. It's better this way. No one here knows me. They don't know my past. The only thing they have to judge me on is what I do right now.

Tonight, I'm wearing black jeans that are so tight they look like they are painted on, and I deliberately forgot to put a jacket over my red boob tube. Yep, Rhys told me to dress slutty, and while I wasn't willing to have my legs out in this cold weather, I totally went a full 360 on the top half.

I had to wait for Ayden to leave my house earlier before I got ready. I know he means well, but if he gave me his opinion on what I can and can't wear, then there would have been a bloodbath! Okay, slight exaggeration, but it would have pissed me off.

He had spent a good hour talking to Rhys about the seriousness of my situation. He'd made her agree to remind me to check in with him every hour and let them know addresses we go to and how we were getting to and from the party.

Ayden learnt quickly that Rhys has an answer to everything. And he also learnt that she's a little cray-cray, which is why I adore her so much. I guess he could see that, so he eventually left us to have our fun night.

As we dance and laugh, two different joints get passed around our group, and I only take it once, not wanting to have a repeat of losing my memory or my wits. I feel so free right now. So light and happy. I know it's a veil caused by the booze mostly, but I don't care. These new friends of mine don't riddle me with the self-conscious anxiety I usually get at parties. They fill me with a sense of peace and belonging.

Is this what normal feels like? If it is, then count me in.

"Incoming." Bell deadpans, and I turn in time to see a tall, dark, decent looking guy approaching us.

"Oh, yes! Look at him, Lexi. He's fuckable and then some. Have at it. I'll take the next guy." Rhys whisper shouts in my ear, letting everyone around us, including the guy, know exactly what she said.

"Hey there. I'm Andy." He's tall, like all guys are to me, but not as tall as Jared. Maybe a similar height to Ayden. He has the sexy facial hair that I seem to like, along his jaw just like Ayden, although now that I take a closer look, it's patchier than Ayden's. Scruffier looking somehow.

"Ah, hi Andy." I'm pretty sure I have a stupid grin on my face as I look up into his brown eyes. It's hard to tell what my face is doing. Shit, that weed must have been strong if I can't feel my face properly. I only had one drag... didn't I?

"You wanna grab a drink with me, ah…" Andy hesitates before leaning in a little closer, "Sorry, what's your name?"

"Oh. I'm Alexis." Jesus, why did I say my full name?

"A very beautiful name, for a very beautiful girl," Andy's eyes soften as he looks at me. Meanwhile, I fight back a cringe. He's full of shit. He's telling me what he thinks I want to hear, and because I'm drunk, a little stoned and horny, I'm totally going to pretend I buy it.

Ayden.

Fuck me, why am I thinking of Ayden? I need to forget about Ayden so he can move on.

"So, would you like to come and have a drink?" He's a persistent fella.

"I'm not that thirsty, but I'll come chat with you, anyway." I smile at him, mostly because the weed is kicking in, and I'm pretty sure everything is going to make me smile right now.

Andy's eyes darken, and he licks his lips before gesturing towards the house. "Let's go then."

For a second, I panic, but I don't get the chance to feel its force before Rhys shoves me forward, and I stumble into Andy's chest. His deep chuckle is close to my ear, and his arms wrap around me. Leading me onto the porch which is bathed in the shadows, he grabs a beer out of an esky and cracks the lid, taking a sip.

"So Alexis," I cringe hearing my full name. Why did I tell him that? I'm thankful he doesn't notice my expression in the dark. "What brings you out tonight?"

"Just wanted to have some fun." I glance behind me. My friends are still in the middle of the yard, by the fire. Not too far away, but far enough that they can't hear me talk. People are spilling out from the shed where the music floats out from, but over here at the back of the house, it's quiet.

"You want to have some fun with me?" Glancing back at Andy, who is now a lot closer to me than he was a moment ago, I feel fear prickle at the edges of my high. Fuck, this guy is straight to the point. No chatting. No getting to know each other. Just straight into it.

"Ah- maybe a little." I'm not so sure now. This was a bad idea. I'm not ready for this. Sure, I'd love to share a kiss with someone, but really, I want that someone to be Ayden. Not Andy, whoever the fuck he is! Glancing back over my shoulder again, I double-check my friends are still where I saw them a minute ago. They are, and Rhys catches my eye. Good, she's keeping an eye on me. That's good, right?

"If there's one thing I can do for you tonight, Alexis, what would that be?" I turn back to Andy, who is now closer again. Like all up in my space type of close. I have to strain my neck back to see his eyes which lock on my lips when I look up to him.

Calm down, Lexi. He's not whipping his dick out. He's just looking at my lips, wanting a kiss, I guess. I can do that, right? I can kiss him? His lips look pretty nice. They aren't like Ayden's lips, but I'm sure they would be soft and warm. I really miss being kissed. Being touched like I'm loved.

"A kiss." The words leave my lips before I can stop them. Whoops.

"A kiss hey?" Andy grins. It's a nice grin, but it doesn't have the sexy dimples like Ayden's grin does.

"Yeah. I need a really good kiss." Why the fuck am I still talking? That's it. No more drinks for me!

"Looks like you came to the right place then, darlin'." Andy's fingers gently brush my cheek.

I flinch, but he doesn't stop. He leans down, and I freeze in place, feeling like I'm about to do something incredibly wrong.

All I can think of is Ayden. But I have to stop thinking about him because he deserves better than me. I will do nothing but bring him down and destroy his kind soul with my bullshit life. I can't have him.

I can have Andy, though, and this meaningless kiss.

Andy leans in, his eyes on my lips. I have to do this, so I fight back my fears and stand on my toes to close the distance. Andy brushes his lips over mine, and I wait for the warm tingly sensation that gives me butterflies... but it doesn't come.

The only thing I feel is repulsed. Without even thinking, I push against Andy's chest, needing to get him away from me. He stumbles back, anger twisting his face, and even though it's dark, I can see it glow red.

"You fucking tease!"

"Hey! Cockhead! Back off!"

The bellow comes from behind Andy, the deep voice very familiar.

Andy spins, addressing the voice.

"Stupid high school sluts! Talk the talk but can't walk the walk!" It's almost like Andy is a different person to the one that approached me only minutes ago. I know, I know. I spoke to him for all of three minutes, but still.

"Yeah? So, you know she's underage then, man! You might want to fuck off now before I make you!"

Andy growls, dragging his hand over his dirty blonde hair. "Fuck this, Trav. Stop inviting the teenage bitches to our parties man!"

Trav? I step around Andy to see Travis Watson, my partner in crime. Literally.

"Travis?" My voice comes out like a squeak.

A cheesy grin spreads over Travis' pimpled face as he moves his eyes to me, but then, he turns to address Andy again. "Fuck off will ya!"

Andy grumbles something under his breath, storming off towards the shed, and Travis steps up to me and places his hands on my forearms.

"If it isn't the one and only, Sexy Lexi." His smile is big, and all I feel is relief. Launching myself at him, I wrap my arms around his neck in a tight hold. "Aww, you missed me, didn't you?"

I nod into his neck, and he chuckles.

"I'm so sorry about the school thing," I say low enough that only he can hear.

Peeling my grip from around his neck, Travis steps back to look me over.

"Forget about that. Are you okay Lex? I fucking freaked when I saw that news report about you. I beat the shit outta Mike when I saw him a couple of days later."

"What?" I screech, "You saw Mike? My brother?"

"Yeah. It was a few days after the news broke. The fucker had the nerve to come knocking to score some dope. Fucking idiot. As if I'm gonna sell to that dipshit. Turns out he went on a bender with the product he was meant to sell, and his dealer cut him off and gave him a week to come up with the cash. I got no idea what happened to him after I laid into him, but his name is dirt in the Valley now, and it has more to do with why the cops are looking for him, and less to do with drugs."

Wow. Mike didn't even try to flee the area. He's either dumb as all fuck, or has a big set of gonads. I'm betting on the former.

My mind is still reeling when arms wrap around me from behind.

"Oh, baby, you did it again, didn't you?" Rhys' voice draws Trav's attention, and she slides her hands seductively over my waist, "Sorry man, she's new to lesbianism. Sometimes she forgets she prefers pussy."

A laugh rips free before I can stop it, and Trav joins me while eyeing Rhys with interest. I turn in her arms and hug her before looking back over my shoulder to Travis.

"Rhys, this is Travis, an old friend."

"Well, I'm glad he's an old friend. For a moment, I thought you were playing pass the parcel with your tongues. Where did that Andy guy storm off to?" Rhys links her fingers in mine while she blatantly checks out Travis.

Travis' brows shoot up. "So, Andy got a tongue in, did he?"

I shoot Travis a dagger, but he just laughs at me.

"Was he a good kisser?" Rhys asks, and I shift uncomfortably as she waits for my answer.

I shake my head.

"Too much tongue? Too sloppy?" Rhys cringes, "He wasn't a muncher, was he?"

"A muncher?" I have no idea what this girl is on about half the time.

"Yeah, you know. Kissed you like he was trying to eat your face." Rhys gags. "I fucking hate munchers."

My brows reach my hairline, and Travis chuckles, this time checking out my new best friend just as she did him a few minutes ago. Great!

"No, he wasn't a muncher. He just wasn't..."

"Wasn't?" Rhys urges.

"Ayden," I whisper.

I know Rhys heard my words when I feel her drop my hand, and she slides her arm over my shoulder, tugging me close. Unfortunately, Travis heard it too.

"Ayden? Who's Ayden?" He asks, his sandy blonde brows tugging inwards.

"Ayden is the guy that saved her from her brother. Then Lexi gave him her V-card."

"Rhys!" I hiss, pushing her off me.

"What? You said this guy is an old friend." She shrugs.

Fuck my life!

Travis starts belly laughing, and I have the overwhelming urge to punch his pimply face.

"Besides. It doesn't matter. You and Ayden aren't a thing anymore, and you're looking for a kiss to rid you of all things Ayden."

Pain claws at my chest. Rhys is right. We aren't a thing anymore, and I know I need to try to move on so that Ayden can too, but it's hard. My heart wants him more than it wants to beat.

"You know Lexi, I'm happy to let you kiss me again. You loved it last time." Oh, Travis did not just go there!

"Say what? You little slut Lexi!" Rhys cries and starts jumping and clapping her hands.

"Seriously?" I hiss at Travis, and he frowns.

"What?"

I shake my head and turn my back on them both, heading towards the fire pit where my other friends are.

"That was the most awkward kiss I've ever seen. Don't do that ever again." Bell, usually so blasé, actually screws her face up when I approach. Did everyone see that Andy guy kiss me?

"You know, Lex, you can totally have the kiss you're craving without thinking about Ayden." Rhys lights up another joint as she skips past me. I turn to see Travis walking into the shed where a lot of the other partygoers are. I'll have to find him again later. He might have more info on where Mike is.

I draw my attention away from Travis and consider what Rhys said. "How?" I ask since she has me curious.

"Kiss me." My brows shoot up at Rhys' comment.

"Jesus Rhys, you can't try and turn Lexi into a licker," Bell argues.

"I don't want to turn her Bell. I want to show her how fun it can be to have both." Rhys wags her brows at both of us, and Bell rolls her dark eyes.

I frown.

"Rhys is bisexual, Lexi. She's greedy and likes dick and pussy." Bell explains, snatching the joint off Rhys.

"Wow. How did I miss that?" I ask.

"It's not like I have it stamped across my forehead. You'd be surprised how many people are bisexual, Lexi." Rhys grins deviously at me. "Oh, the 'Tea' I could share with you."

"I don't have any interest in pussy." I'm one hundred percent certain about that too.

"Don't knock it until you try it." Rhys blows a puff of smoke in my face and offers me the joint. I refuse. I need to be careful. If I have too much, I'll end up having no memory of the night again.

"I'll pass."

Rhys rolls her eyes at my refusal.

"Honestly, though, I can totally give you the kiss you're looking for. You won't even think about Ayden, I promise." Rhys smiles, "Besides, guys fucking love seeing two chicks make out."

Standing in front of me, Rhys takes another drag of the joint. As if my eyes have a mind of their own, they automatically seek out her lips. Fuck, am I seriously considering this?

Holy shit! I think I am. I totally want Rhys to kiss me.

As if I'm possessed with mischief, I shoot Rhys a devilish grin, and she smiles knowingly.

"Pucker up those luscious lips, Lexi." Rhys smiles, moving in, her eyes on my mouth.

She pulls me against her body, and it feels oddly exciting to have a female body pressed up against mine that way. I can feel her curves and the round swell of her breasts. She's a little taller than I am, but not by much.

Holding the joint between her fingers, Rhys lifts it to my lips, letting me take a long drag. Once I'm done, she takes another drag herself and then tosses it over her head. Dale curses and lunges for the joint, but that's all I notice other than the shape of Rhys' lips and how her tongue darts out to wet them as she moves in closer. I close my eyes once I feel her lips touch mine and enjoy the feel of her soft lips as they press against mine. Then Rhys darts her tongue out, and I open to her, hearing her groan as our tongues collide.

Cheers ring out around us. Guys hoot, calling out for us to keep going, and Rhys deepens the kiss making me moan this time. She was right; I can't think of anything but her lips.

Strong arms suddenly wrap around my waist, and I'm ripped away from Rhys before I find myself thrown over a strong shoulder like a sack of potatoes. My world tilts upside down, and it takes me a moment to get my eyes to focus when I see Rhys is in the same predicament. Our eyes lock, and we laugh. She looks ridiculous upside down with her dark hair falling past the knees of the guy that carries her.

"Girl, who's carrying me?" Rhys manages to say between giggles.

I strain my neck, trying to see who it is. It's hard to make sense of anything when I'm upside down, stoned and drunk.

"I think it's Marcus," I whisper-yell. I don't know why I'm whisper yelling. "Wait. Who's carrying me?" *Why is Marcus here?*

Rhys is laughing too much to respond, so I decide to take things into my own hands... literally.

"Who belongs to this fine arse?" I slap the arse and hear a grunt. Rhys laughs even harder.

"Um, Marcus, she's likely to pee on you if she laughs much more," I yell this time and then join Rhys in a fit of giggles.

Rhys slaps Marcus on the arse then, and he wiggles it, laughing.

I decide to play the drums on the arse that is basically in my face, and in return, I get a firm slap on my own arse, and a deep voice snaps, "Behave."

I squeal at the contact and talk to the arse.

"Play fair cute arse." I then pinch said cute arse, and the bearer of it flinches and tries to jump out of my reach. An impossible feat really, since I'm so close to it that I could probably bite it.

Hey, there's an idea.

Before I even get the chance, I find my world the right way up again. My head spins, and I have to throw my hands out to steady myself on the car that has appeared out of nowhere.

When the spinning stops, I lock eyes with Rhys, and we double over laughing again.

"Jesus, they're wasted." Marcus' voice draws our attention, and we try to stop laughing. Really, we do.

I look at Ayden, and I have to fight, very fucking hard, not to go to him and claim that kiss I've been dying for all night. Why is he even here?

"Get in the car." Ayden doesn't sound very impressed. I can't for the life of me figure out why.

"Nah, we're good. Thanks anyway." I try to walk past him, but he steps in my path, and I roll my eyes.

"Dude, we were having fun. Why would we want to leave?" Rhys interjects in a slur.

"Too much fucking fun." Ayden hisses, glaring at Rhys.

"Hey, back off. She's my girl." I say in a childish tone, and Ayden rolls his eyes this time.

"Come on, girls, get in the car." Marcus urges.

"Hey, Marcus. Why don't you make me?" Rhys challenges, and Marcus rises to it, grabbing her before she can get away and throwing her over his shoulder again. She doesn't complain though, just slaps his arse as he carries her around the other side of the car and attempts to put her in the backseat. Somehow Rhys ends up with her legs wrapped around Marcus' hips, and she drags him into the backseat on top of her.

"Christ, you two are a fucking handful," Ayden complains, and I shrug, wearing a big shit-eating grin. "Get in the car, Lex."

I shake my head.

"Really, you're going to make me force you to get in?"

I shrug and grin, still feeling ridiculously mischievous. "You really think you can?"

He steps up to me so quickly that his scent engulfs me, and I sway, nearly moaning. Taking a step back for every step forward he takes, I end up flush against the car, and he leans in. I think he's about to kiss me, but disappointment is a real bitch when I realise that he's only reaching for the handle of the car door to pull it open.

"In."

I poke my tongue out and slip in the front passenger seat, crossing my arms over my chest, pretending to sulk. I'm not really, though. I'm too fucking happy to care right now.

"You have to be kidding me!" I turn at Ayden's voice and see that he's standing outside the back door on the other side of the car, looking pissed. Rhys and Marcus are kissing and grinding their bodies against each other on the back seat.

I can't help but laugh.

Twenty-One

Apparently, the party moved to my house. Well, some of the party, thank fuck. I don't want Uni students coming to my house, or Travis, for that matter. Having him mingle with my pack is a bad idea. Jesus, I need to stop calling them my pack!

"Lexi, come have another fireball shot!" Rhys sings from the kitchen bench where she has shots lined up.

"Ah... No thanks. I'll pass."

"Poo!" She pouts, trying to trick me into feeling bad.

I won't fall for it, though. My head is spinning enough already, and my drunken state is making it extremely hard to fight off the urge to go over to the kitchen table where all the guys are sitting and straddle Ayden. Maybe even slip his shirt off and run my hands over his smooth, firm chest.

OMG Lexi! Stop!

"I'll have a shot, Rhys. Stop pouting!" Bell approaches Rhys and takes not one but two shots, downing them in succession. Christ, she's scary!

"Bitch you said *A* shot, not two!" Snatching the two glasses back off Bell, Rhys rinses them in the sink.

Shrugging, Bell moves back over to the table to peek at the cards Simon holds. "He's totally bluffing." The boys chuckle, and when Simon realises that she's giving his hand away, he glares, but she ignores it.

"What would you know?" Simon hisses, holding his cards to his chest so she can't see them anymore.

Colour me fucking pink; she actually smiles down at Simon. I never thought I'd see the day when Bell would actually smile. "I know you let everyone think you lose on purpose just so you can take your clothes off. But the real reason is that you're actually really shit at poker."

"Ha! Woodie, she doesn't even know you, and she knows you're a loser!" Shaun stirs, using the name I called Simon when he had the hard-on from watching porn in my living room.

I wait for Simon to lose his shit, but it never comes; he just shrugs and gives Bell a wink. I should probably warn him that she will eat him alive if he tries to follow through on whatever that look was he shot her, but it'll be too funny to watch. So, I keep my mouth shut.

Shaun and Rhys fought over the stereo when we arrived earlier, so they quickly compromised and made a combined playlist. Now every second song is my kind of music. Fire up the night by New Medicine starts playing, and I can't help myself. My hips start swaying, and the rest of my body follows.

"Hell yeah!" Rhys downs a shot and comes to dance with me on the other side of the kitchen island.

Tillie and Dale join us then, and I let myself go, feeling the lyrics and beat of the music, singing along and feeling so light and carefree. Hands land on my hips, and my eyes shoot open. I didn't even know I had shut them. It's okay, though. It's only Rhys dancing in front of me. Is it bad that I'd wished it was Ayden? I wonder if he even dances?

"You know, Lex. Every girl should have at least one lesbian experience." Rhys steps closer and starts dancing against my body. Well, not dancing really, more like grinding. I laugh. This chick is hilarious.

"I mean, Rhys is right about that, but don't let her weasel her way into your bed, Lexi. There are plenty of girls out there that would be more than happy to warm your sheets."

I frown at Tillie. I can't tell if she is just offering advice or if there's a hidden meaning, and she's referring to herself offering to warm my sheets. O. K. Shit just got weird.

"I'll be the only one warming her sheets."

The deep voice works like a drug, and I melt, closing my eyes. That voice. His voice. It manages to turn me into molten lava and sends a shiver up my spine at the same time. Strong hands slide over the curve of my hips and wrap around my body from behind, effectively breaking Rhys' grinding hold of me. The heat from a familiar chest against my back renders me useless, and I'm unable to stop myself from relaxing back into him. I can feel every place where our bodies meet. One strong hand on my hip, holding me to him, another hand doing the same across my tummy, his firm chest rising and falling at my back, his hot breath on my neck.

"Well, fuck me. I want Lexi to look like that when I touch her!"

My eyes shoot open at Rhys' words, and I stiffen. Shit. I've let down my wall.

No!

"Girl, she ain't ever gonna look like that for you. She doesn't love you." Bell unhelpfully adds.

As if sensing my change, Ayden slowly loosens his hold on me and steps back. I can't help but turn to him, once again, the invisible magnet leading me to him instead of away.

"Sorry, Lex." His smooth voice is laced with concern, as are those ocean eyes of his that I could happily drown in. "I stepped over the line again. I'm trying. I really am."

The pain behind his words almost sees me cave, give in and throw myself at him. I don't, though, but fuck my life, I really want to.

Glancing over my shoulder, I see that Rhys, Tillie and Dale are looking on expectantly. I love my new friends, but what happens between Ayden and me is private.

"It's okay." Keeping my voice low, I offer him a small smile when I turn back, and he returns it with his own.

Cheers ring out, drawing our attention, and I look past Ayden to see Jared peeling off his shirt. Oh, good god! How is a girl supposed to have self-control around these guys?

"I'm totally down for poker," Rhys growls in my ear as she passes by, strolling up to the table and seductively pokes her arse out as she takes a seat on Marcus' lap.

Tillie jumps up and down, clapping, "Yay, strip poker. I'm in!"

And that's how the rest of the night goes. Fucking strip poker. I don't play, but I watch, and I'm in tears from laughing so often that I eventually have to go and remove my makeup because black mascara starts running down my face.

I barely make it back out of my mum's room when Rhys and Marcus somehow find their way in through the door while Rhys' legs are wrapped around Marcus' waist, and he peels her clothes off while their lips are locked.

That girl has no shame. And I love her!

The party moves to the lounge room, where everyone makes beds on the floor and couches before settling in to watch the movie, *After*. I hover in the doorway, not sure what to do. I'm tired and really just want to go to sleep, but there are too many bodies and too many hook-ups happening in front of me. Bell and Simon are snuggling up while Tillie is in deep conversation with Allister and Shaun, and Dale is not so subtly checking out Ayden, Jared and Garrett. While the last one is kind of funny, it hurts too much to see everyone else, so I turn around and walk up the hall to the staircase.

It's dark and looming, with most of the lights off in the house. To my left, I can hear quiet chatter from my friends in the living room as the movie starts playing. To my right, I can hear grunting and moaning coming from my mum's room. Most of my clothes are in that room. Only some remain upstairs in my wardrobe, while the rest are at Marcus'. I know that if I want to get changed, I'll have to go up there. I had asked everyone to stay downstairs tonight, and they all respected my wish, but I had also hoped I could avoid going up there too. Going up there only results in anxiety. I fucking hate anxiety. I'm so sick of feeling this way, but I need to go up there. I need out of these clothes, and I need a bed.

Taking each step slowly, I silently climb the staircase, placing my feet in the spots that I know will cause the least creaking. If someone were watching me, they would probably laugh at the way I step on the left side of one step, only to stretch out and step on the right side of the next.

I use the torch on my phone to illuminate the area as I go. I should turn the light on, but I don't want to alert anyone to where I am. I just need some space.

It's not until I'm standing in front of my door that I realise something is wrong because where there was a door earlier today when Rhys came over to get ready, there isn't one now.

A hand lands on my shoulder, and I try to scream, but fear constricts my throat as I spin, ready to fight.

"Shhh, Lex, it's just me."

My phone must have tumbled to the floor when I panicked, blanketing us in darkness, but I'd know that voice anywhere. Ayden.

"D-d-door." I stutter, trying to get air in.

Ayden flicks on the switch next to him, filling the space with warm light.

"Hey. Shhh. Sorry, Lex, I didn't mean to scare you." Ayden's blue eyes lock on to mine, his hands rubbing warmth up and down my arms.

"D-Door."

He frowns and then looks behind me, realisation instantly widening his eyes.

"Fuck." His strong hands grip my shoulders, shifting me behind him before reaching in and flipping on the light in my bedroom. Walking in, he checks the window, then the wardrobe and under my bed before moving past me to check the toilet, bathroom and Mike's room at the end of the hall.

I'm shaking by the time he makes it back to me.

"No one is here." He runs a comforting hand up my arm as he takes out his phone and dials a number.

"Get your dick out of Rhys and get upstairs now. Grab Crowley on the way." Hanging up, Ayden pulls my quaking body against his chest, cocooning me in his arms. I want to stay there forever.

"Shhh. It will be okay Lex. I got you. I'm never letting you go."

I don't argue with him, wanting his words to be true, but knowing I have to let him go... just maybe not right this minute.

Heavy steps pound up the stairs, and I know it's Marcus and Jared, but I can't bring myself to pull back from Ayden to acknowledge them. I don't think I could even if I wanted to. With the grip he has on me, he has no intention of letting go of me either.

"What's going on?" Marcus sounds more concerned than I thought he'd be. Ayden just interrupted his sex-fest with Rhys, so I was sure we were going to have a grumpy blue balled Marcus on our hands.

Ayden's body jerks a little, and I imagine him nodding his head toward my bedroom doorway.

"What the fuck?" Confusion laces Jared's voice, and I know he sees what has me so upset.

"I've checked the rooms up here. They are all clear." Ayden's smooth voice rumbles through his chest where my ear is pressed to it, and I never want to leave. "We should check the whole house and outside too. Grab the guys but keep it quiet. Let's not share this with Lexi's new friends. I don't want to freak them out."

"Freak them out? I'm fucking freaked out." Marcus' voice rises the highest I've heard it go since he was about twelve.

"Suck it up, princess. Maybe you need to go back into the room where Rhys is and ask her for your balls back!" I chuckle at Jared's dig at Marcus. I can't help it. These guys make everything feel better, even when we are deep in the thick of it.

A soft chuckle meets my ear, and Ayden's warm hand rubs my back. He's still not letting go.

Marcus and Jared bicker as they head back downstairs, and Ayden finally shifts me away from his chest. I instantly mourn the loss and fight the urge to throw myself back at him.

"Can we go into your room, Lex? Talk with me for a bit?"

He's trying to keep me occupied. Take my mind off the fact that not only have my personal items been going missing, but in the few hours since Rhys and I left my house to go to the party, someone broke in and removed my bedroom door.

Ayden steps into my room but turns back to me when he realises I'm not following.

"Lex?"

What I should be doing is focusing on the fact that there is the hottest guy I've ever encountered inside my bedroom. Every girl's dream, really. But I can't. All I can do is focus on the room itself and fight back the images and memories that plague me every time I step foot inside.

"You don't want me in your room?" Ayden's voice draws my attention again, and I look at him instead of the bed where I had woken from blacking out to Mike looming over me, trying to get his jeans down.

I shake my head, "It's not that. It's the room. There are some pretty awful memories from this room." My voice is soft, a strange numbness washing over me.

Ayden's blue eyes soften, and he steps back to me, reaching out to take my hand. "Let's make some new memories then."

My brows shoot up. Is he insinuating what I think he is?

His dark brows rise, matching mine as he understands my reaction. Then, that sinful grin of his lights up his face. It's a grin that lifts those soft kissable lips at the corner, caving in the dimples that sit just either side of his mouth while his eyes brighten and crease ever so slightly at the corners.

I'm so screwed!

He chuckles, "Get your head out of the gutter, Lex. I just want to talk."

I don't speak but let him tug me into my bedroom to sit on the edge of my bed.

"Were you coming up to go to bed before?" He asks, and I shrug.

"I guess. I think I was trying to get past my anxiety about coming up here because I'm so tired. It's stupid, really. I thought I could sleep up here. How pathetic is that? As if I would be able to sleep up here. I can't even sleep on my own."

"It's not pathetic at all. You should be able to do that if you want to." He's still holding my hand, his thumb rubbing over the back. It's so familiar. So right, but I can't let it be.

"And yet, I can't," I whisper.

"I'll stay up here with you. I can sleep right here on the floor." He points to the floor at our feet with his free hand. My eyes follow, looking to the dirty grey carpet and cringe.

"The carpet is filthy."

"I'll use blankets, don't worry. And it's not that bad." He grins.

"It's bad enough." When did my carpet get so dirty? It has been a long time since I've really paid much attention to my room. Probably ever since Mike moved in.

"Lex." Ayden squeezes my hand, and I glance back up to meet his hypnotising eyes. "I'm not leaving you. I'm staying so you can try to get some sleep."

I don't get a chance to respond when we're interrupted by what one could only assume is a herd of elephants stampeding up the stairs. Moments later, Marcus, Jared, Shaun, Simon and Garrett are bumping shoulders as they try to squeeze through the doorway into my bedroom.

Having them all in here is weird.

"House is clear. No sign of anyone breaking in." Marcus sounds puffed. I bet they raced up here trying to beat each other. *Adorable idiots!*

"The back shed was unlocked, though. No sign of the door which means whoever did this took it with them." Jared adds.

"What do you want to do, Lex? Stay here or go somewhere else?" Garrett asks, and all eyes turn to me.

"Lex?" Ayden urges when I don't respond.

"Stay here. If you guys are here with me, then I'm safe. Safety in numbers. Isn't that the saying?"

"Yep." Simon nods, "where you go, we go. Which is why I'm pissed at you!"

"What? Why?" I frown.

"You had totally planned to ditch us tonight. You were going to sneak off to go god knows where with a chick we don't even know. I mean, she's fucking wicked, don't get me wrong, but still, we don't know if she can or will protect you like we will!"

Shit. Simon is genuinely pissed at me. I'm lost for words. His face, typically wearing a clown grin, is screwed up in anger.

No one speaks, and all eyes remain on me. I guess they all feel the way Simon does.

Well shit! How do I talk my way out of this? And do I want to?

"Sorry," I whisper, casting my eyes to the floor.

"Is that all you have to say? No excuse or explanation?" Simon scolds, and I cringe, shaking my head, keeping my eyes cast low.

"How about you back off Hastings? You don't know the full story." Ayden snaps.

"It's okay, Ayden." I stand, deciding not to cower anymore. Simon is right. I should never have thought about sneaking off and putting myself in danger, especially since I'm fairly sure that Mike is still around. "Simon is right. I should have told you all what my plans were. That was stupid."

Simon grins, "Yes, it was. Don't do stupid stuff again. That's my job."

Chuckles sound out from all of the guys, even Ayden, and Simon steps forward and pulls me to his chest.

"Also, FYI, Lexi. We like parties. You could have invited us too." Simon pouts, and I pull back and mouth another 'sorry'.

"Right well, I'll double-check all the doors and windows again, and we should all get some sleep." Jared declares, effectively ending the conversation.

Each of my pack gives me a grin or a friendly shoulder bump as they file out of my bedroom, leaving me alone with Ayden again.

He doesn't speak but pulls some blankets out from my wardrobe and makes his bed on the floor.

"Ayden, stop."

He freezes mid blanket placement, peering up at me.

"If I ask you to sleep in my bed, are you going to think more of it than two friends sleeping side by side?" I want it to mean more, I really do, but I know it can't.

Ayden stands, dropping the blanket from his grip and rakes his hand through his thick dark hair. God, I miss running my own fingers through that hair!

"I'm always going to think more of things between us, Lex, but that doesn't mean I can't hold my restraint and be the friend you need right now." Honest words match his sincere blue eyes as they seize me in place, unable to move. His candour is confronting yet refreshing.

"I don't deserve you." The whisper slips past my lips and floats across the small space to meet his ears.

Ayden's eyes warm, his right dimple making an appearance as the corner of his mouth heads north. "You're wrong. It's me that doesn't deserve you."

I can see that no one will win this argument, and I can't hold back my grin in return.

"Get in the bed. No touching!"

"What? No spooning?" He's so smug right now.

I'd slap it off his face if I could be sure I wouldn't melt the moment our skin makes contact.

"Definitely no spooning." I ignore his pout and move to the other side of the bed, taking out a hoodie from my drawer.

"You want mine?" Ayden asks, hopeful, but I don't turn to look at him. I shake my head and slip the hoodie over my head. If I wear his hoodie, I'll be powerless to stop myself from giving in to him.

Keeping my arms inside the hoodie, I slip my red boob tube and strapless bra off before sliding my arms in place and turning.

Ayden eyes me as I shimmy my jeans down my legs needing to be free of the tight fabric. I don't say anything because I don't trust myself not to say something that will make him step over the line between friends and, well... more.

Before he can get any more words out, I slip into my bed, a bed I haven't slept in for such a long time. It feels strange until Ayden slips in next to me, fully clothed. Now my bed feels too big and too small all at the same time, yet oddly it feels right. Perfect.

We both shuffle around, trying to get comfy while avoiding touching each other in the small space. Ayden had turned the light off before climbing in with me but left the hall light on. I'm glad he did that. I need the soft glow that filters in through the open doorway. It helps to scare away the shadows that come to life.

Downstairs I can hear the faint murmur of voices and the TV. My house has never felt more like home than in this moment. I wish I could stay here tomorrow, but I know we will have to go back to Marcus', and I'll have to face that lonely lilac bedroom.

"Ayden?" I whisper, raking my eyes over what little I can see of Ayden's face, which is so close to mine. We are on our sides facing each other. Tonight is going to be torture.

"Yeah?"

"Your mum is going to be mad at me for not coming home by curfew."

"Nah, I already covered for you. You're in the clear." His voice is gravelly and sexy as sin as he tries to whisper.

"You shouldn't have done that. No more lying to your mum, remember?"

He chuckles. "It's fine Lex. I didn't lie. I told her you were with me and that we are all staying here. I even sent her a selfie with you in the background."

"What! When did you take a photo?"

"Right before you started dancing." Ayden chuckles.

I need to remember to ask him to show me the picture in the morning.

"How'd you find Rhys and me, anyway? We only told you we were going to a party in Redfield. Come to think of it, why were you there?"

He sighs. "Dale. He added me to SnapChat, and he didn't ghost on SnapMaps. And we were there, Lexi, because *you* didn't check in with me like you promised."

"Stalker much?"

"When it comes to you, always. Not in a creepy way, though." Ayden tries to sound convincing. It's cute.

I giggle. "Oh no, there's nothing creepy about Ayden Mitchell stalking me."

Ayden laughs with me, and when we are done, we both fall quiet again before he speaks.

"Why were you kissing Rhys?"

"I plead the fifth."

"Lexi, you do know that's not relevant in Australia, right?" Ayden's deep voice is laced with humour.

"So everyone keeps telling me!"

"Stop avoiding my question." He chuckles as he speaks.

I sigh, seeking out his eyes in the darkness. From his vantage point, he has a better view of my face with the light filtering in on it. But his face is covered in shadows, all except for those damn panty-melting ocean eyes. It's like they glow.

"Rhys said that kissing her would help me forget about kissing you." The honesty comes out before I can tamper with it and twist it into some sort of half-truth. Damn him and his power to render me useless!

"Did it work?" Ayden whispers.

"I-I plead the fifth."

Ayden chuckles before linking his pinkie finger with mine. Warmth spreads through my body at the contact, making me relax into the mattress, and as if he summoned me to sleep with magic, I fall into a dreamless, peaceful sleep.

Twenty-Two

Seeing Marcus and Rhys' bare arses and tangled limbs on my mum's bed really isn't what I wanted to see... ever! Yet here I am, sneaking past them to get to my mum's bathroom so I can shower. I'm going to make them wash the sheets themselves, because eww!

Showering quickly, wanting to avoid being walked in on, my mind wanders to what I saw and felt when I woke up this morning. Ayden lying next to me is a truly breathtaking sight, but I didn't expect to see that he no longer had his pinky finger linked with mine, but he had my hand in his, tucked under his chin hugging it like it's a teddy.

Fuck me! How's a girl meant to find self-control around that?

"Lexi!" Rhys yells, pounding on the other side of the door, making me jump and nearly slip on the wet tiles in the shower. "I need to pee! Hurry up!"

"Okay! Hold on just a minute!"

I shut off the water and drag the towel over the top rail of the shower to dry my body. I didn't bother washing my hair today, so I'm able to make quick work of drying myself off before securing the towel around me to step out of the shower.

Then I scream!

On instinct, I throw myself back, and at the same time, Rhys reefs the door open, eyes wide, seeking me out. I know the moment she sees it. What someone has written in the fog of the mirror. No, not someone. Mike. It can only be Mike.

I CAN STILL GET TO YOU LEXI.
IT'S ONLY A MATTER OF TIME!!!

Marcus is suddenly in the bathroom with us, and I scream again and cover my eyes with my free hand when I get a full frontal of his junk.

"Lexi! Are you okay?" Ayden's voice gets louder the closer he gets, and before I know it, the small space is filling with Ayden and the guys on his heels.

Curses ring out before Ayden growls at Marcus and shoves him out the door.

"Get dressed!" Ayden hisses at his cousin before turning back to the mirror.

I should be trembling, crying, running, but I'm not. I'm pissed.

"Who showered in here last?" Jared asks, taking his phone out and snapping a picture of the now fading message. With the door open, the steam in the room is escaping, and with it, the message.

"Not me. I'm still dirty from Marcus!" Rhys giggles, and I hear someone make a gagging sound. Probably Simon.

"I did. Last night before Rhys and I got ready for the party. There definitely was no message on the mirror then." I wrap my arms around my body, hoping that I won't lose the towel and flash everyone.

"So, someone came in after you showered? You would have still been here for the message to have been written on the mirror." Garrett says, gaining everyone's attention.

"No. By the time I finished getting dressed after my shower, the steam had cleared because I opened the door and put the fan on. I needed to use the mirror to get ready."

"So, whoever it was, came in last night while you were at the party and removed the door, and what? Had a shower?" Shaun asks, looking as confused as the rest of us.

"Door? What door has been removed?" Rhys asks, reminding us that she doesn't know everything that's going on. I'd thought Marcus might tell her, but I guess he was too busy.

"Ah… come with me. I'll explain." Marcus, who now has jeans on, says to Rhys while giving me a questioning look.

I give him a brief nod, silently telling him it's okay to tell Rhys before answering Shaun's question. "Firstly, whoever came in and did this is Mike. Secondly, he probably did take a fucking shower." A shiver runs up my spine at the thought.

"We don't know that it's Mike doing this." Garrett tries to sound convincing, but his statement comes out more like a question.

"Actually, I'm 98% sure it's Mike," I say, annoyance clear in my tone. The message on the mirror reminds me of the message he sent me a couple of weeks ago when I was in Melbourne.

> *You little slut! I don't know how you got away, but I will find you, and when I do, I'll make our last encounter seem like foreplay! You were never good at Hide and Seek Ali. When you least expect it, I'll be there to catch you!*

I try to move out of the confined space, but there are too many bodies in the way. "Can I get out, please? I need to get dressed."

"Why are you so certain?" Ayden asks, clearly beating Jared to it by the look Jared shoots Ayden.

My shoulders sag when I realise the guys aren't going to move until I've answered.

"Besides the fact that the message is similar to one he sent me a couple of weeks ago, I found out last night that Mike has been seen in the area. Apparently, after going on a bender with the drugs he was meant to sell, he's been trying to score more. I don't know much about that stuff, but the important thing to know is that he's still close by. He probably never left."

"Who told you this?" Jared gets in before Ayden this time.

I don't want to tell them because I'm fairly certain they don't know that Travis and I have history. Yes, that history is criminal, but it's still history. I'm not dumb, though. I know the guys aren't going to drop it, so I should be somewhat honest. Somewhat!

"Travis."

"Travis? Travis Watson?" Garrett asks.

"Yep. I saw him at the party last night. He told me that Mike has been seen around the place."

"So, in other words, Mike approached him to score drugs?" Shaun hisses, making it clear how he feels about Travis.

I blanch a little but try to hide it by turning the other way and pretending I'm frustrated. Ayden's ever-watchful eyes follow my every move in the reflection of the mirror before his eyes narrow. Yep, he caught my reaction. Dammit!

"Who's this Travis guy?" Ayden asks.

I spin and push my way out of the bathroom, not needing to hear them bag Travis. I know he's not the most savoury person to call a friend, but he took the full blame for something I played a part in, so I kind of feel protective of him.

My name is called by Ayden and Jared as I storm off, my body still only covered by the grey towel. I pass through the kitchen, ignoring the weird looks I get from Tillie and Dale. I don't know where Marcus and Rhys went. I sure hope it wasn't upstairs because I need to get dressed, and I need some space.

This shit with Mike has to end. I'm sick of feeling scared and needing to always look over my shoulder. He's a sick, twisted psycho that needs to die... or at least go to prison again. But dying would be better. I need to rid him from this earth, from existence.

Upstairs is quiet and free of visitors, so I make quick work to find clothes and get dressed. Most of my clothes are at Marcus' house now, so with few options to choose from, I slip on my white Bonds trackies and my basic blue K-Mart t-shirt, tucking it up under my bra to crop it.

"How do you make trackies look so good?" Ayden's voice makes me jump, my eyes immediately moving from my reflection in the mirror to where he stands in my doorway, leaning against the frame.

"You really need to move louder around me. I'm too skittish these days." I glare at him, but it only makes him grin.

"Maybe I should wear a cat bell around my neck so you can hear me coming."

"Sounds like a plan." I grin smugly, and he chuckles.

"Tell me about Travis."

Fuck, I was hoping he'd find out what he wanted to know from the guys.

"I'm sure one of the boys filled you in." Stepping back, I sit on my bed and roll on some white foot socks.

"They told me their version of Travis. Now I want to know your version." Ayden steps into the room and around the bed to see my face. Ugh! He's so adorably infuriating!

"They are the same versions, Ayden." Avoiding his eyes, I focus on my shoes, loosening the laces of the white sneakers.

"Nope. Don't think so. You know a different version of Travis. I could tell by the annoyed look on your face when Bossi spoke about him."

"I was annoyed about having a conversation about my psycho brother. That's all." I'm unable to hide my annoyance now, and I hope Ayden gets the hint and drops it.

"Nope. It wasn't the mention of your brother that annoyed you." He's not going to back down! Dammit!

I stand, glaring at Ayden, my sneaker still in hand. "What the fuck do you want from me, Ayden!"

"I want you to tell me the truth! What are you hiding? How can I help you if you hide shit from me?"

"I didn't ask for your help!" My face is on fire. It must be bright red because I'm burning up.

Ayden steps up to me. "Tell me what I need to know, Lexi!" He's so close now, a foot away, his breathing heavy with frustration.

"I don't need to tell you shit. It's not relevant to the Mike situation, so you don't need to know." I growl in a much too girly way.

"Is he an old boyfriend?"

"What? No!" My voice is high, the partial lie not fooling him in the slightest.

Ayden's blue eyes roam my face, boring into my own, searching for answers. "He means something to you." His voice is barely a whisper.

"It's not what you're thinking, Ayden." I huff and drop my butt back to my bed. "He's a friend. A questionable person, yes, but he has been good and loyal to me."

Lowering to his knees in front of me, Ayden takes my shoe out of my hand and slips it on my foot.

If only I were Cinderella, and he were my prince!

"How come the guys don't know about your friendship with Travis?" Intense blue eyes peer up through dark lashes, the storm raging in them like a plea for me to let him in.

I drop my head, sighing again. This information isn't relevant to the situation with Mike, but I can tell he's not going to drop it. It pisses me off, yet I find myself submitting to him.

"We don't have a close friendship, Travis and I. We experienced something together, non-sexual by the way," He doesn't need to know about this kiss, "and Travis has protected me ever since. That's all."

"Any chance you're going to tell me what you experienced together?"

I shake my head.

"Didn't think so." Ayden pats the top of my foot, and I look to see that he has put both my shoes on and tied the laces. He sighs, and I notice the exhaustion shadowing his eyes, reminding me once again that I'm not good for him.

"I need to call the cops and tell them about what's happened overnight. I'll tell them about the rumours going around about Mike being spotted in town, but I'm not throwing Travis under the bus because of the drugs. I expect you and the guys to keep your mouths shut about that too."

"Fine, but if things get worse, I'm not withholding information just to save your friend's drug dealing arse!"

I could kiss him. It would shut him up, that's for sure. It would also open the can of worms I'm trying to keep sealed tight. So, I do what any mature seventeen-year-old girl would do. I poke my tongue out.

Cue his grin... and cue my damp knickers! *Jesus!*

I somehow manage to pry myself away from Ayden's presence and make the call to Officer Zimora. I fill him in with what has been happening, and I shoo everyone but Ayden and Marcus out of my house before he arrives to collect evidence.

Before Officer Zimora leaves, he gives me a lecture about coming back to the house. I have no idea what he said. All I could focus on was that navy uniform and the gun attached to his upper thigh. Maybe I should become a cop; that way, I could look at hot officers all day long! Then I'd own a pair of cuffs. Oh, what I could do to Ayden with a pair of cuffs!

WTF Lexi!!

Okay, it's safe to say that I need a little alone time to get this sexual frustration out!

Since everyone went their own ways after leaving my house, Ayden, Marcus and I return to their place and spend the afternoon lounging around in the living room watching more episodes of Stranger Things. I end up falling asleep while watching TV, so Ayden turned Stranger Things off, so I didn't miss anything, and while I was quietly snoring, they watched the footy.

It's around 5pm when I get a call from Rhys, inviting me over for dinner to meet her foster parents. I never pegged Rhys as a sit-down and have dinner with the parents type of girl, but apparently, she is, so I ask Andrea if she can drop me there, and she gives me her warm smile and nod.

I can tell that Ayden doesn't want me to go when it's time to leave, but I need space from him before I self-combust from all the sexual tension. On the drive to Rhys', Andrea asks me again about what happened at my house, even though Ayden and Marcus already filled her in, and when we arrive, she waits parked on the curb until Rhys answers the door and lets me inside.

Rhys lives in one of the newer parts of Fox Pines. There are houses still being built around her home, and the un-landscaped front yard and pile of dirt indicate that she hasn't lived in the house for long. It's a single-story modern home with large shop-front style windows and a mix of brick and render on the façade. Inside is white. Like white, white. White ceilings, white walls, white tiled floors. The carpet is a light grey, but even the kitchen cabinetry is white. It looks good, just extremely white.

"I'm giving you a heads up. My olds are... annoying. And my brothers are a pain in my arse. You will probably like my older sister. She can be kind of cool for a rock chick wanna be... Sometimes."

My brows shoot up, and Rhys grins, gesturing for me to walk through a door. It's a theatre room, but no one is watching anything. Two dark-haired boys bounce on the armchairs throwing coloured balls at each other, while an older girl with green hair at the tips and blonde roots sits in the corner, too busy on her phone to notice anything else going on around her.

"Archie! Connor! Say hi to Lexi!" Rhys hollers over the giggles from the boys. Hearing her, they both turn to me and wave, saying "hi" in sync.

The first thing that grabs me is that they are Asian or something. I have no idea, but the two boys don't look like Rhys. The next thing that grabs me is that they are identical.

"Twins?" I ask Rhys, and she nods.

"Yep. Twin pains in my arse." Rhys pokes her tongue out at one of the boys. I don't know who's who. "The snob in the corner is Charlotte."

Hearing her sister speak, Charlotte looks up from her phone and raises a very pointy brow at Rhys before turning her green eyes to me. She looks me up and down with distaste and returns her attention to her phone.

"Happy thing, isn't she?" I know I shouldn't be disrespecting Rhys' sister, but I'm sick of arseholes going around being arseholey!

"Oh, she's a real fucking treat!" Rhys snickers.

"Bitch." Charlotte hisses from the corner.

"Mum! Char and Rhys are swearing!" One of the twins yells.

"Oh, don't worry, I heard."

I swing around in shock, instantly recognising the voice. Principal Cynthia Rogan stands before me in a casual pair of blue jeans and a plain white t-shirt. Usually looking perfectly groomed, today Cynthia looks the opposite with her long brown hair up in a messy high bun and a smudge of flour on her makeup-free cheek.

"Well, I can see by the look on Lexi's face that you didn't tell her I am your guardian Rhys," Cynthia states, looking a little annoyed.

Rhys shoots her a fake smile, "It never came up."

"I don't suppose it ever came up that you live with a foster family filled with foster kids?" Cynthia asks while I stand like a stunned idiot. How can Rhys be Mrs Rogan's foster child? Surely, she would try enforcing rules like no nose piercings or black lipstick to her foster kids if she's a Catholic school principal?

"Nope. We have too much other fun stuff to talk about." Rhys says smugly, and I'm sure Cynthia is going to get angry. She doesn't, though. She simply rolls her eyes.

"Dinner will be ready in five minutes. Go wash your hands and wait at the table."

A tornado of dark-haired little boys stampedes past us while Charlotte slowly rises from her chair and swings her hips as she strolls across the room.

"Lexi, I apologise for the rudeness of my children." Cynthia declares.

I don't know what to say in response, so I stay quiet but offer a small smile Cynthia's way, and she returns it before turning and leaving the room.

I glare at Rhys because I really should have known that her foster mum is the school principal.

"Girl, you might be my best friend, but don't think I won't kick your arse if you give me shit about this at school." Rhys crosses her arms over her chest, challenging me. I laugh.

"You're an idiot, you know that?" I ask, and Charlotte snickers walking past us to leave the room.

"She knows you too well, Rhys."

"Shut up!" Rhys snaps, glaring at her foster sister.

We follow Charlotte out of the theatre room, down a long hall to the back of the house where we all sit around a large white dining table to eat. William Rogan, Cynthia's husband, is introduced to me when he joins us at the table, and I experience a very normal dinner, reminding me of dinner at the Grady's or Mitchell's houses.

After dinner, we help with the dishes, and I learn that although Rhys pretends to be tough, she has a soft spot for the twins. Even Charlotte manages to get Rhys to laugh.

"Okay, ask your questions. Let's get the bullshit over and done with." Rhys whines and flops down on her large queen four-poster bed, which is also white.

"This house is very white. Too white for you." I announce, and she lifts her head off her bed to look at me.

"Girl, are you racist?"

I laugh. "You know what I mean. Where's all the colour? Or the darkness. I imagined your room would look like a dungeon."

Rhys bolts up on her bed, "Oh, you've seen into my heart! When I'm old enough to leave this family, I'm totally going to have a dungeon." Rhys lifts her finger to her chin in thought, "Or perhaps a red room of pain, with whips and chains and..."

"Ah-okay. I got it." I cut her off, not really wanting to see too far into her sex-crazed mind.

"I'll let you bring your pack of wolves there to play with you if you're into that?"

"Rhys." I sigh. "When are you going to accept that I'm a one-man girl? Why don't you find a group of guys and have your own reverse harem thing? You talk about it so much. You're obviously into it."

She considers my words and then flops back on the bed. "Maybe. My life is a little complicated. I don't know if I'll ever be able to settle down and have a relationship."

"So... Marcus is just a one-night stand?"

"Probably more like a three-week stand, or friends with benefits. We will have to see how much he annoys me." I laugh at Rhys but also feel bad. What if Marcus really likes her? Should I warn him that Rhys isn't into serious relationships?

"He does have a really pretty cock. I might keep him around for a bit. It's hard to find pretty ones these days." Rhys divulges.

"Rhys!" I scold, shocked at her. I don't know why I'm shocked, though. She is always upfront about this stuff.

"Oh, come on. You can't tell me you like the hoods? Eww! No way! I'm a helmet girl all the way."

"What? Hood? Helmet? What the fuck are you on about?" I laugh because I'm completely lost.

She sits up again, this time crossing her legs, a glint of mischief in her dark eyes. "I can see I have my work cut out with you, Lexi. I would never have guessed you were so green. Or perhaps vanilla is a better word for you."

"I am not vanilla... I think." I frown. Am I vanilla? Isn't that boring? What if Ayden doesn't like vanilla?

WTF! I don't need to think about that because I'm not getting back together with Ayden!

Rhys laughs, "You totally are! That's fine. It's just because you are so green. You said you gave Ayden your virginity, so I'm guessing you haven't seen a lot of cocks in the flesh."

"Rhys!"

"Don't Rhys me! I can tell you haven't." Rhys' dark eyes stay locked on mine as she leans forward a little. "A hood is foreskin. Gross!" She gags, "A helmet is a pretty circumcised dick. So much better when they are in your mouth."

My cheeks heat at her words, but I say nothing, because I think I'm actually learning something. I think.

"I like my men to be circumcised. Some chicks don't care, but I do. If he has a hood, then we are a no go!" Rhys looks so serious right now. She's having this conversation with me so casually like we are talking about baking cakes.

"So, what happens if you're in the heat of the moment, and you see that the guy you're with has an, ah- hood?" I ask, genuinely interested.

"Oh, I never even kiss a guy until I know they are hood free."

"What?" I screech, and she nods. "So how did you know Marcus was hood free?" I can't believe I am having a conversation about Marcus' dick!

"I asked him, of course. Then I made him send me a dick pic to confirm."

My brows reach my hairline, "But you were all over each other in the back seat of the car last night. There was no time to have that conversation between him carrying you out upside down, to putting you in the car."

"Oh, Lexi, Lexi, Lexi. We have been chatting for a few days on SnapChat. I found out about his glorious cock a couple of days ago." Rhys declares with a huge smirk.

"Wow. You work fast."

"Of course I do—no point in beating around the bush when you both want the same thing. Life's too short to hesitate, Lexi. You gotta grab what you want by the balls and claim it." She wags her dark brows, reaches up to her hair, and starts to pull pins out of her buns.

I'm quiet as I watch her unravel each bun to reveal beautiful extra-long dark hair. She's stunning, even with her black lips. She reminds me of a supernatural goddess of some sort.

"So, are you going to ask the questions you want to ask about my family? My past? Better to get that shit out of the way now." Her mood changes, and for the first time since meeting her, I see her confidence wane.

"Rhys, it's none of my business. You don't have to tell me shit."

"Well, isn't that what best friends do? Tell each other everything?" She runs her fingers through her long hair, combing out the knots.

I consider her words. I used to think that until I started keeping secrets from Abbey and until she betrayed me.

"I used to think so. Now I think friendships should be about respecting boundaries. I like you, Rhys. I know you're a good person, and I even like your craziness. I want you to know that I don't need you to tell me things if you don't want to. I won't hold it against you. We all have our demons, remember?"

Before I even know what's happening, Rhys launches herself off her bed and wraps her arms around my neck.

"Thank you." She whispers, and for a moment, I think she may be crying, but when she pulls back, her eyes are smiling as big as her mouth. Pulling away from me, Rhys strips out of her clothes and changes into a Creed t-shirt and nothing else but her black lacy knickers. She has no problem getting bare in front of me, but I turn away because it seems she is right; I am a little green.

"My mum died when I was nine." I turn at the sad words and see Rhys sitting on the end of her bed. "She was into drugs. Loved them a little too much. I found her when I woke to get ready for school one morning. When I found her, I knew straight away that she was dead, so I went next door to Mrs Mabel, and she called the cops. Since no family came forward to claim me, I went into the foster system. I lived in a few dodgy homes during my first year, but then I was placed with Julie and Brian." Rhys smiles. "They were okay, I guess. Julie could be a mean bitch, but Brian was good to me. The best and only dad I've ever known until William. I was with Julie and Brian until I was twelve. I was happy there, but then... something happened... and I had to leave."

I've never seen Rhys look miserable. Pain contorts her face as she remembers her past.

"Anyway," she waves the pain off, "then I was placed with a few more families that couldn't handle me until Cynthia walked into the group home. It's like she sought out the most unstable kid and said, yes, let me take this child to stir up my boring life! Turns out she already had Charlotte, who is more fucked up than I am."

I'm not sure what happened when Rhys had to leave Brian and Julie's home, but she seems genuinely upset about it. It must have been bad, though. I can't imagine what could have happened.

"You're happy here with Cynthia?" I ask, hoping she is. I'd like to keep her around.

She shrugs, "Yeah, they are okay. Bit boring, but that's okay. They let me be who I want to be even though it goes against the school rules. I like the twins, and sometimes I like Charlotte."

Smiling, I take her hand, "Good, because I don't want you going anywhere."

"Oh, no way. You're stuck with me now, so get used to hearing about cocks, and vaginas, and sex, and dungeons, and..."

"I get it!" I laugh, cutting her off.

"Now. Tell me all about Ayden's cock? Is it pretty?"

For fuck's sake!

Twenty-Three

Screaming. It's faint, like in the distance, but it's close enough that I can tell it's screaming. It's a girl's scream. It's too high to belong to a boy. Who's making that noise? She sounds terrified.

Bright light suddenly startles me awake, and my eyes fly open to the tail end of a scream ripping from my throat. I'm in bed. My new bed, in the ugly lilac room, and at the end of the bed stands Andrea, Barb and her husband Tony, who is stark naked, cupping his junk.

I scream again and throw my hand over my eyes.

Oh, man! I've seen way too much Grady nudity this week!

"Dad! Shit dad, get out!" Marcus yells, drawing everyone's attention away from me, and I peek between my fingers.

"Tony!" Barb scolds when she sees his state of undress.

"What? She was screaming. She could have been getting attacked for all we knew. You want me to waste time getting clothes on while she's getting stabbed to death?" Tony still hasn't moved to leave the room, and I peek at Andrea for guidance. The moment our eyes meet, she bursts out laughing.

"Lexi!" Ayden's voice booms from somewhere in the house, his footsteps heavy as he approaches my room.

Andrea is still laughing but trying hard to compose herself, but each time she tries, she loses it again.

"Andie, this isn't funny." Barb hisses, and Andrea tries to stop, but the moment she tries, another wave of laughter hits her.

"Lexi!" Ayden bursts into the room, knocking into Barb, who stumbles into Tony, who trips and loses his hold of his manhood.

And... Andrea practically stops breathing. She hits the floor in hysterics, and Ayden glares at his mum like she's lost her mind.

"Mum! Stop!" Ayden demands, but it only makes her worse.

Meanwhile, tears are coming out of my eyes, streaming down my face, because apparently, I'm laughing too.

"Oh, for goodness sake, Tony, go back to bed; you're embarrassing yourself!" Barb demands, and then Marcus starts to laugh.

Through my blurred vision, I watch as Tony mutters an apology, turning to walk out of the room, flashing us his bare white arse. There's no hope for any of us at this point, fits of laughter turning us into inconsolable idiots.

"Are you all high?" Ayden asks, and Barb glares at him. "What? It's a legit question given what I've walked into."

Barb looks away from her sister, son, and nephew before focusing on me.

"Lexi honey. You were having a bad dream. Are you okay?" Barbs concerned question sobers everyone up, and we manage to stop laughing.

Wiping the tears from my eyes and sucking in deep breaths, I work to compose myself. When I'm finally able to string a few words together, I address Barb's question.

"I'm okay. I'm so sorry for waking everyone up. I shouldn't have tried to go to sleep."

Barb frowns, "Lexi, you need to sleep. Maybe we should take you to a doctor? Perhaps there's something you can take to help you sleep."

"It's not really the sleeping part that's the problem," Marcus speaks up. His dark hair dishevelled. It's a better look for him than his usual near-perfectly groomed look.

"Then what is it?" Barb asks, looking confused.

"The dreams," Ayden answers for me.

The weird thing is, I haven't actually had a conversation with the guys about this. As far as I know, they thought I'm just a big scaredy-cat and can't sleep alone. I hadn't realised they paid that much attention. For some reason, most of the time, when I'm not alone when I sleep, my dreams are kinder or just not there. I don't know why. It's just another fucked up thing about me.

"You know what, Barb, I'll sort this out with Lexi. Why don't you go back to bed?" Andrea steps up to the side of the bed and sits on the edge to smile at me.

"Okay. Let me know if there's anything I can do to help." Barb says, turning and cupping Marcus' chin, standing on her toes to kiss his cheek before leaving the room.

"Thanks, boys. Go back to bed, please." Andrea insists.

"But mum," Ayden complains but stays silent when she shoots him a pointed glare.

"Night, Lexi," Marcus says, yawning and leaving to walk across the hall to his own room.

Ayden doesn't move for a moment, his eyes locked on me, concern etched across his face. Why do I have to be such a freak? He doesn't need this in his life. None of them do. They are all good people in this house. They at least deserve to have an uninterrupted night's sleep. I really need to call my mum tomorrow and see if she can come home yet.

"Ayden, off to bed, please." Andrea urges, and Ayden's eyes finally leave me to look at his mum.

"Fine. Night." He sounds like a grumpy child and looks like it when he walks out the door, grumbling under his breath. It's hard to hide my amusement from Andrea.

When we're alone, Andrea takes my hand. "You want me to sleep in here with you? Or I can grab my laptop, and we can watch a movie if you like?"

Is she really offering to deprive herself of sleep just to babysit me? Is that what she would do for Ayden? Even as I think it, I know it's true. She would. If he needed her, she would be there. As much as that sounds nice, it's kind of weird to me since she's not my mum. In fact, if my mum offered to do that, I'd still probably say no. I guess I'm just too damaged to be a normal child.

"Thanks for the offer, but I'll be okay. I'm so sorry for waking everyone up."

"Don't be silly. There's no need to apologise for that. I just wish I could help you." Andrea's warm smile reaches her caramel eyes.

"You are helping me. You've given me a roof over my head. A safe place to stay. Meals. It's so much more than I've had in a long time."

"Perhaps. But you are so young, too young to be having such worries." Andrea sighs, "Are you sure you don't want me to stay with you?"

"I'm sure. Thank you." I offer her a warm smile hoping she buys my confidence.

Standing from the bed, Andrea cringes, "It's possible we will all be having nightmares about Tony tonight. Did you see how white his arse was?"

I burst out laughing, and Andrea joins in. She finally leaves me alone and returns to her room when our laughter dies down, but I can still hear her giggle to herself as she walks away from my room.

Since sleeping is out of the question, I decide to settle in for a night of reading. Through tired eyes and overwhelming exhaustion, I keep nodding off while I try to read, but dreams drag me back to my reality each time which makes for a very long night.

My Monday morning starts with a trip back to school for my mandatory counselling session with

Mr Matthews. Typically, my visits with him are spent deflecting, but today I push aside my pride and open up. I can't deal with re-living the assault by Mike or my dad's strange behaviour, but I talk a little about my mum, as well as the things that have been going missing from my house. Our hour session goes quickly, and before I know it, I've caught the bus back to Marcus' to an empty house since everyone is at work and school. I try to ring my mum, but she still won't take my calls. I do my usual search on the internet to see if anything pops up about Mike or my dad, but there's nothing as usual. I sit in the lounge and try to watch TV, but there's nothing on. It's a lonely feeling when I'm in someone else's house, so I'm thankful when I go to the kitchen in search of food and come across a note on the bench with my name on it.

Lex, there's a surprise for you in the garage! xx Ayden

A smile instantly engulfs my face, and I rush out to the garage. Lifting the heavy roller door, I push it all the way up, and my eyes widen when I lock onto my gift. Hanging from a ceiling beam is a shiny new boxing bag. I squeal and do a girly jump and clap my hands. Jesus, this guy has the ability to turn me into a sappy chick!

Taking out my phone, I line up a shot and take a selfie with my new bag behind me before sending it to Ayden. He replies, straight away.

Ayden Mitchell
You look happy! I take it you like it?

Lexi West
Hell, yes, I like it! I LOVE it!

Ayden Mitchell
:)

Lexi West
Thank you!

Ayden Mitchell
No need to thank me!

Lexi West
Are you kidding? Of course, I need to thank you. How can I make it up to you?

Ayden Mitchell
You don't want to know the answer to that!

Lexi West
Yes, I do!

Shit! Wait! No, no, I don't. I mean, I do, but I know what his answer will be, which will just complicate things.

Ayden Mitchell
What I really want is to feel your soft lips on mine again. BUT because I can't have that, all I want is for you to be happy.

Fuck me! Seriously! Why does he have to be so good at making me weak at the knees? Now all I'm thinking about is his lips.

Lexi West
I am thrilled with the bag!!!
I'm gonna enjoy kicking the shit out of it!

Ayden Mitchell
That's my girl!

Why do I think I can resist him? And why am I trying to? Ugh!

Frustrated, I decide to take it out on the bag, which is what I spend the next hour doing. It helps to get out my pent-up anger and pass the time and not think about the fact I'm alone and lonely. That feeling doesn't last.

As if someone has walked over my grave, my skin chills, and a ripple of warning runs up my spine. Someone is behind me. I know it as much as I know Ayden will never give up trying to win my heart. The same heart that races as I continue punching the bag, not wanting to let whoever it is know that I'm aware of their presence.

All my instincts are screaming at me to run, but since I'm fairly certain it must be Mike behind me, I don't want to run because I'm going to kill him! He needs to pay! He needs to be gone forever. It's the only way I know I'll ever be able to walk down the street and not need to look over my shoulder.

As soon as I feel the slightest shift in the air behind me, I spin around, throwing my fist out. A firm hand catches my gloved fist mid-air, and I come face to face with Muz.

"Is that any way to greet a visitor?" Muz drawls past the unlit cigarette hanging out of his mouth.

Gasping, shocked to see him here, and disappointed that it wasn't Mike because I'm ready to get that shit over with, I rip my hand out of his grip.

"What the fuck are you doing here?"

"Lexi, Lexi, Lexi. Such a little firecracker, aren't you?" Muz is wearing a blue cap which makes him seem less menacing, but his dark eyes still hold evil intent.

"You need to leave!" I hiss, standing as tall as my 5'5" height will allow me.

Muz grins, reaching into his pocket and pulling out a lighter to ignite the cancer stick sitting between his lips. Taking a deep drag, he blows the smoke to the side before speaking again, "Pretty girl. I've come a long way to visit you. You really need to work on your people skills."

"What the fuck do you want?" I still haven't moved. I don't want him to see an ounce of fear from me, even though I'm scared shitless right now.

"Where's lover boy?"

"Busy. Now fuck off!"

Muz chuckles before shooting me a smile that's nowhere near nice and then lifts his shirt so I can see the gun tucked into the front of his black jeans.

He did the same move when Ayden and I ran into him in Melbourne a few weeks ago.

"I'll ask again. Where's Aydo?" His raspy voice sounds less impressed this time.

I shouldn't poke the bear, but I do because I'm sick of these arseholes trying to control me with violence and threats. I can play that game too!

"And I'll tell you again, he's busy. Now fuck off!"

Muz moves fast, tugging the gun out and aiming it at my head. My heart just about leaps through my chest as I look down the barrel of what looks like the same gun he pulled on Ayden and me last time. Then... I lose my mind.

With heavy breathing, a heart that's ready to burst, and legs that shake ever so slightly, I take a step forward so the barrel of the gun presses against my forehead.

"Do it!" I hiss through my teeth.

"Pretty girl, what are you doing?" His dark bushy brows draw together in confusion.

"I'm making this easy for you. Pull the fucking trigger and put everyone out of their misery already."

My words make him flinch before he frowns again. He takes a step back but doesn't drop the gun, so I step forward, pushing my head against the barrel again.

"What the fuck is wrong with you?" He growls and steps back again.

"What's my problem?" I ask, anger consuming me. "What's my fucking problem?" I scream, stepping forward into the barrel again. "You are my fucking problem! People like you are! I'm fucking sick of arseholes like you who think it's okay to control people with violence, especially women! Fuck you Muz! Fucking pull the trigger or fuck off!"

Muz is static. Not moving, face blank in shock. Then he lowers his arm and the gun and drops his head back in laughter.

"Aydo's a lucky son of a bitch to have snagged you. I never thought I'd say this, but I'm jealous as fuck."

My shoulders slump, and I sigh. "Muz, I'm serious. Ayden's busy. You need to leave." Turning my back on him then, I step back to the bag and start my punching combination.

Movement out of the corner of my eye drags my attention away from the bag, and I watch Muz sink down onto the battered couch along the side wall.

"What are you doing?"

"Sitting. Waiting." Muz says simply, "You need to widen your stance. It will give you better balance and control."

My brows shoot up. "You're giving me boxing advice?"

"Use it. Don't use it. What do I care?" Muz says, his voice slurring slightly with tiredness. His olive skin seems paler than the last time I saw him, and the dark shadows under his eyes indicate that he's either not well or hasn't slept in a while. I can sympathise with the latter.

"Did I say you could sit there?" I snap, and he grins up at me from the couch as he lays back in the corner, looking like a lazy king on his throne.

"I don't need your permission, pretty girl."

I throw my hands up in frustration. "How about you tell me why you want to see Ayden, and I'll pass the message on? I'm sure he has your number or something."

"Nope. I'll wait. Where is he? Work or school?"

"None of your damn business." I throw him a dagger that doesn't bother him in the slightest.

"That's where you're wrong. Aydo is my business."

"Care to explain?" I ask, wanting to know more. I can't for the life of me figure out why he's here in Fox Pines.

"Not really." He yawns. "Why aren't you scared of me?"

His question takes me by surprise. The fact that he doesn't think I'm scared of him means my acting skills have improved tenfold. Maybe I have a future as an actress.

"The real question is, why aren't you scared of me?" I ask.

A deep gravelly belly laugh rips from Muz, his hand slapping over his tummy like the act causes him pain. Shit, maybe he's injured.

"You're fucking hilarious, you know that?" Muz chuckles. "I can see through it, though. You're deflecting. You're very good at it."

I shrug. "It's a skill that can't be taught."

That makes him laugh again. I'm on a roll here. Maybe I should be a comedian instead of an actress?

"Tell me, Lexi, why aren't you at school?"

I shrug, "They couldn't handle me, I guess."

He laughs again. Yep. Comedian it is.

"You drop out?"

"No! Just taking some time off." It's a half-truth, right?

"Really? By choice?" He looks smug, his grin revealing a missing tooth in the upper left side of his mouth. That's new.

"Nope." I start hitting the bag again. Muz is obviously going to stay even if I don't want him to.

"Damn girl, you get suspended or something?"

"Or something." My vagueness makes him chuckle.

"You really are a surprise, Lexi. Aydo's a lucky guy to have you."

"He doesn't," I say the words before I can consider the consequences.

"Trouble in paradise? What happened?"

"You happened!" I snap and grab at my gloves, trying to rip them off.

"Me? What did I do?"

"Really? What did you do?" I growl, finally freeing one hand and tossing the glove at his head. He dodges it, smiling. "You forced Ayden to snort that shit. He was fucking clean, and you destroyed him!" I'm yelling now, my temper at the surface, ready to kill.

"I gave him options, pretty girl. Not my fault he chose badly."

My other glove meets his head this time, and it gives me a brief moment of satisfaction at the smacking noise it makes. He's up and in my face so fast I barely see him move. Instinctively, I throw a punch, landing it on the side of his slimy face before he locks my wrists in his grip and pulls me flush against him.

"Your sassiness is making me hard. If you don't want to get fucked, you might want to calm the fuck down!" His voice is low and menacing, reminding me of Mike.

"Get your hands off her!" Muz loosens his grip when he hears Ayden's voice, but he doesn't let go. He turns his smirk towards Ayden, who is standing in the driveway with the guys and Rhys all flanking him.

"Finally, I've been waiting for you, Aydo. Me and your little piece of arse have just been catching up. Oh, wait." Muz chuckles, "Not your little piece of arse anymore, is she?"

"I'm here, so let her go." Ayden steps forward, and my pack, including Rhys, follow suit.

"Take a step closer, and I'll put my gun to her head," Muz growls.

Ayden's eyes widen, and he stops moving. So do the others.

"Jesus Christ!" I spin, the action causing the grip Muz has on me to break. "Stop wasting everyone's time and cut to the chase." He falters a little when I push him away from me.

"Lexi, be careful," Jared growls.

"It's fine Jar. This idiot isn't going to shoot me." I turn back to Muz, "Are you?"

He grins. "Nah. Not today, anyway." Then he shoots me a wink.

Everyone but Ayden looks confused. He grins, too, like he's in on our secret.

"She's been giving you a hard time, hey?" Ayden asks Muz.

"Nothing I couldn't handle. Sure is feisty, isn't she?"

They both chuckle. What the?

"Are you two done?" I snap, and Ayden turns serious again.

I'm standing against the workbench between Ayden and Muz. I will not cower behind my friends. No. No way. If something goes down, I'm stepping in front of them!

"Why are you here?" Ayden asks.

"You and I need to have a little chat. Turns out your dad somehow influenced Ringo to cut me off. I need you to get your dad to reverse that, or someone is going to pay."

"Cut you off how? Like out of the family?" Ayden asks, confused. Everyone stands behind him, quiet and curious.

"More like *cut* me out of the business," Muz explains, his lips curling as he says the words.

"But Ringo isn't in your business," Ayden states, his blue eyes darting to me every now and then, checking to see if I'm okay.

"No, he isn't, but the motherfucker has connections, and he got them to cut me off." Muz takes out his smoke packet and pulls out another cigarette, lighting it and inhaling deep.

"How did my dad get Ringo to do that?" Ayden looks calm right now, but the hunched form of his shoulders tells me he's anything but.

"Fucked if I know. Probably threatened to go to the police again. It doesn't matter how he did it. I just need you to get him to undo it."

"My dad won't do that." Ayden frowns, speaking the truth.

"Well, then. I'm going to be your little bitch's shadow until it's done. The longer you keep me waiting, the closer I'm going to get." The threat Muz delivers is real.

"The fuck you will!" Ayden hisses, launching himself towards Muz, but skids to a stop when I step between them.

"Move, Lexi!" Ayden growls, his face turning red in anger. So naturally, I don't, and I cross my arms over my chest, raising my blonde brow in challenge.

"Really? You're going to protect him? He put a fucking gun to your head." Ayden hisses, his pretty face turning red.

"He what?" Rhys speaks up for the first time, anger turning her gaze dark.

"Rhys, it's fine. He's too much of a pussy to pull the trigger." I step aside and turn to Muz again. "Isn't that right?"

Muz chuckles, shaking his head as he slips his gun back into the band of his jeans.

"Tick-tock Aydo. Time's ticking!" And with that final word, he walks away.

Everyone else is silent. Stunned.

I, however, slip my gloves back on and start pounding away at the bag.

Twenty-Four

Apparently, tonight is 'let's all gather together and do our homework at Marcus' house' night. I'd kind of thought the guys would back off now that I'm safe with my temporary living arrangements. As usual, I'm wrong.

Ayden's mum and Marcus' parents aren't due home until after 6 tonight, so Rhys and Marcus disappear upstairs as soon as we come in from the garage. Ten guesses as to what they are doing. It's only 4pm, so they have plenty of time to "study". Meanwhile, the rest of us cram into the living area to do homework no one cares about. Since the teachers have been emailing me work, I have plenty to do as well. It's been hard to concentrate, though. Every time I look up, my eyes meet Ayden's. I don't think he's getting any work done either.

I'm about to cut my study session short when Ayden stands up from the couch and takes the three steps across the small space to where I'm sitting cross-legged on the floor. My eyes follow his every movement as he shifts my books aside and sits where they were, bringing him extremely close.

He mimics the way I'm sitting and holds out his phone with his earphones attached. One of my blonde brows shoots up, but he doesn't speak, just nudges them in my hands.

Sitting face to face like this with him is intimate. He is so close, with only centimetres between our knees. I have no option but to look into his piercing blue eyes, making my face instantly heat. He notices it too. I can tell he's trying to hide the grin that wants to show itself.

I glance over Ayden's shoulder to see that Jared is the only one paying us any attention. His eyes are squinted a little, not really a glare but close to it. Shaun and Simon are too busy looking at something on their phones, and Garrett looks deep in thought with his brow furrowing, his teeth biting down on the top of his pen.

Returning my attention back to those blue eyes that lure me in, Ayden takes an earbud in each hand, brushes back my hair from my ear and inserts a bud before repeating it on the other side. His scent wraps around me as he leans in, and I fight the moan that wants to escape. My eyes dart past Ayden again to see that all the guys are watching this time.

When Ayden pulls back, I think he's going to play me something on his phone, but he doesn't. Reaching into his hoodie pocket, he pulls out some card-sized pieces of paper. I glance back to his eyes in question, but he gives nothing away. He's nervous, though. I can tell by the edge of fear in his eyes and the slight tremble of his hand.

Then he holds up a piece of paper.

> *I'LL NEVER FORGIVE MYSELF FOR THE WAY I TREATED YOU THAT DAY IN MELBOURNE.*

My heart instantly aches. Not for me, but for him. Even though I haven't said the words, I know deep in my heart that I forgive him. I should probably tell him.

He puts the card down between us on the floor and then reveals another.

I'M NOT PERFECT.
I STILL CARRY DEMONS.
I STILL HAVE MEMORIES THAT I WISH I DIDN'T REMEMBER.
BUT...

Shit, But? But what? He places that card down on top of the first and then reveals another.

I WILL NEVER LET MYSELF FORGET THAT DAY.
THE LOOK ON YOUR BEAUTIFUL FACE.
THE HURT IN THOSE SWEET INNOCENT EYES.

"Ayden." I try to speak, but he quickly silences me by placing a finger over my lips.

For a moment, his eyes lock onto my lips where his finger rests, longing written all over his face.

Oh my god. I'm going to cave. Shit!

No, Lexi, don't give in. He deserves better!

Pulling his hand away, he returns his attention to the cards, placing the one in his hand down and pulling out another to show me.

I DON'T DESERVE YOU LEXI.
ESPECIALLY AFTER WHAT I DID.
BUT THE PROBLEM IS...

He's killing me. It's torture the way he's dragging this out. But I also don't want him to stop. Again, he places that card down and reveals another.

I NEED YOU!

"Ayden."

Again, he stops me from speaking, this time by shaking his head.

He repeats the steps, putting the card down and holding up a new one.

LISTEN TO THE LYRICS OF THIS SONG.
IT'S NOT COMPLETELY ACCURATE.
BUT SOME OF THE LYRICS RING TRUE.

Ayden leans forward, unlocks his phone, and presses play.

I instantly recognise the song. It's called 'Prove how I love you' by Archer 9.

I do as Ayden asks and focus on the lyrics. As the words are sung, he holds up more cards when he wants me to pay attention to certain lyrics.

YOU ARE THE CURE FOR MY EMPTY SOUL
A POTENT DRUG DRAGGING ME FROM THE DARK HOLE

He puts that card down and holds up another in sync with the lyrics.

I NEVER WANTED TO HURT YOU THAT WAY
I JUST WANTED TO KEEP YOU AT BAY
UNTIL I COULD FIX THE MESS IN MY HEAD
I'M SORRY FOR THE HURTFUL THINGS I SAID
BABY, PLEASE
LET ME PROVE HOW I LOVE YOU

Keeping that same card in his hand, he holds it up each time the chorus plays.

Then he holds up a new one.

KNOWING THAT YOU HAVE SEEN
THE FUCKED UP PART OF ME THAT IS MEAN
BRINGS ME CRASHING TO MY KNEES
BABY FORGIVE ME, PLEASE
TAKE ME BACK INTO YOUR EMBRACE
PULL ME OUT OF MY DARK PLACE
BABY, PLEASE
LET ME PROVE HOW I LOVE YOU

Then he holds up the chorus card again when it returns to the chorus.

By the end of the song, I am fighting to hold myself together, and then he holds up one last card after the music stops.

IT'S TRUE.
YOU ARE MY DRUG LEXI.
I NEED YOU MORE THAN I NEED AIR.
YOU ARE MY GIRL.
AND I FUCKING CRAVE YOU SO MUCH IT CONSUMES ME.
PLEASE TAKE ME BACK.
PLEASE REMOVE THE LINE.
PLEASE LET ME BE MORE THAN YOUR FRIEND.

A tear slips free, and Ayden leans in to remove the earbuds from my ears. The room is silent, but I know we still have company. I can feel their eyes on us, watching our exchange. I can't handle the eyes. I can't handle being so close to Ayden and not being able to touch him. I stand abruptly and race out of the room as tears fall freely. Before I even realise what I'm doing, I'm out the back door and in the garage clutching onto the punching bag that hangs from the ceiling. The gift Ayden surprised me with this morning.

"Lex." Ayden's pleading voice comes from right behind me. I hadn't even heard him follow.

His warm hand lands on my shoulder, turning me to him.

"Talk to me." His eyes are begging, and fuck me, I want to give in. But I can't, so I shake my head. "Help me understand why you won't take me back." His beg nearly undoes me.

"You deserve better than me, Ayden. You deserve to heal and move on and find someone whole and not ruined by vile acts. You deserve to be with someone that can be happy."

"You see, this is the problem. You think you're not good enough for me, but the thing is, Lex, I think I'm not good enough for you. We both have pasts. Both carry baggage and bad memories.

But don't speak of happiness as if you will never be happy. We were happy until I fucked it up. You were happy, despite the horrible things that happened. You had times of happiness with me. We can have happiness together if we stop pushing each other away."

I want to believe his words. I want to have what he's offering. But it would be wrong of me to drag him down like that, so I shake my head.

Taking hold of each of my shoulders, Ayden rubs his hands up and down my arms. It's like he's trying to give me comfort, but also like his need to touch me is giving him comfort. I should push him off, but I can't bring myself to do it.

"What if we are stronger together, Lex?"

"What if we're not?" I whisper, looking up at him through the veil of my dark lashes.

"There's only one way to find out. Please remove the line." He begs, his hands lifting to cup either side of my head near my ears.

I shake my head and pull away from him, needing space. I can't think clearly when he's close like this. I spin towards the door, but Ayden grabs my upper arm and turns me back to him, anger reddening his face.

"You said I took your decision away from you when I decided to have the drugs and not allow you to have any. How is this any different, Lexi? I fucking want you, and I know you want me too, but you are making the decision for both of us. For what? A what if? Fuck that! What if we get our happily ever after together?" He lets go of my arm, his hands fisting in frustration in his dark hair. "Be honest with me, dammit! Do you care about me?"

"Fuck it, Ayden! Yes, I fucking do, okay! I feel like I can't breathe without you, and it fucking hurts!"

His eyes darkening is the only warning I get before Ayden's mouth crashes into mine. Lifting me in his arms, my legs wrap around him, clamping tight as a small whimper escapes me. My back slams into a wall and I revel in the sting it brings as my hands fist in Ayden's hair, keeping him in place. Our tongues clash as our desperation takes over, and our moans fill the room the moment our pelvises grind against each other.

I feel like crying because fuck I have missed him so much. To have his touch that I have ached for, his lips that I have craved to taste again, and his scent wrap around me like a safety blanket feels like too much, yet not enough. I know now that if he is ever taken away from me again, I will surely die from the pain.

I switch my thoughts off before I spiral and let myself feel every little thing, from the way one of his hands kneads my arse cheek to the other, mimicking it at my breast. The way he has me trapped between his firm body and the garage wall means I can hardly move, but I don't need to; Ayden has things covered.

His hand leaves my breast and travels down between our bodies to the place I crave his touch the most. The first brush of his hand nearly sends me over the edge.

"Tell me this is okay, Lex." Ayden's breathless voice breaks the silence, and I nod.

"Yes. Fuck yes."

Ayden chuckles against my mouth, taking a moment to taste my lips again before speaking. "This is going to be quick, baby. I'll do slow to you after, but right now, I need to fuck you here against this wall."

"Yes." I cry out when his hand slips under the band of my trackies. I'm desperate for him. The need to have him impossibly close is all-consuming and his not so gentle words about fucking me against the wall sends a pool of moisture between my legs.

Warm fingers slip between my folds and slide inside, feeding the need that's building inside me.

I lose my connection with his lips as I throw my head back, so close to going over the edge as he fills me with two fingers. My hips surge forward, seeking more, riding his hand and fingers as they work their magic until an intense orgasm rips from me.

I'm yelling. Or screaming. I can't be sure, and I don't care. This feels too good. Ayden feels too good.

"Fuck, you're hot." Ayden hisses, drawing my attention as he struggles with the tie on his sweatpants before he finally gets them undone and releases his hard length.

Before I get the chance to admire it, he drops my feet to the ground, pulls my pants free of my body and then lifts me back into the same position before he slams into me. Deep. I scream and pulse around his cock while he grunts, burying his face into my neck.

"Fuck you feel good." His words have no restraint, not like the last time we were together, and I love it. I think I like this version of him better.

He thrusts his hips, sliding in and out of me hard and fast as his pleasure builds. Warm needy fingers return to my breast, but when he finds my t-shirt covering it, he growls and reefs it up and over my head in one smooth motion, all while continuing his thrusts. He doesn't bother trying to unclasp my bra; instead, he pulls the fabric of the cup down, freeing my aching flesh.

I cry out again when his lips cover my nipple, his tongue swirling over the peak before his teeth lightly graze it. That's all it takes to send me over the edge again, and my release clamps down on him sending him over too.

Our heavy breathing is all that can be heard in the silence of the garage. We stay in the same position for a few minutes. Me wedged between Ayden and the wall, legs wrapped around him while he stays seated inside me.

It's only when I feel something warm and wet between my legs that I realise we didn't use protection. *Shit!*

"Ah- Ayden?"

"Yes, beautiful?" His husky voice nearly makes me forget about our dilemma.

"We kind of forgot to use protection."

Ayden pulls back, dark brows furrow as he realises his mistake.

"Oh, fuck Lex. I'm so sorry. Shit. I didn't even think." He looks so upset. I shouldn't laugh, but I do.

"It's okay. I've only ever been with you, so I'm clean, but my pill taking has been screwed up over the last month."

Ayden scans my face, his ocean eyes holding so much emotion. He lifts a hand and brushes back my wayward hair. I bet it resembles a bird's nest right now. I must look ridiculous.

"We'll go get the morning-after pill. I really am sorry Lex. I didn't do that on purpose. I'm clean too. It's only been you. No one else for a long time, and I've been tested. I can get tested again if you like?"

I smile. "Stop apologising. It's fine, I believe you."

Ayden returns my smile. "So, just to be clear. This is you taking me back, right?"

I laugh. "No way! That was just sex. I was horny."

Ayden's mouth opens in surprise, and then he grips my bare arse and squeezes. "You little minx. You're going to pay for that comment." Ayden slaps my bare arse then, and I can't help it... I fucking grind against him.

"Well, would you look at that? Someone likes to be spanked." Ayden's blue eyes are filled with a combination of lust and amusement.

"What? No, I don't." I disagree, but he slaps my arse again, and this time I moan at the same time as my hips thrust forward, searching for more.

"Oh yes, you do! This is going to be fun trying out new things to see what you like. I'm going to make you come so many times that you're going to pass out." He slaps me again, and I arch my back, throwing my head back. "Can you feel me inside you, Lex? You've made me hard again." Then he slaps my arse and bites my neck at the same time. I nearly come. Again!

"I need." I manage to breathe out, not entirely sure how to finish that sentence.

"I know what you need, beautiful. Let me take you to my bed and give you what you need."

"Yes." I nod right before he slaps and bites in unison. I start to ride his cock while he struggles to walk, carrying me to the staircase and up the stairs to his room. By the time we are inside the door of his loft, he's unable to make it any further, so overcome with need that my back meets the floor, and he fucks me hard until we are both screaming again.

Twenty-Five

After making me scream on his loft floor, Ayden finally gets me to his bed, where he sends me over the edge two more times before Rhys lets herself in. Like a creeper, she stares at us from the opening of the curtain divider with mischief written all over her face. Then her dark lips spread into a grin before she says, "Thoroughly fucked Lexi looks hot!" Then she skips out of the loft, calling out that she'll message me later to find out if Ayden has a pretty cock. When Ayden asks me what she means, I shake my head and tell him not to question the things that come out of Rhys' mouth.

Returning inside the house not long after Rhys departs, we find that Shaun, Garrett and Jared have already left as well, but Simon is still doing homework with Marcus in the living room. I tried my best to tame my hair and splash cold water on my face to take away the flush on my cheeks before we came inside. I must have failed, though. It was as if I was walking around with a flashing sign above my head saying, *'Lexi had sex... multiple times!'* because Marcus frowns when he sees me, and Simon raises his brows before nodding, a knowing grin tugging at his mouth.

It doesn't take me long to decide to do a runner after that, and I leave Ayden with the boys while I hide in my room until Barb arrives home a little after 6 pm with chicken and chips for dinner. Ayden deliberately sits beside me at the dinner table and holds my hand underneath it every chance he gets. Marcus notices but doesn't frown at us again, so hopefully, things between him and me will be okay. He has been getting busy with Rhys after all.

Once the day finally comes to an end, I feel the usual dread of going back up to that lilac bedroom and attempting to get some sleep. Besides my mind reeling from Muz's visit earlier and how easily I fell back into Ayden's arms, I know nightmares are hovering in the shadows, waiting to plague me. I'm so exhausted yet too scared to go to sleep, but then my door creaks open just after 1am, and my ocean eyed boy sneaks in, slipping under the covers and snuggles up to me.

Then, as if he willed it once again, my eyes close for a soundless night of sleep.

I don't know why I fought so hard to give in to my feelings for Ayden. Well, I do know, but I don't know why I thought I could fight it. The way we came together in the garage is unlike anything else I have ever experienced. No one else has the magnetic pull on me the way Ayden Mitchell does. Some of the lyrics from the Archer 9 song he had me listen to, meant the same for me as they did for him. He is the cure for my empty soul. He is the potent drug that drags me from the dark hole. Even now, while he is at school, just thinking about him and the things he did to my body has me walking in the clouds like I'm high.

My Tuesday morning may be quiet and lonely when everyone is at school and work, but I could honestly sit and stare at a blank wall all day, just thinking about what Ayden and I shared while I anticipate the moment he gets home from school.

The ringing of my phone pulls me out of my Ayden trance, breaking the silence in the kitchen where I've been sitting for over an hour. When I look at the screen, I answer it without hesitation.

"Hi, Val."

"Lexi." My name is whispered, "There's someone at your house."

"What? Who?" I bolt up from the barstool, taking the stairs two at a time to get my shoes from up in my room.

"I don't know, but they must have a key or something because they pulled into the garage and closed the door," Valarie whispers down the line again.

"Val. Why are you whispering?"

"Ah- I don't know. It just seems like I should because I'm a spy."

I laugh, "Okay, Val. So, a car pulled into my garage and closed the door. Did you see who was driving the car?" That's probably a stupid question.

"No." She whispers again. "But the car was silver, if that helps?"

"Silver." I repeat, "My dad's car is silver."

"That would make sense then because your dad would be able to get into the garage, right?" Val says, her voice a little louder this time.

"Yes, he would. Thanks for calling me Val. I'll take it from here."

"Okay, bye." Val hangs up before I can say bye too. She's a weird kid, but I adore her.

Sliding my sneakers on, I grab a hoodie out of the drawer and take off for my house. I know deep down that this is a bad idea given what my dad did to me, but I'm sick of fearing him, and he needs to learn that I will not be pushed around anymore.

Like I said, probably a bad idea.

As I take the back streets, I consider calling the police first but decide against it. I need answers from him, and if the cops fail to do their job, then I'll never get them. Cutting through a park and a laneway, I have the odd feeling that I'm being followed as I enter my street from the opposite end. Val's house comes into view first, and I see her jet-black hair in the window as she spies on the street below. She's never at school. I've never asked her why. Maybe she gets home-schooled?

Spotting me, her dark eyes widen, and a big toothy grin spreads over her face as she waves. Grinning back, I wave too and then stop by the fence that divides our houses. My house looks normal. No blinds or curtains are open, so I can't see inside, but I can hear noise coming from inside the house.

Nerves stop me from moving forward. I'd be an idiot to go inside without letting someone know. I think about sending Ayden a message, but he will freak and ditch school. I don't want him to do that. He needs to focus on passing year eleven.

Taking my phone out, I hit Officer Zimora's contact and wait as it rings out before going to voicemail. It's not ideal, but I leave him a message and then suck in air as if it will give me extra courage before I walk up my front path.

Sweat pops out over the back of my neck, reminding me that I am shit scared as I walk. I don't stop, though. Either my dad is inside, or Mike is. If they are together, then this probably won't end well for me, but I still don't stop. The heroine from Uppercut Princess wouldn't back down. So, neither will I.

My hand trembles as I turn the handle and push the door open. I'm instantly met with mess strewn down the hall and noise coming from the back of the house. At first glance, you would think my house was being robbed, but I see my dad's wallet and keys on the hall table and know that he's here.

"Dad?" I call from the door, and the noise from the kitchen area stops. Heavy feet move across the tiled floor right before my dad steps into view at the end of the hall.

I don't know what I expected. Maybe a look of remorse or even relief to see that I'm okay, but instead, my dad glares at me, looking annoyed that I interrupted him.

"Alexis. What are you doing here?" Hearing his voice in person is conflicting. Part of me has missed him, so it's nice to hear. The other part of me, the smarter part, knows the words that are laced with distaste come from the monster who left me at the mercy of his sick and twisted son.

"I don't have school today." I lie.

He frowns, studying me for a moment from the other end of the hall.

"Right. Well, either help me or stay out of my way." He spins on his heel and disappears into the kitchen.

Drawers open and close, cupboard doors slam shut, and the sound of a stack of papers being tossed draws my attention. Slowly I step further into the house, leaving the front door open behind me, and carefully step over discarded papers scattered down the hallway.

Entering the back part of the house, I watch my dad frantically search through every cupboard, every drawer, every shelf, looking for something.

He sees me looking and frowns. "Where is it?"

"Where's what?" I ask, confused as hell. I feel my phone vibrate in my pocket but ignore the incoming call.

"The file Alexis!" He's angry. Barely holding it together if the fact that his face is nearly purple is any indication.

The file? Mum spoke about a file over the phone a couple of weeks ago. She wasn't making sense.

She'd been concerned that Mike had already found it and said something about the money still being in the accounts, so he probably didn't have the file. It was confusing as hell, and she made no sense. But now, my dad is here, tossing the house looking for a file. What fucking file?

"What file dad?" I ask, which just fuels his anger. Heavy steps pound toward me, and I watch my dad's fury contort his face and take over his entire body.

"Tell me where it is, Alexis!" His deep voice booms, bouncing off the walls as he stands before me with his fist raised.

With our close proximity, I can see that his blue eyes are darker than usual, and his blonde hair is a frazzled mess. This is a very different Maxwell West to the one I thought I knew. I glare at his raised fist and curl my lip, stepping towards him instead of away.

"I don't know what file you are talking about. What makes you think I know where it is?" My voice is calm, low, but filled with anger. There's a big chance my dad is going to strike me, just like his son did only weeks ago. But I will not cower anymore. I jut my chin up and focus on controlling my breathing. I don't want him to see even the slightest bit of fear in me.

My pocket vibrates with another incoming call. It could be Officer Zimora returning my call. I probably need to answer it, but now isn't the right moment. Not when my dad is so close. I can't risk him getting my phone again. If he does, I'll lose my ability to call for help.

"Of course, you know where it is." My dad spits, "Your mother would have made sure of that. Now, stop playing games and tell me where it is!" As the last words leave my dad's mouth, he grabs my upper arm, much the same way he did the night I sprung him with his mistress in the restaurant. His hold is tight and biting, which causes me to cry out in pain.

"I suggest you take your hands off her!"

The deep voice comes from behind me, surprising my dad so much that he instantly drops his hold on me and steps back. His blue eyes widen, focused over my shoulder.

I'm just as shocked to hear that voice, but I don't let it show, and I don't turn around. Right now, it's better if my dad thinks the thugged up gang member behind me is on my side. Better the devil you know and all that.

"Who are you?" My dad growls, glancing at me before returning his confused gaze to Muz.

"I'm your worst fucking nightmare if you lay hands on Lexi like that again." His voice is calm but every bit as menacing as his words.

"Uh- yeah, okay. Fine, I'll keep my hands to myself. No need for the gun."

My brows shoot up at my dad's words, and I dart my head around to see that Muz has his gun trained on my dad.

"Really? A gun?" I ask, and he smiles at me like he's proud. *Idiot!*

"It gets results."

He's not wrong. I shake my head and turn back to my dad.

"Look, dad. I don't know what file you are talking about. Mum has said nothing to me. Why don't you tell me more about the file so I can help you find it?" Of course, if I knew where it was or came across it, I wouldn't let him get his hands on it. It must be pretty serious if he's so desperate to get it back.

"God damn it!" Dad hisses and almost rips his hair from his scalp, clutching it tightly at both sides above his reddened ears.

"How about you answer your daughter, daddy dearest?" Muz growls, and I roll my eyes. Why is he even here? I thought we'd managed to get rid of him yesterday, but I guess I was wrong.

Apparently, he was serious when he said he will be my shadow until Ayden speaks to his dad to try and get Ringo back on his side.

"Lexi, is everything okay?"

The innocent tone of Valarie's voice meets us all, and I spin quickly, putting my hand on top of Muz's, pushing down to lower it and the gun, as I look over his shoulder. Val is standing just outside the open front door, looking in on a scene that will make no sense to her. I'd like to keep it that way.

"It's all good Val. My friend and I are just chatting with my dad. I'll call you later, okay?"

"Friend, hey?" Muz whispers, a slight grin tugging at the corner of his mouth. He hasn't taken his eyes off my dad, all while my hand remains over his, keeping the gun pointed down toward the floor out of Val's view.

"That guy is your friend?" Val asks, scepticism filling her tone.

"A friend of sorts. It's okay Val. Head back home." The last thing I need is her getting hurt. I'd never be able to live with myself if something happened to her because of me.

"The little bitch better hurry up and go. I'm getting hard with you standing so close to me." Muz growls through his teeth, and I glare at him.

"Call her a bitch again and see what happens, arsehole." I quietly hiss so only he can hear.

"You've gone and done it now. I'm hard as a fucking rock. Wanna feel?"

I ignore Muz and return my gaze back to Val. She looks worried, her big dark eyes staying locked on me, searching for a sign that I'm lying. I mean, I am, in a way. Nothing about this situation is okay, but I can handle it. She doesn't need to be here for this.

I nod at her, "Really, Val. It's okay. I'll talk to you later."

She eyes me warily for another moment and then walks away, her small steps fading up the path.

"Did I say you could get that out?" Muz hisses, pushing me aside and raising the gun again. I spin to see my dad holding his phone in his palm, his fingers hovering over the screen.

"I need to make a call about the file." My dad offers, and Muz gives him a nod of approval.

"On speaker!" Muz adds, and my dad dials a number.

"Hello?" My mum's voice fills the room.

"What the fuck!" I frown. How did my dad just call my mum? He's not meant to know where she is, let alone have a direct line to her. I haven't even been able to talk to her.

"Ruth. No more fucking games. Tell me where the file is!" My dad booms at my mum, and in response, she laughs.

It's a foreign sound to hear my mum laugh. It's not just any laugh either. It's the kind of laugh that says *torturing you is too much fun*.

"Who's Ruth?" Muz whispers behind me.

"My mum," I answer before stepping closer to my dad. I can feel Muz follow close behind.

"Max. Honey. The answer is the same as every other time you have asked. I don't know where it is." My mum sounds good. Almost too good. Is it even her on the other end?

"Bullshit Ruth. Just tell me where it is, or I'll rip this fucking house apart." Spittle flies from my dad's mouth as he speaks, his face almost purple with anger.

"Go for it, honey. Tear that house to pieces all you want. You'll never find it."

"See, you do fucking know where it is! Tell me, or I'll be visiting your bed tonight to fucking squeeze the life out of you."

"The fuck you will!" I scream and storm towards my dad. His eyes widen, and he darts around the kitchen island before Muz snatches my hand and pulls me back.

"Let's see how this plays out, pretty girl," Muz whispers in my ear as my mum laughs through the speaker.

"A lot of good that will do, Max. Killing me will ensure you will never get your hands on the file! I'm afraid you will need me alive if you ever want to see it again."

What the fuck is in this file?

"Fine, Ruth. How about I finish what Mike started with Alexis? I'll be sure to call you so you can hear her take her last breath."

Muz releases me and storms around the island bench, taking my dad off guard and shoving the barrel of the gun against his temple. He whimpers.

It should scare me, right? That's my dad that Muz is holding a gun to. It takes me a moment to realise that my breathing has sped up, and my pulse is out of control. I'm not scared. I'm fucking furious. The words, *pull the trigger*, is on the tip of my tongue, but I hold them in because what the actual fuck, Lexi! Wanting people's heads blown off isn't me. Is it?

"Always such a drama queen Max. Unfortunately for you, if you kill Lexi, you have the same problem. You need her to access the file."

Ruth laughs down the line, none the wiser that her husband has a gun pressed against his head and that her daughter is letting it happen.

"When did you become such a bitch?" My dad hisses, tears springing to his eyes when Muz pushes harder against the gun, digging the barrel into his skin.

"Maybe when you started sticking your dick in all of your assistants." Venom drips from my mum's words. I've never heard her so strong.

"Better than your shrivelled up hole!" My dad gets those vile words out before Muz kicks his legs from under him, sending him to his knees. With a grunt, he rights himself, glaring up at Muz from the floor.

"You'll never find it, Max. It isn't even in the house, you moron." My mum's laugh cuts off when she ends the call, leaving my dad yelling in frustration at the top of his lungs.

He tosses his phone across the kitchen, and it smashes against the cupboard before falling into pieces to the floor.

Ragged breathing fills the room, coming from both my dad and me. His, in frustration from the conversation he just had with my mum. Mine, from the anger and fury that has been hovering near the surface since I left Melbourne. It wants to leap free and unleash on my dad.

Sirens sound in the distance gaining all of our attention. If they are on their way here, it means that either Officer Zimora heard my message or Val called the cops.

"I need to go." My dad leaps up from the floor before stilling when Muz shoves the gun in his face.

"What do you wanna do, pretty girl?" Muz asks, keeping his eyes locked on my dad.

If I make Muz hold him here, then he's going to get caught by the cops too. We live in Australia. Handguns are illegal unless you have a special licence to own one. He's a criminal, I know that, but he also protected me here today, despite acting like a dick.

"Let him go. The cops will catch up with him soon enough." I say, defeated and annoyed that he's going to get away again.

Muz nods, and the moment he lowers his gun, my dad runs out of the room. Moments later, I hear the garage door opening and his car start.

"You should go too," I tell Muz, looking around at the mess strewn about by my dad.

"You sure you don't want to turn me over to the cops?" He asks, and I turn to him.

"I mean, I can if you want?" I shrug, and he chuckles.

"Hard pass. See ya, pretty girl." Muz slips the gun back into the front of his jeans and walks towards the backdoor.

"Muz!" He stops when he hears my voice, turning back to me. "Thank you."

A big smile spreads across his face, reminding me he's not such a scary guy, especially when he's not holding a gun.

Twenty-Six

♥

I spend a couple of hours answering questions after the police arrive at my house. Val had called them, and Officer Zimora turned up a few minutes after the patrol car in plain clothes because it was his day off. Once again, they take the evidence they need, including my dad's smashed phone, and then Officer Zimora drills me for information about the file my dad had been looking for. I couldn't tell them much since I don't know what this file is, but like them, I sure want to know since it's sending my dad over the edge, and my mum is using it against him for his infidelities.

While I wait for the officers to finish up inside my house, I notice Val is missing from her usual perch at her window. Maybe she got in trouble for spying again. Who knows? I hope she is okay, though. I don't know what I'd do without that little raven-haired girl in my life.

After updating Andrea with what happened over the phone, Officer Zimora offers to drive me home, but instead of dropping me back at Marcus', I get him to drop me at Abbey's. It's probably a bad idea, but I have too many uncertainties in my life, and I need to start clearing them up. Abbey is one of those uncertainties. I don't understand why she has turned on me, but I'm determined to find out.

I sit on the sidewalk, enjoying the warmth the spring sun brings, scrolling through SnapChat, out the front of her house. I wait for about thirty minutes before she makes an appearance, and she doesn't see me there as she walks up the street with her head buried in her phone. I stand and wipe the grass off the back of my black leggings, watching her approach.

"Abbey."

My voice causes her to stop in her tracks, her eyes darting up from her phone to see me standing mere feet in front of her. She looks different. Tired. Dark shadows sit under her eyes, and weight loss has sunken her cheeks. Her sun-kissed skin isn't glowing as much as usual, and even her blonde braid seems dull.

Worry flits across her face briefly before it's covered up with impatience.

"What are you doing here?" She snaps like I'm the one who did her wrong.

"Why do you think I'm here, Abbey? I want to know why you have turned on me?"

Sighing, her shoulders drop, and she looks down to her feet. "You wouldn't understand."

"Try me," I say simply.

"I can't." Abbey shakes her head, glancing back up at me momentarily, her brown eyes not seeming as bright as usual.

"What did I do, Abbey? I've wracked my brain trying to think of what I did to you that would cause you to end our friendship."

"I can't talk about this." Abbey's voice wavers before she continues. "I'm sorry, but I have to go." She steps around me, walking briskly up her front lawn.

I turn and catch up.

"Why did you show Tasha the pictures I sent you? Why did you tell her my secrets? Why did you let her spread lies about me? Why did you stand by and watch her hit me when you know everything I've been through?"

Tears spring to Abbey's eyes as she stops walking and looks at me but glances away quickly. It was enough for me to see the pain behind her brown eyes.

"Look Lexi, I'm sorry, okay." Abbey declares, looking back at me. "I've made some bad decisions lately, and I can't take them back. There is no way of making up for what I've done. You should stay away from me. Now I need to go."

"Wait!" I grab Abbey's wrist, and she flinches in pain. It's not pain I've caused either; it's pain that's already there. Frowning, I let go, not wanting to hurt her. "What's wrong with your wrist?"

Abbey tries like hell to cover the pain she's feeling, but the thing is, I've known her since we wore fairy wings and silly tulle dresses to the park. She can't hide that from me.

"It's nothing. I have to go." She practically runs the few steps up to her front door before disappearing behind it.

I still have no idea what's going on, but just like things with my mum and dad, there is definitely more to Abbey's betrayal than what I thought. I know it deep in my heart. Yes, she betrayed me, but not to be one of Tasha's minions. She betrayed me for another reason, but for the life of me, I can't think what it could be.

My phone buzzes in my pocket, so I turn away from Abbey's house and answer it while I start walking.

"Where's my girl? Marcus had to duck home and grab his stuff for footy training and said you weren't there." Ayden's voice instantly calms me. I don't know how he does that, but I'm grateful.

"Ah- I'm walking back from Abbey's."

"Why were you at Abbey's?" Ayden asks, sounding confused.

"It was time we had a chat," I say, simply picking up my pace.

"And how did that go?"

"I still don't know why she's turned on me, but I do know that something more is going on." I look around as I walk, paranoia always present. Shit, why did I think walking alone is a good idea?

"Oh? Why do you think that?" Ayden asks. He sounds puffed, his breathing ragged.

"A few things she said, and a feeling I have." I say, "Ayden, what are you doing?"

"Jogging." He huffs.

"Why?"

"You look beautiful today Lex. The way those leggings hug your arse... mmm."

"What?" I squeak, realising he knows that I'm wearing my leggings. I didn't have them on this morning when he left for school, so how does he know? I look around frantically, thinking he must be somewhere that he can see me.

He chuckles down the line. "I can see that pretty pink blush from here."

Searching the area, my eyes catch his tall frame walking towards me on the other side of the street.

"Weren't you walking home?" I ask, shocked to see him as he crosses the street to get to me.

He shrugs and then bends over, his hands braced on his knees as he puffs. "I was." Puff. Puff. "But then you said." Puff. Puff. "That you were walking." Puff. Puff. "From Abbey's." He stands taller then, gaining his breath. "So, I turned around and ran here instead of going home. I was just down the road."

I frown. "But how'd you know where Abbey lives?" If it were Jared or Marcus, then that would be understandable because we grew up together, but Ayden hasn't been to Abbey's before.

"SnapMaps," Ayden says. I look at my phone and realise that at some point, Ayden must have ended our call.

"SnapMaps?" I ask. "I don't use the map feature on SnapChat."

"Ah, yeah. It was Jared's idea to turn it on so we could find you if something happened."

"What? Like trying to hide from you guys at school, or if I run off to a party with Rhys?" I shove my hands on my hips, not impressed.

"Hey, he only turned it on after the party. But yes, we all want to keep you safe."

I frown, and he laughs before reaching out to my hip and pulling me to him.

"I missed you." He says before leaning in to capture my lips in a searing kiss.

My arms know what they want, and they wrap around his neck as he draws me closer, tasting me with his tongue.

"I need to get you home where I can show you how much I missed you today." Ayden draws back, his blue eyes fllttlng from my lips to my eyes.

"I like that idea."

We walk quickly, both of us needing to get behind closed doors to continue that kiss. I use the time to tell Ayden about what happened at my house. It didn't go well. He's pissed off big time because I didn't call him and didn't let him know what went down until now. He's also pissed because Muz showed up, even though he helped me.

When we arrive back, he doesn't even ask me if I want to go up to his loft; he just decides for me and drags me up there, slamming the door behind us. I'm not saying I don't want to go up to his loft because hell yes, I do, but playing hard to get is kind of fun because it seems to piss him off more. Something I realise I like doing.

I know, I know, I'm messed up!

"Get your clothes off!" His words are demanding, and for a brief moment, I panic. Mike's face flashes through my mind from when he said similar demanding words to me.

"Oh fuck. Lexi, I'm so sorry." Ayden's face contorts from the *sexy dominant annoyed at his girlfriend* look, to shame and sorrow. He saw the panic on my face. I obviously didn't hide it in time. He steps towards me, but I step back. Determination fuelling me. I need to get past this shit.

"Say it again," I demand, and he frowns.

"What?"

"Say the words to me again," I demand.

"No. Lexi I'm sorry I…"

"Fuck it, Ayden. Say the words to me again, dammit!" Angry heat pools behind my eyes.

"Why?" He whispers, confusion in his gaze.

"Make new memories. Isn't that what you said up in my bedroom the other night?" When he nods, I continue, "Make new memories with me,

Ayden. Help me replace the old ones with ones I want. Say. It. Again."

Understanding dawns in his blue eyes, and he parts those kissable lips.

"Get your clothes off."

I raise an unimpressed brow at him, "Really? That's all you got? I think I'll pass."

He chuckles, "You sassy minx. Get your clothes off now!"

A shiver runs down my spine at his demanding tone. Yes, I like this side of him. "Again."

"Lex, I won't say it again. Get your fucking clothes off!"

That does the trick. Heat pools between my legs and need fills me. Biting my lip, I lift my t-shirt up over my head and drop it to the floor. The heat in Ayden's eyes is so addictive, I couldn't stop now if I tried.

Hooking my fingers in the waistband, I drag my leggings down slowly and watch his eyes as they follow my hands until I step out of the fabric.

"You're mine." He growls the words, and I raise a brow.

"Really?"

"Yes."

"What if I don't want to be yours?" I tease, making him growl again.

"You can fight it all you want. You're mine, and that's all there is to it." He licks his lips. "Bra off."

I do as he asks, reaching back to unclasp my bra, trying to shake off Mike's voice when he demanded the same thing. Again, my face must show my vulnerability, and when Ayden's face drops, I shake my head at him, throwing him a glare and letting my bra fall to the floor.

"Lex. Maybe this isn't a good idea."

"Let me ask you something," I say, standing as tall as I can, pushing out my chest and drawing his attention to my pebbled nipples. "Do you like being dominant like this? Is this part of you?"

"It doesn't have to be." He answers as his eyes watch my hand lift to my breast, and my fingers graze over my nipples.

"That's not what I asked."

He sighs. "Yes, I like it. Yes, it's part of me." He answers honestly.

"Then stop holding back. I like this part of you, Ayden. I may freak, I may even get upset, but I will tell you to stop if I need you to. If I don't say stop, then don't. I know it sounds messed up but help me work through this shit so I can be... normal."

Ayden's chest rises and falls as his breathing becomes deeper and faster before he nods.

"Fine, get in the shower then."

I freeze.

Ayden's breathing quickens, and his nostrils flare. He ducks his head for a moment, looking to his feet and shakes his head. I can see this is killing him, I didn't tell him to go that far, but maybe it's exactly what I need. The quicker I face those demons, the quicker I can be a normal girlfriend.

I can tell he's about to apologise again, so I move past him, my legs shaking a little as I head towards his bathroom. Turning on the light, I step inside the small white space keeping my back to him.

"Lex." He pleads.

"Keep going," I beg, a tear popping free.

"You still have clothes on. I said everything off." Ayden's voice gives away how much he is struggling, so I suck in a breath and turn to him, holding my head high. He moves to step towards me when he sees my face, but I shake my head slowly, and he stops and sighs.

"Take your panties off. Let me see what's underneath." His voice is husky but firm.

I bite my lip and do as he says, sliding them down slowly. What Ayden doesn't know is that I'm getting turned on right now. If he wasn't so wrapped up in his head with concern for me, then he'd see the heat in my eyes. I desperately want to reach out to him, but I need to see this through for a little bit longer.

"Get in the shower and turn it on. Leave the door open." Ayden demands, and I do as he says.

I don't feel humiliated or violated right now like I did with Mike. With Ayden's heated gaze travelling over my body, I feel beautiful, desired, wanted. I let the water flow over me, warming my skin before I turn back to Ayden.

"Wash your hair." He demands, and I obey. It's hard to concentrate on the task at hand, though. Not when I can see the hardness behind his school pants. I do a pretty crappy job of washing my hair, anticipation adding to the desire building in me.

"Turn around and face the back wall," Ayden growls, and I move slowly, making sure he can see my confidence before I turn. "Now, bend over and wash your legs. Slowly!"

Fuck. This hits home big time. Mike's voice fills my head, and my breathing quickens.

I can do this. I can do this.

I will my legs to stop shaking as I take the bar of Ayden's soap off the ledge and slowly bend. I remind myself that the eyes watching me this time are Ayden's. They are ocean eyes that own my soul. They are eyes that drink me in and show me love.

I hear the moment Ayden gets a view of my most intimate part when I've bent fully, rubbing the soap over my ankles. His quick intake of air is followed by a moan. I feel like I'm about to spiral, my heart racing so fast that I fear it's going to explode. The problem is, I can't tell if it's because I'm scared or excited. So, I test myself. It's the only way I'm going to know. Taking another deep breath, I widen my stance, running the soap up the inside of my leg just past my knee. A lust-filled moan escapes Ayden, and pure need pulses between my legs.

Fuck yes! New memories!

"Stand up and turn around." Ayden's voice is gravelly. Husky. And damn if that's not a turn-on of its own.

I obey once again, coming face to face with the guy I'm sure is an angel sent down to save me.

"Wash between your legs. Wash that sweet pussy for me."

My eyes squeeze shut as I focus on Ayden's voice. Mike said something similar, and I need to get his voice out of my head.

"Say the last part again," I whisper loudly.

Ayden clears his throat, "Wash that sweet pussy for me."

I open my eyes to meet his as I do as he asks and wash over my aching sex. Ayden's breathing is as rapid as my own, and he moves to the fly of his pants and pulls down the zip.

"Drop the soap." He demands. This is new. I wasn't asked that last time, but that's okay. I'm no longer there in that bathroom with my half brother. I'm here inside Ayden's shower, with his eyes watching my every move, so I do as he demands and drop the soap.

"Touch yourself." He growls, so I do. I let my hands roam over my aching breasts, first one and then the other, before dragging my hand towards the place that is desperate to be touched. Desperate to be filled.

Ayden lets his pants and jocks fall to his ankles as he takes his hard length in his hand and pumps. "Show me how you like to be touched, Lexi."

I comply, my fingers finding my nub and circling. A moan escapes, and I move my feet apart further as I seek more with my fingers.

"You are so fucking beautiful, Lex. Look at what you do to me." He keeps pumping while he works to step out of his pants.

As my fingers work, my eyes dart from his pleasure-pained face to his straining hardness that looks almost painful. I bite my bottom lip, moaning again, and then Ayden is in the shower with me, pinning me to the wall.

Moaning. Panting. Kissing. Water falling. These are the sounds that fill the room. I'm desperate to have Ayden inside me, but he has different ideas. My eyes widen when he drops to the floor of the shower and lifts my leg, hooking it over his shoulder. Then I forget to breathe.

His blue eyes meet mine as I look down and watch his tongue dart out to taste me between my legs, and I hold my breath, my hips surging forward, seeking more. My head tips back as Ayden kisses and laps at me in the most intimate way possible, and then he draws his head back.

"Look at me, Lexi." He growls, and I immediately look back down at him. "Don't take your eyes off mine. Keep them open, or I'll stop."

Exasperated, my mouth forms an O before I snap it shut when his mouth seeks out my heat once again. It's hard. Really hard to keep my eyes open. It's also incredibly intimate, having to keep my eyes on his while he builds the pleasure inside me. His blue eyes glow with satisfaction when he can tell how close I am to exploding, so he adds his fingers, sliding them inside, and I do what he set out to do. I explode, over and over and over.

I've barely recovered when my leg is dropped off Ayden's shoulder, and I'm lifted against the wall. Before I've even locked my legs around him, Ayden surges inside, filling me. We both cry out, the pleasure taking over as Ayden starts to pump inside me. He starts out slow, but it doesn't last long. He is fevered with need, and his pace quickens.

"You feel fucking amazing." He grinds out before latching onto my neck.

My nails dig into his shoulder blades, probably marring his tattoo, but I don't care. He's leaving his mark on my neck, and I'm leaving mine on his back.

Ayden shifts his legs wider and leans back a little, the new angle hitting a different spot, and after three thrusts, I'm screaming out in pleasure again before Ayden quickly pulls out and follows with his own release.

We are panting in exhaustion. Our bodies wrapped around each other, not willing to let go.

"Are you okay?" Ayden asks between breaths, and I nod.

"Ayden?"

"Yes, beautiful?"

"You're mine," I claim, and he pulls back to look at me.

"Fuck yeah I am." He smiles before claiming my lips again.

After we pry ourselves away from each other, we use the shower to actually wash before drying off and moving the party to Ayden's bed to cuddle. I like this part. It's just as special as the other part, I realise as we lay together, stroking hair, cheeks, arms, and entwining fingers. It's almost as if we can't help but touch each other.

We lay in a tangled mess, and my mind wanders to the last few days and the times Ayden and I have come together like a force of nature.

"Penny for your thoughts."

I giggle at Ayden's words. He used the same words when we were at his dad's, and I bargained the penny as a kiss instead. That's when I got my first kiss from him.

"I feel older when I'm with you when it's just the two of us. I can't explain it, but I always feel like such a bratty teenager whose opinion doesn't matter, but I feel like I matter when I'm with you. I feel like I'm relevant."

Warm lips brush my shoulder. "Lex, you are the only thing that matters. You are what makes me relevant. You are everything."

His words are raw and filled with emotion. My body needs him, my lips seeking his out to ease their craving. This connection we have is beyond anything I could have ever imagined experiencing with another person. It's like my heart aches when he's not close enough.

The whole thing fills me with overwhelming happiness, which just reminds me that there is still too much darkness chasing me, ready to drag me down. I need to start exorcising my demons, so I start with the one that I have a little more control over.

"I need to tell you something." I blurt into the silence.

"You can tell me anything, Lex." Ayden encourages, stroking his fingers up and down my arm.

"Travis Watson. My friend. You know the one the guys don't think too highly of?"

"Yeah, the one that got done for the vandalism at school?" Ayden asks to confirm, not sounding too impressed.

My heart sinks. Shit. Shit. Shit. What if he thinks differently about me? What if it ruins what we have?

"Lex, you know you can tell me anything. No judgement here." He can obviously sense my hesitation. "Just remember, you're speaking to a drug addict who treated you in the worst way possible a few weeks ago. There's nothing you can say that will make me think differently of you."

Taking a deep breath, I nod and duck my head. I don't want to see the disappointment in his eyes when I tell him this truth about me.

"It was me," I whisper.

"What was you?" Ayden asks, his fingers moving to my chin and lifting my head so he can see me.

"I was the one that was with Travis when he broke into the school and trashed it."

Ayden frowns. "You?"

I nod, closing my eyes. I don't want to see his opinion of me change.

"You broke into the school and trashed it?"

My eyes fly open when I hear humour in his voice. I nod.

"You?" He asks, clearly not believing me, which just pisses me off.

I sit up, annoyed and throw off the covers. The moment I stand, I find myself pulled back into the bed with Ayden's arms wrapped around my middle. Pushing me down to the mattress and pinning me to the bed, Ayden looms over me, trapping my arms above my head as amusement caves in those adorable dimples.

"Get off me, Ayden," I warn.

He shakes his head. "No, I'm not letting you run off every time something gets hard or doesn't go your way. I'm sorry for not taking you seriously, but I am now. Tell me about that night."

I glare at him, "Are you going to get off me?"

"No way. You feel too fucking good underneath me." He admits. It's then that I notice the hard bulge pressing against me in the most sensitive way.

I roll my eyes. "Fine, I'll tell you, but you better give me another orgasm for it."

"So needy. Luckily, I'm more than happy to comply." Ayden proves this by pushing his pelvis forward, causing friction that makes us both moan.

Shit. I need to focus and tell him about that night before I get lost in the pleasure he conjures up inside me.

"I was kind of spiralling, I think. Tasha had one of her parties, and apparently, I ended up in the shed with the stoners getting high. This is just what I've been told because I can't remember much." I moan again when Ayden slowly, teasingly rubs his length over my clit.

"Keep going." He whispers. Jesus, this is torture. I'm just going to spit it out and move on to orgasmville.

"I started walking off from the party. Travis was outside and went with me so I wouldn't be alone. We ended up at the school. I remember smashing a window with my fist."

Ayden freezes, "What? You punched a window?" I nod, "Were you hurt?"

"A few cuts. Shit Ayden, don't stop." I growl in frustration, causing him to chuckle. He starts moving again, sliding between my folds.

"Then what happened?" He whispers.

"We trashed the Art room then moved on to the canteen because we were hungry. I woke up the next day with not much of a memory and a feeling like I did something bad. Travis told me all the details in exchange for a bag of weed which I stole from Mike before going to another party and getting high again and waking up on my ex-boyfriend's lap, straddling him with our clothes on. But we didn't have sex which was a good fucking thing because I saved myself for you. Yes, keep doing that." I rush it all out and dig my nails into Ayden's arse cheeks as he slides inside, and we ride another high together.

Afterwards, through panted breaths, Ayden growls. "Who the fuck is your ex-boyfriend, and where can I find him so I can punch the shit out of him?"

Twenty-Seven

Mr Matthews is lost for words. I never thought I'd see the day when I would be successful in my pursuit to shock the guy, yet here we are.

"Are you being serious right now?" He asks, and I nod.

In line with me opening up from our session on Monday, in today's session, I go for gold and verbally vomit everything that happened over the last two days since seeing him. There's the visit from Muz, the song with Ayden, the sex with Ayden, yes, I told him about that. Then I told him about the call from Val, the visit from my dad, that Muz showed up with a gun, the missing file that my dad is searching for, the phone call between my parents, the cops turning up, the visit to Abbey's, the therapeutic sex with Ayden, oh and the little chat Andrea had with me last night about having unprotected sex before giving me the morning after pill, which Ayden organised with her. Yep, that happened.

"You've got a lot going on." Mr Matthews says, taking a sip of his water. He's probably wishing it was vodka.

"Yeah, well, you wanted to know what happened since our last appointment two days ago."

"Yes. Right. Well, with all of those things that happened, is there anything in particular that you would like to discuss in more detail today?"

I shrug.

"How about this Muts guy?"

"Muz." I giggle, correcting Mr Matthews.

"Oh, right. Muz. You said he threatened you, but then he protected you. Do you know why?"

"No idea. Maybe he's hoping it will win him brownie points with Ayden, so he talks to his dad about helping Muz." I shrug, leaning forward to grab a handful of M&Ms from the bowl on the table between us.

"How about what's happening between your parents. That must be confusing." Mr Matthews scrubs his hand over his shiny bald head. It's so shiny, I could probably see my reflection in it.

"Well yeah. I have no idea what's going on. I just need the cops to hurry up and catch my dad and brother. It's driving me crazy having to look over my shoulder all the time."

"Yes, I can imagine it would." Mr Matthews agrees.

My attention is caught by my phone buzzing, and I pull it out of my hoodie pocket. The boys' group chat is blowing up. I shouldn't look while I'm in my appointment with the school counsellor, but I do.

Jared-Crowley
What the fuck is Tasha's problem?
I'm over that bitch trying to bring Lexi down!

Garrett-Cole
Someone needs to put her in her box.

Simon-Hastings
Grady man, get your bitch to sort Tasha out.
She'll put her back in her box and
bury it so no one can find it.

Marcus-Grady
Hastings, if you call Rhys a bitch one more
time, I'm going to dick punch you until
you've got a fucking vagina!

Mr Matthews clears his throat. "Lexi, can you pop your phone away, please?"

I look up to him briefly, but I'm drawn back to my phone when another message comes through.

Shaun-Bossier
Ha! Take that, Hastings!

Simon-Hastings
Everyone is so touchy these days!

Ayden-Mitchell
Can someone fill me in?
What's happened now?

Jared-Crowley
Today's rumour is that Lexi was Travis
Watson's accomplice in the school vandalism.

Oh shit!

Ayden-Mitchell
Fuck! Are you sure it's Tasha spreading it?

Marcus-Grady
Who else would it be?

"Okay, Lexi. I think we are done here." Mr Matthews' clipped tone gets my attention.

"No. Wait!" I panic; my knee starts jiggling up and down.

Mr Matthews frowns at my knee. "What's just happened?"

"Ah. Um. Ah." Shit. I can't tell him about my part in the school vandalism... can I?

"This is a safe zone, Lexi. You can tell me anything, remember?"

He says that, but can I really, without him legally having to divulge information to the authorities? My phone keeps buzzing with incoming messages, but I slide it back into my pocket. I can read them on my way home after this.

"Hypothetically speaking, if I told you something that happened that may be illegal, would you be obligated to report it?" I rush the words out and wait quietly while Mr Matthews thinks up his answer.

"You mean like hanging around with a gangster that pulled a gun on your dad? That sort of illegal?"

Well shit. I hadn't thought that through when I verbally vomited that information, had I? I shrug. "Kind of, I guess, but maybe more like if I did something illegal like holding a gun to my dad's head?"

"Did you?" he asks, and I shake my head and frown.

"No! This is hypothetical."

He sighs. "I do have an obligation, Lexi. A Duty of Care that if you are behaving in a way that breaks the law, or is harmful to others or yourself, that I must report it."

"Right," I say and then throw a smile on my face. "Well, it's a good thing I'm a stellar law-abiding citizen then, isn't it?" I laugh, but it's forced.

Mr Matthews frowns, studying me.

"Oh, look at the time. I should go." I glance at my wrist to a watch that isn't there and stand ready to get the hell out of Dodge.

"Lexi, what's happened?" Mr Matthews asks, walking hurriedly behind me as I make a mad dash towards the door.

"Nothing. All g. Mr M. See you in a couple of days."

I don't hang around to hear what Mr Matthews says next because I'm out the door and down the hall in the blink of an eye. I should go home, but I don't. I send the boys a message to meet me where Rhys hangs out at recess, and I sneak up to the back of the school and wait it out.

The bell has barely gone when I see Ayden round the corner, his eyes locking onto mine.

"Are you okay?" He doesn't give me a chance to answer when he reaches me and claims my lips. My panic starts to subside a little, and I know it's from the drug that is Ayden Mitchell.

I nod when he pulls back and cups my face to look into my eyes.

"I need to come clean," I whisper, and Ayden's eyes swim with concern.

"It's only a rumour, Lex." He whispers back.

"You know it's not Ayden."

He frowns, "So? You don't have to tell anyone else. It just looks like another desperate attempt by Tasha to bring you down."

"I know. But I just feel like I need to be free of all the lies. I fucked up Ayden. Bad. Travis shouldn't be the only one that has to pay for it." I step back from Ayden's hold when I hear the banter of the boys float around the corner.

Ayden gives me a small grin. "I get it, Lex. You do what you need to do. I'll be right by your side."

"You will?"

"Yes. I will." Ayden's support is overwhelming. I could cry if I let myself, but I won't because I'm sick of my eyes leaking.

"Here's our girl. This place is so boring without you, Lexi." Simon bounds up to me and lifts me into a spin from behind, causing me to squeal.

When he puts me down, I'm met with a high five from Shaun and Garrett, a hug from Jared, and a playful shoulder bump from Marcus. Rhys and her crew haven't made it here yet, so now is the best time to get this conversation over and done with.

I give the boys a quick rundown of the night I broke into the school with Travis and watch a mix of emotions flit across their faces. By the end, I can't look at them. My shame is too much and seeing it in their eyes will surely kill me.

"Okay, then. We should still redirect the focus to Tasha. No one will believe the crap she is trying to spread, anyway." Marcus says, and the other boys nod.

"Only it isn't crap, is it? It's true." I counter, and Simon catches my eye. He's smiling.

"It's our secret. They don't need to know that. Fuck Tasha. She's been nothing but a vindictive cow to you. It's time to take her down."

"I think I'm in enough trouble already." I can't afford to get busted for anything else.

"Nah, not you Lex. We should get Rhys to handle this." Marcus says, just as the crazy chick in question appears behind us.

"Get me to handle what?" Rhys asks.

"Tasha," Marcus says regarding Rhys. Their eye contact gives away that they are more than just friends with benefits, but that's the only sign that there's something more going on between them.

"Ooooh, Yes. I'd be happy to bring her down." Rhys rubs her hands together, and everyone laughs. Everyone but me.

"No." All eyes turn to me. "I really just want to ignore her. She will hate that more. I don't want to make a big deal about Tasha, and I also don't want anyone else getting into it with her either. People can see who she really is. She's digging her own grave. Let's just leave it to Karma."

"Oh, poo. That's boring." Rhys stomps her foot, lightening the mood again.

The rest of my new friends arrive then, and the conversation quickly disperses. Ayden is just about to take my hand in his when it's snatched up by Jared.

"I need a moment with Six." Jared glares at Ayden, who returns it but doesn't try to stop Jared when he leads me away from the group into the trees.

"What was that about?" I ask Jared once he stops walking and turns to me. He doesn't drop my hand.

"What?" His innocent reply makes me roll my eyes.

"The glare you shot Ayden. What's your deal, Jar?"

He is either swirling his tongue or biting the inside of his cheek right now. It's hard to tell. But his blue eyes, which aren't quite as bright as Ayden's, roam my face and search my eyes.

"So, you guys are back together now?" He asks, his tone cold.

My shoulders drop, and I sigh. I don't need this shit from Jared right now. But he's my friend, so I guess we have to sort this out.

"Yes, we are."

"So, you just forgave him for the way he treated you?" There's venom in Jared's tone, and I hate hearing it from him.

"Let's get something straight. I forgave him immediately because the situation was fucked, and I'm not going to have you judge him since you weren't even there to witness anything. I didn't take him back when he returned because I thought he deserved better."

"Lex, I wasn't there because you shut me out. For months you have done that, and you keep springing surprises on me. I could have fucking helped you every step of the way!" Frustration sees Jared drag his hand through his ash blonde hair, messing up his styling. "Why the fuck would you think Ayden deserves better than you? If anything, you deserve better than him. Much better. Fuck Six! I thought we were friends?"

Jared's words sting. I hadn't meant to shut him or anyone else out. But I had until Ayden came along. I could argue that Jared didn't fight hard enough to make sure I was okay, but that's not fair. He didn't know, and what's done is done.

"I'm sorry I didn't come to you. I've told you before I was ashamed. I still am, but I'm trying. Don't make me regret opening up to all of you." I'm snappy now because, fuck, I don't feel like I deserve this attack from Jared.

Jared hangs his head, pressing his forehead to mine. "Sorry, Six. I get a bit crazy when it comes to you."

We are quiet for a few moments, both of us gathering our thoughts.

"I'm really into him, Jar," I admit, my voice quiet, and he draws back, a frown creasing his forehead. "Can you please be happy for me?"

Jared studies me for a few long agonising moments, and then his face softens, and he nods. "I am happy for you Lex. Just an overprotective arsehole. You know that."

I nod. "I do."

He chuckles.

"Can I go back and see him now? Recess is nearly over, and I'll have to go back home." I really just want Ayden to come with me. How tempting it is to spend the day in bed wrapped in his arms. It sounds like heaven.

"Yeah, I guess." Jared smiles and releases my hand, walking beside me as we weave back through the trees to return to our friends.

Ayden's eyes are on the tree line, and he spots us immediately as we walk back out. His jaw ticks, and I can tell that he's holding a hell of a lot of restraint right now. I don't make him wait any longer, going straight to wrap my arms around his neck, pulling him down for a kiss.

It's not a passionate kiss because Ayden is too tense, his mind elsewhere.

"Sorry, bro. Just needed a minute with our–ah, with Lexi." Jared's fumbled words cause Ayden to glare, a growl coming from deep within his chest.

Oh my, I do like that growl.

Jared throws his hands up in surrender just as the bell rings, indicating the end of recess and my brief time with Ayden. As if he feels the same disappointment as I do, Ayden tugs me close and buries his face in my neck.

"I don't want to be away from you, Lex. It's a form of torture."

I giggle at his agonised tone, and then I moan from the nip he delivers to my earlobe.

"Make sure you don't have any homework tonight. I want your time." I whisper right before he takes my lips in a kiss that's filled with promises.

"You know Lexi, you still haven't told me if he has a pretty cock. Stop avoiding me. I expect a full debrief after school. I'm coming over." Rhys whisper yells in my ear, effectively cutting short my lip-lock with Ayden.

"Sorry, Rhys. She has a prior engagement with me and my extremely pretty cock after school." Ayden teases, leaving me in shock, and Rhys wearing a big smirk. I caved last night and told him about Rhys' obsession with good looking cocks.

"See you later, beautiful." Ayden kisses the tip of my nose and shoots me that panty-melting wink of his before walking off with the boys to class.

"Fuck me, I think I just came in my knickers." Rhys drawls, running her tongue over her lips.

I turn and slap her arm, "Eyes off, or we aren't friends!" It's a joke, and she beams, flashing me white teeth behind her black lips.

"See you after school. I'll give you an hour of fuck time before I burst in and kidnap you from Ayden's dick... I mean loft. I'll get Marcus to keep me busy while I wait." Wagging her dark brows, she walks backwards, thrusting and gyrating her hips.

I can't help but laugh. That girl is as crazy as they come, and I love her for it. When she finally disappears around the corner of the building, I walk along the tree line until I reach the school fence and jump over it. I feel lighter, somehow. Like admitting to my part in the school vandalism has lifted another burden I carry. Of course, it's not completely gone. I won't feel free of it unless I come clean to the principal. Cynthia may be obligated to go to the police with that information. I just need to figure out if I'm willing to face up to that punishment and scrutiny from my peers or if I'm just a coward who's willing to let someone else carry all the blame.

Even as I think it, I know I'm going to come clean. Maybe I'll get Andrea to drive me over to speak with Principal Rogan tonight. I'd like to do it before my suspension is over, just in case she expels me. There's no point in wasting anyone else's time at this point.

Twenty-Eight

Instead of walking back to Marcus', I catch the bus. I know the walk is only ten minutes, but the bus ride is only 5 minutes and a lot safer than walking the streets when Mike may still be in town. As soon as I step off the bus at the end of Marcus' street, my phone rings. The moment I see Val's name on the screen, I know something is wrong. I've learnt that a text from Valarie is a *details* thing or just conversation, but a phone call always means something is wrong. I don't hesitate to answer the call.

"Val?"

There's muffled noises down the line before I hear a piercing scream. Val's piercing scream.

"Val!" I yell, already running.

"Help!" Val's plea is the last thing I hear before the line goes dead.

No! No! No!

As I run, I try to call her back, but she doesn't answer. I try her house phone, but there's no answer there either. My lungs burn, and tears sting my eyes as I sprint through the quiet streets of Fox Pines, desperate to get to Val.

As I round the corner of my street, I call Ayden.

"Lex, what's wrong?" His voice is frantic down the line. He knows I'd only call if there was an emergency.

"I don't know. Val called, screaming for help. I'm nearly at her place. Call the cops and ditch school. Meet me there!" I don't know why I called Ayden and not the cops, but all I know is that I want him here, and I know he will do everything he can to get help to me.

I hang up, cutting him off. The word "No" made it to my ears, though.

I skid to a stop in Val's driveway. There are no cars in sight, but her front door is wide open. I don't hesitate; I bolt forward, and when I reach the threshold, I hear Val whimpering.

"Val?" I call, and her whimpering gets louder, coming from the back of the house where her kitchen overlooks their backyard and orchard. I move fast, looking around cautiously as I go past a formal living room that doesn't look like it's ever been used and a small office that looks like it's used too much.

The whimpering gets louder as I approach the back of the house. I stop briefly at the bottom of the U-shaped staircase to listen for any sounds upstairs, but it's silent up there. The only noise is straight ahead.

I don't wait any longer and bolt into the large space, glancing from a small living area to the grand dining table and the oversized Tasmanian Oak kitchen.

My breath catches, seizing in my lungs when I see my sweet innocent twelve-year-old neighbour tied to a chair in only a pair of knickers.

"No." The whisper escapes, finally letting air in, and I lurch forward towards Val. She is crying, her voice muffled by a gag tied around her head and shoved in her mouth.

"Shit Val. It's okay. I'm here." I cry, reaching to pull the gag free from her mouth.

Her eyes widening over my shoulder is the only warning I get before my head is ripped back by my hair, and I'm thrust into the corner of the island bench. I hear myself scream, and my vision wavers before I fall into darkness briefly. Once the moment passes, I try to focus on who is in the room.

"You fucking little whore. Did you really think you could get away from me?"

"Mike." The whisper falls from my mouth, and my half brother smiles like he's proud. He's looking a bit worse for wear. Scratches that look like they were caused by fingernails run down his left cheek, and a bite mark is bleeding badly on his arm.

Good girl, Val!

"You and I have unfinished business, little sis, and this time, no one is coming to save you!"

That's what he thinks. How dumb does he think I am? I mean, yes, I'm stupid enough to not call the cops and wait for them instead of storming in here. I never claimed I was perfect!

"Let her go!" I demand as if I have bargaining power. I know I don't, not with Mike, but I need time. Time to keep Val alive and drag this out so the cops can get Mike. I can do this. For Val. For me.

The sickening laugh that haunts my dreams fills the room, and I let him see my cringe. I hate this motherfucker!

"Oh no, little Valarie here is going to watch what I do to you, so she knows what's to come, and then you will swap places and watch me break her in."

"Fuck you!" I scream and launch myself off the floor at Mike like I'm a crazed, bloodthirsty monkey. I clamp my knees to his waist and shove my hands into his hair, fisting them tight and pulling hard as I throw my head back and then slam it forward to head butt him.

It sounds good, right? Head-butting someone. I've seen it on the badass movies, and while it manages to render him useless briefly, it has the same fucking effect on me.

I see stars, and my grip on him falters, sending me to the floor while he stumbles back into Val, knocking her chair over. The sickening crunch of her head hitting the hard tiled floor echoes in the room and brings me back to the present.

Mike is holding his head, trying to shake free the stars he's obviously seeing, but I can't focus on him because my eyes are locked on Val's unconscious face and the blood pooling from the back of her head where it impacted on the floor.

No! Val!

I scramble across the floor to get to her, but a choking hand wraps around my throat from behind, and I'm pulled up against Mike's body.

"Look what you've gone and done. Now the little snitch can't watch what's going to come her way." Mike's vile breath hits the side of my face before he drags his tongue up my cheek, just like he did last time in my bedroom.

As much as I want Valarie to be okay, part of me hopes that if I'm not able to get us out of this situation before Mike gets to her, that she dies, so she doesn't have to experience what Mike is promising.

Mike's grip on my neck tightens, "Time to play, Ali."

I struggle to get air in as Mike uses his free hand and slips it up my hoodie, grabbing my breast and squeezing so tight that I cry out, pain shooting through the sensitive flesh. I kick out my legs as I try to pry his hand loose from my neck. When that fails, I reach back and do what Val did. I use my nails and try to scratch his face and neck.

I succeed in getting him to loosen his grip, and the moment I'm free, I use my new punching skills and aim for his nuts, giving him the dick punch I've dreamed of doing for weeks now. I move quickly out of the way as he tumbles to the ground, and I launch myself towards the other bench where the knife block is.

Just as I've slipped one free, which is disappointingly very small, Mike's heavy weight slams into me from behind, winding me on the edge of the bench before spinning me and throwing me across the kitchen. I slam into the fridge hard, more wind getting knocked from me, making it impossible to breathe. Tears flood my eyes as my lungs scream for air.

Mike takes his time to reach me, obviously still in pain from my dick punch, so I pick up the knife I dropped just in time to take a slice at his hand and arm when he reaches for me.

"You fucking bitch. You're not coming out of this alive, Ali. I'm going to fuck every hole you have and then carve more holes with that fucking knife and fuck them until you've been dead for hours. By the time anyone finds you, they won't even recognise you!"

The venomous yell from Mike sends chills over my skin and takes more of what little breath I can get in. The good thing about his scream is that someone has to have heard it.

I'm still trapped, cornered in Val's kitchen. I need to get this fight outside, preferably out the front, away from Val and closer to other people. I stagger to stand and look around frantically, trying to figure a way out of this kitchen.

As if sensing my train of thought, Mike hisses like a snake, and I see his fist at the last second before pain slices through my skull, and everything goes black.

I've been here before. Been in this place of nothingness. It's just as peaceful as it was last time; the only difference is me. I'm not the same person as I was last time when I felt like giving up. When I felt like I had nothing but my shame to live with.

This time, my heart pumps with determination. With love. With purpose. This time, I am strong!

My eyes fly open, and deja vu hits. Mike is standing over me, although this time I'm not naked. My hoodie is gone, and so is my top. Right now, he's tugging my pants down over my feet, leaving me in my bra and knickers laying on the hard surface of the large fancy dining table.

I lay still, closing my eyes again, so he doesn't notice, biding my time until I can strike. I hold my breath when I feel his rough, callused hand glide up my leg and rub over a place I only ever want Ayden to touch. I'm not strong enough to bite back my whimper, and upon hearing it, he digs his fingers into the fabric of my knickers.

I bolt upright, my hands grabbing for Mike's head, and I latch onto his cheek, sinking my teeth in, blood filling my mouth. He wails in pain and lifts me, making me lose my grip and throws me as if I weigh nothing at all. My body skims the surface of the island bench, and I land hard on the tile floor, mere feet from Val's still unmoving form.

"When are you going to accept your fate bitch?" Mike growls, coming around the bench and leaping on me, pinning me to the ground. The taste of his blood still coats my tongue, and I gag when I see the dangling flesh of his cheek as it hangs by a thread. "You're going to pay for all the trouble you have caused." Mike's threat is followed by his hand gripping the side of my head. He spits in my face and then lifts my head, only to slam it back onto the hard floor.

I immediately see stars, unexplainable pain shooting through my skull, and nausea rolls my stomach. The impact affects my entire body, and I can't seem to move. I try to scream, but I can't find my voice.

Holy shit! I'm going to die. This is it. This is the moment when my life, that I just started to see a hopeful future in, ends.

I can hear Mike hissing venom at me, but the ringing in my ears is too loud, and his rough hand slaps my face. The action shifts my head, and I can see Val now. She looks peaceful, like she's asleep, but her skin is so pale. If she's not already dead, then she's not far off.

I'm sorry, Valarie. I never wanted you to get hurt.

Rough hands wrap around my throat and squeeze, and right when I accept that I'm about to die, the hands vanish, and so does the weight on my body. I still can't move, and I try to hear over the ringing in my ears. I think I can hear yelling. Things are smashing.

I try with all I have to move but can't. Something warm and wet is soaking my back. It feels too thick and oozy to be anything else but blood. I must be bleeding from somewhere. Maybe that's why I'm feeling faint.

"Lexi!"

My name! Someone is calling my name.

"Lexi!"

I hear it again, but I can't turn my head to see who it is.

"Get up, Lexi! Run!"

There's the voice again.

It's not Ayden's voice.

It's not Officers Zimora or Reynolds' voices.

Wait! I can hear sirens. They are very distant, but I can hear them.

My body gets jolted as a form lands next to me, blocking my view of Val.

"Lexi! Run!"

That face! It's Muz. I try to answer him and tell him I can't move, but no sound will come out of my mouth.

Mike comes into view, reaching down and punching Muz in the face. Blood sprays from the impact, going in my eye. I blink rapidly, trying to clear the red from my vision, but it doesn't help. Everything is tinted red. Muz returns punches to Mike as the sirens get louder.

Yes, Muz! Kill him!

The metallic smell of blood engulfs my senses, and my head starts to spin. I try to force my eyes to stay open, try to keep my eyes trained on Muz and his fierce fight against my brother. It's no use, though. Blackness dots my vision and starts to tunnel my view. My eyes drift closed, and again I try to force them open, needing to see that Muz is okay, but I'm too weak. They shut against my will, darkness closing in on me.

The last thing I hear is the loud crack of a gunshot before heaviness drags me down deep, consumed in nothingness. Suffocating. Buried.

To Be Continued

BURIED

THE HEAVY HEARTS SERIES

BOOK THREE

https://books2read.com/HeavyHeartsBook3

♥

SARAH JD'S BOOKS

IN READING ORDER

SERIES ONE

THE HEAVY HEARTS SERIES

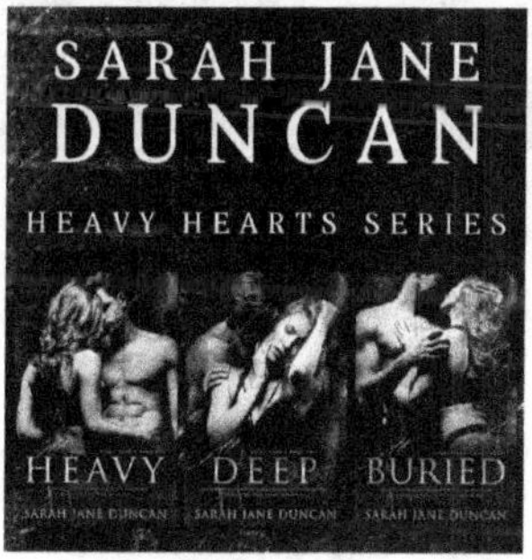

HEAVY

https://books2read.com/HeavyHeartsBook1

DEEP

https://books2read.com/HeavyHeartsBook2

BURIED

https://books2read.com/HeavyHeartsBook3

SERIES TWO

THE INSATIABLE SERIES

INSATIABLE KITTEN

https://books2read.com/Kitten1Books

TAINTED KITTEN

https://books2read.com/KittenBook2

VICIOUS KITTEN

https://books2read.com/KittenBook3

STAY CONNECTED

To stay connected and be in the know
about future works that may include some of
the side characters from The Heavy Hearts Series,
join my Facebook Readers Group:
SARAH JD'S VICIOUS KITTENS
https://www.facebook.com/groups/
sarahjaneduncanreadersgroup

Visit
Sarah Jane Duncan at
sarahjaneduncan.com
for updates!

Join my VIP Readers list and receive
monthly newsletters jam packed with updates
about your favourite characters!
https://sarahjaneduncan.com/newsletter/

Sarah JD, also known as Sarah Jane Duncan is a dark romance author, living in the beautiful Gippsland region in Victoria, Australia, with her high-school-sweetheart-turned-hubby and three grown children.

When she's not busy writing, Sarah can be found sewing dance costumes for her daughter or helping her hubby in their family business.

Sarah writes about females who have to fight against the odds to find their power, find their voice, and find their truth. The heroines in Sarah's stories possess the strength that only comes when you have to fight for your life!

CPSIA information can be obtained
at www.ICGtesting.com
Printed in the USA
LVHW100048280323
742726LV00005B/338